THE FAMILY HE WANTED

Tears glimmered in her eyes.

Without thinking, he pressed his hand against her face. A teardrop escaped, trailing down her cheek as she stared up at him.

That was as far as he should have taken it. Except she took that last step and wrapped her arms around his waist. All the times he'd hugged her, held her, it had felt like friendship. Today, right now, she was a woman in his arms.

But then she looked up at him, eyes wide, lips parting, breath hitching in her throat. A devil perched on his shoulder, calling out instructions, goading him into doing something he damn well shouldn't do. Not when it was Jana in his arms, hurting and confused.

All he could think about were her lips and lowering his mouth to hers.

All Rights Reserved including the right of reproduction in whole or in part
in any form. This edition is published by arrangement with Harlequin
Enterprises II B.V./S.à.r.l. The text of this publication or any part thereof may
not be reproduced or transmitted in any form or by any means, electronic or
mechanical, including photocopying, recording, storage in an information
retrieval system, or otherwise, without the written permission of the publisher.

This book is sold subject to the condition that it shall not, by way of trade or
otherwise, be lent, resold, hired out or otherwise circulated without the prior
consent of the publisher in any form of binding or cover other than that in
which it is published and without a similar condition including this condition
being imposed on the subsequent purchaser.

® and ™ are trademarks owned and used by the trademark owner and/or its
licensee. Trademarks marked with ® are registered with the United Kingdom
Patent Office and/or the Office for Harmonisation in the Internal Market and
in other countries.

First published in Great Britain 2010
Harlequin Mills & Boon Limited,
Eton House, 18-24 Paradise Road, Richmond, Surrey TW9 1SR

From Friends to Forever © Karen Templeton-Berger 2009
The Family He Wanted © Karen Sandler 2009

ISBN: 978 0 263 87980 3

23-0710

Harlequin Mills & Boon policy is to use papers that are natural, renewable
and recyclable products and made from wood grown in sustainable forests.
The logging and manufacturing processes conform to the legal environmental
regulations of the country of origin.

Printed and bound in Spain
by Litografia Rosés S.A., Barcelona

FROM FRIENDS TO FOREVER
BY
KAREN TEMPLETON

THE FAMILY HE WANTED
BY
KAREN SANDLER

⊚™ MILLS & BOON®

FROM FRIENDS TO FOREVER

BY
KAREN TEMPLETON

Karen Templeton is the mother of five sons and living proof that romance and dirty nappies are not mutually exclusive terms. An Easterner transplanted to Albuquerque, New Mexico, she spends far too much time trying to coax her garden to yield roses and produce something resembling a lawn, all the while fantasising about a weekend alone with her husband. Or at least an uninterrupted conversation.

She loves to hear from readers, who may reach her online at www.karentempleton.com.

To Gail, for giving me this opportunity.
Did I say "Yes!" fast enough for ya?
And to my five boys,
for turning out to be such fine young men.
You guys haven't always made life easy,
but you've always made it fun.

Chapter One

Perched on a stool in a stifling New England kitchen that was not hers, chopping potatoes into a plastic bowl that was not hers, either, Lili Szabo thought, *Not exactly how I envisioned my life at this point,* orphaned and alone and vulnerable to things like spontaneous invitations to visit American relatives who, with few exceptions, she either didn't know or barely remembered—

"Are you done yet, sveetheart?" Aunt Magda yelled from across the room, and Lili glared at Self-Pity and said, *You. Out. NOW.* Finally it shuffled off, grumbling, and Lili smiled for her mother's older sister.

"Go. Enjoy your party, everything's under control."

"In zis house? Nefer!" Magda Vaccaro said, her heavy accent as proudly worn as her sculpted blond hair and theatrical makeup, even though she'd left both Hungary and the circus life behind more than forty years before. Her normal attire ran to tight pants and even tighter tops, but today she dazzled in a mirror-and-sequin-encrusted East Indian dress of tentlike proportions, worn with high-heeled mules and much tinkly jewelry. Next to her flamboyant aunt, Lili felt practically invisible in her white eyelet sundress. But then, most people disappeared next to Magda, who didn't need a spotlight, she made her own.

Then her Uncle Benny came in, Robert De Niro playing Santa Claus, to filch a sample of whatever Magda was setting out on a platter, stealing a kiss at the same time, and Self-Pity whispered, *I'm ba-ack,* and Lili sighed, suddenly weary of being the good one. The dependable one.

The cautious one.

"Any sign of Tony yet?" Uncle Benny asked, and Lili's head snapped up. Of course, in an Italian family, Tony was a common name. He wasn't necessarily talking about *that* Tony—

"Not yet," her aunt said with a sympathetic sigh. "But zen, he hesn't been on time to anysing since Marissa died. Such a shame."

Okay, so they were talking about *that* Tony. Except after all this time it was highly unlikely *that* Tony still existed, anyway, even if he hadn't been a recent widower—less than a year, wasn't it?—or the father of three little girls. What on earth could she possibly have in common with him now?

What did you have common with him then?

There was that, Lili thought, pretending not to watch as Benny swooped down on a laughing Magda to give her another kiss, sending a wink in Lili's direction as he strode from the room, a man happy in his world. And anyway—Lili slammed the next potato chunk into the bowl—if Tony was this late, maybe he wouldn't show at all.

Marginally cheered, she stood to upend the potatoes into a pot of boiling water, watching them succumb to their fate, ignoring Self-Pity's snickering in her ear.

* * *

"Do we *have* to go?"

His hands full of wriggling, giggling two-year-old—jeez, it was like dressing an eel—Tony Vaccaro could feel his oldest girl's frown from ten feet away.

"Yeah, baby, we gotta," he said, even though putting on the everything's-fine face wasn't exactly at the top of his list, either. But nobody turned down an invite to his Aunt Magda's annual birthday bash. And lived to tell about it. "Besides, it'll do us good to get out of this house. Interact with other human beings." Dress yanked over a little blond head, Tony shoved a hunk of his own damp, too long, not blond hair off his forehead. Josie seized the moment to bounce off the bed. "Besides—" he grabbed the squealing toddler, bouncing her right back "—you got something more pressing on your social schedule? JoJo! Sit still, for cryin' out loud, lemme get your shoes on—"

"Ohmigod. You can't let her wear *that!*"

Tony shut his eyes. Exhaled. Twisted to face the scowl barely masking the still raw pain in Claire's nearsighted eyes, the same pain that periodically throbbed in his own chest, that her mother had died and there hadn't been a damn thing he could do about it, that his little girl was still hurting and he couldn't do a damn thing about that, either.

That there'd been problems between him and Marissa, before she'd gotten sick, that had just laid there like a bleeping grenade between them, ignored until it was too late.

Then he noticed, framed by far too much light brown hair on either side of Claire's shoulders, the beginnings of a pair of somethings that had not been there yesterday, and his lungs seized.

Put those back, we can't afford them, hammered inside his head as a tiny person strangled his neck, peppering his cheek with noisy kisses. Got him every damn time, those kisses. Tony looked at his youngest daughter, wrinkling her nose at him.

"What's wrong with what she's wearing?" he said.

Grinning, Josephine patted the ivory lace bibbing the red satin dress she'd somehow not only found in her crammed closet, but had demanded to wear as only a two-year-old named after an empress could. "I'm pretty, huh, C'are?"

Claire shoved her blue-steel-rimmed glasses farther up on her nose. "Uh, Dad…that's a Christmas dress?"

"And your point would be?"

"It's *July?* She'll roast. Not to mention she's gonna get mustard and ketchup and crap all over it."

"Don't say c-r-a-p," Tony said, wearily, finally getting the baby's butt planted long enough to close the Velcro tabs on her glittery little sneakers—which even he knew didn't go with the dress—before setting the baby on the bare wood floor. Like a wind-up toy, she chugged over to the toy chest Tony had just filled to gleefully empty it again. "Especially in front of your baby sister," he said, dodging Super Grover. "And the dress is gonna be too small by next Christmas, anyway, so what's the big deal?"

Claire's hands landed on her hips, chewed fingernails dotted with her mother's purple nail polish. "Who the *heck* wears a Christmas dress to a backyard barbecue? Like, ohmigod?"

And who the *heck* was this kid? Swear to God, Tony never knew from one day to the next who was gonna come out of her bedroom door, like she was trying on different personalities to see which fit the best. The grief counselor said the Jekyll and Hyde thing was a coping mechanism. Tony's money was on early-onset puberty.

"Don't say ohmigod, you know your mother hated it. But hey, you wanna try getting the baby into something else, go for it. Call Daph, wouldja? We're late."

Claire stomped back to the door, bellowed, "Daphne! We're leaving!" then stomped back to Josie's white dresser with a decided sway to her not-so-little butt that leached the blood from Tony's face. If she was anything like her cousins, one day the baby fat would reorganize itself into curves and Tony was gonna be a dead man. As was any boy dumb enough to get within fifty feet. "Mama said she bought that dress for me," she said quietly. "So maybe I'd like to save it for my little girl. Or something."

Ah, hell.

This had nothing to do with the baby wearing the dress. What this was, was Claire's wanting to stop her world from spinning out of control. Kid always had freaked out if God forbid they drove a different way to school, or changed a room color, or had spaghetti on Tuesday night instead of the usual Monday. Her mother dying?

Damn miracle she was functioning at all.

Wasn't like he couldn't relate, Tony thought as, baby shorts and T-shirt in hand, Claire hooked a zooming Josie around the waist and flung her back on the twin bed she didn't even sleep in yet. He'd kill for "normal" again. For what he'd had—they'd had—even a few years ago.

"Hey, JoJo, let's wear these instead—"

"No!" the baby said, arms crossed, matching her sister scowl-for-scowl as she pointed imperiously to the dresser. "Put back! Right now! I wanna wear *this!*" Then she scrambled off the bed—again—howling in protest as Claire grabbed for her. Again.

Tony's cell rang. With a grimace at the read-out, he answered it.

"Tony?" his mother-in-law said. "Is that the baby? Is everything all right?"

"Yeah, Susan, everything's fine. Minor fashion crisis, that's all. What's up?"

"Just making sure we're still taking the girls tomorrow. Although we certainly don't mind coming for them tonight—"

Josie's caterwauling ratcheted up another decibel or two. "Are you *sure* everything's okay?"

"Positive. And forget it, you don't need to be drivin' down from Boston that late. I wouldn't dream of puttin' you two out like that."

"You wouldn't be putting us out, honey, you know that." When Tony didn't answer, Marissa's mother switched tactics. Slightly. "Then…you don't mind if we keep them Sunday night, too?"

"Nah, of course not. The girls love it there, with the pool and everything. Not to mention you guys spoilin' them rotten," he added with a slight smile.

"Just doing our jobs," Susan said, her faux cheer wilted a bit at the edges. "You know, if we got them tonight, they could attend church with us in the morning, then go someplace nice for lunch—"

"Got it covered," he said softly.

"We're only trying to help, Tony," Susan said, just as softly, and Tony sighed, because they really were. And the kids were crazy about them. Not to mention their two-story colonial in Brookline with the cook and the housekeeper and that pool. And besides him they were the closest family the girls had, Tony's folks having both died within the past five years and his brothers and sister scattered all over the freaking country—

"Daph!" Claire shrieked as the seven-year-old came pounding into the room. "What on earth were you *doing?*"

"Gotta go," Tony mumbled, cutting off Susan's "Tony…?" His phone clapped shut, he slowly faced the child who looked most like him, with her dark jumble of curls and deep brown eyes.

Deep brown *don't look at the mess, look at the cute* eyes.

"Daph, for God's sake—"

"I was watering the 'matoes an' Ed got in the way of the

hose, an' then he ran through the mud where I'd just watered, an' then he rolled in it…" Her eyes lowered to the mud-splattered devastation from the chin down, then lifted again. "An' then he shook."

Ed, their affable, terminally clueless boxer/shepherd mix—their weirdly clean boxer/shepherd mix, having efficiently transferred ninety percent of the mud to the child—grinned up at him, panting.

"So I see."

Her contrite smile punching dimples in round cheeks, Daphne held out grubby hands bearing a stack of smudged envelopes and catalogs. "Mail came."

"Thanks," Tony muttered as he took it, refusing to dwell on the muddy footprints Daph would have left in her trek to get the mail. Halfheartedly, he riffled through the usual assortment of bills, credit card offers and Don't Let This Be Your Last Catalog! warnings from Marissa's favorite mail-order companies, frowning when he came to the slightly damp, oversize envelope from their lawyer—

"You want me to change?"

"What?" Tony glanced at the walking, cute-as-all-hell mudslide in front of him. "Uh, yeah, sweetie. But hurry, we're sposedta be there by five."

"Won't take but a sec," Daphne said, bounding down the hall to her room, as Tony clamped the rest of the mail under his arm to tear open the envelope from the lawyer. Inside was a short note on Phil's letterhead, wrapped around another sealed envelope…addressed to him in Rissa's handwriting.

"Tony," he silently read over the loud rushing in his ears, "I have no idea what this is about, but Rissa asked me to send it to you when she'd been gone at least six months. I know it's been more like nine, but frankly, I forgot about it until now. If you need me for anything, let me know. Phil."

What I need is a new lawyer, Tony thought, turning to Claire, who'd apparently—since the baby was still a vision in satin and lace—given up the good fight. "Let me dump this stuff on my desk, then we can get outta here, okay?"

Except he'd barely reached the small bedroom office at the end of the hall before he ripped open the second envelope and skimmed the letter.

Twice.

"…I'm so sorry, and I know this is taking the chicken's way out, but I just couldn't figure out a good time to tell you…"

"Dad? You okay?"

The letter clutched in his hand, Tony wheeled on a frowning Claire, standing in the hall with the baby perched on her hip.

"Sure. Fine." Swallowing back the howl lodged at the base of his throat, he crossed to the battle-scarred Melamine desk to stash the letter in the top drawer, then fumbled for the Super Dad switch in his brain before turning back, game face firmly in place. "You guys all ready to go?"

"You sound funny—"

"Somethin' caught in my throat," Tony pushed out, thinking…nine months ago? He thought he'd been through hell.

Turns out he'd barely gotten through the front door.

Fine. If Dad wanted to pretend everything was cool, Claire could, too. Except she knew when he was faking being okay and when he was really okay. Not that he'd been *really* okay since Mom died, but she knew he was trying his best. For their sakes. Because kids weren't supposed to be sad, or something lame like that. Whatever.

Then he said they were gonna *walk* the six blocks to Aunt Magda's and Uncle Benny's, and she heard herself say, "Are you *kidding* me? You want us to die of sunstroke or what?"

"You've all got hats," Dad said, sounding mostly normal again as he struggled to get the Empress—that's what they sometimes called JoJo, on account of her being named after some dude's wife two centuries ago—into her stroller. "I think you'll survive six blocks. Think of it as being ecologically responsible."

"Or cheap," Claire grumbled with a longing look over her shoulder at their old Volvo wagon, sitting in the driveway. One fist wrapped around the stroller handle, Dad tugged a receipt out of his jeans pocket and handed it over.

"What's this?"

"That's how much it cost me to gas up the car yesterday."

"Holy crap."

"Don't—" He sighed. "Yeah."

Then it occurred to Claire that maybe she should cut Dad some slack, since this obviously wasn't one of his better days. "C'n I push?" she asked, reaching for the stroller. Yeah, Josie could be a pain in the butt, but she could be really cute and lovey and stuff, too. And Claire tried to help out with her little sisters as much as possible, so Dad wouldn't feel like he had to do everything. Especially since she'd overheard Nana and Gramps talking about how it would be so much easier on Dad if Claire and her sisters came to live with them. She loved her grandparents and all, but…no.

"Go for it," Dad said, moving over so Claire could take the stroller.

"The walk will do us good," she said, feeling all tingly inside when Dad's hand landed on the back of her head. She looked up at him, smiling, letting out a little breath of relief when he smiled back. Even if it was the kind of smile that made Claire's insides hurt. Basically Dad was pretty cool, if a little crazy sometimes, although they didn't see the crazy so much now. As awful as Claire'd felt when Mom died? She knew it'd hurt Dad a hundred million times more.

Which was why she couldn't tell Dad about how she'd found Mom crying one day, before they knew she was sick. Mom made her swear to never say anything to Dad, or anybody else, that it was a secret.

Claire didn't much like keeping secrets—they always made her feel like when you want to throw up but you can't because you're in school or church or someplace. But Mom said it would only upset Dad if he found out, so Claire said okay. And Claire never, ever broke her promises.

Even ones she was sorry she'd made.

Daphne's hot—but clean—hand in Tony's, they walked the six blocks underneath a bleached sky, the hot, sticky silence broken only by the stroller's bumping over the cracks in the old sidewalk and Josie's babbling. Not a leaf stirred in the sycamore trees fronting the sturdy New England Victorians, erected a century ago when families were huge and building materials cheap. The early summer humidity clung to everything like plastic wrap; Marissa hated this weather, the way her hair would always corkscrew into a tangled, frizzy mess—

The memory slashed through Tony like a rusty knife, reopening still-infected wounds, now rancid with disbelief and shock. His pace slowed when his aunt and uncle's house loomed into view a half block ahead. How could he do this, go to some party and pretend like everything was fine when his guts were bleeding all over the damn place? But what choice did he have? Especially since turning back would mean facing a barrage of questions from Little Miss Never-Miss-a-Thing pushing the stroller.

So he'd do the playacting thing for a couple hours. At least the kids would get fed. One less thing to worry about, he thought as they approached the old brick foursquare where Benny and Magda had raised six kids.

Uncle Benny opened the door, immediately pulling Tony into a brief, but deadly, bear hug as a stiff-legged golden retriever and a cotton ball toy poodle eagerly rushed the kids, woofing and yipping and wriggling and licking. From every corner of the house, laughter taunted him.

"You made it," Benny said, clapping Tony on the back before Tony squatted to spring Josie from her stroller while the other girls hovered nearby. "We were beginning to think you wouldn't show. Aww…gimme the little cutie," he said, holding out his arms to Josie, who clung more tightly to Tony, shaking her head. His uncle laughed, not in the least offended.

Instead he grinned at the girls. "God, you two are getting so big! Unbelievable, huh? Hey—most of your cousins are upstairs. Even Stacey," he said to Claire. "You should go on up."

Daphne the Invincible was gone in a flash, but Claire hung back, forehead creased, eyes worried, obviously picking up on stuff Tony did not want her picking up on. Now or ever. Looping an arm around her shoulders, Tony wondered how soon they could leave. "Stace is here? So Rudy and them came down?"

"Just for the day. They had to find somebody to watch the inn." Benny smiled for Claire. "Stace was askin' about you, wonderin' if you'd be here."

Claire's eyes shifted to Tony's, torn. "Go," Tony said with a little smile. And a not-so-little push. Because if he had a hope in hell of getting through the next couple of hours, he had to stay out of range of that all-too-knowing look.

"Hey, Tone," Benny asked as Claire finally trudged off. "You okay?"

"Yeah, sure, I'm fine—"

"Tony?"

His head jerked up, toward a voice he hadn't heard in a thousand years and a pair of blue eyes as laser-sharp as he remembered, and before he could catch his breath Josie wriggled to get down, then ran over to this woman she'd never seen in her life. Her arms wrapped around Lili Szabo's knees, she looked up at her adoringly, and Tony felt like somebody had just shoved him off a damn cliff.

Chapter Two

"Oh my goodness," Lili said, her smile threatening to fry
what was left of Tony's brain as she lifted Josie into her arms.
"Is she yours? She's adorable—"

"What on earth are you doin' here?" Her smile faltered,
and Tony felt like a jerk. A blindsided jerk, but a jerk all the
same. "I'm sorry, that came out bad, but, damn—"

"No, it's okay," she said, hiking Ms. Chunkers higher on
her hip. A hip much more, um, *there* than he remembered.

"How long has it been?" he asked, realizing Benny had
disappeared. "Twelve years?"

The smile flickered to life again, giving him a flash of the
slightly crooked eyeteeth she'd been so self-conscious about.
God knows why. "Fourteen, actually."

"Fourteen. Right. God." He paused. "So what brings you
back?"

"My mother died," she said softly, swinging Josie from
side to side, making her laugh. "A month ago—"

"Jeez…I'm sorry—"

"It's okay, it wasn't unexpected," she said in her pretty accent. "A blessing, actually, when she finally let go. In any case, afterward…" She touched her forehead to the baby's. "I thought the change would do me good."

She was still skinny, mostly, except for a couple of crucial places that weren't, judging from the way that dress was fitting. And it wasn't like she'd turned into a bombshell or anything, because she hadn't, she was still just little cousin Lili with the too-wide mouth and long, ordinary brown hair that curved slightly on the ends. Although the glasses were rimless now, and her mouth seemed fuller or something—

"Tony? Are you feeling all right?"

—but she'd been the only person, Tony now realized in such a rush he got dizzy, who'd ever really *gotten* him. At least, the eighteen-year-old "him" who'd been so cocksure about what he wanted.

And that hadn't included his fifteen-year-old, slightly geeky Hungarian cousin visiting for the summer after her father died and the rest of her family toured Europe with their high-wire act. The only person, friend or relative, willing to keep him company when a stupid-ass skateboard accident shattered his leg, his summer and whatever hope he'd had of going all the way with Marissa Pellegrino.

Who he *had* wanted, with a single-mindedness bordering on obsessive.

"It's been a rough few months," he said, the words out of his mouth before he had any clue they were there, and Lili gave him that same disingenuous smile that had kept a cooped-up boy from totally losing it that summer, a moment before she gave him a one-armed hug…and she was soft and warm and strong and giving, no longer smelling of grape soda and potato chips but of something sweet and musky and honest, a scent way past dangerous to a battered, stunned man whose life kept falling in the crapper.

Then she leaned back slightly, her hand still on his arm, drawing him into the calm behind that smile, and he knew the exact instant when she saw what nobody else did, when those deep blue eyes said, *Come in out of the storm, where it's safe.*

As if.

I know that look, Lili thought, her Empathy Alert System spiking to at least orange level as she gazed into those dark, haunted eyes and saw a man struggling not to fall apart in public—

"She's probably getting pretty heavy," he said, taking the baby from her.

—rather than, say, the slightly dulled, stoic grief of someone who'd lost the love of his life several months before.

A thought which did nothing to mitigate the flush still stinging her chest and cheeks from before she'd stumbled into all that sadness and shock, when she'd spotted Tony across the room and her brain simply stood aside and gave her hormones the floor, those rowdy hooligans yelling *Taller! Broader! And did you notice the mouth, perchance?* in her ear.

Can we say, inappropriate?

Not that she and Tony were real cousins, since her parents and Tony's weren't related to each other, except by Magda and Benny's marriage. Not a single gene shared, anywhere. Still. What hadn't been right then still wasn't right now. Her hugging him, that is. Because they never had before. Although it was no big deal, everybody hugged and kissed in this family, that was just the way with these Mediterranean types, even those three generations removed from the home country.

And the tingling would subside. Eventually.

As would the instant, mortifying reversion to lovesick teenager indulging a forbidden fantasy.

"How old is she?" Lili said, smiling, unable to keep from touching the silky blond hair. To keep the slight sting of longing at bay.

"I'm this many," the little girl said, holding up two fingers.

"Oooh, big girl. And what's your name?"

"Josie. You're pretty."

Lili flushed even more. "Thank you, sweet lamb. So are you."

"I know," she said, and Lili laughed, before some female cousin Lili didn't really know carted off the child—Tony's gaze followed, protective and sad—and then it was just the two of them, awkward and bufferless.

Then Tony smiled for her, a very different smile from those he'd first spared for her that summer, when his entertainment options had been reduced to hanging out with a younger cousin who wasn't even cool by Hungarian standards. "Wow. It's really you."

"It really is."

But he'd never been snide or condescending. And by the end of the summer, the smiles had come more readily, as well as the conversations and laughter, easing Lili's chronic awkwardness. No surprise, then, that she'd developed a huge crush on him. Except he'd had a girlfriend and she was going back to Hungary, anyway, and…well.

The crush, thank God, had eventually faded. The memory of all that kindness and patience and honesty, however, hadn't. That he should be going through such hell now broke her heart.

"You have other children?" she asked.

"Yeah," he breathed out. "Two more girls. They're around somewhere, I'm sure you'll meet them."

"I'm sure I will." Then she said, "I'm so sorry about Marissa," and Tony actually jerked, the pain blossoming anew in his eyes as his mouth flattened into a grim line, and she thought, *Put a foot in it, why not?*

But before she could think of some way out of the tangle she was rapidly making of the conversation, she was nearly thrown off balance when her—their—aunt wrapped one arm around Lili's waist, releasing enough perfume to fell oxen at twenty kilometers.

"Tony, sweetheart! You made it! Now my birthday is complete."

Lili watched, amazed, as Tony seemed to shrug off his pain like an ill-fitting coat, then leaned over to kiss their aunt on the cheek. A move which brought his pheromones close enough to wink at Lili's hormones, those sad, neglected things. "Like I'd miss it, Aunt Mag."

Their aunt laughed, then squeezed Lili's waist. Harder. "And hesn't our Lili turned into a lovely young voman?"

Oh, dear, Lili thought, until Tony leveled an unexpected, and unnervingly steady, gaze on her and said, "Yes. She certainly has," and she could barely hear for all the stampeding hormones.

Before they trampled her to death, she spun around and ran.

"No, you come vis me," Magda said when Tony started after Lili, instead steering him toward the back of the house.

"But—"

"She'll come out ven she's ready. Like a kitty from under ze bed."

His aunt gently pushed him out onto the deck, the clinkety-clanking of a dozen bangles mingling with the roar of count-less gabbing Vaccaros, where the summertime smells of freshly cut grass and seared meat and beer taunted him with their overtones of joviality and predictability and normalcy. Trying to ignore the hot, sudden sting of sexual awareness, he scanned the crowd of husbands and wives and kids— laughing and arguing and fussing at each other—jealous as all hell and not even trying to deny it.

"Why's Lili here?" he said, more sharply than he probably should've.

"Is a long story," Magda said with a tinkly wave. "You can esk her yourself, later. For me?" she squealed, when another of her kids arrived bearing grandchildren and presents.

She'd barely floated off when a hearty clap on Tony's shoulder blasted him out of his thoughts—Rudy Vaccaro, big as a damn mountain and the cousin closest in age to Tony. They'd hung out a lot together, both as kids and after, and Tony had really missed the bastard since he'd moved. Rudy pressed an ice-cold, and very welcome, Bud into Tony's hand. "Good to see you, man."

"Yeah. You, too. Only don't even think about asking me how I'm doing." Rudy would understand the warning. And not question it. Still, below a buzz cut that should've made him look a lot scarier than it did, sympathy swam in sharp blue eyes.

"Wouldn't dream of it," he said as Violet, his still-new, cute-as-a-bug wife came up beside him.

"C'mere, you…" Violet yanked Tony down for a hug, her mess of orange curls ticking his chin before she let go, giving him a shrewd look. "How're the girls?"

"Doin' okay," Tony said, scanning the crowd for Lili. Not having a clue why. "Considering."

"Saw the baby earlier," Violet said. "Celeste was showin' her off like she was her own. God, she looks exactly like you. Except for the blond hair, obviously," she added, having no idea her words were like an ice pick to the heart.

Rudy lifted his own beer to Tony. "You and the girls should come up for a cuppla days—"

"Absolutely!" Violet said when Tony demurred. "We're booked most weekends, but we sometimes have openings during the week. And you're off from school all summer, right? It would do the girls good. And the boys would love it!"

"Yeah, Stace would be in heaven, havin' all those kids to boss around. God, I thought thirteen was a pain-in-the-ass, that's nothin' compared with fourteen. If we ever have another kid?" Rudy pulled his wife close. "And it's a girl? I'm seriously considering shipping her off to boardin' school between the ages of twelve and eighteen."

"Oh, right, you'd curl up in a ball and die if Stace wasn't around…"

Violet's jabbering faded to white noise when Tony spotted Lili creeping out onto the deck, arms crossed and eyes darting around the yard, and the stinging started up again, bad, *real* bad, bad enough to sound some heavy-duty alarms—

"Excuse me, I need to, uh…"

Run like hell. Throw up. Have my head examined.

Rudy and Violet's heads turned as one, then back. Matching grins. Hell.

"Hey," Rudy said, "you should bring Lili with you. She said she's never been to New Hampshire." Tony gawked at the man like he'd lost it. "What? It's not like I'm suggesting something untoward or anything. And anyway, in a cuppla weeks," he added with a discreet nod toward his mother, "she might need some serious rescuing."

"Yeah, yeah, I'll think about it, thanks," Tony muttered, giving Rudy a final arm slap and heading toward Lili—who'd clearly seen him—before she could bolt.

Except…this was nuts, this was just *Lili,* for God's sake, all that stuff about her getting him—or whatever—was just his sleep-and-sex-deprived, shocked brain shorting out. Playing tricks. Really dirty tricks. So he'd talk to her, right? Clear this whole crazy thing up.

Except as he closed the gap between them, he saw her take a deep breath, then smile, a smile that said, *I don't understand, either,* and a little voice inside him said, *Maybe not so crazy.* Which could only mean he was one step removed from certifiable.

And yet, he kept walking.

Lili stood, frozen, watching Tony charge toward her, telling herself she wasn't afraid of him, exactly, it was her own messed-up feelings—feelings perhaps dismissed a bit prematurely—giving her pause.

Especially when he marched up to her, all dark in the face, growling, "Why'd you run off?"

"Don't be ridiculous, I didn't—"

"Like hell. And I'm guessing you're fighting the urge to do it again."

"Just as you fought against coming over here?"

Her face burned again, at her own boldness. At the sudden spark of something close to self-hatred in his eyes. "You have no idea," he said softly, and she thought, *This can't be happening.*

Lili glanced around, but nobody seemed to be paying the least bit of attention to them. Then she met Tony's eyes again, and her stomach jumped at the way he was looking at her, as though he was being ripped apart inside.

"What's this about, Tony?"

He slightly smiled. "Beats me. Except…" He clasped her bare arm, smartly moving her through the sea of bodies and out into the yard, heavy with the scent of Aunt Magda's prized roses.

"Where are we going?"

"Over there, in the shade," he said, nodding toward the huge old oak on the other side of the yard, sheltering a sturdy tree house worn smooth from two generations' worth of kids.

Including the teenage Lili, who'd spent countless hours that summer stargazing through a million quivering leaves and giving her heated imagination its head. Now, as then, heavily flowered rhododendrons, set in a rainbow tangle of pungent marigolds and petunias, smothered the wooden fence, but the circular stone bench girding the old tree was new. She started to sit; Tony dragged her back.

"Bird poop. Better sit on the grass instead."

"And…aren't there just as many droppings in the grass?"

"Yeah, but at least you can't see them. No, wait," he said, stripping off the unbuttoned, lightweight shirt he wore over his T-shirt and chivalrously spreading it on the ground. "Grass stains are a bitch to get out of white fabric." When Lili gave him a bemused look, he shrugged, his heart-wrenching attempts at acting normal at such odds with the pain etched in his features. "At my house real men do laundry. And Daphne's made me a kick-ass expert on grass stains."

Her heart beating overtime, Lili kicked off her sandals and folded herself onto the soft cotton shirt. Tony dropped onto the grass beside her, close enough for his scent to spark the achy, bittersweet memory of unrequited longing. "Better?" he asked.

"Yes. Much. Thank you." She offered him a slight smile, then squinted back at the house. "I never have been all that comfortable around large groups of people."

"Why do you think I rescued you?"

She paused. "And not yourself?"

With a soft laugh through his nose, Tony leaned back on his elbows, his hooded gaze aimed toward the house. "Normally I'm up for these clan gatherings, but today…" His jaw clenched, he shook his head before taking a long swallow of beer. "Except no way in hell would anybody let me stray from the herd."

"So you decided we could stray together."

"Yeah. Just like old times, huh? You and me against the world."

"Is that what we were? United against everybody else?"

His mouth tilted. "Sure felt like it. I was mad as hell about my summer being screwed, you were pissed about your family dumpin' you off on Magda and Benny—"

"I was not! Especially since it was far better than the alternative."

Tony chuckled, and she smiled. She'd told him back then that, despite her father's assumption she'd join the act, by the time she was ten it was painfully obvious she had neither the talent nor the enthusiasm for the trapeze. It had taken a bit longer for the family to accept that Lili hated *everything* about circus life. Tony, however, had understood it immediately.

"Makin' you the only kid in the world who wanted to run *away* from the circus."

She shrugged. "But won't our being out here by ourselves invite…speculation?"

"Rather deal with that than the nagging. And at least this way they'll leave us *both* alone. For the moment, at least."

A breeze blew her hair into her mouth; she tugged it out, tucking it behind her ear. "Tired of being the strong one, are you?" she said quietly, not looking at him. This time when he laughed, there wasn't an ounce of humor in it.

"You always were one scary female, you know that?"

"About as scary as a newborn kitten. And you didn't answer my question."

"Not gonna, either," he said, tilting the can to his mouth again, only then seeming to notice she was empty-handed. "Hey—you want anything…?"

"No, no…I'm fine. So. Magda says you teach school?"

"Yeah," he said, his shoulders relaxing. "High school phys ed. Coach the football team." He paused. "Not exactly living the dream I had way back when. But then, how many people do?"

"You don't sound terribly unhappy about that."

"Now? No. Then…" He blew a stream of air through his lips. "That busted leg screwed up any chance I had of even making a college team, let alone a shot at the pros. So I did the next best thing and majored in PE." His mouth curved. "Smartest move I ever made." Then he sighed. "Damn, Lil— it's like no time's passed at all."

Too true, she thought, sternly telling her heart and her hormones and everything else yipping in her ears to be quiet. "I know what you mean."

"Even so…something's changed."

"It *has* been fourteen years."

"I'm not talking about the way you look. Although you look good. Maybe still a little on the reserved side, but good—"

Lili looked down at her dress. "What's wrong with what I'm wearing?"

"I didn't say anything was wrong with it, I said you looked good, didn't I? And you know that's not what I mean. There's something different about *you.* You were quiet, sure, but…why'd you take off like that, when we were talking before?"

She brought her knees up, tucking her full skirt around her legs before hugging her shins. A burst of laughter went up from the deck; Lili shooed a fly off her arm, then said, "Because I'm not sure what you want from me. It really does seem as if…as if no time's passed at all. That everything's exactly the same, even though…" Frowning, she let her eyes touch his again. "Nothing is."

Tony's eyes narrowed slightly before he made a soft, derisive sound through his nose. "I'm not sure what I want from you, either," he said, and Lili mentally stood aside to let the disappointment shuffle on through, even as she chided herself for the moment's foolish detour. Even ignoring the fact that they'd only ever been friends—for a single summer a million years ago, at that—Tony was a recent widower. One plagued by heaven knew what other issues. What on earth had she expected? A fairy tale?

"Are those your other two girls over there?" she said, steering the subject into hopefully safer territory.

Tony sat up to get a better look at the crowd, briefly bumping her shoulder. "The little curly-headed demon runnin' around with Rudy's stepsons?" he said, sagging back. "That's Daphne. She's seven, so smart I can barely keep up and gets dirtier faster than any of her boy cousins could even dream of. And the one wearing the Patriots hat and the grump face, hanging next to Stacey? That's Claire. She'll be eleven in a couple months."

"Oh, my…she's going to be a knockout, isn't she?"

"And I could have happily gone all day without you sayin' that. Although…she's been, uh, eating more since her mother died. My mother-in-law keeps making these not-so-subtle comments about Claire's diet. Like I'm gonna deny the kid the occasional bag of French fries on top of everything else she's been through?"

"Of course you're not," Lili said, her heart twisting at the obvious conflict behind his words. Not that she was any expert, but she imagined that wanting what was best for your child and wanting to make her happy weren't always compatible goals. Josie ran across the deck, not watching where she was going; Claire caught the baby as she tripped, giving her a kiss before their aunt scooped the toddler back up into her arms.

"Claire's very good with Josie, isn't she?"

"Yeah," Tony said after another moment. "She is. Bossy as hell, though. With all of us. Supposedly that's normal for the oldest kid. Especially after a loss."

"Which I suppose accounts for the frown currently aimed in our direction?"

"Don't take it personally. Claire frowns at everybody." He

sighed. "At every*thing*. What I don't get, though, is how she can be so self-assertive one moment, so insecure the next."

Without thinking, Lili laid a hand on Tony's forearm, solid as iron beneath her fingertips. "It's early days yet," she said softly, and his eyes bounced off hers.

"That's what I'm hoping."

Suddenly self-conscious, Lili folded her arms around her legs again to wiggle her bare toes in the grass at the edge of the shirt, meeting his oldest daughter's laser-bright glare from across the yard. "You're doing a good job with them. I can tell."

"Some days I'm not so sure," he said after a moment. "But nobody can say I'm not tryin' my best. My kids…they're my life, you know?"

"Obviously," Lili said, thinking, *You've grown up very nicely indeed, Tony Vaccaro.*

A thought that could make her extraordinarily sad, if she let it.

"Who's that?" Claire said, following Stacey to a couple of beat-up lawn chairs on the other side of the deck. "The woman with my dad?"

Her older cousin glanced over as she dropped into a chair. "That's Lili." She reached over her head to twist her long, shiny, dark hair up with a band so the ends all fanned out. On Stacey, it looked totally cool. Claire tried it once and looked like an alien. "Aunt Magda's niece. She's visiting for the month, I guess. From Hungary. Wouldja mind handing me a Coke from that ice chest? God, it's hot out here."

Thrilled at being asked to do something for her fourteen-year-old cousin—the rest of her older cousins usually ignored her—Claire plowed one hand through the cold, slippery cubes to get a Coke, casting a quick glance over her shoulder before sliding out one for herself, too. She'd already had one today, Dad would have kittens if he caught her with another.

Not to mention Nana, ohmigod. The chest slammed shut, Claire handed Stace her drink, then sat next to her, shifting several times before realizing no matter what she did, she was never gonna look as good as Stace, not with her stupid short legs. Or her dumb lumpy hair which never looked nice no matter what she did with it.

Being ten sucked. The older kids could do whatever they wanted, practically, and everybody loved the younger ones because they were still cute. What was super sucky, though, was being old enough to know when something was going on, but too young to do anything about it.

Claire popped the tab off the soda and glared some more at her dad and this Lili person. At least she wasn't touching him anymore, because that had just been, like, five kinds of wrong. Like she was trying to act like his girlfriend or something—

"Oh, God," Stacey said, laughing. "I know *exactly* what you're thinking. About your dad and Lili?"

Claire's cheeks warmed. "Who said I'm thinking anything?"

"Yeah, right. It's, like, so written all over your face. It's okay, I felt the same way when we first moved to New Hampshire, and Dad and Violet started making eyes at each other?" She skootched down in her chair, her eyes drifting closed. "I was all, *Get a room*—in my head, I mean—except not really, because that was so not what I wanted to happen."

When Stacey didn't say anything else, Claire squinted over at her. "But it did happen," she said, wondering if Stacey thought this was supposed to be making Claire feel better. Sweat was beginning to pop out in little drops on her upper lip. Ew. She really wanted to go back inside, but then Stacey might think she was a baby. "Violet and your dad got married."

Stacey shrugged, her eyes closed. "I got over it. But anyway, it's totally different with your dad and Lili."

"Why do you think that?"

"First off, my dad said your dad was like seriously in love with your mom. Kids are ridiculous, they break up and two days later they're with somebody else." Her eyes still closed, she did the little shuddering thing. "But grownups take for*ever* to get over a broken heart. I mean, yeesh, it took my dad, what? Twelve years? Second, they're just friends. Or were, apparently."

"Were?"

Stacey opened her eyes to peer at Claire from underneath lashes with about five coats of mascara. "Baba said Lili was here before, like before I was born. So this isn't any big whoop, it's just them catching up and stuff. Anyway," she said, snuggling back into the chair, "Lili's going back to Hungary at the end of the month. So trust me—you've got absolutely nothing to worry about."

"You sure?"

"Claire. They're, like, almost *related*. Nothing's gonna happen, okay?"

When Stacey closed her eyes again, Claire finally took a sip of her Coke. It burned her throat all the way down, making her choke so hard her eyes watered. Dad looked over, frowning, to make sure she was okay.

She waved, slipping the soda behind her so he wouldn't see.

"Is Claire all right? Should you go check on her?"

"She's fine," Tony said, finishing up his now-warm beer, trying not to react to the genuine concern in Lili's voice. Even as a kid herself, she'd been great with the younger cousins. Nice strong maternal instinct, there. "She also thinks I didn't see her drinking her second Coke of the afternoon."

"A minor offense, all things considered. And isn't it diet, anyway?"

Her accent was much lighter than his aunt's, usually, except when she got emotional. When she stopped thinking so hard about the words and let her feelings do the talking. He hadn't realized how much he'd missed it.

"Yeah, except the caffeine buzz will keep her awake half the night. Nothin' worse than a ten-year-old insomniac." He scratched his head as an icy wave of comprehension surged through him, that he sure as hell wouldn't sleep tonight, either. Or for God knew how many nights after. "Except a thirty-two-year-old one."

Lili curled to pluck at a clump of clover near her polished toes—a light pink that hardly seemed worth the bother. "So. Are you going to make good use of me or not?"

Tony jerked. "Excuse me?"

Her eyes slid to his, accompanied by a slight smile. "I'm as good a listener as I ever was. If you'd like to tell me what's really bothering you…?"

Tony sucked in a breath, both because she'd caught him off guard and because until that moment he'd had no idea how he'd *kill* to give this horrible, sick feeling inside him some air. Instead he crushed his beer can and said, "So what have you been up to for the past…what is it again? Fourteen years?" When she didn't answer, he glanced at her, then turned away again. "I can't. Not yet."

"It hurts that much?"

"Dammit, Lil—"

"Sorry," she whispered, the word as caring as a touch. And almost as devastating to his self-control. Thank God, then, she said, "I have two degrees in linguistics—I'm fluent in five languages now—"

"Impressive."

"Not really. I already spoke them when I started university—the one good thing about all that touring around Europe as a kid—but the grammar needed a bit of tidying up. So I do a lot of freelance translation work. Textbooks, novels, that sort of thing." She paused. "And I almost got married."

"Almost?" Tony said over the totally unexpected jolt to his midsection.

"Years ago. Right about the time my stepfather left my mother." She smoothed the dress's hem over her toes. "For a twenty-two-year-old."

"Ouch. When was this?"

"About five years ago."

"Damn, your mother really had it rough, didn't she? But I don't follow. What'd one have to do with the other?"

Lili tucked a long strand of hair behind her ear, a nervous gesture he remembered from before. "Mama was devastated, as you can imagine." *More than you know,* Tony thought as she added, "So it was obvious she couldn't be alone. None of the boys could take her in, since they were all still travel-ing with the act. So I decided to move out of the flat I'd been sharing with some university chums and back in with her until my wedding, assuming she could come live with Peter—my fiancé—and me in our flat afterward. Except Peter never really got on with my mother. The idea of our all living together, even temporarily…" Her mouth thinned. "He made me choose."

"Nice guy."

She shrugged, then said, "The ironic thing was, Mama and I had actually been estranged for a while before that. And yet when she needed me, I never even thought twice about being there for her. Because that's what you do, isn't it? When a parent or child needs you, you're there. Peter's not under-standing that was a deal breaker."

"And what've you been doing since then?" When she didn't reply, Tony felt his eyebrows lift. "Cripes, Lili—you took care of your mother for five *years?*"

"Obviously I hadn't intended things to play out the way they did. Or for her to get sick. But at the beginning…" She frowned, still staring at her toes. "I'm not sure what happened, to tell you the truth. Maybe I had a delayed reaction to my own breakup, or maybe I just enjoyed getting to know my mother again, going shopping and preparing meals together, catching up on movies and books. Talking."

Her head propped in her palm, she smiled at him. "We became very good friends, during that time. Much closer than we'd been before. I honestly never felt burdened. Not even when she became ill. If anything, I was simply grateful that I could be there for her. In many ways, especially in the beginning, it felt very…safe." She sighed. "Although I suppose most people would see it as not being very brave. Which I suppose I'm not," she added with a shrug. "I mean, here I am, completely free for the first time in years, and what do I do? Come stay with my aunt and uncle for a month. How weird is that?"

"Okay, you might have a point there," he said, making her laugh, the sound deeper, richer than before. "But you know something? Screw other people. It's your life, live it the way you want to. As for you not being brave…" He shook his head. "Goin' against your family about the circus, being there for your mother, telling your fiancé to basically go take a hike…hell, Lili, you've got more guts than probably ninety percent of the people on this planet."

"You're very kind."

"Only calling it as I see it. And just for the record, that fiancé of yours was a selfish bastard who didn't deserve you. *Or* your mother."

A sudden grin lit up her eyes behind her glasses. "Spoken like someone who didn't know my mother."

"Was she anything like Magda?"

"Worse."

"Oh."

Lili chuckled, then released another breath, wrapping her arms around her legs. "Still. I feel a bit like Rip Van Winkle waking up after his very long nap, trying to figure out where I fit in this strange new world of being on my own."

Up on the deck, Uncle Benny said something that apparently cracked up their aunt, making her laugh so hard she had to lean on him to catch her breath. And the look on his uncle's face…

"You believe in love at first sight?" Tony asked out of the blue, thinking of how Benny and Magda met so many years ago, the cop falling head over heels for the circus girl after seeing her perform.

Following his gaze, Lili said, "The kind that sneaks up and surprises you? Yes, I suppose. Even though it's completely illogical."

"Not sure logic's got much to do with love."

Lili's eyes swung back to his. "Wow. Deep," she said, sending something gentle and warm and hugely dangerous snaking through him, at how easy it was, being together like this. Then he caught Claire watching them again, vibrating with worry, reminding him that nothing was easy. That being a grownup meant you couldn't just run with something because you wanted to.

His wife's apparent unfamiliarity with the concept notwithstanding.

Tony smirked. "One thing I'm not, it's deep. Just your average everything's-right-there-on-the-surface kind of guy."

"Nothing wrong with that. Still. I sometimes think the best love is the kind that happens almost effortlessly, like a plant that takes root on its own."

"Like weeds?"

She laughed again. "Like wildflowers. Certainly, there was nothing effortless about my relationship with Peter. Not that even the strongest love doesn't need tending, of course, but I should have known when it became such a struggle—" Biting her lip, she swung apologetic eyes to his. "Sorry. Don't mean to bore you with tales of my woebegone love life."

Better than mine, Tony thought, as, like a distorted St. Nicholas behind a curtain of shimmering heat waves rising from the grill, Uncle Benny called everybody to dinner. Because more than once it had occurred to Tony, too, that it wasn't right, him and Marissa having to struggle so hard to keep the flame going those last years. Sure, all marriages took work, but when every single conversation becomes a chore, you know something's wrong.

He just hadn't known how wrong, Tony thought, thinking of the letter, crushed into a drawer in his office, crushing him inside—

"Are you coming?" Lili said, already on her feet, her gaze direct and honest, her sandals dangling from one hand and the breeze blowing her hair. Tony stood, the urge to touch her— to connect with her generosity and goodness—so strong it was like an electric shock to his heart…even as he knew how unfair to both of them it would be to follow through on the impulse.

Because who was he kidding, he knew damn well what he wanted from Lili, had known from practically the minute he laid eyes on her, and it made him sick, what he was thinking. Made him realize how bad off he was, even entertaining the idea of using Lili to soothe the anger and the grief and the black, bottomless loneliness threatening to suck out his brain.

"You go on. I'll catch up later."

He wasn't at all surprised to see the confusion in her eyes. That, he could deal with. The understanding that immediately followed, however…

Damn near killed him.

All Claire wanted to do, when she saw Lili heading her way, was run. But there was no way that was happening, especially since Aunt Magda dragged her over to introduce them. When Lili held out her hand, Claire figured she didn't exactly have a lot of choice about taking it or not. At least it wasn't clammy or anything, and she didn't hang on too long, or try to hug her and act like they were going to be BFFs or something. Lili was pretty, but not like Mama. Mama was *gorgeous*—

Then she got, like, stuck in Lili's eyes, which were seriously the bluest eyes she'd ever seen, only they weren't cold like you'd expect. And her smile was just, you know, normal and stuff, not like she was *trying* to be nice or anything. So why Claire felt her face get all hot, she had no idea.

"Lili's visiting from Hungary," her aunt was saying, and Claire said, "Yeah, I know, Stacey told me," then excused herself, which she knew was rude but she couldn't help it, she felt like she was gonna cry and she didn't even know why.

Breathing hard, she ran down the deck's steps and out into the yard, toward Dad, who was sitting in the grass again with his arms folded over his knees, resting his head on them. When she sat beside him, though, he looked at her, smiling a little.

"You look like I feel," he said, and she shrugged.

"I'm okay, I guess."

Dad reached over and squeezed her shoulder. "Where's your sisters?"

"Daph's still with Violet's boys, I think. And Kevin and Julianne just got here…look," she, said, pointing to Rudy's youngest brother, laughing at Josie trying to take his eighteen-month-old daughter by the hand and lead her God knew where. Well, actually, Pip was Kevin's daughter, but Julianne's niece, except now they were married so she was Pip's mom, too. It all made Claire's head hurt.

"Pip doesn't look any too sure about going with Josie," Dad said.

"Smart kid," Claire said, and Dad actually laughed.

"I see you met Lili," he said quietly, and Claire got that tight feeling in her chest again.

"Yeah. You gonna come eat?"

"Not hungry. But you go on."

"I could bring you a burger or something—"

"That's okay, baby—"

"We could eat out here, just you 'n' me."

After a moment, Dad nodded. "Sure. That'd be cool." When Claire got up, dusting off her bottom, Dad added, "We can leave right after the cake, if that's okay."

Her eyes all stingy, Claire said, "Yeah, fine," and ran back to the deck, through all the laughter bouncing off her like hailstones.

Chapter Three

Still mulling over Tony's very obvious dismissal two hours earlier, Lili gave the kitchen sink a final rinse just as her aunt and uncle hauled in yet more leftover food from the backyard.

"Didn't I tell ya you made too much?" Uncle Benny grumbled, hefting a bowl of barely eaten potato salad—yes, the very potato salad Lili had spent an hour making—onto the kitchen table. "I keep tellin' her," he now directed to Lili as she set the sponge on the back of the sink, "nobody eats like they useta, when the boys were teenagers. And half the time, the wives are on some diet or other. Unless they're pregnant."

He said this with a pointed look for Mia, Lili's only female cousin, carting in a platter of unclaimed burgers and hot dogs. Tall and thin, her warm brown waves caught in a ponytail, Mia gave him a pointed look right back. "Jeez…nosy, much?"

"What?" Benny said when Magda swatted him. "Her and Grant, they've been married a year, already."

"Pops? They have this thing called birth control? So, you know, you can plan when you have kids?" Then she slapped her head. "What am I saying, you guys had six kids in, like, five minutes."

"Benny on baby bump watch again?" Grant said, dragging a sloshy cooler into the kitchen, and Lili was glad nobody expected her to take part in the conversation because every time she clapped eyes on the man her tongue went numb. Rich, handsome, funny—her cousin had seriously hit the jackpot. Except Lili would take an ex-jock athletic coach she could actually talk to over Mr. Adonis, any day—

Stop that.

"Like you guys don't have enough grandkids already, yeesh," Mia said, sharing a quick glance with her husband that Magda did *not* miss.

"Vat's going on?"

"Nothing, Ma," Mia said, giving her mother a huge hug, and Lili felt the sting of missing her own. "We gotta go, I got an anniversary party in the Hamptons tomorrow—"

"Oooh…" Magda's eyes lit up. "Enybody famous?"

"Nope. Just loaded. C'mon, kiddo," she said to her step-daughter, Haley, a six-year-old pixie with blond curls, as Grant embraced his mother-in-law. Mia gave Lili a hug, too, said how great it was to see her again, then they were all gone, leaving Lili alone with her aunt and uncle, their two dogs and enough food to feed Eastern Europe. For a week.

As the dogs danced around, tripping over each other, Magda surveyed the leavings, sighing. "It must be ze heat. At Thanksgiving they eat like locusts. Okay, Benny, you know ze drill. Tupperware, now, and keep it coming—" She stopped, noticing the sparkling sink and surrounding counter. "Honestly, Lili—I nefer in my life knew anyone who likes to clean like you do. My own children, zey would rather parade nekked down the street zen clean. You, I nefer even have to ask, you just do it."

Lili shrugged. "I've always liked cleaning. Putting things to rights. It's…soothing."

Magda narrowed her eyes. "You are a strange young woman," she said in Hungarian, and Benny, seated at the table, groaned.

"Aw, Mag…you know I hate when you do that."

"Hah! You remember efter we met, before I spoke English as good as I do now? How your parents vould talk in front of me, and all I could mek out was Magda zis and Magda zat. I zink zey call zis payback."

Lili laughed. "It comes from too many years living with messy brothers in tiny circus trailers. It drove me crazy. And Mama. So I'd clean while they were performing." She skimmed a finger over the clean counter. "I still like wresting order out of chaos. Not that your kitchen's chaotic—"

"Sveetheart, my *life* is chaos," she said, and Benny said, "Hey," and her aunt swooped around the kitchen table to hug him from behind. "I *embrace* chaos," she said, giving him a big kiss on his bearded cheek.

"Not me," Lili said as parts of her conversation with Tony came roaring back. "I've always avoided it at all costs." As in, her life being a series of choices based on whatever was least likely to cause her *agita*. For instance…she could have pushed Tony harder to open up about whatever was bothering him, especially when it was perfectly obvious how little she would have had to push. But did she? No—

"And yet you decided to come stay with us?" Benny said. After another ineffectual swat, Magda tugged him out of the chair and gave him a gentle shove toward the door. "What? You're throwin' me outta my own kitchen?"

"Yes. Lili and I need to talk. Voman to voman."

"Auntie—"

"And no beck-talk from you," Magda said, pointing a freshly-applied acrylic fingernail in her direction. Lili momentarily considered sliding down the drain. Especially after her aunt's heartfelt sigh, once Benny had gone.

"Ven you were here before, I was so vorried about you, zat you were—vat is zat expression? A square peg in a round hole? Ze quiet one, always vis her nose in ze books. So…" a glob of potato salad smacked into a container "—afraid of…putting yourself out zere. But I zink, is just a phase, she'll grow out of it."

Lili frowned. "Because I didn't get the circus gene?"

"Of course not, did I say that? And I couldn't be prouder of you. Five languages! And *two* degrees! But zat summer, I vatched you change from zis scared little bunny rabbit into a confident young voman—"

That was Tony, Lili thought, something sharp clutching her throat as she burped the lid over the Jell-O salad. *Tony did that to me.* For *me*—

"—only now," Magda said, "I see you and zink, vat heppened? I'll tell you vat happened—my sister let you give up your life for her—"

"But it wasn't like that! And anyway, you know as well as I do what a mess Mama was. If it hadn't been for me—"

"She vould hef put on her big girl panties and gotten on vis things! And maybe she vould hef done somezing better than just vaiting out ze last five years of her life!"

Lili frowned. "Are you implying I somehow held Mama back?"

"I'm not implying anyzing, I'm saying point-blank. And it vorked both vays. The two of you held each *other* back. For God's sake, Lili, you vere going to get married!"

Ah. "It's okay, auntie, since I eventually realized that wasn't who I needed at that point in my life. And he obviously didn't need me." She shrugged. "Mama did."

"But you were hurt."

"Of course I was hurt," she said, surprised at the twinge,

even after all this time. "It's a bitch, discovering someone isn't who you thought he was. Mama and I…I suppose we were both dealing with the same feeling of betrayal. Although obviously mine was on a much smaller scale. But it's all good now," she said, lifting her chin. "My heart's all healed. Stronger than ever, in fact."

"You zink hearts are like bones, zey're stronger for being broken?"

"Perhaps," Lili said with a slight smile. "And anyway, I believe things work out the way they're meant to. Except…"

"And how did I know there vould be an 'except'?"

The containers all filled, Lili sat at the table, frowning. "The day Mama died, I stood in the middle of the kitchen and realized I was nearly thirty and still had no more idea about what I was supposed to do with my life than I did ten years ago. Because you were right, earlier. About my not fitting in anywhere." A smile tugged at her mouth. "Ever since I was little, I was both the circus brat who didn't fit in with other 'normal' kids, as well as the oddball in the family. Now I feel as though everyone else caught the boat, leaving me stranded on the shore."

"Oh, sveetheart…" Magda sat with her, cupping Lili's cheeks in a gesture so much like her mother's Lili's eyes stung. "Trust me—zere's more zen one boat."

Lili laughed. "I certainly hope so, or I'm screwed."

Smiling, Magda folded her hands together. "So how does one go about finding one's purpose?"

"That's the part I haven't figured out yet. I suppose my translating work is useful, but it's not exactly fulfilling."

That got a thoughtful frown. "You need to be needed, yes?"

"Yes, I suppose that's it."

With a sharp nod, her aunt got up to pluck a couple of plastic grocery bags from underneath the sink, filling them with some of the storage containers. "Everybody in my femily, they tell me I'm crazy for vanting to marry somebody I barely know, somebody I can barely even talk to." The first bag filled, she started in on the second. "But efter two dates with Benny, I know he's a good man, and he needs me." After plopping in a loaf of whole grain bread some kind, misguided soul had contributed to the cause, Magda turned, smiling. "Not zat he could *tell* me. But vords...too often zey come from ze head, and not ze heart. It's what a person does zat counts, no? Who he is."

The bags filled, Magda hefted them off the counter, crossed to the table and held them out. "Don't just sit zere, get up off your skinny little butt and take zese."

"And...what am I supposed to do with them?" Lili asked, taking the bags.

"Ve can't eat all zis food, it vill go bad. Nobody else needs it, either." She grinned. "Tony, on ze ozzer hand..."

"Oh, no—" Lili tried to hand the bags back, but Magda folded her arms so she couldn't. So Lili swung them back up on the table and folded *her* arms.

"I am not going over there on some...some mission of mercy."

"And vy not?"

"You know full well vy—*why* not."

"Zen meybe you should explain to me."

"The man's just lost his wife. And Claire looks at me as if I'm carrying some flesh-eating virus. How am I doing so far?"

"You vant to be needed? I nefer see anybody needier than Tony right now."

"True. But it's not me he needs."

"I'm no so sure of zat. Lili," Magda said when Lili released a breathy laugh, "you zink I don't see the special bond you two hed before?"

"Oh, please. To Tony, I was just a little sister. An annoying one, too, no doubt."

"I am not talking about how Tony felt about *you*. But iz easy for a young girl to develop feelings for an older boy, yes? Especially a boy who treats you with such kindness?"

Lili's eyes narrowed. She'd never said one word to her aunt—or anybody else, for that matter—about her crush. That dumb, she wasn't. Even then. "Where are you going with this?"

Slowly, Madga smiled. "You remember the diary you lost, ven you were here before?"

"Yes, I…" Heat roared up her neck. "You found it."

"I might hef," Magda said, pretending to inspect her nails like some character from an old movie. "I might hef read some of it, too. Before I knew vat it was, of course. So," she said mildly, "you hef two choices. Tek the man ze demmed food, or I mek your life a liffing hell." At Lili's dumb-founded look, the older woman shrugged. "Vat ken I say, I fight dirty."

In spite of herself, Lili chuckled. And grabbed the bags' handles. Although she sincerely doubted even Magda would stoop so low as to show Tony—or anybody—the embarrassing ramblings of a lovesick fifteen-year-old, once again it was just easier to go with the flow. To do what was expected of her than to fight.

"Car keys?"

Her aunt dug them out of her pocket and handed them over. Smiling.

Soon after, Lili backed out of the driveway in Magda's pine-scented Ford Focus, the bags safely tucked under the passenger side dash. At the first stop sign, however, she started laughing all over again.

Because that diary? The one Magda threatened, however obliquely, to show Tony?

Completely in Hungarian.

She chuckled all the way to Tony's house.

While Josie happily batted at a flotilla of bath toys in the sudsy tub, Tony sagged against the wall between the toilet and the tub, sighing. The minute he'd walked back in the house an hour before, Fear had greeted him every bit as eagerly as the dog. And as messily. Tissues, meat trays, diapers—strewn from kitchen to front door. Although the argument between Child 1 and Child 2 about who was supposed to have put the rotten beast outside handily pushed Fear into a corner of his brain. However, unlike Ed—who at least had the good sense to cower and look guilty—Fear simply sat there, biding its time. Waiting to attack.

To pulverize him like Ed had all those meat trays.

"Hey. You 'sleep?"

"Not really," Tony said, as half smiling, he opened his eyes. Her chin propped on the rim of the shell-pink tub, Josie was watching him through water-spiked lashes like Tony was a damn miracle or something. Fear inched a little further out, teeth bared.

What if—?

"Dad!" Daphne yelled up the stairs. "Aunt Magda just pulled up in the driveway!"

Frowning, Tony scrambled to his feet, grabbing a towel off the rack. In one motion he yanked the baby out of the tepid water and wrapped her up like chubby little burrito, then tramped down the stairs. Except it wasn't Magda standing in his doorway, weighed down with bulging grocery bags, but Lili, all big eyes and soft smile and grownup curves, and he had to squelch the urge to yell *Run! Get out while you can!*

Then it occurred to him the woman was perfectly capable of fending off lunatic men with easily excitable libidos. Especially those who couldn't do anything even if they wanted to, since there were three children—

Ed woofed.

—and a dog in the house.

"Oh, my goodness," Lili said, dumping the bags to pat her thighs. Ed went nuts. *Nuts.* "Aren't you a wonderful doggy, yes, you are—no, no!" Much laughter as she tried to dodge his slobbery kisses. "What's his name?"

"Ed."

"Yes, Eddie…I love you, too—!"

"It's Lili," the ever-helpful Daphne said, looking up at him.

"I can see that," Tony said, hiking the soggy baby farther up into his arms. "Runnin' away already?"

Wiping dog spit off her chin, Lili grinned. Even if the grin did look a little undecided. "Tempting, but no. However—" she shoved Ed's head out of one of the bags to pick them up again "—she thought you might like some of party leftovers—"

"Dad? Who is it…? Oh."

"Hello, Claire," Lili said, her smile genuine but careful. At Claire's mumbled response, Tony cleared his throat and she sighed and said, "Hi, Lili," back. Not like she was over-joyed, but it was a beginning.

Except then she said, "You want me to get the baby ready for bed?" at the same time Daphne, already in her night-gown, said, "You gonna read to me tonight, or what?"

"Oh, I'm sorry," Lili said. "I didn't mean to interrupt your routine—"

"Not at all." The baby handed to Claire, Tony took the bags from Lili's hands, getting a good strong whiff of something pretty and kinda spicy which did a real number on his head—among other things—and what shreds of common sense he had left told him nothing good could come of this, even as he thought that was nuts, because there was no *this,* and wasn't gonna be.

"Come on in," he said.

Standing in the entryway with her arms crossed, Lili valiantly tried to ignore Claire's thundercloud face as Tony ducked into the kitchen, dumped the bags, then popped back out, striding over the well-worn, earth-toned braided rug.

"Coming, cupcake," he tossed up to Daphne, draped over the banister like a rag doll. Then to Lili, with a quick, nervous smile as he hooked one hand around the newel post and swung himself onto the stairs, "I'll be right back. There's soda and stuff in the fridge, if you want—" Halfway up, he pivoted to hunch over the banister. "Whatami thinking, you probably have plans or something, right?"

"Um…not really, no. But I can't stay long, I, er, promised to watch a video with Magda later." Lili nodded toward the kitchen. "I could put the food away, if you like."

"Oh. Sure. Claire, you mind showing Lili the kitchen—?"

She smiled. "Unless you moved it, I remember where the kitchen is."

"And I have to put the baby to bed, anyway," Claire said, stomping up the stairs past him, her baby sister expertly balanced on her hip. Lili watched as Tony's gaze followed them both for a second before he gave her a tight smile.

"Kids," he said, shrugging, then lightly banged his palm on the banister. "Right. Well. See ya in a few."

Ed, aka her New Best Friend, followed Lili into the kitchen, where he collapsed with a groan onto the mosaic-patterned linoleum. Underneath a pleated forehead, soulful brown eyes kept watch as she surveyed the familiar, eerily quiet room that had once been command central for Tony's large family, with Rhea Vaccaro the generous, iron-fisted general in charge of it all. The floor, dark wood cabinets and mustard-colored countertops were the same, but a huge, gleaming two-door refrigerator had usurped the old almond model, and on one rusty-red wall a trio of large paint swatches in bright, clear blues and greens hinted at changes to come.

Long overdue changes, Lili mused as she emptied the plastic bags, then tugged open one of the refrigerator doors, bringing the dog instantly to his huge feet, floppy ears perked. Eyes firmly clamped on the container in her hands, he slowly lowered his hindquarters to the floor. Looked from container to Lili to container again.

Chuckling, Lili popped it open and pulled out a hot dog. Looking as if he might weep with joy, Ed gingerly accepted the offering, only to gulp it down in a single chew—

"He's not supposed to have people food," Claire said behind her, making her jump. "It gives him really disgusting gas."

"Oh! I'm sorry," Lili said, blushing as she dove into the fridge and began rearranging innumerable deli packages, leftover Chinese take-away and half-eaten yogurts to fit in her aunt's offerings. Behind her, Ed burped, and Lili felt like slime.

Only to choke back a laugh when Claire said, "You are *so* not sleeping in my room tonight." Then, "So you were here before?"

Lili twisted around. The intense, suspicious glare was at complete odds with the girl's slouched stance, the tightly tucked arm over her round stomach, the constant twisting of a strand of hair around and around her finger. *Déjà vu,* she thought on a spike of sympathy.

"Ages ago," she said mildly, wedging containers of vinegary, red cabbage slaw and macaroni salad in amongst the chaos. Noticing that the cottage cheese sell-by date harked back to late spring, she removed it, setting it on the counter. "When this was still your grandparents' house."

"Dad's parents, you mean? They're both dead now."

"I know," Lili said with a quick, hopefully sympathetic smile. "I liked them both, very much."

"I don't really remember them. Daph wasn't even born yet."

The first batch of goodies tucked safely in their new home, Lili stood to retrieve the rest of the containers. Desperate for another conversational topic, she nodded toward the paint swatches. "I think I like the second one from the right best. How about you?"

"What?" Claire followed Lili's gaze, then seemed to realize what she was doing to her hair, perhaps because somebody had been on her case about it before. She tightly crossed her arms. "Those are from before Mom got sick. Dad hasn't had a chance to paint back over them yet."

"Paint over them? Instead of choosing one of the new colors—?"

"The red's fine. I like it."

Got it, Lili thought, plunging into the depths of the refrigerator again to shove in the hot dogs which she somehow doubted they'd ever eat. Telepathically communicating his willingness to help everyone out on that score, Ed looked up at her. And burped again.

"I suppose a new color would take some getting used to," Lili said, backing out of the fridge and shutting the door. Ed plodded off to sulk. "But sometimes it's fun to change things around, don't you think?"

"Not really," the child said with a where-do-people-come-up-with-these-things? expression. She pushed up her glasses. "Stacey says you're from Hungary, too."

"Stacey…oh, right. Rudy's daughter." *Any time now, Tony,* Lili thought as she stretched out the used plastic bags on the same pebbled glass table where she used to eat peanut butter and banana sandwiches, hand-ironing them as flat as possible before folding them into obsessively neat little squares. "That's right, I am."

"You don't sound like Aunt Magda, though."

"That's probably because I've been speaking English since I was little, whereas my aunt didn't learn it until she was already an adult."

"So how long are you staying this time?"

The words lashed across the spacious room like a whip, one wielded by a deeply wounded child still unsure of her footing in her fragile new world.

"A few weeks. I'm just here for a visit."

"Do you have a boyfriend back where you live?"

The absurdity both of the question and the situation almost made Lili laugh. And wouldn't *that* be a huge mistake? "No. I don't. Not there or anyplace else." She paused, empathizing with the fear behind the questions. The threat Lily represented to a child who'd recently lost a parent, to whom the idea of replacing that parent was far more odious than the void left in her absence. No matter how ungrounded her worries.

"Your father and I are old friends, Claire," she said gently, not surprised when the intelligent, slate-blue gaze sharpened behind her glasses. "Hardly that, even, since we haven't seen or talked to each other in so long—"

"And you're cousins, too, right? Like, family?"

"Only by marriage, not by blood. But cousins can be friends, too—"

"Ten pages," Tony said from the doorway, "and Daph was gone…" Frowning, he looked from Claire to Lili, then back to Claire. "What's going on?"

Claire pushed herself away from the counter. "Nothing. I'm going to read for a while, if that's okay."

"Sure, honey." Tony watched her leave, then turned back to Lili. "Did I miss something?"

"Only the glaring overhead light and the two-way mirror."

"What…oh." Tony sighed. "Gave you the third degree, did she?"

"Apparently my bringing leftovers set off alarms."

"Yeah, well, those alarms have hair triggers. Anything and everything sets them off these days. I'm sorry. I guess it's that protective thing kicking in again."

"So I gathered." Lili hesitated. "She reminds me a great deal of myself, after my father died. The rampant distrust, I mean."

"Didn't seem that way to me," Tony said, and she frowned at him. "Sure, you were kinda withdrawn, after you first got here. But I never felt like you were on guard or anything."

That's because I never felt I had to be on guard around you, Lili thought, saying, "I was pretty much over it by then." She nodded toward the wall. "She's having trouble with changes, I take it?"

That got a dry chuckle. "There's an understatement. I keep trying to get her to pick a color, she keeps nagging me to paint it back the way it was. Been going on for months."

"Her mother chose the colors?"

"Yeah," he breathed out. "So I thought maybe it would help, you know? Keep Marissa's spirit alive, or something." He cleared his throat; when Lili looked over, every muscle in his face had tensed. "Shows how much I know."

"Give her time." She paused. "Give *yourself* time." Feeling suddenly awkward, Lili gathered her stack of obsessively folded bags. "I should go," she said, starting out of the room, only to jump when Tony caught her arm.

"You saved my sanity that summer, Lili. I don't know if I ever told you in so many words, but you did."

She let his gaze wander in hers for several seconds before saying, "And…I suppose this might seem like a good opportunity for a repeat performance."

Tony's brows crashed over his nose. "Is that what it was? A performance?"

Oh, no, you won't, she thought, her spine tightening. If she'd held on to her self-respect as a naïve fifteen-year-old, damned if she was going to let it go now. "If by that you mean, was it a chore, keeping your company? Of course not. After all, you helped me through a bad patch, too."

He seemed to relax, if only just. "Even though it couldn't've been much fun for you. I was pretty much a pain in the ass, as I recall."

"Not any more than my brothers," she said with a smile, which he briefly returned. Lily weighed her options, skittering away like a frightened mouse ranking high on the list. But he had steered her through the worst of her grief that summer, and turning her back on him now wasn't sitting well. After all, she was only there for a few weeks, she might as well make herself useful.

"You were a good listener, too, Tony. Then, I mean—"

"Seems to me I didn't have a whole lotta choice," he said with a rueful smile. "What with my leg being in a cast and all."

"Oh, you had a choice. And I'm serious—if you need someone to talk to, I'm happy to return the favor."

"Like you don't have anything better to do than listen to a guy bitch about his sucky life?"

"Depends on the guy," she said, immediately regretting it.

Tony's eyes darkened slightly before he turned toward the refrigerator, sighing when he opened the door. "Man, FEMA would have a field day in here."

"Excuse me?"

"Never mind," he said, shutting the door again to lean heavily against it. Frowning. Obviously thinking. Then, "You ever sometimes feel like you're shoveling sand? That no matter how fast you dig, the hole just keeps filling back up?"

Fifteen years earlier Lili'd experienced firsthand the devastation the untimely death of a parent wreaks on a family.

Now, the haunted look in Tony's eyes, in Claire's, brought the memories flooding back. But she imagined Tony wasn't seeking solace as much as a sounding board. So instead of a lame, "I'm so sorry," she instead zeroed in on the practical. "Do you have help? With the house and such?"

"On a PE teacher's salary? No damn way. I mean, I manage—of course I *manage*—and the girls spend at least part of every weekend with Marissa's parents, giving me a chance to get the place cleaned up without bein' interrupted every two seconds. In fact," he said with what could only be described as guilty relief, "Susan and Lou are comin' for the girls after church tomorrow, bringin' 'em back Monday night."

"You? Clean house?" She smiled, remembering Rhea Vaccaro's telling tales on her poor, immobile son, in particular about the assorted disgusting things she'd found growing in his room over the years.

"Since it's not gonna clean itself, yeah." He rubbed the back of his neck. "Although I kinda let things slide there for a while, after the funeral. Kids got away with murder for those first few weeks, too. Well, the younger two did. Claire basically took over until her sorry father realized crawling into a corner and ignoring the rest of the world wasn't an option."

Another flash of pain crossed Tony's features before he pushed away from the refrigerator to grab a glass from the drainboard, filling it at the tap. "But I had no idea how exhausting it was, taking care of three kids, keeping track of everything they're supposed to do and doctor's appointments and…all of it. Don't get me wrong," he said, turning, "before Marissa died, I pitched in, of course I did, changing diapers and doing the shopping sometimes and folding laundry. But didn't take long to see that my 'helping out' was nothin' compared to what Marissa did, day in and day out."

"But…you were working, weren't you?"

He smirked. "Makin' a buncha teenage boys run laps or

shoot hoops isn't exactly what you'd call strenuous. Keeping three kids alive and a house off the condemned property list?" Staring blankly at some spot past Lili's shoulder, he took a long gulp of the water. "I've never been so tired in my entire life—"

"Daddy?"

They both turned to see a very sleepy Josephine toddling toward them in shortie pajamas, her blond hair all rumpled, a very strange, long-legged bird clutched in one arm. "Hey, cupcake," Tony said, immediately squatting to gather the tiny girl into his arms. "Whatcha doin' up?"

"Firsty," she said, yawning. "It's hot."

"Yeah, I know," Tony said, balancing her on his hip while he refilled the same glass he'd just used. "Daddy's really gotta do somethin' about the air conditioner, huh?"

Solemnly nodding, the toddler took a single sip of water, then shook her head. "That's 'nuff," she said, sinking against Tony's chest with her thumb plugging her mouth. Not a second later she'd fallen back to sleep. Lily smiled.

"She's absolutely precious," she whispered, not even trying to ignore all the broody feelings rising up like warm yeast inside her.

"Like this, she is," Tony said, but with such tenderness in his voice it brought tears to Lily's eyes. Then he began inching toward the door. "Well. I need to get her back to bed—"

"Yes, of course. I've stayed longer than I should have, anyway." She followed father and snoring daughter out of the kitchen, signaling to him to go on, she'd let herself out. But as she was leaving, she turned to catch Tony watching her, his gaze steady and questioning in a way that made her stomach jump. Because whatever else was, or wasn't, going on, he certainly wasn't looking at her the same way he had that summer.

Which, she thought as she stepped out into the soupy night, only made her question her sanity, that she was even considering the idea that had come to her a few minutes ago…

Chapter Four

Shortly after noon the next day, Tony opened his door to find Lili again standing on his porch, this time brandishing a mop and bucket filled with cleaning supplies, and he thought, *Please, God, no.* Ed did his happy dance and peed on the floor. In another life, Tony might have done the same thing. The happy dance, not the peeing. In this life, however…

Lili calmly dug into the bucket, ripped off a paper towel and handed it over. Tony dropped the towel on top of the pee, only to realize he was barefoot. He squatted to wipe up the mess, while Ed madly licked the air a half inch from Tony's face, sorry as all hell.

"Magda sent you again?"

"No, this time was my idea. I thought of it last night."

Tony stood, this time noticing Lili's loose, blah-looking gray T-shirt flopped over some seriously short shorts. Deep in whichever gland was responsible for noticing things like short shorts, a tiny, defiant spark erupted, momentarily obliterating the fact that, except for the girls, his life was hell on a stick.

He finally dragged his gaze back up to a smile flashing in a glowing, scrubbed-clean face behind adorably crooked glasses, and the spark cleared enough for her words to register. "Thought of what last night?"

"That while I'm here, I could help you clean the house. I assume the girls are gone?"

"Uh, yeah—"

"Good." Lili pushed past him, ponytail swishing as she and Ed headed with definite purpose toward the kitchen, one of them trailing a faint cloud of something flowery—probably not Ed—which Tony only half noticed because his gaze was glued to all that smooth, pale skin below the hem of those very, *very* short shorts.

Dude. Wrong. "What are you," he called to her back, slightly dizzy and more than a little pissed, "my own personal Merry Maid?"

"I like to clean," she said, disappearing into the kitchen. A second later, a disembodied, and apparently disappointed, "You started without me?" floated back down the hall.

Tony ambled to the kitchen doorway, where he crossed his arms across his own baggy T-shirt, worn over a pair of ancient gym shorts unfit for anyone to see who didn't share his last name. "We did eight o'clock mass, the girls were gone by ten. So, yeah. Since I had no idea you were coming. But hey, I haven't gotten to the bathrooms yet."

He could have sworn he snarled that last part. Lili, however, actually brightened, her eyes as clear and blue as the water in some tropical paradise brochure. "Wonderful!"

"Jeez, Lil—I was kidding—"

But she was already gone, mop in hand and cleaning supplies merrily rattling. Tony caught up with her at the stairs, nearly tripping over the stupid dog as he lumbered up after her two steps at a time. Not only were the legs easy on the eyes, but they moved at the speed of light. "I'm serious, I can't let you do this—"

"Oh, dear. Did you wash the dog in this tub?"

Ed lifted deeply offended eyes to Tony.

"No. Just Daph."

"How can such a little girl get so dirty?"

"It's a talent," Tony muttered, doomed, as, on a happy sigh, Lili grabbed a bottle of tub cleaner, squirted some into the tub, then dropped to her knees, sponge in hand.

"You're insane," Tony said. Now ogling her butt. Which was amazingly…round. Ed plodded over to see if he could help, but his butt wasn't nearly as interesting as Lili's.

Tony thought she might have shrugged while she scrubbed. Then she actually started humming. Transfixed, Tony dropped onto the toilet lid to watch her. She glanced up, a piece of hair snaked into her eyes. "You're not supposed to be watching, you're supposed to be cleaning, too," she said, and her damned pretty accent and damned laughing eyes and damned round butt nudged aside the self-pity he now realized he'd been clutching to him like Nonna Vaccaro that ratty black shawl she used to wear. Not a lot, not completely, but enough to see a glimmer, maybe, of pale light beyond the murky little world he'd been calling home this past year.

Then he thought of Marissa's letter and the glimmer went out.

"Already did the kitchen, remember?"

Another glance—this time, she'd apparently caught the sharpness—but she simply shrugged and turned on the squeaky old faucet. "Is there laundry, then?" she said over the water roaring into the old porcelain tub. "Or something else you need to do?"

"There's always something else that needs doing," Tony mumbled, too tired to keep up the Big Bad Ogre routine, too amazed to stay mad at her. The tub rinsed, another bottle appeared out of the depths of the Magic Bucket, this one dispensing foam all over the fixtures and tile. A little more scrubbing, a little more butt-wiggling, and shazam. Gleaming fixtures and sparkling tile.

"How'd you do that?"

"I have my ways." She flapped her hands at him. "Move."

Still seated, Tony lifted his eyes to hers. "You are not cleaning my toilet."

"Don't be ridiculous, I've been cleaning lavatories since I was seven. So go," she said, poking at him with the dry johnny mop. "You're cramping my style."

Defeated, Tony stood to leave, only to turn back when he reached the doorway, his earlier annoyance pretty much disintegrated, replaced by a gratitude so sudden and profound he nearly wept. "Thanks."

She grinned up at him from over his open toilet. "That's more like it," she said.

Two hours later, the bathrooms clean, beds stripped and changed, the living room vacuumed and dusted, Lili found Tony out in his backyard, on his hands and knees in the middle of the overgrown vegetable garden taking up half of it. The plot was nearly choked with weeds, which he was attacking as though each one was a personal insult.

"We've had so much rain, and I haven't had a chance to get out here in weeks." He straightened, removing his billed hat to wipe his forehead on the hem of his shirt, a move that revealed the midsection that time forgot. As had Lili.

"When on earth do you have time to work out?"

His shirt hem still in his hands, Tony gave her a curious look. Which is when she realized she'd said that out loud. Oops. "I lift weights a couple times a week. Try to get in a run whenever I can, if nothing else to take the edge off the stress. Hauling a two-ton toddler around doesn't hurt, either."

He bent over again to yank out another clump of weeds. "Keepin' in shape at least gives me some illusion of control, you know?"

Lili sat on the edge of the back porch, hugging her knees. "Want some help?"

"You've already done more than I should've let you. Forget it." Sitting back on his knees, he squinted over the tangled mass of vines and plants, shaking his head. "This wasn't my idea. The garden, I mean. Marissa had the green thumb, not me. But the kids wanted to keep it goin', so I said okay."

"Gardens are a lot of work."

"Tell me about it."

"I'm serious. My grandmother spent half the day during the summer in hers. It was twice the size of this one, of course, but…do the girls at least help?"

"Yeah, they do. Some. Daph more than Claire, but she does her bit, too." He tugged out a particularly vicious looking clump of weeds, tossed them aside. "This shrink or whatever we went to after Rissa died, she said it was important to keep as much continuity as possible, that it would make the transition easier. A lot of people—" he got up, moved over to a line of straggly tomato plants, weighed down with several dozen ripe fruits "—the first thing they do when somebody dies? They make a major change right away—sell the house, move someplace else, whatever. But that's like runnin' away from the grief instead of dealing with it, adjusting to life with the new hole in it. Plenty of time to make changes later. Just not right away."

He gave her a look one might have construed as a warning glance, then nodded toward the porch. "You wanna hand me that basket over there? Shoulda picked these puppies days ago."

Lili looked behind her, spying the bushel basket a few feet away. She retrieved it, the hot sun pouncing on her when she walked out into the garden. Instead of handing it to Tony, however, she began gently twisting the swollen, warm tomatoes off the plants, carefully setting them in the basket. "I see a lot of spaghetti sauce in your future."

Beside her, Tony sighed. "Actually, I'll give most of these to Magda and them. Rissa did a fair amount of canning and stuff, but it's not my thing. Here, let me take that, it must be getting pretty heavy."

As she pulled off two more tomatoes, Lili sneaked a peek at Tony's face, drawn and determined. "I hope the girls appreciate you're only doing this for them."

One corner of his mouth twitched. "Putting them first…it's my job, isn't it? If it's not good for them—" he glanced over "—it's not good, period—"

"Yo! Mister V.!" boomed from the side of the house. "I see your sorry old car sittin' out here, so I know you're home!"

"Hollis Miller?" Tony yelled back, grinning. "That you?"

A moment later, an equally grinning dark face framed in short braids appeared over the back gate. "Nobody else, Mr. V. Oh, sorry…didn't mean to crash the party—"

"Not at all…come on back! Lili Szabo," he said after the kid swung open the gate and joined them in the yard, his tall, spindly frame nearly lost inside an oversized baseball jersey and baggy pants that puddled around huge trainers, "this is Hollis Miller, one of my kids who graduated last year. Lili's sort of a cousin, visiting from Hungary for a few weeks."

White teeth gleaming in one of the most beautiful faces Lili had ever seen, Hollis extended his hand. "Pleased to meet you, Miss Szabo." Then bright, mischievous eyes flashed to Tony. "'Sort of a cousin'?"

"Her mother's sister married my father's brother."

The kid looked puzzled for a moment, then laughed, holding up his hands. "Whatever, man. Hey—my mother and me, we just moved into that new apartment complex a few blocks away," Hollis said, pointing east. "I was out getting the lay of the land when I spied that old rust bucket of yours and thought, No way, this must be Mr. V.'s place. So looks like we're neighbors." The boy turned his bright smile on Lili. "This dude saved my sorry *ass,* and that's no lie."

Tony choked out an embarrassed laugh. "I wouldn't go that far—"

"No, what you did was go above and *beyond,* man. If it hadn't've been for Mr. V.," he said again to Lili, "I probably wouldn't've even graduated, and that's the truth." He scanned the yard. "Whoa. Serious garden. In *serious* bad shape. You trying to grow your own national forest or what?"

Lili sputtered a laugh; Tony shot a brief glare in her direction, followed by a sigh. "Yeah. I know."

"Hey, man…you need some help? I usedta spend summers with my great-aunt in Virginia when I was a kid, she had a vegetable garden so pretty it'd make you cry. Anything you wanna know about vegetables and stuff, I'm your man."

Tony perked up. "Actually, that's not a bad idea. I'd be glad to pay you—"

"After everything you did for me? Forget it, helping you out's the least I can do. I gotta run now, but I got some time on Monday morning. I don't have to be at work until noon. That okay?"

"That would be great," Tony said. "In the meantime… *please* take some tomatoes and cukes off my hands. No, really," he said when the young man started to protest, "you'd be doin' me a favor."

"Mom's gonna bust something when she gets a load of these," Hollis said when Tony found another, smaller basket and loaded it up with vegetables. "She's always complaining about how those pitiful things from the grocery store taste like plastic." Basket in hand, grin firmly in place, the young man nodded to Lili, saying how nice it'd been to meet her, then strode back to the front.

"Well. It appears you now have a gardener," she said, the almost worshipful look on the boy's face now indelibly etched on her brain. "Not to mention a fan for life. What on earth did you do—?"

"Hey, we got all this stuff, and that bread you brought from Magda's…wanna stay for lunch?"

She decided he hadn't heard her. "Sure, why not?"

Compared with the blistering heat in the yard, the clean, tidy kitchen felt cool and inviting. A breeze even teased the lightweight curtains over the windows. They worked as a team to pull together their simple meal, one similar to what she might have eaten back home in her grandmother's country kitchen in northern Hungary—bread and cheese and cabbage salad, the fresh vegetables warm from the garden.

"Sorry about the air conditioning," Tony said after they took their food back outside to eat on the porch, nearly as cool as the kitchen. "Or lack thereof. My folks had central air installed when I was in college, but when it goes on the blink it's a pain in the ass to fix."

"Please don't apologize, I'm not used to it much, anyway, except at school and in public buildings. My mother's apartment got wonderful cross breezes, but even when it was still…" She shrugged, popping a piece of tomato into her mouth. "Heat doesn't bother me."

"Does anything?"

Lili frowned at him across the chipped, wrought-iron table. "What a strange question."

"Didn't mean it to be. It's just…I've never known anybody to take things as they come like you do."

Lili tore off a piece of the crusty bread. "I wasn't always that way. But with enough practice—and enough time—one can get better at anything."

"Is that why you're here now? Giving yourself time to adjust?"

"I don't know. Perhaps." She sighed. "Although it's not as if I expect to have a major revelation about what to do with my life simply because I'm here. I still have to decide what I want to be when I grow up. Where I am when that happens is immaterial."

Tony rocked back in one of the iron chairs that matched the table, his arms folded over his chest. "Any clues? About what you want to do, I mean?"

"Nary a one. But what keeps going around in my head is…shouldn't I be making a difference? Adding to the world instead of just existing in it?"

Tony looked amused. "You wanna be famous?"

She laughed. "Dear God, no. I just feel I should be doing more, somehow. Even if I don't yet know that's supposed to play out. What's so funny?"

"Hearing American slang in that accent, that's all," Tony said, looking almost halfway relaxed. "Tickles me every time."

"I watch a lot of American TV and movies, read magazines, to keep up. For my translation work? I guess a lot of it's rubbed off."

His expression suddenly pensive, Tony looked out over the garden. "For whatever it's worth…" His gaze returned to hers, giving her gooseflesh. "I'm glad you decided to come."

"You're just glad someone else cleaned your bathrooms," Lili said lightly.

"Won't argue with you there. But it's not just that." Focusing again on the garden, he brought his hands up to link them behind his head. "You make a difference, Lil," he said softly. "Just by bein' yourself."

Her face warmed. "You're embarrassing me."

"Deal with it," he said, then scratched his chin for a second before clamping his hands behind his head again. Except this time he didn't look even remotely relaxed. "Right before we came to the party yesterday? I got this letter. From Rissa, through our lawyer."

Lili felt the blood in her veins chug to a standstill. "What? But—"

"She'd apparently given it to him sometime before she died, I don't know when, it wasn't dated." He paused, a muscle clenching in his jaw. "She confessed to havin' an affair."

"Tony, no…" The dog put his head in her lap; absently, she stroked the smooth, stiff fur on his neck. "Is that what you didn't want to talk about?"

"Yeah. But it seems kinda pointless keeping secrets from somebody who's cleaned your toilets." His attempt at humor didn't even begin to mask the pain working its way to the surface. He lowered his hands. "I mean, I knew we were having problems for a while there, but…I had no idea. None. But you wanna hear the kicker?"

Although Lili braced herself, nothing prepared her for the agony that now shrieked in his eyes when he faced her. "Judging from the dates she gave? There's a good chance Josie's not mine."

Chapter Five

It had felt even better than Tony had imagined, finally giving
vent to the putrid feelings inside him. But only to Lili.
Because in a world where damn little was a sure thing
anymore, Tony knew this about her: She wouldn't go crazy
on him, and she wouldn't go blabbing to the family.

"Oh, dear God," she finally whispered. "Are you sure?"

"About the timing? Yeah. Not that there were many gaps
in that department," he said bitterly, thinking how stupid he'd
been, assuming because things were still more or less okay
in the bedroom, they were okay otherwise. "But if she was
foolin' around with somebody else at the same time…" He
slammed his hand on the tabletop, making the dog jump. Lili
didn't even flinch.

"Did…did she *say* the baby might not be yours?"

"Yeah. She did. I mean, sure, I'll have a test done and all
but…"

Lili reached over and wrapped her hand around his. "It's going to be all right—"

"You don't know that!" Tony said, yanking free. "Nobody knows that! Especially considering the insane number of things that have gone wrong over the last year! So spare me the pats on the head, okay?"

She pulled back, her arms crossed over her ribs, but otherwise seemingly unaffected by his outburst. Tony got up to lean hard on the porch railing, the paint completely peeled off in places. Like his life, peeling away bit by bit.

"Sorry, I shouldn't've blown up on you like that."

"As you can see, I survived."

Tony almost smiled, only to blow out a harsh breath instead. "Funny how you can look back, see the clues you totally missed. We argued a lot, mostly about stupid stuff. Now I'm wondering…did Rissa feel trapped? Like maybe marriage hadn't turned out the way she thought it would?"

"In what way?"

"Damned if I knew. She'd never really come right out and say what was bugging her. Like she expected me to, I dunno, figure it out on my own. I mean…"

He turned to Lili. "I thought she understood exactly what she was getting. *Who* she was getting—a jock who wasn't gonna suddenly turn into some brainiac businessman or somethin'. Yeah, there was that time Lou—her father—suggested I come into the restaurant with him, but they couldn't've been serious about that. I mean, come on—what the hell do I know about runnin' a restaurant? Not to mention the god-awful hours. It was like I kept tellin' her—maybe teaching high school PE wouldn't exactly make me rich, but I figured the time it left me to be with the girls was a fair trade-off, right?"

"I would think so—"

"Or maybe it was this house," he said, frowning up at the sagging porch ceiling, over at the fence in dire need of repair.

"My mother left us the place when she died, all we had to pay for was the utilities and taxes. And at first Rissa said it would be fun, fixing it up. Making it ours."

He looked back at Lili. "But renovating a house like this takes big bucks, it's not like we could march into Home Depot and say, 'Make it happen.' More than once she hinted at wanting to move closer to her folks, who left Springfield about ten years ago. Closer to *Bahston*—" he deliberately exaggerated the flat accent "—to a better neighborhood."

Lili's forehead creased. "What's wrong with this neighborhood?"

"Nothing, really. But the city's been through some rough patches. Like a lot of the kids who live here…" His brow knotted as his brain switched tracks yet again. "And that was *another* sticking point. Me not wanting to leave my kids. A lot of 'em, their family life sucks, maybe school's not exactly their favorite place to be. But…"

Tony gave his head a sharp shake, feeling like a thunderstorm was brewing inside him. "But they need somebody to see past the 'tude and the bluster to the real person in there. To tell 'em, hell, yeah, they've got potential—"

"Like Hollis?"

"Yeah. Like Hollis. Like a hundred others like him, kids who know I don't take any crap off them but I respect 'em, too. Sure, there's plenty of days when my head feels like it's gonna split wide open from banging into that brick wall, when I get a kid in class I can't reach, or run into a dead-end because of some bureaucratic crap or other. It's not *fun*. But it's a helluva lot more than blowin' whistles and keepin' track of the basketballs. I mean, when they get out on that basketball court or football field—" his hands came up, fingers taut around an imaginary football "—and I see the light in their eyes, that this…this is someplace where they can forget about everything but the game, that moment, where they can just be *themselves,* white, black, Hispanic, Asian, whatever…and *damn,* that feels good."

Scratching the dog's ears, Lili smiled slightly. "I imagine so. But Marissa never understood that?"

"See, that's the thing," Tony said, dropping his hands. "I thought she did. At first, anyway. Used to be, she'd come to the kids' games, ask me how they were doing, how my day went. But I don't think she ever really got it, that what I do? It's not just a job." He dropped onto the end of an old chaise, looking out over the tangled mess of the garden. "Then she got pregnant with Josie." He blew out a humorless laugh. "That's when the bottom really fell out."

"Now you know why."

"Yeah, guess so." Leaning forward, he clasped his hands between his knees. "Although at first I just chalked it up to the pregnancy itself—after Daph, she'd made it more than clear she didn't want another kid. And I thought we'd been careful, but…" He shook his head. "Not that she wasn't okay with the girls—I mean, sure, she'd yell at 'em sometimes, name me a mom who doesn't—but me? Unless it was to talk about the house or the kids, I might as well not have existed." He scraped a hand across his jaw. "Crappiest nine months of my life."

"And let me guess. Nobody knew."

"Are you kiddin'? After everything we went through to convince our parents we weren't making a mistake getting married so young? No damn way. Even so, I said I'd go to counseling, whatever she wanted. No dice. Frankly, I was worried maybe she even wouldn't bond with the baby. But whaddya know—soon as Josie was born, it was like the old Marissa was back. Acted no different with Josie than she had with the first two. Cuddled with her just as much, always right there if she so much as made a peep…"

He felt his eyes sting. "She was a great mom. Whatever

problems the two of us might've had—no matter what I know now—nothing can change that. And anyway, after the baby came…she started acting like she wanted to make things up to me, even though of course I no idea that's what she was doing. Then…"

He ground one fist into his palm. "Then she got sick. Just when it looked like maybe we could get things back on track. Went through her like wildfire. Chemo, radiation—nothing even made a dent. Although…this is gonna sound crazy, but—"

"What?" Lili said gently.

"It was almost like she didn't *want* to fight it. Like…like the guilt was literally eatin' her up. The thing is, if I'd've known, if she'd've just come out and told me, maybe we couldn've worked through it somehow."

"Do you really think that would have made a difference?" Lili said, even more gently. "In the outcome?"

"Judging from what she wrote me? I think she died in the kind of pain that has nothin' to do with the body."

Lili frowned slightly, then got up and walked to the porch railing. "And now she's passed that guilt on to you."

Tony's head jerked up. "What? No—"

"I know you're not asking for advice," she said, turning. "As if I'd have anything to offer on that score. But why are you taking so much of this on yourself? Yes, of course it takes two to make a relationship work, and it takes two to make it fall apart. But your wife's having an affair…" Her eyes sparked. "That wasn't your fault. And for *God's* sake, neither was her death."

His mouth twisted. "You think I sound off my nut?"

"No. You sound like someone trying to make sense out of something that makes no sense whatsoever. Only sometimes…things simply *don't* make sense. And all the mental juggling in the world won't change that."

A long, ragged breath left his lungs. "But all these thoughts…they're battering the hell outta me, Lil. First I'll think Josie looks exactly like Claire did at that age, she *feels* like my kid, whatever the hell that means. The next minute I'm scared to death I'm gonna answer the door one day to find some dude standing there, demanding his daughter. Except then I think it's been too long, if somebody else is the father, maybe he never knew. Maybe Rissa never told him, because *she* didn't know. She didn't go into details, for all I know maybe it was a one-time fling. Or…or maybe it wasn't, maybe she'd planned on leaving me, but her getting pregnant was a deal breaker with the other guy. Then I think, dear God—if Josie's not mine, do I tell her? When? And Marissa's parents…how on earth do I tell them—"

"Tony, Tony…" Lili crossed to kneel in front of him, taking his hands in both of hers and pulling him into those damn eyes of hers again. "For God's sake, you're going to make *yourself* sick with all this worrying and wondering. Have the test done, as soon as possible. Then figure out what comes next. But all this conjecturing is pointless."

"Maybe I don't see it as pointless," he said flatly. "Maybe I see it as bein' prepared for the worst. I've been raising that little girl virtually on my own for the past year," he said through a thick throat. "That feeling you get when you see the baby for the first time, and they reach right in and grab your heart… You think I'm gonna suddenly love her less if I find out my blood's not in her veins?"

"No. Of course not."

Tony's eyes dropped to their linked hands as the stupid dog came over to flop on his back, hoping for a tummy rub. "It would kill me, losing Josie. Losing any of 'em."

Her eyes followed his. She let go, like she suddenly realized what she was doing, then stood. "Just as it killed you to lose Marissa?"

Palming his head, Tony said, "I just wish I knew what went wrong. It's like there's this hole inside me where the answered questions should be." He lifted his eyes to Lili. "Only there's nothin' to fill it up."

To avoid those tortured eyes, Lili squatted again to pat Ed's stomach, the sense of déjà vu so strong it nearly made her dizzy. Memories of Tony's lying on that very chaise fourteen summers ago, his leg immobile as they talked about whatever crossed their minds; her mother's nearly identical laments, after Leo's betrayal—the recriminations, the transferred guilt, the lot. And hadn't she berated herself for months, after Peter so cavalierly shrugged and walked away from their two years together, certain *she'd* been the flawed one, somehow?

She supposed there were two kinds of people in the world—those who believed nothing was their fault, and those who believed everything was. How odd, when it was obvious that things were rarely that cut-and-dried.

"Swear to God," Tony said with a soft, deprecating laugh, "I had no idea that was all gonna come out. But you being here…in some ways it's like being in a time warp. Even then, I felt like I could talk to you in a way I couldn't to anybody else."

Lili forced herself to catch his embarrassed smile in the porch's shadow, not sure what she felt when he looked at him. Sympathy, she supposed, mixed in with a little irritation. Then she thought of his expression when he talked about his students, his obvious pride in Hollis, and her stomach free fell. She did her best to smile back.

"So everything's the same between us as it was then?"

Their gazes held for several seconds before Tony stood, eventually going down the steps to the netted cherry tree close to the house, ablaze with clusters of bright red fruit. "Whaddya think—these look ripe to you yet?"

For a moment Lili felt as though she'd picked up the wrong

book, confused because she couldn't find where she'd left off. But she finally joined him, pulling a firm, warm fruit off the tree and popping it into her mouth.

"Not yet," she said, making a face as the sour juice exploded over her tongue. "Another week or so, I think."

"You nut," Tony said softly. "You didn't hafta do that."

"What's life without a little risk?" she said, spitting out the pit.

He turned away again, the hot, heavy breeze ruffling his already messy hair. "So you can't feel it?"

"Feel what?"

His eyes found hers again. "That of course it's not the same between us. How could it be? We're not the same people we were then."

The knotty, sturdy tree trunk poked between her shoulder blades when she leaned against it, her hands tucked behind her back, the shade a welcome relief from the searing heat. Except, this close to Tony, *relief* was a relative term.

"Perhaps we're not so very different," she said. "Not at heart. For instance, I see the same person I did that summer. Just one who's been tried and tested."

Tony palmed the trunk, barely six inches over Lili's head, his earnest, direct gaze sending a chill through her. "How come you never returned my e-mails? And don't tell me you didn't have the Internet then, because Aunt Magda told me you'd write to her from your library's connection."

Lili pushed herself away from the tree. "What would have been the point?" she murmured, gasping when he caught her arm.

"The point is, I thought we were friends. When you left...I missed that. Missed you."

A strand of hair tumbled free of the elastic band holding it back; she jerked it behind her ear. "Did Marissa know you were e-mailing me?"

Letting go, Tony frowned slightly. "What does that hafta do with anything?"

"Did she?"

"I dunno. Maybe. Why?"

Lili hesitated, then said, "It turned out my mother's main reason for sending me away that summer was so she could marry Leo. Without it 'upsetting' me."

"What does that have to do with—?" At her sharp look, he lifted his hands and went with the flow. "But I thought your dad had just died?"

"Not even six months before, to be precise." Lili's mouth flattened. "I'd met Leo exactly once, for about five minutes."

Tony swore. "And how did she think keepin' it a secret *wouldn't* upset you?"

"I doubt she was *thinking* much at all, to be blunt. Being on her own—being alone—petrified her. Obviously. To the point where she was more than willing to let someone else do the thinking for her. She told me later the quick marriage had been Leo's idea."

"This is same jerk who dumped her, right?"

"Yes. And no, the irony was not lost on her. But my point is…I was still reeling that summer. Which you know. To come home and discover my mother had betrayed my father's memory…"

"Your father, hell," Tony said softly, pulling her into his arms. Startling the life out of her. "She betrayed *you*. Damn, honey…I can't imagine how rough that must've been for you."

Tears welling in Lili's eyes as she settled against his chest, her hands curled underneath her chin. "It felt worse than the grief," she said after a moment. "In fact, I was so upset that I went to live with my grandmother, because I couldn't bear to be around my mother and *him*. In any case, I was so wrapped up in feeling sorry for myself that my time here didn't even feel real." *You didn't feel real.* Blinking, she pulled away, lifting her eyes to his. "I read the first few e-mails, but they felt as though they'd been written to someone else. After a while I marked them as 'read' and moved on." She shrugged. "I'm sorry."

"Yeah. Me, too." At the edge to his voice, she frowned. "Dammit, Lil—you should've talked to me. Told me what was goin' on, what you were feeling—"

"And what could you have possibly done?"

"Listened."

And he would have, she thought, in a way nobody else ever had. Even now, twisted up in his own problems as he was, his umbrage on her behalf for something that had happened half a lifetime ago vibrated from him like an aura. The man *cared* about other people with a bone-deep sincerity that could make a girl fall in love with him, if she weren't careful.

Lili reached up to place a quick, light kiss on Tony's rough cheek, breathing in the scents of dark, damp earth and sweat, the soap he'd washed up with before lunch. "I somehow doubt Marissa would have been okay with that," she whispered, then walked away. But when she reached the porch, she turned back. "If you like, I could come back again next weekend. To help you clean?"

His gaze burned into hers, dark and troubled and smoldering with something even she had no trouble recognizing. Something that, if she had a grain of sense, would make her rescind her offer on the spot. "You really are nuts," he said, barely smiling.

"Then I'm in good company."

His chuckle followed her all the way back to her aunt's.

Tuesday morning, ten a.m. Vibrating with suspicion, Claire yanked back the kitchen curtain, her backpack thudding to the floor. "Who the heck is that?"

Tony's in-laws had just dropped the girls off, after begging to keep them an extra day. The garden turning out to be, according to Hollis, an inch away from hopeless, the kid had returned early that morning to continue his mission. Right now that meant battling Ed for the remaining ripe tomatoes. Judging from the kid's periodic shouts, the dog was winning. Dog really would eat anything.

"That's Hollis," Tony said mildly, his arms full of Josie, his head full of Lili. Like it had been all weekend. If he'd thought the path he'd been headed down before had been dangerous, this was a one-way road to hell. The odd kick to the groin, he could handle. That was…reflex. Hormones. Annoying, but easily dismissed. Okay, maybe not that easily, but at least manageable—

"He usedta be one of my students. Now he's our gardener. Sort of."

The kick to the center of his chest, though… Uh, boy. That was bad news. Really bad news. The kind of bad news you can't forget even after you change the channel—

"We have a *gardener?*" Daphne said, giving Tony raised brows. "Like Nana and Gramps have a gardener?"

"Not exactly," Tony said. To air, as it happened, since the child had already disappeared to accost the unsuspecting young man currently trying to tame their cantaloupe vine before it ate the neighbor's children.

"Daph!" Claire yelled out the window. Like that was gonna do any good.

Tony laid a hand on her shoulder. "It's okay, honey. If anything, Hollis should be afraid of Daph—"

"Why do we need help with the garden?"

"Because Mom's not here, and I suck at gardening, and you guys are too young to keep it up. You want a garden? Hollis is part of the deal."

Claire shot him a wounded look, grabbed her backpack

and stomped out of the room. "And he's staying for lunch, too!" Tony yelled in her wake, because he could.

Then he immediately felt like a bum for yelling at his kid, so he tramped upstairs after her, Josie giggling as they bounced up each step. Claire was sitting on her bed—legs crossed, elbows jammed on knees, scowl firmly in place—on some cutsie cartoon character bedspread which she refused to give up, despite both its threadbare state and her seven-year-old sister's declaration that it was for "infants." But at five, Claire had said she wanted a pink room; Marissa had obliged her with the pinkest room in the history of little girls. Pink, and frilly, and so intensely girlyfied Tony felt like Shrek every time he walked in.

"So how was it at Nana's?"

Claire shrugged. "She taught Daphne the breaststroke."

"What about you?"

"I already know the breaststroke."

"No, I mean, did you swim?"

"Yeah. But only because if I hadn't, Nana would've been totally on my case—Was everything all right? Was I feeling okay?" She shrugged again. "So I swam."

"You usedta love swimming."

"It's not much fun anymore."

"Because…Mom's not around to swim with you?"

"I guess."

Josie crawled off Tony's lap and over to her sister to pat Claire's shoulder. "Don't be sad, C'are," she said, practically twisting herself upside down to see Claire's face. "It's okay." With a wobbly smile, Claire pulled Josie into her lap, resting her cheek on top of her sister's head.

Tony forced air into his lungs—somehow he was gonna have to find a way to get that DNA test done soon, before he lost his mind altogether. But it wasn't like he could take everybody with him to the testing place, or leave the girls with somebody and take JoJo without it looking weird—

"Dad? What's wrong?"

"Nothing, honey. Just got a lot on my mind."

"Like what?"

"Like...I was just thinking about...how nobody likes change. But it happens anyway. And even when it seems like our own world has come to a grinding halt..." He reached over to push her hair away from her face. "The rest of the world keeps chugging along. The longer we sit around, cryin' in our beer about how we wish things were the same..." He shook his head. "The more we get left behind."

Her eyes lowered, Claire picked at a loose thread in the bedspread's quilting. "I know that," she said quietly, then lifted watery eyes to his. "It's just...it's like every time I turn around, something *else* is different. And I feel like I can't keep up."

"Yeah," Tony said, thinking about the last few days, about Marissa's bombshell and Lili's reappearance and the five million mixed-up thoughts zooming around and around his brain like one of those insane motorcyclists in the cage at the circus. "I know what you mean."

When Josie crawled off her big sister's lap, and then the bed, to pull one of Claire's old books off her shelf, Claire reached for a bedraggled Clifford the Big Red Dog Tony had brought home for her before she was born.

He half smiled. "Bet you don't remember how you useta say his whole name, every time, when you were little."

"I still do," Claire said, her own lips tilting slightly.

"So you still have Clifford," he said, "And we're still living in the same house. And school's the same, so you've got all your friends, right?"

"Yeah," she said, hugging the dog. "And...I've still got you and Daph and Ed and JoJo..." She looked up at him. "I guess lots of stuff's still the same, huh?"

"So, see? There ya go."

The shabby toy returned to its place of honor in the center of her pillows, Claire leaned against Tony as Josie "read" *One Fish, Two Fish* at their feet. "Feel better?" he said softly into her tickly hair.

She nodded, then leaned back, her expression dead serious. "Just promise me something."

"And what's that?"

"*Please* don't get married again."

"Not planning on it," Tony said, even as the feel of Lili's lips grazing his cheek scooted through his brain.

And kept on going.

Chapter Six

"Hot damn," Lili heard behind her when Hollis came in through the back door the following Saturday afternoon. "You got some *serious* cleaning mojo! Hey, Mr. V.!" he yelled down the hall. "Come see what this woman did to your kitchen!"

"For heaven's sake, Hollis," Lili said, peeling off her rubber gloves. "It's not that big a deal." Although she had to admit surveying her handiwork definitely gave her a warm, bubbly feeling inside. Something she'd tried, in vain, to explain that morning to her aunt, who eventually tossed up her hands and clack-clacked away on her spindly heeled mules, muttering in Hungarian.

Hollis snorted. "I usedta think my mother was the Queen of Clean, but this puts her to shame. Although you did not hear that from me—"

"Holy cow."

Tony's words provoked another sort of warm, bubbly

feeling entirely. The kind that came from sharing chores with a man who had no clue how good he looked in a sleeveless sweatshirt. One whose smile took some coaxing these days to come out of hiding, but, oh, was it worth the effort. Tony walked past her to the stove, all bulging shoulders and hard calves, to run a finger along the metal strip edging the cooktop. "How did you *do* that?"

Lili shrugged, pleased at the oblique compliment. "What can I say, dirt quakes in my presence."

The smile came out and Lili lost her breath. "Obviously. Damn, you're amazing," he said, and their gazes locked, and her heart sort of seized up, until Hollis cleared his throat, breaking the spell.

"I should go," she said, grabbing her cleaning bucket, and Tony said, "Actually, why don't you both stay for dinner, since it's so late? Marissa's parents should be back with the kids in about an hour, I could do burgers on the grill or something."

"Sorry, man," Hollis said, "but Mom's got people coming around, I gotta stop by the store and pick up some stuff. So later, yo. Tell Daph to keep an eye on the cukes." Grinning, he let himself out the back door, and Tony turned to Lili.

"So that leaves you."

"No, it doesn't. For many reasons. Not the least of which is that I've been vanquishing grease harking back to the mid-nineties all day—"

"Hey!"

"—so I'm sweaty and my hair's a wreck and I smell funny. Hardly fit to meet your in-laws."

"So go get cleaned up. Like I said, you've got an hour."

Rolling her eyes, she started for the door. "And how come the kids are coming back tonight, anyway? I thought their grandparents kept them through Sunday."

"They got plans for tomorrow or something, I didn't get

all the details." He gently clasped her shoulder, making her turn. Making her fall into those earnest eyes. "I'd really like you to come for dinner."

"To…what? Run interference?"

"Hardly. I can handle my in-laws, believe me. But I'd like them to meet you. What?" he said at her headshake. "We're all family, right?"

"I'm not sure they'd see it that way. And what if they get the wrong idea?"

Comprehension flitted across his features before, sighing, he crossed his arms over his chest. "You know, I spend my entire life bendin' over backward to make everybody happy. And that's fine, that's my job. But every once in a while, I like to do something for *me*. Like watch a movie nobody else wants to see. Eat a whole bucket of hot wings by myself." Lili laughed, and Tony smiled, although it wasn't nearly enough to dispel the cloud darkening his eyes. "It's the little things that keep you sane, you know? And right now, what I want is for you to let me feed you. To say thanks for demolishing twenty years' worth of grease from that stove. Is that too much to ask?"

You have no idea, she thought, even as she said, "Of course not. Except…this isn't really about thanking me for cleaning, is it?"

His nostrils flared when he sucked in a breath. "Problem with manual labor, it gives you far too much time to think. Especially when you've got a lot to think about." He paused. "Okay, maybe I could use the moral support."

"Now was that so hard to admit?" she said, smiling.

The look he gave her sent her scooting out the door.

A half hour later—showered, dressed and mentally bolstered—Lili let herself in through the partially open front door, following the throbbing rock music to the den at the back of the house, where Tony sat in an old leather recliner with a beer in his hand and the dog at his feet. The dog leaped up—*Ohmigod, you're back!*—his greeting much more enthusiastic than Tony's, who barely grumbled a "Down, you stupid mutt" as he stared at the empty fireplace.

Divested of crazed dog, Lili perched on an ottoman near the hearth. "Let me guess," she shouted over the noise. "You've been thinking again."

"One of the hazards of havin' a brain." Tony aimed the remote at the CD player to lower the volume before looking at her, his expression misleadingly blank. He, too, had scrubbed up, now wearing jeans and a clean T-shirt spouting some witticism, his bare feet shoved into a pair of well-worn moccasins. His gaze flicked over her before a small smile curved his lips. "You flyin' blind tonight?"

"Contacts. I don't wear them much. They bug."

"S'okay, you look good in glasses." He hoisted the beer can in her direction. "I like your hair like that. The dress, too. Nice color."

Lili reached up to touch her hair, quickly piled on top of her head. The dress, though, was nothing special, just some bland, bomb-proof jersey number that traveled well. In a blue that made her eyes brighter.

"Thanks," she said as Tony tilted the beer can to his mouth, muttering, "I'm a jerk," after he swallowed.

"Oh, dear," she said, making him frown at her. "Are you drunk?"

Chuckling, he shook his head. "From one beer? No."

"Then why do you think you're a jerk?"

The smile died as he stared at the hearth. "Because I'm taking advantage of your good nature."

Lili poked his ankle with her toe, getting another frown for her efforts. Tough. "I'm not a pushover, Tony. I make my own choices. If I really hadn't wanted to accept your invitation, I wouldn't have."

Another nod preceded his collapsing back into the chair. "Good to know. Still. I don't wanna come across as some sonuvabitch user."

"Not possible." Grabbing his hand, Lily dragged him to his feet. "Especially since you promised me food."

But when she tried to let go, he held fast. "This is just like before, isn't it? You not letting me wallow."

"I don't let *anybody* wallow. Wallowing only gets you stuck in the mud. Look, I hurt for you, for what's happened. And I'm angry for you, too. But I'd like to think I can be there for people without—what's that you Yanks call it? Enabling them?"

His gaze rested in hers for a moment before he headed toward the kitchen, not speaking until he'd yanked a package of frozen hamburger patties out of the freezer compartment and thunked them onto the counter. Then he leaned heavily on the edge, shaking his head. "I've been thinkin' about what you said, about how sometimes things just don't make sense, but…" He pulled out a knife five times larger than he needed to pry apart the patties. "It just won't let go, Lil. That all the signs were *right* there in front of me, and I totally missed 'em."

"And *I* repeat—that wasn't your fault."

"It is—" he whacked the first two burgers apart "—if you've got your head so far up your ass—" and the next ones "—you think as long as nobody's actually fighting?" He jabbed the knife between the last two patties so hard one went skittering across the counter. "It's all good."

Still brandishing the knife, Tony shut his eyes, breathing hard. Lili gently pried the potential weapon from his hands, setting it far out of reach before wrapping her arms around this strong, macho man who was hurting so badly and had no earthly clue what to do about it. Not surprisingly, he shrugged her off.

"I'm fine, I'm…" He retrieved the errant patty and

dumped it back on the plate with its friends. "I *loved* her, Lili. And I had no clue. None." His tortured gaze cut to hers. "And what I really can't figure out is if she didn't see fit to tell me at the time what was goin' on, why the *hell* did she bother tellin' me at all? And why so long after her death?"

"I don't know," Lili said, even though she knew he didn't really expect an answer. And it had still only been a matter of days since Marissa's bombshell; the endless whys had plagued her mother for literally years—an experience that, if nothing else, had taught Lili patience.

Which was partly why she hadn't pressed Tony about the DNA test. After all, there was no guarantee the result would be in his favor; she couldn't imagine how terrifying that prospect might be. In his shoes, she'd probably be dragging her heels, too.

"But while you're trying to figure it all out," she said, picking up the platter of frozen burgers, "at least you're not going through it alone."

His eyes grazed hers. "For as long as you're here, anyway. Right?"

"Right," she said over the sudden, sharp ache in her chest when he smiled.

A breeze cooler than Tony might've expected wicked the moisture from his skin, carried the grill's charred-beef-scented smoke into neighboring yards. He flipped the burgers, annoyed that it was a perfect summer evening, thick with the roar of lawnmowers and whine of weed whackers, with kids' clear, high shouts as they splashed in above-ground pools or kicked a soccer ball in the street. The kind of evening where you'd sit out and smell the sweet, rich scents of honeysuckle and newly cut grass as you watched giggling kids chasing fireflies....

He rubbed a wrist across his own eyes, stinging from a sudden barbecue backdraft. Or so he told himself, his thoughts knotted up inside his head like a Twister game gone bad. Like it wasn't bad enough that the night reminded him of a hundred others, of him and Rissa sitting on that porch, feeling the breeze and smelling the honeysuckle running riot along the back fence and laughing at the kids. Then he had to invite Lili over, on top of it? To what? Hold his hand?

Yeah, chalk that one up to a brain fart of epic proportions.

He started slightly when she nudged his arm, handing him an thermal tumbler of something with ice in it. "Lemonade," she said, sitting on the arm of an Adirondack chair Rissa had bought at some end of season sale. "I found a can of concentrate in the freezer."

"Thanks," Tony mumbled, taking a sip, shuddering from the tartness. Not looking at her. Lili'd made herself scarce, once he'd put the burgers on. God only knew what she'd been up to.

She cleared her throat. "When do you expect the girls?"

"Any minute…actually," he said at the sound of a car pulling up out front, "I think that's them now." He looked into those steady blue eyes, even bigger without her glasses. "You ready for this?"

"As I'll ever be," she said, standing and smoothing her hand over her dress just as

Daph barreled out the back door to wrap her arms around Tony's hips. "Burgers! Yes!!!" she chirped, as one by one, everybody else drifted out. Or, in Susan's case, floated, in a soft, crinkly skirt that brushed her ankles and a neat white top pulled in at the waist with one of those silver Native American belts. And lumbering behind came Lou, his father-in-law, in a designer golf shirt that was too bright, flashing a genuine Rolex that was too big, even on Lou's beefy wrist.

Catching sight of Lili, Josie inexplicably ran toward her— jeez, she'd only seen Lili once, twice at the most—hands raised. Lili eagerly obliged, swinging his little girl into her arms and hugging her with a gentle fierceness that stabbed Tony right in the gut.

As expected, his in-laws' expressions weren't a whole lot different from Claire's, the child giving Tony a "What the hell?" look that might've been funny on somebody else's kid. Although he had to hand it to Susan, the woman was a master at hiding what she was really thinking—she didn't need no stinkin' Botox to keep her face frozen when it suited her purpose.

"Go wash your hands, guys," he said in a low voice, smiling for Rissa's parents after the kids ran, shuffled or toddled off. "Susan, Lou," Tony said, pissed that they were jumping to conclusions, even more pissed that maybe they weren't jumping all that far. "This is Lili Szabo, Magda's niece from Hungary. She's staying with Magda and Benny for a few weeks. Lili—Lou and Susan Pellegrino. Marissa's parents."

Without missing a beat, Lili stepped forward to pull an obviously startled Susan into a hug. "It's so lovely to meet you," she said, letting go to include Lou in her gaze. "Although I'm so sorry to hear about your daughter. My deepest sympathies."

Marissa's mother pressed one hand to her chest, the white-tipped fingernails shiny and square and as perfectly even as her teeth, bared in a smile so stiff it had to hurt. "Thank you, Lili, that's very sweet. And it's nice to meet you, too." To be fair, Tony had seen plenty of genuine smiles from the old gal over the years. This wasn't one of them. "Claire was telling us all about you." Her gaze swung to Tony's. "That you two knew each other from before?"

"A long time ago," Lili said smoothly. "We weren't much more than children. I wasn't, at any rate. Um…the hamburgers are nearly finished—why don't you stay for dinner with us and the girls?"

The smile still in place, Susan's eyes smoothly slid to

Tony's, underneath short blond hair that swear to God hadn't budged since his and Rissa's wedding. "Is the meat freshly ground? And lean?" She glanced in Claire's direction, then lowered her voice. "Because some of us are watching our weight, you know."

Tony let the prickle of irritation play on through before he said, "I suppose it was freshly ground before they froze it. Lean I don't know about. But they're skinny, does that count?"

Judging from the flicker in those bland gray eyes, she got the message. "Of course it does, sweetheart. And I know how hard it must be on you, trying to make sure *every* meal's nutritious—"

"Tony made a salad, too," Lili said, taking the woman by the arm and steering her back toward the kitchen, and Tony wondered what "he'd" made it out of, exactly, since it'd been a while since he'd hit up the produce aisle. Yeah, they had tomatoes and cukes out the wazoo, but the leafy green stuff might be kinda iffy. As he transferred the charred excuses for hamburgers to a paper plate, Lou came up beside him, blessing the world at large with his cologne. Even so, Tony'd always liked his father-in-law, the son of a factory worker who—the Rolex notwithstanding—was still just an average Joe from the old neighborhood who'd done good.

"Those look great," he now said, and Tony laughed.

"You gotta be kiddin' me? You own one of the best restaurants in Boston, and you're salivatin' over a bunch of burnt, pre-pressed burgers?"

The older man shrugged, his hands in his khakis pockets. "Reminds me of when I was a kid. Bad burgers, rubbery hot dogs, hot off the grill—now *that* was summer. These days it's salmon and chicken breasts and grilled vegetables. That's not summer, it's hell."

"Susan's just watching out for you. Making sure you eat right so you'll be around for a long, long time."

"Killin' me with kindness, is what she's doin'," Lou grumbled, but with a *yeah, you're right* shrug and grin.

Maybe Susan went overboard with the worrying, and maybe Lou sometimes flashed his success more than Tony might've liked, but at heart they were good people. Good people who'd defied *their* parents when they'd fallen in love and wanted to get married, good people who were still devoted as hell to each other after more than thirty years. Finding out Marissa had cheated on Tony would be like a stake to the heart. If Josie ended up not being his...

Tony pulled a hamburger bun out of the package and plopped it on a plate. "Here. You get dibs."

"Yeah?" The older man surveyed the plate, then said, "You pick. But you got enough to stick two patties on there? Just for God's sake don't tell Suze, she'll make me eat bean sprouts for a week. Yeah, like that. You got mustard? Ketchup?"

"Over on the table. So I take it the girls didn't give you any trouble?"

"You kiddin'?" Lou said, pumping the ketchup bottle. "They're angels, all three of 'em. Although JoJo..." Chuckling, he smothered the burger with ketchup, then went for the mustard. "She's somethin' else. Knows exactly what she wants and goes after it. Doesn't take 'no' for an answer, either. Just like her mother. You got pickles?"

"In the fridge."

"Forget it, then."

"I should call the kids—"

"No, wait a sec, I wanna talk to you." Lou smashed the top half of the bun over the burger, sending mustard and ketchup squirting out the sides, before taking a seat at the table and looking out at the girls, now back outside. Daphne and Josie were playing ball with Ed—so much for the clean hands—while Claire sat listlessly on one of the swing seats, keeping an eagle eye on her sisters.

"That one's got the world on her shoulders, doesn't she?" Lou said softly before taking an enormous bite of his burger. "Since her mother died, I mean." At that moment, the dog accidentally knocked the baby over. Even though she was obviously unhurt, Claire was instantly on her feet, pulling Josie to her and giving the dog hell. "See what I mean?"

"Actually," Tony said, on guard, "she was like that before. Kid was born with the mother hen gene."

"True. But you know what I'm talkin' about, right?"

Yeah, he knew. That Lou was about to bring up a subject Tony had fervently hoped they'd buried along with Marissa, after Lou had taken Tony aside and expressed concern about how Tony would be able to take care of three kids on his own. "Lou, don't."

"What? Try to make you see reason? I got a good manager for the restaurant now, I hardly ever go in, maybe once, twice a week. Suze and me, we got more time on our hands than we know what to do with—"

"Then travel, for God's sake," Tony said. "Go build houses for Habitat for Humanity. Join a swinging singles club, I don't care—you're not getting my girls." Trying to control his breathing—and his voice, since he didn't want the girls to hear—he added, "I know you and Susan had issues with Marissa marrying me to begin with, that you never thought I was good enough for her—"

"That's not true, Tony, and you know it." At Tony's lifted brows, Lou sighed. "Okay, so maybe it bothered us, at the beginning, that Rissa didn't really understand what she was getting into. The two of you were so damn young, Tony—of course we were gonna worry. But it had nothin' to do with you, I swear. And anyway, you proved us wrong. When I saw how you were suffering, when Rissa got sick…"

Lou looked away. "We're not talking about taking 'em from you, Tone. Just…helping out. Until they're a little older, a little easier to take care of. In the meantime, there's this good private school, just down the road from us—"

"The kids are fine where they are, Lou. They're fine *here*. I know…I know how hard this has been on you, Rissa being your only kid. But you can't have mine."

Finally, the old boy nodded. "Exactly what I told Suze you'd say. If that's how you feel…" He lifted his hands. "Then that's how you feel."

Right. Like Tony didn't damn well know that while Lou might be conceding the battle, the war was far from over. But nobody was getting his girls, he thought, watching Josie throw her arms around Ed's neck and give him a great big kiss on the snout.

Nobody.

"That's better," Susan said, returning to the kitchen from the downstairs bath after she'd gone to "tidy up." Seething from the exchange she'd just witnessed through the kitchen window, Lili watched her cross to the counter, where she'd left her large, obviously expensive designer bag, to fish out a tube of obviously expensive designer lotion, which she then squirted into the palm of one hand. "Sorry I took so long, but that sink looked as though it hadn't been cleaned in a month—"

Lili's jaw dropped. "How could it possibly be that dirty? Tony just cleaned it!"

Susan frowned. "How do you know that?"

"Because…because he told me, that's what he does on Saturdays, when the girls are gone. Cleans house. But children are messy! And Daphne just washed her hands."

Frowning slightly, Susan said gently, "Of course children are messy. But a clean house encourages them to be neater, don't you think?"

Lili thought of all the clean sinks and floors her brothers

had trashed immediately after she'd scrubbed them and almost laughed. Thought of the kitchen she'd spent all afternoon cleaning which had apparently either escaped the woman's notice or which obviously didn't meet Susan Pellegrino's impossible standards. "Not in my experience. And Tony's doing the best he can, he's wonderful with the girls and he loves them so much—"

Blushing, Lili faced the window again, her arms tightly crossed over her stomach.

"Lili? Is everything all right?"

Keep your mouth shut, this is none of your business, you don't know these people, Tony can take care of himself—

"I didn't mean to eavesdrop," she said as calmly as she could manage, "but…" She turned back. "You and your husband want the girls to come live with you?"

Her expression once more slipping into neutral, Susan walked over to the window, massaging lotion into her knuckles. "Lou and I have been discussing the possibility for a long time," she said softly. "I hadn't realized he'd bring the subject up tonight, though." Her gaze swung back to Lili. "What did Tony say?"

"What do you think he said? The very idea appalled him."

Susan sighed. "Not that I'm surprised. I'd just hoped…" She cleared her throat. "It's just…you people from the large families, you have no idea what it's like when you lose your only child. The crater it leaves in your hearts. Your lives." Tears glimmered in her eyes. "The girls are all we have left of Marissa. And we can offer them so much, take the burden off Tony, at least for a while—"

"The girls are all Tony has left, too! How could you even consider taking them away from him?"

"We're only thinking of what's best for them. And for Tony, too. He's obviously overwhelmed, even if he won't admit it—"

"Then help him—help the girls—right here!" Lili said,

startling herself. "Hire a housekeeping service or an au pair or something! And you already see the girls, what? Nearly every weekend? That's already a lot more than most grand-parents get!"

Susan calmly returned to her open bag, snapped shut the tube of lotion and dropped it back inside. "Clearly, Tony has a very staunch ally."

Realizing how close she'd come to showing her hand—a hand that wasn't even hers by rights to begin with—Lily strode back to the counter and the undressed salad. "Tony was...very sweet to me, the summer I was here," she said, dousing the pale greens with olive oil. The only lettuce she'd found in the vegetable bin was a head of old iceberg, the outer leaves wilted and rusty. But the inside was at least edible, if boring. "He didn't have to be, but he was. Especially since he was already going out with your daughter. I've never for-gotten his kindness, that's all."

"And now all these years later," Susan said, "you've got his back."

"Something like that, I suppose."

"You're blushing."

"It's warm in here."

After a long silence, Tony's mother-in-law said, very gently, "Lou and I weren't initially big fans of Tony and Marissa getting married. We felt they were too young, that Marissa was limiting her opportunities..." Shaking her head, she smiled slightly. "But our daughter is...*was* extraordi-narily stubborn. As is Tony. We finally realized he'd do anything to have her. Do anything *for* her. He's..." The corners of her mouth lifted. "An admirable young man. Very...honorable. Decent." She paused. "Lou and I think the world of him."

"They why do you want to take away his children?"

"We just want to help, Lili. That's all. But my point is..."

Susan came to stand beside Lili, her expression earnest. "He loved our daughter very, very much. And a love like that…well. I'm sure you're smart enough to put the pieces together."

Lili met the older woman's gaze. "That Tony's heart is still broken?" she said, deadpan, wondering what this woman would think if she knew the truth. "That he's no more ready to form another attachment than he is to fly? Of course."

"Oh, I think this goes beyond his being ready. Seeing what he went through, during Marissa's illness and…after…" She picked up the garlic salt, frowned at it, then put it down again. "Of course he might remarry—one day, when the children are ready to accept someone in Marissa's place—but I think it's safe to say he'll never love anyone again the way he loved our daughter. You might want to keep that in mind. And you might want to watch how much vinegar you're putting on that salad."

Lili slammed down the bottle. "Do you really think you're saying something I don't already know? That I can't see how much pain Tony's in? And Claire…" She lowered her eyes for a moment. "Even if I weren't returning to Hungary in a few weeks, I know all about trying to wedge yourself into a space when you know you'll never fit. I've had plenty of practice, believe me."

She dumped in a little more olive oil to counteract the vinegar. "But—forgive me for speaking out of turn—you've got no right deciding Tony's entire future, either. Or how or what he's supposed to feel. A man that good, that giving, deserves to be loved." *For the long haul, dammit,* Lili thought, madly mixing the greens as something fiery blossomed inside her. "He also deserves to be supported, not rescued. Because—"

"Burgers are ready," Tony said, popping in the back door, frowning when he clearly realized he'd interrupted their conversation. When he looked at Lili, she gave her head a small shake. Dear God—another dozen words and she'd have come this close to letting his secret slip.

"So's the salad," she said brightly, clamping her hands around the bowl to carry it outside, knowing full well the look Susan gave Tony behind her back.

Chapter Seven

A good half hour passed before Tony found a moment talk to Lili without anybody else in earshot. Burger in tow, he casually lowered his butt onto the chair opposite hers at the outside table, feeling like he should be passing off a brief-case of stolen dough. "What the hell happened in there?"

Lili sighed, her eyes fixed on Susan, pushing Josie in the baby swing. "I overheard Lou's suggesting they take the girls. I guess I came to your defense a little strongly."

Tony looked up from his burger. "You did that for me? And the girls?"

"Duh." She shoved a piece of anemic lettuce into her mouth, muttering, "How dare they?" around it.

Ed slinked past; Tony grabbed him to snag a crumpled napkin out of the his mouth. "Just a regular little she-wolf, aren'tcha?"

"Grrr," she said, and he smiled, thinking that her crazi-ness—and by now, he had no doubt she was as crazy as the rest of the family—was like unexpected fireworks in a starless sky. Fleeting, yeah, but still nice.

"Like I said—I can handle Marissa's parents. Lou backed right down, if you noticed."

Lili's eyes touched his. "For how long?"

Tony bit into his burger. Set it back down on the plate. "They mean well. And this whole thing is killin' 'em, I know that. Doesn't mean they have a shot in hell of gettin' the girls." He gently bumped her knee with his. "But thanks for bein' on my side—"

"Lili!" Daphne called from the garden. "The radishes're coming up! Come see!"

"Guess I've been summoned." Her salad abandoned, she smiled slightly at Tony. "Just being a friend," she said, and the fireworks burst again, that brief moment of surprise, of sucked-in breath and amazement. "However, as soon as I've admired Daph's radishes, I think I'll take my leave. To stay longer would only cause more anxiety."

Tony tensed. "What makes you say that?"

"Um…Susan warned me off?"

"You're kidding."

Lili let out a dry laugh. "Not that it was necessary. I mean, I've just spent the better part of the last several years in isolation. Of my own choosing, yes. But I'd be a complete fool to walk right from that situation into one where…" Her mouth clamped shut.

"Where, what?"

She stood, glancing away for a moment before returning her gaze to his. "I told our aunt I missed being needed. But that's only half true. Because what *I* need, is to be *wanted*. For myself. And…I don't think that's happened, really. Ever. And despite what you say," she said, her words coming faster and faster, "I know when you look at me you're only seeing an older version of who I was fourteen years ago. You were

angry and vulnerable then, and you're even angrier and more
vulnerable now—"

"Li-*li!*"

"Coming, sweetie!" she called to Daphne, then turned
back to Tony. "And that's perfectly okay, Tony, I swear. I'm
glad to be your friend, to help however I can. But…" She took
a deep breath. "Susan's warning was unnecessary."

Tony looked deep into Lili's eyes, gone a cloudy blue as the
sun tilted west. "Any reason why you're telling me all this?"

"Yes," she said simply, then brushed past him and out into
the yard, where she squatted by Daph with her arm around
her waist, while Claire—and Marissa's mother—kept a
watchful, wary eye on the whole proceeding.

Well. That just shot to hell the prospect of sleeping *that*
night, didn't it?

You know, really, none of this has anything to do with you.

During the week or so since the cookout, Lili had probably
reminded herself of this indisputable fact no less than a
hundred times. As in, every time she thought of Tony. Which
happened approximately every five minutes of every waking
hour. Since clearly she was never going to sleep well again,
that was a lot of thinking about Tony.

"Which will never do," she muttered to herself, smartly
turning the page of the British chick lit novel she was translating for her Hungarian publisher, although she'd read the
same page three times with no comprehension whatsoever.
Might make translating it a trifle difficult.

They hadn't seen each other since then, there being no real
reason to. Good thing, since Lili couldn't get the look in
Tony's eyes when she left out of her mind. A soulful look,
like an unclaimed dog at an animal shelter, resigned to its fate.

Doesn't matter what sort of signals he was sending out—

And even she knew there were signals, unintentional or no.

—the man's an emotional wreck.

She turned a page.

So you did the right thing, laying it on the line like that.

She shifted on her aunt's plastic-shrouded sofa, wincing when the backs of her thighs stuck.

And anyway, he was only using you as a sounding board—

The book sailed across the living room to bounce off the fireplace hearth. The obese retriever hauled himself to his feet to go investigate, only to collapse again with a groan. Groaning herself, Lili sank into the corner of the sofa, pouting like a teenager. Because she liked Tony. Liked being around him. Missed him when she wasn't. And all the logic in the world couldn't change any of that. She'd never really had to deal much with wanting things she couldn't have—not for years, at least—and doing so now was not sitting well.

Beside her, the landline rang. Without even checking the display, Lili plucked the phone off the end table.

"Lili?" said a slightly familiar voice. "It's Violet. Rudy's wife? We met at Magda's birthday party—" this came out nearly like "patty" "—a couple weeks ago?"

"Oh. Hi, Violet. Magda and Benny aren't here—"

"That's okay, it's actually you I wanna talk to, anyway."

"Me? Why?"

"Okay, I know this is last minute," the redhead said, "but we had a cancellation—an anniversary party, the family was supposedta take the whole inn—from Wednesday through Friday. I tried calling Tony, but his cell's not picking up and I'm just gettin' his machine on his home phone. But if you guys could make it then, that would be great."

Sure the cushions had muffled her hearing, Lili struggled to sit upright. "What do you mean, *you guys?*"

"Uh-oh…he didn't say anything, did he?"

"Um, no…"

"Honestly, men. Can't live with 'em, can't kill 'em." She

laughed. "You must've thought I was a few sandwiches short of picnic, goin' on and on when you had no clue what I was talking about. Anyway…when we were down there, we invited Tony and the girls up, said he should bring you, too. So consider this your official invitation—"

"Um…" Lili lunged for the first thought that scuttled across her brain. "That's very sweet of you, really…but I think Tony's got plans for the rest of the week. With the girls."

"Really? Rudy's mom seemed to think they were just rotting away in that big old house, not really doing much of anything. So what could it hurt to ask, right? Because God knows when we're gonna having another opening like this for the rest of the summah. He's never been up here, and you must be goin' batty by now at Magda's. Don't get me wrong, I love her to death, but Mag's like one of her rich desserts, she's better in small doses. Right?"

Lili waited for the dust to settle, then chuckled. "That's very true." Then she had a thought. "I suppose I could come up on my own?"

"If it doesn't work out with Tony, sure, why not? Hey, you like to shop? We've got an outlet mall up heah that'll knock your socks off…"

After a few more minutes devoted to the wonders of southern New Hampshire, Violet rang off. The buzzing in Lili's ears had barely stopped, however, when the phone rang again. Seeing Tony's name on the display, she flinched as though pricked by a thorn. Letting the answering machine pick up was certainly tempting. As well as cowardly and childish. Besides, she supposed she should at least *tell* him about the invitation.

"Oh, good—it's you." Was it bad that his voice sent actual shivers up her spine? Was it worse that Peter's voice had never tingled a single vertebra? "I need to ask a favor."

"Why are you whispering?"

"Because apparently I'm raising bats," he whispered. "Do you think you could come over and watch the older girls tomorrow morning while I take…" his voice softened even more "…JoJo to get the test done? I hate to ask, but you're the only one who knows, if I ask anybody in the family they'll be all over me with a hundred questions—"

"I'd be glad to," Lili said, because what else was she going to say? "What are you going to tell the girls?"

"That I'm taking the baby in for a check-up. I figure—"

The next part of whatever he was said was muffled as he apparently put his hand over the phone. A few seconds later, he was back.

"Sorry about that. Anyway. The kids aren't exactly big fans of the doctor's office, so nobody's gonna wanna tag along."

"Er…Claire's not exactly a big fan of me, either."

"For an hour, she can deal. I mean, unless you're uncomfortable…?" This said with a slight begging edge to his voice.

"I suppose I can deal for an hour, too. What time do you want me there?"

"Nine?"

"Nine it is. Oh! I almost forgot! Violet just called, something about our going up to their inn?"

"Crap, I didn't think they were actually serious."

"Apparently, since you never mentioned it. But the invitation's for Wednesday through Friday. I told them you were busy, but Violet didn't shake off that easily."

Tony almost chuckled. "No. She wouldn't." Then he sobered. "You told 'em I was busy?"

Lili couldn't quite read his tone. "I thought…I didn't think…yes," she finally said. "Because we couldn't possibly go up there together. For obvious reasons."

A second passed before Tony said, "From everything I've heard, it's a really great place."

"I'm sure it is, but—"

"And hey—free vacation."

Lily sat up a little straighter on the sofa. "You can't possibly think this would be a good idea?"

"Oh, I think it's a terrible idea," he said, not a hint of humor in his voice. She heard his screen door bang open, a car going by, the drone of a cicada. "You and me, together—"

"With the kids, of course," she said, her stomach going all jittery.

"Somehow, I don't think having the kids around would make much difference one way or the other, but that's just me."

She stilled. "What are you saying?"

"What the hell do you think I'm saying?"

"You're…attracted to me?"

"Duh," he said, and she pressed her hand to her mouth. "God knows, I don't wanna be, I can't act on it, I can't think of anything worse for either of us—"

Earth to Lili.

"—but yeah. I am. And if I wasn't so braindead I probably wouldn't've said anything. But I'm tired…" She heard him push out a sigh. "I'm tired of secrets, Lili. Tired of pretending." For some reason, she visualized him leaning one hand against a support post, the phone clamped to his ear. Saw him so clearly, in fact, her hand lifted, as though to touch him. *Silly girl.*

Now she pushed out a sigh littered with a thousand shards of unfulfilled dreams.

"But I'm also tired of us bein' cooped up in this damn house, this damn *town*," Tony said. "So I'm thinking, maybe a couple days away wouldn't be such a bad idea. Maybe it would maybe help Claire shake that freakin' cloud that follows her everywhere." He paused. "Maybe it would give me something to do beside sit here and worry about…the results."

Oh, she thought. "How long does it take?"

"Forty-eight hours."

Her heart twisted, knowing it would be the longest two days of his life. "So take the kids, why do I have to go?"

"Because you've never been to New Hampshire," he finally said, then hung up.

"Why can't *I* watch Daphne while you're gone?" Claire said the next morning, shadowing Tony from room to room as he looked for Josie's other sandal. Which, natch, had gone missing in the middle of the night even though he distinctly remembered putting them both on top of her toy chest before her bath.

"Because you're ten and it's against the law," Tony muttered, thinking, *Oh, hell,* when he spotted the damn shoe next to the dog's water dish. Josie clinging to his hip, he squatted to pick up the sandal, breathing out a profound sigh of relief that, except for a couple of canine tooth dents in the rubber, it was otherwise intact. He plunked down on a kitchen chair to insert foot in sandal. "And there's way too many cops in this family to take that chance."

"But why is *Lili* watching us?"

"Because everybody else was busy," Tony said, wondering how many lies, white or otherwise, the average parent dispensed over the course of eighteen years. Or longer. "And what've you got against Lili, anyway? She's a nice lady."

Claire gave him one of those if-I-have-to-explain-what's-the-point? looks. The same one he'd seen way too many times from her mother. Once upon a time, he'd found it endearing. "That's probably her now," he said when both the doorbell and the dog sounded. "Go let her in."

"Daphne can do it."

"See?" Tony said, getting to his feet. "Exactly why you can't watch her on your own, you'd let her open the door to anybody."

Claire's mouth fell open. "Ohmigod! Of course I wouldn't do that! You just *said* it was Lili! God—"

"Well," Lili said brightly from the kitchen doorway, Daphne at her side and more grocery bags dangling from her hands. Amused eyes bounced off Tony's before settling on Claire. "What did he do this time?" she said, and the girl's gaze flew to hers.

"He…" Her cheeks flamed. "Nothing."

"Really?" She looked at Tony again. "Because I could have sworn I heard you teasing the poor child."

"Naw, I was just—"

"My father," Lili said to Claire, "would tease me to distraction. Of course, eventually I realized that was his *strange*—" another glance at Tony "—way of showing his love. But when I was your age? Torture, I tell you. Pure torture."

Wow, point to you, Tony thought as Claire regarded Lili in stunned silence for several seconds before curiosity apparently got the better of her. "What's in the bags?"

Lili grinned. "I thought we could make plum dumplings," she said, blue eyes sparkling behind her glasses.

And behind Claire's glasses, The Look of Utter Horror. "You mean, with actual *plums* in them?"

"Well…yes. It's, um, a traditional Hungarian dish, I used to love when I was a child—"

"I don't *think* so," Claire said, storming out of the kitchen. She was halfway up the stairs before Tony caught up with her.

"Claire. Come back here. *Now.*"

She turned, miserable. "You know I hate plums, Dad, they make me gag—"

"I understand that. But Lili didn't do anything to warrant that reaction. So you march yourself back down and apologize—"

"Tony," Lili said behind him. "That's not necessary, really—"

"Yeah. It is. Claire?"

Her arms tightly folded over her chest, she glowered at the riser below her for a moment, then came down the stairs far enough to see Lili. "I'm sorry," she mumbled, then lifted her eyes. "But I really *don't* like plums. Would it be okay…" She shoved her hair behind her ear. "Would you mind if I stayed in my room and read instead?"

Lili glanced at Tony, who nodded, before saying to Claire, "Of course not. You go right ahead." Then she turned to Daphne, who was tugging her skirt. Leave it to that one to have a front row seat. Kid lived for this stuff.

"I'll help you make them." She was also a world-class brownnoser.

"Oh. Good. Thank you. Why don't you go unload all the bags onto the kitchen table, then, and I'll be right in?"

His middle child skipped off, humming happily, as his oldest tromped upstairs. A moment later they heard her door click shut. "Sorry about that," Tony muttered, grabbing both baby and car keys. He turned to Lili, who, as usual, seemed remarkably unfazed by it all. "Civilizing kids is a lot harder than it looks."

She smiled. "She'll be fine. *We'll* be fine."

He wanted to kiss her so badly he thought the top of his head would come off. "Well," he said, lowering his eyes to the baby. "Guess I can't put this off any longer."

Tony was nearly out to the car before he realized Lili had followed them to stand in the driveway with her arms crossed, a breeze fluttering her flippy little skirt around her knees. "I take it you haven't mentioned the New Hampshire trip?" she said as he belted Josie into her car seat. He straightened; she'd messily twisted her hair up with a couple sticks poking through it, so half of it was floating around her face. In the sunlight, it had a lot more gold in it than he would've thought.

"No. Not yet. When I get back's soon enough. That way

they have less than twenty-four hours to drive me nuts about it." He propped one hand on the car's roof, still cool in the early morning shade. "I thought you didn't wanna go."

Strands of hair teased her cheeks for a moment before she said, "Actually, I do. Very much. Whether I should or not, though…" She glanced up at the upstairs window.

"Her room's in back, she can't hear us. But it's okay, you don't hafta spell it out."

"I just don't want to add to anyone's distress." Her cheeks flushed. "I'm only here for the summer, Tony. And heaven only knows when I'll be back. If I'll be back."

"Because you're gonna go off and find your life and all that."

"Right," she said, the corners of her mouth lifting. "So the logical side of my brain thinks I should probably keep my distance." Her gaze speared his. "For many reasons."

"And what does the illogical side of your brain think?"

"That logic is hugely overrated. That—" her blush deepened, making her eyes even bluer "—that I don't exactly have a lot to show for nearly thirty years of doing the 'right' thing, do I?"

Tony slammed shut the car's back door and yanked his open, knowing his frustration had virtually nothing to do with her and everything to do with feeling like he was the butt of some sick joke. Finally he looked back at Lili, knowing damn well what he should do and not having the least interest in doing it, for probably much the same reasons as her.

"Why don't you see how it goes with the girls today?" he said mildly. "Then let me know tonight what you decide."

"Fair enough," she said, turning back to the house. This time, though, it wasn't her backside he was fixated on, but her hair, flashing gold in the morning sun. He could practically feel it, slippery and warm between his fingers, against his mouth…

"I am so screwed," he muttered, climbing behind the wheel and jerking the gear shift into Reverse.

* * *

"Over there, Ed!" Daphne yelled at the dog, who'd been doing acrobatics for the past ten minutes trying to catch a fly and keeping both Lili and her sous-chef in stitches. The dog spun around, snapping several times at the buzzing insect until, frustrated, he started barking at it.

"Yeah, that'll show it," Lili said, and Daphne dissolved into at least her tenth giggle fit of the morning.

"Look, Lili! He got it!"

"Are you sure?"

"Uh-huh—he's chewing!"

"Ewwww," they said at the same time, then cracked up all over again—

"What on earth is going on in here?" Claire said from the doorway, clearly annoyed at being left out of the fun.

"Ed caught a fly!" Daphne said from stool next to the counter where she'd been smushing together confectioner's sugar and cinnamon with a fork. "An' then he ate it! Hey, Claire—you should come help—we're making plum dumplings!"

"I'd rather eat the fly," Claire grumbled, sidling over to the fridge and trying not to show interest in the proceedings. "Sheesh, it was so noisy down here I couldn't read."

"Sorry," Lili mumbled, exchanging a look with Daphne, who giggled again. And then brushed her forehead with the back of her hand. Sugar everywhere.

"Come on, Claire," the little girl said, dimpling at Lili. "It's fun."

"Claire doesn't like plums," Lili said mildly, cutting the already made potato dough into squares. "Actually, neither do I, unless they're in dumplings."

The ten-year-old edged closer, eyeing their workstation. "That's…weird."

"Isn't it? We're ready to wrap the dough around the fruit. Wanna try?"

"It looks messy."

"Oh, it is," Lili said as Daphne trooped from counter to table with the bowl of cinnamon sugar in her hands. And splotches of flour on her face and bits of potato in her hair. At Claire's gasp, Lili bit her lip to keep from laughing.

"Ohmigod, Daph! What happened to you?"

"Daph helped make the dough," Lili said, and Claire looked at her as if she'd just announced they'd invited Martians to lunch.

"Nana's picking us up in an hour to take us shopping! In the *Cadillac!*" Tears bulged in her eyes. "She'll have an absolute fit when she sees Daphne!"

This was news to Lili. "Oh?" she said, pinning the child with her gaze. "Funny, your father didn't mention it."

"That's because…he d-didn't know. Nana just c-called and said she was on her way."

Lili could call the child on the lie, since the phone hadn't rung. And for a moment she had to fight the blow to her own ego that Claire would go to such elaborate lengths to get away from her. Then she remembered what it had felt like to be a ten-year-old who basically hated her life.

"Well, not to worry…Daph's washable." Then, out of nowhere, she heard herself add, "Nobody expects you to be responsible for your sister, Claire." She paused. "Or anybody else."

"That's what I keep *trying* to tell her," Daphne put in, waving her hands. "That she's not in charge of me and JoJo. But will she listen?" The younger girl blew out a sigh. "No."

Tamping down another laugh, Lili got up to gently lead a sniffling Claire to the sink, where she dampened a paper towel. "Put this on your eyes, it will keep them from getting puffy."

Removing her glasses to press the compress to one eye, the girl peered at Lili with the other, glimmering with cautious trust. "Mom used to do this, too. With the towel."

"It's a girl thing," Lili said. "So. We have an hour?"

"Yeah, about."

"That's plenty of time to finish and for Daphne to have her shower. And if you don't wish to help—"

"No, it's okay." She shrugged. "It's not like I've got anything else to do." The towel abandoned, Claire frowned at the squares of dough already laid out on the floured table. "So what's next?"

Her heart fluttering at the small step toward détente, Lili showed Claire how to wrap the dough around chunks of sweet-tart plum, pinching the edges closed to form little balls before lowering them into the big pot of boiling water on the stove. Both girls—and Ed—stood in rapt attention beside her, although the dog couldn't see inside the bubbling pot.

"How do you know when they're done?" Claire asked.

"When they pop up. Like that!" Lili said, smiling, as one by one the dumplings bobbed to the surface of the bubbling water, which she carefully removed with a slotted spoon. "Now we roll them the breadcrumbs," she said, transferring the platter of hot, cooked dumplings to the table to be gently coated in fragrant, buttery breadcrumbs.

"And now the sugar?" Daphne asked.

"And now the sugar."

Lili stood aside, quietly coaching the girls as they sprinkled the warm, crunchy dumplings with the sugar mixture, the fragrance of cinnamon and warm fruit and butter filling the old kitchen, filling Lili's head with silly notions she dared not indulge for long. The dumplings all frosted and sparkly under the fake Tiffany lamp suspended over the table, Claire looked at her—without a frown—and Lily nearly groaned with yearning for a home and family of her own.

"Can we eat one?"

"Not yet. Better give them a few minutes for the fruit to cool. I don't want you to burn your mouths."

"And you," Claire said to Daphne, "go take your bath. Hair, too."

Lili frowned at the younger girl. "Can you do that alone?"

"Of course," Daphne said as she slid off her chair. "I'm not a baby, sheesh." Then she pointed at them. "But no eating the dumplings until I get back!"

Then she trounced off, potato-flecked curls fluttering indignantly. A moment later, Claire got up, too, looking unsure of what came next.

"It's okay," Lili said, "you can go."

"Don't you need some help cleaning up?"

"That's all ri—" *Oh, for heaven's sake—are you insane?* "I'd love some help. Although it seems Ed's already taken care of the floor," she said, watching the dog frantically sucking up every crumb he could find.

The giggle was short, and barely audible, but it was definitely a giggle.

They worked in virtual silence for several minutes, Lili hardly daring to breathe for fear she'd break the spell. Finally, though, she heard a soft, "It must've been so cool, growing up in the circus."

"Oh. Well…not so much, actually."

She could feel the girl's frown. "How come?"

"Traveling all the time sucks, if you don't like it. And it's deadly dull if you're not performing."

"You didn't?"

"Oh, dear God, no. My father used to say I was the most uncoordinated child in Hungary."

"That's awful."

She laughed. "But true. All I wanted, when I was your age, was to be normal. To go to a normal school and do normal things." She let out a dramatic sigh. "To have parents who didn't wear tights and sequins, who didn't *fly,* for goodness sake!"

A second giggle made Lili's heart jump. "Yeah, I could see how that would be a little strange."

"For the other circus kids, that *was* normal. And they loved it. For me…no. It didn't help, either, that I had the self-esteem of a slug." Claire frowned. "I didn't like myself very much."

There went that curious look again. "Why?"

"Because…I was all pointy angles. And clumsy. And my nose was too big and my mouth too wide, and I hated these—" she pointed to her protruding incisors "—because my brothers called me Vampira all the time. And," she continued as Claire giggled *again,* "I never felt I had anything in common with the other kids my age. Sometimes, I was tempted to wonder if I really *was* a vampire kid my parents had gotten from the gypsies or something."

"I know how that goes," Claire said with a solemn nod. "Not about the vampire thing, but the rest of it? Yeah." She looked at the dumplings. Taking her cue, Lili leaned over and touched one.

"I think they're ready."

"Oh. Um…shouldn't we wait for Daphne?"

"She'll never know." Lili held out the plate to her. "Unless you tell."

The child reached for one, then pulled back, frowning. "But I hate plums."

"Do you really hate them? Or just think you do?" When Claire's eyes shot to Lili's, she shrugged, even as she suddenly felt so strongly for the little girl she ached. *I know how hard it is,* she wanted to say, *forcing yourself to try new things. To move past "safe."* "One bite. If you don't like it, I promise my feelings won't be hurt."

Claire hesitated, then gingerly—as though the dumpling might explode—plucked one off the pile. After a few seconds' intense contemplation, she jerked her hair behind one ear and took the tiniest bite possible…only to shudder when the tart fruit juices hit her tongue. Lili held her breath, fully expecting the girl to spit it out. Instead, she not only swallowed, but took a second bite. Without shuddering, this time.

"So…what's the verdict?"

A shrug preceded the rest of the dumpling vanishing into her mouth. "S'okay," she said, chewing. "Once you get used to it." *One could say that about most things in life,* Lili thought as the child asked, "May I have another one?"

"Go for it."

Claire wriggled into a kitchen chair, to better savor her treat, apparently. In the midst of catching a dribble of plum juice on her chin, however, she said, "Are you just being nice to me because of Dad?"

So much for détente. "I could ask the same of you, you know."

The girl's eyes flashed to hers. Then she shrugged, a small, sad what's-the-point? gesture that completely cancelled out the spoken, "Whatever," that followed it.

Sighing, Lili dropped into another chair to meet the girl's eyes. "Claire, I know there's…stuff between you and me, even if I'm not completely sure what that stuff is. But for a few minutes, I thought we'd moved beyond that. At least I had." Far too perceptive by half, the child watched her, waiting. Lili sat back in the chair, her arms folded over her chest. "I'm not going to pretend I know exactly how you're feeling—that would be beyond stupid—but sometimes, when you get certain expressions on your face? They remind a lot of the expressions I used to see in my own mirror. So I feel, just a little, as if I've known you for a long time. And that's a good thing."

Claire took another bite, her brows knit as she turned the remaining chunk of dumpling over and over in her fingers. "So Dad has nothing to do with it?"

"Well, obviously I wouldn't even be here if it weren't for him. But he's not why I'm being nice to you. I'm being nice to you because…you're a very interesting person."

"Me?" Claire said, pressing plumy fingers to her white top. Oops.

"Yes, you. You've brave, you're not afraid to speak your mind, which a lot of women—" Lili raised her hand "—have problems with. And you clearly love your sisters and father very, very much."

"You think I'm brave?"

Lili smiled. "You ate the dumpling, didn't you?"

Still frowning, Claire licked her fingers, then looked straight at Lili. "If I ask you something, will you tell me the truth?"

"I'll certainly try."

"Do you like Dad or not? And I don't mean as a—" she made quote marks in the air "—friend."

Lili leaned over, picking a dumpling off the pile and biting into it. *Perfect,* she thought as juice dripped down her chin. Claire handed her a napkin. "Yes," she said, wiping her mouth. "I do."

Claire's eyes never left hers. "Does he like you?"

"You'd have to ask him that, I can't answer for him." She took another bite, wiped her mouth again. "But I can say that, sometimes, with grownups…liking each other doesn't mean…" She searched for the right words. "Doesn't mean serious, or forever, or…anything, really. Sometimes, the timing's all wrong, or there are other things, or people, you have to think about." Finishing off the dumpling, she shrugged. "It's complicated."

The child let out a long sigh. "Yeah. Tell me about it."

Lili smiled, even though her stomach felt as if she'd eaten the entire plate of dumplings on her own. "Even if…things were different, I think it's pretty safe to say your father would never do anything to upset you. Or push you into something you're not ready for." Lili paused. "And neither would I."

The girl's eyes lifted again. "You promise?"

"Cross my heart," Lili said, doing just that, then said, "You see, the timing isn't good for me, either."

"You mean…like you don't want a boyfriend right now?"

Lili's mouth twitched, even as she realized she was having trouble with that logic thing again. That her pull toward Tony was in direct opposition to an almost desperate need to figure out who she was and what her place in the grand scheme of things was supposed to be. "You're an incredibly smart little girl, aren't you?" she said, and Claire lowered her eyes, blushing. Then she added, "If something's right, it has to be right for everybody. Does that make sense?"

Claire reached for another dumpling before finally nodding. "Yeah, I guess," she said, just as a dripping, towel-clad Daphne appeared in the doorway. "No fair! You said you wouldn't start without me!"

Her hair a mass of sopping corkscrews, she tromped across the tile floor, leaving behind a trail of wet footprints, to snatch one of the dumplings off the pile and shove the whole thing into her mouth. A moment later she ran to the trash can to spit it out, then to the sink for a glass of water which she gulped down as if her mouth was on fire. "Grossioso!" she said once she came up for air. "And you people actually *ate* those things?"

Claire and Lili looked at each other and burst out laughing…a moment before the doorbell rang.

"I'll get it," Daphne said, letting out a shriek when Claire nearly tackled her to the floor.

"You can't answer the door, you're naked!"

"Am not, I'm wearing a towel!" Daphne yelled after Claire as the older girl stormed out…only to return a few seconds later with a puzzled look on her face.

"I looked through the peephole, just to make sure it was

Nana? But it's not, it's some guy I've never seen before. So I didn't open the door."

"Good girl. Was he holding a clipboard? Pamphlets?" Lili'd already gotten the lowdown from Magda, who you opened the door to and who you didn't.

"Did he look like a weirdo?" Daphne put in.

"He looks *fine*," Claire huffed. "I just don't know him."

"Ed, come," Lili said, beckoning the lean, mean, fly-eating machine to follow her and the girls down the hall. Grasping the dog's collar, she opened the door.

"Maybe I help you?" she asked the square-jawed man on the other side, blond and crisp and creased, the type of man whose life was probably governed by some bit of technology smaller than a deck of cards.

Then he said, "This *is* Tony Vaccaro's house, isn't it?" and Lili got a very strong feeling that life had just come crashing down around his perfectly coiffed head.

Chapter Eight

Within like a second of Lili's opening the door, Claire got one of her bad feelings. She even felt the back of her neck prickle, like when she was little and had to go pee in the middle of the night, and the house was all dark and spooky.

Without thinking, she took Daphne's hand and inched closer to Lili. The stranger didn't look at either of them. With his sunglasses on, Claire couldn't decide if he was angry or sad or both, but whatever it was, his face creeped her out.

"Tony's not available at the moment," Lili said, fighting to keep Ed, who on his hind legs was nearly as tall as Lili, from jumping up on the man. Only to lick him, but the guy didn't know that. "Who shall I say was here—?"

"Will he be back soon?"

"If you leave a number, I could have him call you."

Claire noticed Lili didn't invite him inside to wait. Also, that she blocked both Claire and Daph with her body. But instead of answering, the man turned and went back down the steps and out to his car, a small, fancy one with no top, like Gramps drove.

"Who was it?" Daph asked after he drove away.

"I have no idea." Lili let Ed go, then closed the door, looking from Claire to Daph. "Neither of you recognized him?"

"Uh-uh," they both said. Claire noticed Lili's hands were shaking, a little. Then she smiled and told them to go get dressed, they didn't want to keep their grandmother waiting. Except before she'd finished her sentence, practically, the door opened—everybody jumped, including the dog—but it was only Daddy and JoJo. Daddy gave Lili a really weird look, and she gave him one right back.

Which only made Claire's neck prickle even harder as she and Daph went upstairs.

Tony waited until he was sure the girls were in their rooms before spinning on a very pale Lili. "What happened?" he whispered, setting Josie down. "You look like you just saw a ghost."

"No, no ghost," she said, palming her cheek before lifting her eyes to Tony's. "A real live man. Here, asking for you. Well-dressed, light hair. Couldn't tell his eye color, he was wearing sunglasses. But he drives an expensive looking sports car. A Jaguar, perhaps. Silver."

His mind racing, Tony crossed the entryway on autopilot to wrest one of the dog's toys out of Josie's hands, barely hearing the baby's howl of protest. "Don't know the car. But..." After another glance upstairs, he turned back to Lili. "Who else could it be?"

Shaking her head, Lili sat on the boot-and-scarf bench by the front door, smiling when Josie made a beeline for her and crawled up into her lap. A second later she'd snuggled against Lili's chest with her thumb in her mouth; Lili gently palmed the baby's head, stroking her fine hair. "Why does this feel so good?" she asked, shifting slightly to settle Josie more securely on her lap.

Even over the sudden surge of acid in his gut, Tony's mouth twitched. "So you don't sell 'em to the highest bidder when they hit puberty?"

Lili chuckled, resting her cheek on top of the Josie's head as she looked up, her eyes soft with sympathy. "When will you know? About the test?"

The bench creaked when Tony lowered his carcass beside her. Josie immediately decided she wanted him again. "Sometime Thursday," he said, strongly tempted to put the kid in the car and strike out for parts unknown.

A quick, light squeeze of his wrist preceded, "If it's still okay, I would like to go to New Hampshire with you and the girls."

He twisted to look at her profile. "You sure?"

"I think Claire and I came to an understanding," she said over the sound of little feet clattering down the stairs. "I even got her to giggle."

"You're puttin' me on."

"Not a bit of it. More than once, even." As Tony shook his head, amazed, Lili added, "Although if she still has a problem with my tagging along, I won't go—"

The girls hit the bottom of the stairs at the same time the doorbell rang, giving Tony only a second to frown at their strangely spiffy outfits before Daph rushed to the picture window in the living room and announced, "Okay, this time it really is Nana!"

"And why is that?" he asked his red-faced—and usually glib—oldest daughter. But before she could answer, his mother-in-law swept through the door, all tanned and toned in a neat little tennis dress and sparkling white shoes to match.

"No, Ed, get *down!* DOWN! Honestly, Tony, you really must get that dog in obedience school—hello, darlings!"

Susan said, dispensing hugs and kisses like she hadn't just seen the kids the day before...a flurry of activity that came to a screeching halt the instant she laid eyes on Lili.

"Oh," she said, obviously confused. "Lili. How nice to see you again—"

"Dad had to take JoJo to the doctor," Daph said before Tony could muzzle her, "so Lili stayed with us. We made plum dumplings, but they're seriously gross—"

"They were not," Claire put in.

"Were, too—"

"What do you mean," Susan said, "you took the baby to the doctor?"

"You ate plum dumplings?" Tony asked, flummoxed.

"Yeah," Claire said with a little smile at Lili. "They were actually pretty good—"

"Are you all right, sweetie?" Susan asked, palming JoJo's forehead.

"She's fine," Tony said. "Just a check-up."

"Oh. Well, then." Susan gave him a funny look, then smiled for her granddaughters. "Are you two ready to go?"

Tony looked at Claire again. "Go where?"

"Their grandmother invited them to go shopping for school," Lili said. "Sort of a last-minute thing, I gathered."

And yeah, he caught the slightly puzzled looks on both Claire's and Susan's faces. God save him from female conspiracies. "But school's not for weeks yet."

"Then now's the best time to shop," Susan said, taking Daphne's hand, "before the stores get crowded." Then she smiled at Tony, and he remembered Marissa talking about her and her mother's shopping expeditions, all-day affairs that often included pedicures and lunches at fancy restaurants...a tradition they'd kept up until nearly the end. He hated shopping, himself, but he could tell how much this meant to Susan, being able to do with her granddaughters what she could no longer do with her own daughter. "And besides," she said, looking genuinely happy for the first time in months, "tell me I'm not saving you hours of agony."

Tony chuckled. "Okay, you got me there. But they wear uniforms, so don't buy 'em a lot of stuff they can't wear. And they gotta be home by five, 'cause we're goin' on a trip tomorrow and I wanna get an early start."

At that, all eyes veered to him.

"What kind of trip, Tony—?"

"Really? Yay! Where are we going—?"

"What if I don't wanna go?"

"It's just for a cuppla days," he said to the group at large, "up to visit Rudy and Violet in New Hampshire. I didn't know about it myself until yesterday." He paused, not really wanting to do this in front of Susan, but better now than to a couple of cranky, malled-out kids. Then, because Susan would only find out later, anyway, he added, "And I've invited Lili to go along."

Daphne squealed another "Yay!" and wrapped her arms around Lili's hips, Claire went into dour mode and Susan looked like she'd just been goosed. Lili, however, bent over to look into Claire's eyes.

"But only if it's okay with you," she said softly.

Claire frowned. "Really?"

"Really—"

"Please say yes, Claire," Daphne said, clinging to Lili. A move obviously not sitting well with Susan. "Please?"

After a moment, Claire sighed. "Sure, why not?" she said, and Lili smiled, and all manner of untoward thoughts rose up in Tony's brain, despite his mother-in-law's pointed glance in his direction before she opened the front door.

"Girls, why don't you go on out to the car? Tony? We should, um, probably discuss what the girls need for school. Would you mind coming out with me for a moment?"

Leaving Josie behind with Lili—and trying to ignore Lili's raised brows—Tony followed Marissa's mother. "Don't start, Susan," he said in a low voice as soon as they got out on the porch and the girls were safely in the car. "I know what you're thinking—"

"What? What am I thinking? Besides the fact that you're rushing into another relationship when Marissa hasn't even been gone a year yet?"

Tony's face heated. "I'm not rushing into *anything*. Rudy and Violet invited us up to their inn on the spur of the moment and asked me if I'd like to bring her along, so that's what I'm doing. And that's *all* I'm doing."

"And did you see how attached Daphne already is? Did you?"

"Daphne attaches herself to everybody she meets, she's always been that way—"

"And what happens when Lili leaves?"

"She'll get over it."

"And will Claire?"

"What are you talkin' about? Claire's barely warming up to the woman—"

"And when she does," Susan said, genuine worry in her eyes, "she's going to fall hard. Harder than she's ready to deal with this soon after losing her mother. Tony…" She laid a hand on his arm. "I know how horribly lonely you must be. But for the children's sake, for *your* sake, please don't do anything you'll regret later—"

"Not about to. After everything I've been through these past months…" His throat working overtime, Tony looked away from the still-fresh pain in his mother-in-law's eyes. "Lili's a friend," he said at last. Which was true, his increasingly frequent more-than-friendly thoughts about her notwithstanding. "And if she can help Claire act and sound like a little girl again, instead of a crotchety old woman, I'm not gonna stop her."

"*We* can help her do that!"

"No, you can't. Because every time she looks at you, she sees her mother. Worse, she sees how much pain *you're* still in. And that's not to put down how much you and Lou have helped us, or how much you love the girls or they love you. Not at all. But I saw something in Claire's face today that I haven't seen in a long, long time, something good, and it just seems stupid not to run with that, you know?"

"It's just…" Susan's mouth thinned. "We don't want *you* to get hurt again, either," she said, then popped on her sunglasses, took a deep breath, and headed toward the Caddy, her tennis shoes barely making a sound on Tony's shady, root-cracked walk.

Lili scooted away from the window, crouching in front of Josie—who'd dragged her toy basket from the living room into the vestibule—just as Tony came back in. The door shut behind him, he leaned against it, one hand still on the knob. "So how much of that did you hear?"

She flushed. "What makes you think—?"

"Lili. Please."

"I got the important bits," she said on a rush of air, wrestling a stuffed cat out of Ed's mouth and handing it back to Josie, who sternly wagged her finger at the dog and said, "No, no, Ed—mine!" Lili smiled. "That she's worried about the girls becoming too attached to me." Her eyes met his. "That you're definitely not looking for…entanglements right now. Which we'd already established."

Tony pushed off the door, shoving his fingers into the front pockets of his jeans as he watched the baby. "Looking, not looking…either one takes more energy than I've got." Then he dropped back onto the bench, tightly gripping the edge on either side of his thighs. "But I had to say something to get Susan off my case. Off yours, too—"

"Yuck," Josie said, making a face before conking poor Ed on the head with the toy. "Kitty all wet. Bad Ed. Bad doggie."

At Ed's *What did I do?* look, Lili chuckled. Josie handed the soggy kitty to her; pensively wiping it on her skirt, Lili said, "You're giving me far too much credit about Claire, though."

"She *giggled*, Lil. Do you have any idea…?" He cleared his throat, then sagged against the bench's wooden back, pressing his thumb and forefinger into his eyes before saying, "Did the guy say he'd come back today?"

"He didn't say much of anything, really. Do you…do you want me to stay?"

"No, you go on," he said, smiling for Josie when she pranced back to him and crawled into his lap. "Wouldn't be anything you could do if he shows up again, anyway—"

"*My* daddy," Josie said, patting Tony's muscled forearm before threading her silky little arms around his neck. "Kiss kiss?"

"You got it, cutie," Tony said, bouncing a kiss off her puckered lips, looking at Lili over the baby's shoulder when she hugged her daddy again.

And the love and fear and longing in those deep brown eyes nearly did her in.

The early morning sun beating down on him at the end of the driveway, Tony checked his watch for what must've been the tenth time in as many minutes. Over in the yard, Daph and Josie and the Ed—who was going, too, Rudy had said their own dog, Simon, would get a kick out of it—were running around in circles and making enough noise to set off car alarms in Alaska.

"Maybe she changed her mind," Claire said, leaning over the open tailgate to shove in her backpack and not trying all that hard to hide her disappointment. Tony inwardly swore, thinking Susan was right, it *was* dumb, letting the girl get close to somebody who wasn't hanging around.

Maybe even dumber than letting *himself* get close to somebody who wasn't hanging around.

"Nah," he said, shooting Claire a smile before staring down the street, like he could will Lili to materialize. "I'm sure something must've just held her up."

"Did you call her?"

"Several times. Yes, both her cell and Magda's landline. Nobody answered...wait. Is that her? That's her, right? See, what did I tell you, that she'd be here, right?"

Claire frowned. Okay, that might've been overkill.

A minute later, his Uncle Benny pulled his verging-on-vintage Pontiac up behind the Volvo, leaning out of the window to yell, "Sorry we're late, this one—" he aimed a thumb in Lili's direction, a blur of arms and bags as she scrambled out of the passenger seat "—had to make a last-minute stop at the Rite Aid, and I got a flat, can you believe it? Haven't had one of those in probably twenty years—"

"And I forgot to charge my cell," Lili said, hot-footing it to the tailgate with a purse large enough to stash Ed in hanging from her shoulder as she dragged a small rolling case behind her. "And of course nobody was home to tell you what was going on..." Tony came up beside her to heft the case into the car, and she was very close and very warm, her scent rising up off her in brain-melting waves, and when he looked down into those oh-God-I'm-so-sorry eyes behind her glasses...

Uh, boy.

"S'okay," he said, one brand of anxiety sloughing off only to be replaced by something far scarier the instant she smiled. Fortunately, one of them had the presence of mind to break the eye contact—not Tony, however—after which they both thanked Benny for bringing her. Waving, his uncle backed out of the driveway and drove off.

The next five minutes was spent making sure the car was packed and the girls were emptied, that somebody had remembered to bring the dog's food and dish and diapers for the baby, whose potty skills were sketchy at best, and suddenly Tony heard Daphne say, "Isn't that the man who was here yesterday?" and he snapped his head around so hard his neck cracked.

Then he glanced at Lili, who nodded. And frowned. "Should we go inside?"

"Not necessary," Tony said mildly, offering a clearly troubled Claire a quick smile before he walked out to the street and down the half block to where the silver Jag was parked. At his approach, the man removed his sunglasses and got out, not looking a whole lot better than Tony felt. Wasn't until he got right up to the guy, however, that his stomach sank to his knees.

"Holy crap. Cole *Jamison?*"

The dude shot a quick look around, like Tony shouldn't've said his name out loud. Then his gaze veered to Tony's driveway. To Josie, safe in Lili's arms.

"You first," Tony said in a low voice.

"You're leaving?"

"For a couple of days. Don't worry, I'm not skippin' town. Well?"

Cole almost didn't seem to hear him, staring instead past Tony's shoulder, while Tony tried to absorb the irony. Two high school jocks, one from a blue-collar Italian family, the other from the same country-club set as Rissa's maternal grandparents, both with a thing for the same girl. How smug Tony'd felt, when he'd "won."

Cole's hand trembled when he rubbed his mouth. "She looks like me."

"She looks like Marissa," Tony said calmly, taking a sick, perverse pleasure in Cole's poleaxed expression.

"My family and I were away. In Europe. We got home day before yesterday, and there was this, this *letter*…"

"Yeah. I got one, too."

Finally, olive-green eyes met Tony's. "She never told you?"

"Nope. Up until a couple weeks ago, I had no clue." Tony shoved his hands in his back pockets. "Your wife know?"

Cole blew out a soft, humorless laugh. "No. It was—"

"Save it. I really don't give a damn."

"It was a fling, that's all," the guy said anyway, more than a little desperation edging his words. "Lasted less than a month. For what it's worth, Rissa called it off."

"That supposed to make me feel better? Or you?"

Cole's eyes widened, then shifted back to Josie. "Do you know…?"

"If she's mine? Not yet. In the works, though."

"When will you—?"

"In a couple of days. Hey—wanna go halfsies on the lab fee?"

Angry, scared eyes shot to his. "Not funny."

"No, it's not. But then, neither is finding out the kid you had every reason to believe was yours might not be."

"It wasn't—"

"Supposed to happen? Yeah, I got that."

Now panic flooded the jerk's face. "Sarah—my wife—she can't find out about this. It would kill her—"

"Dad?" Claire yelled from the car. "Are you coming?"

"Yeah, baby, be right there." Tony turned back to Cole. "One question—do you *want* to know?" A long moment passed before the man finally nodded. "Then you got a card or something?" Tony said over the sensation of riding out a hurricane in a rowboat. "So I can get in touch with you," he added irritably when the guy gave him deer-in-headlights.

"Uh, yeah." He fumbled for his wallet, pulling out an

embossed business card which he handed over. "Call my cell, nobody answers that except me."

Tony stared at the card for a second, then blew out a breath that barely dented the nausea. "Look, your wife's not gonna hear about any of this from me. No skin off my nose. But if the baby does turn out to be yours…?"

"I don't know," Cole said softly. "I don't…" After sparing Tony a final, helpless look, he ducked back into his fancy little car and sped off.

"Dad?" Claire asked, worried, when Tony and Josie reached the Volvo again. "Who was that?"

He caught the concern in Lili's eyes before he smiled at his daughter. "Somebody I went to school with," he said, swinging the baby into her car seat. "Guess he decided we should catch up with each other. Okay…" Josie strapped in, he clapped his hands. "Let's get this show on the road!"

As kids and dogs piled in, Lili looked at him over the car's roof and mouthed, "You okay?"

"Depends on what you mean by 'okay'," Tony muttered, sliding behind the wheel, taking a moment to steady his breathing. Soft, strong fingers briefly squeezed his knee, but he knew better than to look over. Knew in any case she wouldn't be looking at him, either. Instead, he yanked the shift into Reverse and backed out of his driveway.

"You know," he said quietly a few minutes later, when the kids were making such a racket they couldn't've heard fighter jets go over, "if you'd gotten here on time—"

"He would have missed you. I know."

Desperate to change the subject, Tony glanced over. "What was that sudden trip to the drugstore all about, anyway?"

"Just, um, needed some personal things," she said, giving him an embarrassed please-don't-make-me-spell-it-out look.

"Oh. Sorry," Tony muttered, wondering if a denser human being ever walked the planet.

Chapter Nine

Chasing a giggling, barefoot Josie around his room at the inn, taking things away as fast as she could grab them, Tony barely heard the soft knock. "Yeah, it's open—"

"Mine?" Josie said, clutching the faded, antique-looking doll, eyes wide.

"No, baby, it belongs to the people who live here—"

"Lili!" Still holding the doll hostage, she ran over on her chunky little legs and thrust the doll in Lili's face. "Pretty dolly!"

"Oooh, very pretty." Lili glanced at the crib set up on the other side of the spacious room, where Tony had already dumped Josie's favorite "friends." "But…" She crossed to the crib, snatching one of them out of it. "What about…?" She looked to Tony, holding up the goofy, long-legged bird.

"Harvey."

"Haavey," she said, imitating his accent so perfectly Tony

had to smile. "Harvey thinks you forgot him," she said, pulling a comically sad face, then hugging the bird to her. "He's sad, he wants his JoJo."

Josie looked skeptical for a moment, then dumped the doll on the floor and reached for her toy, roughly stroking him. "It's okay, Harvey," she said, her pronunciation the same as Tony's. "Don't be scared, I'm here." She yawned. And screwed her palm into one eye. "I won't leave you."

Tony's breath caught, before he dared to meet Lili's eyes. Eyes filled with caring so deep, so genuine, he had to look away.

"Your room okay?" he said, hauling his sleepy girl up into his arms.

"It's lovely, yes. The whole inn's beautiful. And it's so peaceful up here. Now I'm really glad I came. Where are the other girls?"

"Daph's off playing with Violet's boys, and I'm pretty sure Claire's with Stacey. And this little critter," he said, blowing a kiss into her neck, "needs to take her nap."

"No," she said, giggling, trying to wriggle free. "Don't want nap! Not s'eepy."

Tony swung her up and over the railing, gently plunking her into the crib. "Then you can have a nice, quiet rest with your friends, how's that?"

But the baby clung to the crib rail, her large, watery eyes darting around the strange room. A moment later her arms shot up, her face crumpled. "Don't wanna stay here! Wanna go wif you!"

"Okay, how about…" Tony looked over at Lili, then nodded toward the door between his room and the girls'. Her eyes following his, she nodded back. "Lili and I are gonna be right in here," he said, walking over and pushing open the door so she could see the other room. "I'll sit in that chair, okay? So you can see me?"

That got a skeptical look, followed by an even more skeptical, "P'omise?"

"Promise."

Arms shot up again. "Hug?"

Tony obliged, ignoring the pain, the fear, as the little girl whispered, "Love you," against his cheek.

"Love you, too, cupcake." Finally, a very wobbly Josie laid down on her side, Harvey safely tucked against her chest and eagle eyes pinned to where Tony said he'd be. Except even before they left, the eagle eyes were at half-mast.

"She'll be out in less than a minute," Tony whispered as he ushered Lili into the other room. Feeling like he was about to suffocate, he raised both windows, then opened the door to the hallway, letting in a welcome breeze. Then, with a weary sigh, he sank into one of the red plaid chairs. Lili lowered herself onto the edge of the nearest Colonial-spreaded twin bed, her gaze intense.

"So what happened?" she asked quietly, since obviously there'd been no opportunity to talk about his face-to-face with Cole before this. "And why are you looking at me like that?"

Because the four hours between the drive and lunch and getting settled in had given Tony lots of time to reconsider the wisdom of constantly unloading on the woman. "I don't get it. Why you care so much. It's not like you have a personal stake in any of this or anything."

Several seconds passed before she said, with some heat, "You know…if you think I'm being nosy, just say so."

"No, it's not that—"

"Then I *care* because I just do. About all of you. That *is* the stake I have in this. So deal with it."

Somehow, that didn't help. But Tony replayed the conversation, anyway, even as he realized it didn't sound any better out loud than it had the previous hundred times it had repeated itself in his brain.

"Do you think Cole would even want Josie?" Lili asked when he'd finished.

"I have no idea, to tell you the truth. But he didn't exactly lie across the driveway so we couldn't leave, either." Tony pushed himself out of the too-soft chair to pace the room, idly picking up assorted items from Daphne's exploded gym bag and setting them on the bed where she'd already set her favorite ball-gowned Barbie against the pillows. The contents of Claire's bag, on the other hand, were—he opened a bureau drawer and smiled—already neatly installed in their temporary quarters. "I'm guessing he doesn't know, himself," he said, shutting the drawer, then turning to Lili. "Although if you want my take on it, what has him scared spitless is his wife finding out."

"But he does want to know the results?"

"So he said."

"So what does this mean?"

"I don't know what it *means,* okay?" Tony said, finally giving in to the hopeless, helpless fury he'd been holding back all morning. His gaze swung to the baby, now out like a light in the other room, and his heart hurt with loving her. With the sick fear that he might lose her, that the test would say he wasn't her father and Cole Jamison would get over himself and tell his wife and they'd decide it was okay, they'd work it out, Josie could come live with them—

"It's like everybody expects me to be in charge," he said, his voice strained as he leaned one wrist against the door-frame, staring at his little girl, "to know what I'm doing. Only every damn day somebody decides to change the freaking rules." He swallowed past the golf ball in his throat. "I'll do anything to protect my babies, Lil. But it's like every day I know less and less how I'm supposed to do that."

Tony hardly reacted at first when Lili's arms wrapped around his waist from behind, her hands pressing into heart as her cheek did against his spine. Then he tensed, dreading the shushes, the crap variations on "It'll be okay, you'll see." They never came. Instead she simply held him, held tight, then tighter still, until his breathing got back to something like regular again and the vicious red haze cleared from his eyes.

Releasing a long, shaky breath, he curled the fingers of his free hand around one of hers. "I'm okay now."

He felt her head lift. "Are you sure?"

"Yeah."

But even as her arms slipped away, Tony turned, seeing again that refuge in her eyes he knew he was in no place to accept, no matter how desperately he wanted it. Saw, too, something else, something that blotted out reason but good, something that brought his hands up to her shoulders and his mouth down on hers, that sucked in her brief gasp of surprise and kept on going, like by kissing her he could somehow glean a little taste of sanity in the midst of all this chaos. Then her hands were on his back, strong hands from all the scrubbing and dough-rolling, kneading rock-hard muscles through his T-shirt as her mouth opened under his and the kiss became like a freaking runaway train, totally outta control, a rush to end all rushes, and he thought, briefly, *Definitely not little Lili anymore—*

Then reason tapped Tony on the shoulder and cleared its throat, and the train derailed. His hands still clamped on Lili's shoulders, Tony broke the kiss, seeing confusion in her eyes that must've mirrored his own.

"Sorry," he muttered, looking away.

"For…?"

He forced his gaze back to hers. "You're kidding, right?"

"It was just a kiss, Tony—"

"Just a kiss? *Just* a kiss? Jeez, honey—if that's what you consider *just* a kiss, I'm almost afraid to think what you'd call *spectacular.*" He pivoted, raking his hand through his hair. "In any case, I haven't kissed another woman since Rissa—"

His wife's name caught in his throat, like a bite of something gone down the wrong way.

"Yes, I'd rather imagined that was the case."

He turned back. Caught the insane blush he'd apparently missed the first time, a blush at total odds with the way she was standing there, all calm and collected. Strange woman.

Strange, incredible woman.

"I, uh…" He nodded toward the other room. "Need to stick around, in case JoJo wakes up. You mind keepin' an eye on the other girls until we come down?"

Her gaze unwavering, Lili shook her head. "Of course not. Maybe you can get some rest, as well. With everything going on—"

"Yeah, that's a good idea," Tony said, walking her to the door. Deliberately not touching her. Making himself crazier than he already was. "See ya later, then."

"Undoubtedly," she said with a small smile stretching slightly swollen lips, then left.

Tony shut the door behind her and walked back into his own room, sinking onto the edge of the double bed with his face in his hands, thinking, *Good goin', bonehead.*

He lifted his eyes to stare at his own tight smile in the dresser mirror in front of him. Kissing the woman had been dumb enough. Kissing her in front of an open door?

In a house full of kids?

Somebody sure as hell was looking out for his sorry ass, that's all he had to say.

Daphne crashed through the back door and out into the big backyard, breathing so hard her chest hurt. Both dogs ran at her, barking and jumping; she pushed right through them and kept going, not stopping until she reached the very back, practically throwing herself through the tire swing hanging from the biggest tree she'd ever seen. The tire smelled funny, and the way it bounced made her tummy feel kind of icky for a second, but then she dug her feet into the dirt and twisted the swing all up and let go, spinning and spinning and spinning in a cloud of dust, the dogs and the trees and George and Zeke running from the house toward her a great big blur, like maybe she could spin what she'd just seen out of her head…

"You gonna barf?" Zeke asked when she stopped, feeling like her eyes wouldn't stay still. Zeke was six, only a year younger than her, so she was better friends with him than she was with George, who was almost eleven.

She shook her head. "Uh-uh," she said, then twisted herself up again. "I make myself dizzy lots. It's fun—"

She'd just gone up to her room to get some fruit rolls out of her backpack to share with the boys. Except when she'd gotten to the door, there were Daddy and Lili—

Again, the world spun, faster and faster and faster, until the boys stopped the swing, jerking her back. George was looking at her funny, his face all serious underneath his orange hair. "You okay?"

Daphne wriggled back out of the swing, swiping at a smudge of dirt across her pink T-shirt. It didn't come off. She shrugged, tucking the secret deeper inside her, where she could turn it over and over in her mind until she decided what to do with it. How she felt about it. Right now, though, she felt kinda fizzy inside, like when they'd watch the Macy's parade on TV while the Thanksgiving turkey was cooking at Nana's, and Daphne knew that meant Christmas was *finally* coming. Which of course made her feel sad about Mom, and how weird last Thanksgiving and Christmas were without her—

"Yeah, sure," she said, pushing the sad thought away. "Hey, wanna play hide-and-seek? I'll count." She turned to the tree and covered her eyes. "One…two…three…"

Behind her, she heard the boys and the dogs all run off. Still counting, Daphne uncovered her eyes and leaned her forehead against the tree, wondering why, if she wasn't dizzy anymore, everything still seemed to be spinning.

Lifting her head, she called out, "Ready or not, here I come!"

The next morning Lili followed her nose to the sunlight-flooded kitchen, all yellows and creams and touches of red, where Violet was mixing up batter of some kind in a large ceramic bowl and dogs roamed, hopeful. While Ed stood sentry over the proceedings, Simon—best described as a living haystack—plodded over to give Lili a quick schlurp with his tongue.

"Simon! How many times have I told you, don't lick the guests?"

"It's okay," Lili said. Eyeing the coffeemaker.

Violet grinned. "Help yourself. Mugs're right in the cupboard." She measured out a half cup of sugar, dumped it into the batter. "Another early riser, huh?"

"I like the quiet," Lili said, hugging her coffee to her as she settled at the table.

"Lord, me, too."

"Anything I can to help?"

"Nah, just pullin' everything together so I'm ready to go when the rest of 'em haul their lazy butts out of bed. Figured I'd do waffles. Everybody likes waffles, right?"

She set the bowl on the back of the stove—"Damn dog loves waffle batter, go figure"—pulled down a large skillet from an overhead rack and clanged it on the stove, then poured her own coffee.

"Let's go sit outside. Enjoy the peace while it lasts."

The back porch off the kitchen faced a yard with so many trees it looked like a park, through which Lili caught a glimpse of mountains, gilded by the morning sun. A warm breeze danced through a million leaves, the sound so soothing she closed her eyes, savoring. Violet chuckled softly.

"Yeah. It's like that," she said, smiling when Lili opened her eyes again. "I'm glad you guys could get up here."

"Me, too." She took a sip of the strong, rich coffee. "Was this always your house?"

"Oh, God, no," Violet said with a cross between a laugh and a snort. "Although it's been part of my life since I was a kid."

"Sounds intriguing."

"That's one way of putting it. My mother usedta work here, as a maid, so I did, too, in the summers before I got married." Her mouth flattened. "The first time. When my first husband left me and the boys, Doris—she's the former owner—took us in, in exchange for me helpin' her after her husband died. She promised to leave the inn to me, only when she died, there wasn't a will, and her daughter sold the place." She lifted her mug. "To Rudy."

"Oh, dear," Lili said, and Violet shrugged. Then she smiled, holding her jumble of orange curls off her face.

"Only when Rudy found out? I think he felt worse than I did. So he invited the boys and me to come live here, anyway, help him out while he was fixing the place up…and then, when he was movin' furniture around in Doris's old room? Damned if he didn't find the will." She leaned back, resting her feet on one of the empty chairs. "Funny thing— if he hadn't've told me, I would've never known."

"But he did?"

"Yeah," she said on a wondering sigh, then looked at Lili, a half smile pulling at her mouth. "He did." She faced front again. "The lawyer said easiest thing would be to go in as partners. So we did. In more ways than one." She took a sip of her coffee, not looking at Lili. "So what's goin' on between you and Tony?"

Lili's own mouthful went down the wrong way. "Isn't that a little personal?" she said when she stopped coughing.

"Hmm…I'm guessing you didn't notice the beard burn before you came downstairs yesterday?" When Lili's hand flew to her cheek, Violet chuckled. "But it's okay, I don't think anybody else did, either. Except me, of course."

"There's nothing going on," Lili said quietly, intent on those the mountains. "Not of any significance, anyway."

"Got it," Violet said, only to then add, "You know what's botherin' Tony?"

Lili's eyes cut to Violet's. "Bothering him?"

"Yeah. Rudy and me, we were talkin' about it last night, after you guys all went to bed. Tony seems, I dunno. Not like he's sad or grieving, but like he's…worried or something."

"He just has his hands full," Lili said, hiding once more behind her mug, "with the girls and everything."

Although she found Violet's slight squint unnerving, it wasn't Lili's place to divulge that Tony was waiting for a phone call that could quite possibly shatter his world. Even more than it had already been.

"So what's next for you after you go back to Hungary?"

At that, a clammy feeling came over her. "I'm not sure." She smiled, although it was an effort. "Figure out what I'm supposed to be doing with my life, I suppose."

"Yeah, been there," Violet said on a sigh, then fell quiet for a moment. "You know, I read this article once somewhere where you were asked to name the last five winners of a bunch of important awards, like the Oscars and Nobel Peace Prizes, stuff like that. People at the top of their games, you know? Then you were asked to name the five people who'd meant the most to *you* during your lifetime. A lot easier to come up with that last list, huh?"

Lili smiled. "Definitely."

Violet twisted in her chair. "When I was a kid, I useta

dream about doing something important one day. Not necessarily being famous, just bein'…somebody. And here I am," she said, waving her mug at the scene in front of her, "reconciled to the fact that I'm never gonna find a cure for any disease, or solve the energy crisis, or win a gold medal. But ya know, what I do here, providing a haven for people who're maybe looking for a few stress-free days…I think that's important. Being there for my kids, for Rudy… they'll remember that. We all have our place, our purpose. It's not what you do, it's how much of *you* you put into it, right—?"

"Hey," Rudy said, filling the doorway. "I don't pay you to sit around and drink coffee all day."

Unperturbed, Violet grinned at Lili. "Isn't he cute?" she said, then faced her husband, chin cradled in hand. "Since you don't *pay* me anything, looks to me like you don't have a lot of say in the matter."

"Yeah, well, there's a buncha hungry people millin' around in your kitchen, wondering what happened to the cook."

Violet shrugged, doing an exaggerated yawn and stretch before finally hauling herself out of the chair, yelping slightly when Rudy lightly smacked her behind as she passed him.

"So hard to find good help these days," Rudy said, wagging his head as he gallantly held out one arm to usher Lili back into the kitchen, where her gaze immediately latched onto Tony, Josie in his arms, arrowing through the swarm of small Vaccaros toward the coffeemaker. Although he'd obviously just showered and shaved, the pouches underneath his eyes and creases bracketing his mouth—as well as the slight wince at Zeke's shriek of laughter when Ed jumped up to give him a kiss—spoke of a man who had not slept well.

This is not your problem to fix, Lili thought, again, turning away to smile for Daphne, already seated at the extra-large kitchen table, her face already dirty. Then she briefly caught Tony's eyes and realized what day it was, that the poor man must have felt as if his cell phone was a time bomb.

"Hey," Rudy said as the room filled with the spicy scent of sizzling sausages, "weather says it's not gonna be too hot today. So who's up for a hike later? There's some great trails around here. And it's been months since I've been able to go traipsing through the woods with my kids. Tony?"

"Sure, sounds great," he said with a fleeting smile as he strapped Josie into a high chair. "And no groaning from you guys," he said to the girls, who looked less than thrilled with the prospect. "It'll do us good, to get outside. Commune with nature."

Daphne shrugged, but Claire looked as if she'd been consigned to clean latrines for the next six months. Then Stacey, Rudy's teenage daughter, said she wasn't feeling well and would he mind if she begged off, which of course gave Claire the excuse she needed not to go, and then Violet said a new cleaning lady was coming so *she* couldn't go and besides somebody needed to stay with Josie, right?

Rudy crossed his huge arms over his chest. "Does *anybody* wanna go with me?" he said, sounding so bereft Lili laughed.

"You've still got the boys, and Daph. And Tony and me." Simon woofed behind Ed, who spun around in place three times before joining in. Ed, Lili had already learned, was always up for an adventure. "And the dogs."

"Forget it," Violet said, carting a plate stacked with waffles to the table. "Last time this *thing*," she said, nudging Simon out of the way with her knee, "went on a walk with you, it took me a week to get all the burrs off him. Only way he goes is if you shave 'im or make 'im wear a wet suit."

"Party pooper," Rudy said amidst a chorus of giggles from the table as the kids watched the exchange. Especially when Simon dropped to a lying position to watch Violet's comings and goings, his expression baleful through drooping, spiky eyebrows.

What a simple, rich life Rudy and Violet had made for themselves and their kids, Lili thought, her gaze drifting to Tony, patiently feeding a two-year-old. Why wouldn't that be enough?

"Actually," Claire suddenly piped up, "maybe I will go."

Tony glanced at his daughter, relief evident in his smile. "Glad you decided to grace us with your presence," he said, his gentle teasing filled with nothing but love for his prickly, moody child.

Then Claire's gaze swung to Lili, once more laced with so much wariness she felt the ridiculous sting of tears, as if she were a child herself. She'd thought they'd moved past that—

Oh, dear God—had Claire seen them kiss?

Except they'd all spent the rest of the day together yesterday. Surely the child would have said something if she'd seen them? She certainly didn't seem to have any qualms about speaking up otherwise. So, no, Lili decided, relaxing slightly. Whatever that look had been about, she sincerely doubted the kiss was the culprit.

Then she reminded herself…what did it matter, anyway, whether Claire liked her or not? Wanted her company or not? Trusted her or not? Perhaps, in another world—a world where little girls who'd just lost a parent didn't resent anyone attempting to take that parent's place—she might have reason to indulge a few fairy-tale fantasies, of being what this broken family needed. What Tony needed.

But Lili knew better than anyone that a child's unconditional love wasn't interchangeable. From everything she could gather, Marissa had been a good mother, the kind of mother whose death leaves a gaping hole in her children's hearts.

The kind of woman, she thought, stealing another glance

at Tony, whose betrayal leaves another kind of hole, even deeper and wider. A hole only a fool would attempt to fill.

Whatever her purpose was, being with Tony and his daughters wasn't it.

Hardly a revelation, of course. But for some reason the message seemed to register this time. Oddly, though, instead of making her sad, Lili felt suddenly free. Free to simply enjoy the moment, free to offer whatever comfort and support she could to Tony without endangering her own peace of mind.

Free to love him without all those pesky expectations and hopes and worries about reciprocation.

She dug into her waffles and sausages with more enthusiasm than she'd felt for anything in weeks.

If Tony'd thought a hike was somehow gonna take his mind off the dreaded phone call—not to mention unrelenting replays of that anything-but-*just*-a-kiss—he'd been wrong on both counts. Although on some level, he could at least appreciate how pretty it was up here, the blue skies and the yakkety-yakking brook and the blinding sunlight—

Okay, so maybe he wasn't exactly in the right mood for this.

At least the girls, far enough ahead with the others that the forest would occasionally swallow them up, seemed to be having a good enough time. Daph was, anyway. As usual. Because Daph was made of rubber—everything bounced off her or she, it. Like him, though, Claire was there in body but not at all in spirit, tramping dutifully along behind the boys, looking like she'd rather have a cavity filled.

"I cannot tell you how much I empathize with her," Lili said a couple of feet away, making Tony start. There was something different about her this morning, but damned if he could put a finger on it. Not that she was moody or anything. But then that was the thing about Lil, she never seemed to get pissy for no good reason. Of course, the real test was tol-eratin' each other for the long haul—

"In what way?" he said, removing his head from his butt.

"Feeling a bit like an alien life form, desperately wanting to be part of the human race."

"You should say that to her."

"I did, as it happens. The other day, when we were making the dumplings." She smiled. "When she giggled." Then the smile faded. "Now she's back to looking at me as though I have fleas."

"You do realize she looks at everyone like that?"

"I suppose I did, too, at that age. And well beyond."

"You? A pain in the butt?"

"Hard to believe, I know." Her eyes flicked to his, then scampered away. "For a while I thought perhaps she, um, saw us." Her cheeks reddened. "Yesterday. In their room."

"I sincerely doubt it," Tony said, his own face prickling as well. "Claire's not exactly one for keepin' secrets—"

"Hey, guys," Rudy yelled back. "There's a falls up ahead, if you'd like to stop and rest for a minute. The kids can go wading!"

"Just make sure Daph takes her shoes off first," Tony called back, even as he realized something was building in his brain, something about to come crashing out of his mouth, and he had like exactly one second to stomp on it or—

"You know that jerk you were gonna marry?"

Lili stumbled over a tree root, righting herself before Tony could grab for her. "I used to know him quite well," she said, deadpan. "What about him?"

"If it'd been me? I would have lived with *Godzilla's* mother if it meant getting to kiss you on a regular basis."

She stood, frozen, for several seconds before starting forward again. "It wasn't *that* good," she mumbled.

"Uh, yeah, it was. I can't imagine what—"

Okay, he could stop right there. Had damn sight *better* stop right there.

"You can't imagine…?"

"Never mind."

He heard a huff. "And one of the few things that *really* annoys me is people who don't finish their sentences."

"Fine," he said, turning. "I can't imagine, if you kiss like that? What you must be like in bed. And don't look at me like that, you asked."

She blinked at him for several seconds, then started walking again. "I think this is one of those places we're not supposed to go?"

"Hey. I'm a guy. We're always at that particular place. And anyway, I tried to stop. You wouldn't let me."

Silence dropped between them like a giant army boot. They hiked another fifty feet or so in that throbbing quiet—except for the deafening chatter of roughly five bazillion birds—until they reached the falls. The boys and Daphne were already in the water at the base of the falls while Claire hung back, too cool for school. Although even Claire looked impressed by the scene. As well she should.

Tony tilted back the brim of his ball cap, trying to take it all in. Grumpy as he was, he still had to admit it was like something right out of a freaking travel brochure. They weren't talking Niagara or anything, maybe a twenty-foot drop, but between the trees soaring all around them, the gurgling stream tumbling over and around glistening black rocks, the water sparkling from the spears of sunlight cutting right through all those trees…it was something else.

"Wow," Tony said at the same time Lili said, so softly he almost didn't catch it, "I have no idea what I'd be like in bed. I'm a virgin."

Chapter Ten

And you told him this, why?

Staring at the roaring waterfall, Lili felt Tony's gaze bore through her. Certainly, it wasn't any of his business. Nor did her sexual experience have the slightest bearing on their relationship. And yet, his comment had provoked something inside her, shoving the words out of her mouth.

"That's a joke, right?"

Her brow knotted, she looked at him, only to nearly laugh at his incredulous expression. "Not at all."

"But…you said you were engaged…?"

"Peter was very old-fashioned. And I was still quite young."

"Excuse me, but Peter must've been *dead*. And that was how many years ago?"

Facing the falls again, Lili shoved her hands her shorts pockets. "You know, when I told you about taking care of my mother, I said it was my own choice? Well, this falls into the same category. Until Peter, I'd never met anyone I cared to take my clothes off for. When he didn't seem particularly interested whether I did or not…"

"You were scarred for life, what?"

She softly laughed. "Of course not. But neither did I see that…misstep as an excuse to *lower* my standards, either." Looking back at Tony, she said, "It's not as if I took some vow of chastity, or had any deep-seated fears about sex, or any of that. I simply wanted to be *in* love when I *made* love."

"It can't be that simple."

"Why not? Sex for its own sake has never interested me." She paused, took a deep breath. "And until recently, I've never felt I was particularly missing out."

Lili could feel Tony's eyes on her face again, knew he was much too smart to not get her point. Granted, there'd probably be scant opportunity while they were here to use any of the condoms from that last-minute trip to the drugstore, but her buying them certainly spoke to a major shift in her thinking. And heaven knows hope had flared, however briefly, with that not-to-be-believed kiss, when she'd felt more than ample evidence of Tony's interest in taking things further. At least physically.

But then, as she'd said, she wasn't naïve. Simply because *she* didn't/couldn't/refused to separate sex from love, she was well aware the same wasn't true for the vast majority of the human population. Especially the male half. After all, an erection was only an instinct-driven response to physical stimulus—

Tony's ringtone startled her out of her thoughts. He yanked the phone off his belt as though flames were shooting from it, only to simply stare at the display, letting it ring.

"Tony?"

"It's them."

"Answer it," Lili said softly.

Finally, he lifted the phone to his ear. "Hello?…Yeah, this is him." Expressionless, he faced slightly away; Lily watched, barely breathing, her heart cracking when his head dropped forward, his eyes squeezed shut. "Yeah," he mumbled after a moment, looking up. "I'll do that. Thanks."

For several seconds, he stood still, staring blankly at his other children, Daphne laughing and splashing in the water, Claire sitting on the edge of the stream, hugging her knees as though trying to hold herself, and her life, together.

"Tony?" Lili whispered, tears stinging.

"You mind leavin' me alone for a sec?" His voice…it didn't even sound like Tony. And it killed her, watching him refuse to cower under yet another blow, helpless to do a single thing to comfort him. Not that there were any words. But at the moment she didn't dare even lay a hand on his arm without arousing suspicion.

"Of course not. Do you…I think we should probably head back home, don't you?"

At last he shifted his gaze to hers. There was nothing there. Nothing. No pain, no anger, certainly no real comprehension. But far worse than that, there was no Tony. However, even as fear rippled through her, he took a deep breath, gave her a small smile. "I'll let you know."

She left him then, to pick her way down the slippery bank to the stream's edge, where both Rudy and Claire shot her questioning glances which she didn't return. Instead she forced herself to join in the children's play, even removing her shoes and socks to wade in the freezing water. Her heart, however, stayed with the man on the other side of the stream, his eyes fixed on them…but his mind, Lili suspected, was very, very far away indeed.

Even numb with shock, Tony realized he needed to pull himself together, pronto. Not if he didn't want a buttload of unwanted questions to come crashing down on his head. So after a minute or two, like he'd already done God knew how many times over the past year—okay, longer, ever since he and Rissa started having problems—he got up off his sorry ass, plastered a smile to his face and acted like everything was okay.

Never mind that all he wanted to do was go straight back to the inn, haul Josie into his arms and hold on for dear life...followed by wanting to punch something until his knuckles were bloody.

Naturally Claire got to him first, her little pinched face and concerned eyes getting to him in other, far more painful ways. He preempted the inevitable interrogation, though, by plunking down on the damp ground beside her to remove his shoes and socks.

"You're not actually going in there?"

Thank you, Diversionary Tactic #356.

"I actually am. Everybody else is. Except you. Look, even Lili's in the water," he said, and she looked over and waved, and he suddenly remembered their conversation before The Phone Call, that she'd never had sex, a conversation that seemed blurry and faded and irrelevant, now that he knew for sure—

Tony doubled over, using the excuse to stuff his socks into his shoes as a cover for feeling like he'd just been gutted. He'd thought the *not* knowing was horrible? This was a hundred, a thousand times worse.

Steeling himself, Tony got up to carefully wade into the icy stream, the sharp sting of cold making him catch his breath, making him wish it would go right through his bloodstream to freeze his heart so he couldn't feel the pain. Lili's eyes glanced off his before just before Daphne splashed her; she gasped, then spun around to grab the giggling seven-year-old in her arms, and Tony's heart ached ever harder, at how messed up everything was.

Everything.

I can't make everybody happy, dammit! he wanted to scream, his head pounding as he thought how fathers were a lot like doctors—even if they couldn't fix things, they shouldn't make things worse, either.

Somehow, he got through the rest of the morning, and the walk back, and lunch, sticking closer to the kids than usual, until Violet gathered up all the females and took them to the outlet mall and Rudy went off somewhere with the boys, leaving Tony with Josie and the dogs.

And the looming prospect of making the worst phone call of his life.

By the time they hit up the third store, Lili could feel her poor credit card trembling deep in her purse, whimpering, "Please! No more! I'll do whatever you want, just please stop swiping me through those machines!"

Blithely ignoring the plastic's pleas, she surveyed the acres of pretties before her. Who knew a simple holiday in New Hampshire would release a latent desire to shore up the sagging U.S. economy?

Not to mention her sagging spirits. Although there'd been far too much laughter and loud music and chatter in the car on the way here for Lili to obsess about Tony's plight, it still murmured in the back of her brain, a white noise that was anything but soothing. The good news was, however, that the expedition had seemed to perk Claire up a bit, as well, even if she'd spent all the cash her father had given her on things for Josie, rather than herself. But while Lili still caught the occasional wary look, she also noticed the girl seemed to stick closer to Lili than the others.

Interesting.

Now, as Stacey led Violet straight to Juniors, Lili took Daphne's hand and gave her a stern look. "Okay, cutie—last store. It's now or never."

"But I can't decide," Miss Dimples said, clearly determined to take *her* cash—currently keeping Lili's whimpering credit card company—to the grave.

"Yeah," Claire said as, for the third time, she looked longingly at the racks of clothes. "We just went shopping with Nana, it's not like we really *need* anything."

"Oh, yeah—khaki jumpers and white polo shirts, whoo-hoo," Lili said, leading them smartly toward the Girls' section, figuring if indulgent auntie was the only role she was allowed in this little scenario, she would play it to the hilt.

"And blue sweaters," Daphne put in.

"Oh, well, then," Lili said, and Daph giggled.

"Besides," Claire said, moving toward a table of embroidered, beaded hoodies in assorted shades of blindingly bright, "I already spent all my money on the baby." Lili watched as the girl delicately traced one finger over a silky curlicue; Daph, too, grabbed one of the hoodies, holding it up to her for a second before yanking it on. Two sizes too big, it came halfway down her thighs. And looked absolutely adorable.

"This is so cool!" she said, her dark curls spilling over the hot pink fabric.

"You should totally get it, Daph," Claire said, nodding. And tucking her hand behind her back. "It's really pretty."

The smaller girl frowned at the price tag. "Do I have enough money?"

Claire checked. "Plenty," she said, the torn look in her eyes speaking volumes—that she wanted, but for whatever reason thought she couldn't, or shouldn't have. Now Lili wondered if Claire's insistence on buying toys and outfits for Josie had been a thinly veiled diversionary tactic so she wouldn't have to deal with the inevitable body issues that arose when buying clothes for herself.

Well, that's just crazy, Lili thought, marching over to the table and skimming the choices. "Which is your favorite

color, Claire? Red? Orange? Oh—how about this turquoise?" she said, yanking it off the pile and unfolding it,
the dark pink and purple embroidery and beads shimmering in the store's lights, and for a brief moment she was
twelve again, watching her mother pour herself into a
spangly, sparkly costume Lili would never wear. "What do
you think, Daph? Wouldn't this be perfect with Claire's
hair color?"

"Yeah, totally. Try it on, Claire—"

"Oh, no, I don't think so—"

"Just so I can see how it looks on you. Because I think…"
Lili scanned the pile for one large enough to fit her. Bright
yellow. With turquoise and purple embroidery. Toss in a pair
of wings and she could hide out in the rainforest. "I'm going
to get this one," she said, tugging it over her head.

Finally Claire put hers on, too. "Wow, it's…big."

"That's the style," Lili said. "Hey—now we all look like
Hollis!"

Daphne giggled and even Claire grinned, walking a few
feet away to admire her reflection in a mirror. "Except Hollis
wouldn't be caught dead in beads."

"Another reason why it's good to be a girl. Right, Daph?"

"Yeah," she said, fist-pumping—

"But I spent all my money already," Claire said.

"Oh, this is my treat. For you, too, Daphne."

"Thanks!"

"Really?" Claire said, still looking at her reflection.

"Really."

"Holy bejeebers!" Violet called across the store at them,
shielding her eyes with her hand. "Those bright enough?
They'll be able to see the three of ya in Canada!"

Lili and the girls all burst out laughing, then removed the
tops so Lili could pay for them. As they carted them to the
cashier, Daphne said, "Nana's going to *totally* hate these."

Prying the quaking credit card from her wallet, Lili glanced at Claire. Who shrugged. "She'll live."

At least this, Lili thought, handing everything to the girl behind the register as the worries she'd held off all afternoon about Tony and Josie roared back, flooding her heart.

Josie down for her nap, Tony and the dogs went out onto the empty front porch. Buoyed by the beasts' silent *Go on, man—you can do this* expressions, he dragged Cole Jamison's business card out of his wallet, punching in the number before he lost his nerve. Cole picked up on the first ring.

"Jamison here…. Hello? Is anybody th—"

"She's not mine."

Cole sucked in a breath. "They're sure?"

"They do a double test. So, yeah. They're sure."

A pause. "Still doesn't mean I'm the father."

"Excuse me?"

"Without *my* DNA, there's no way of proving the kid's mine."

Dropping onto a wicker chair by the front door, Tony rubbed his eyes, trying to make the pieces of this ridiculous puzzle fit. "Look, you idiot," he said softly, "it's not like I *wanted* the test to turn out this way. I mean, I should be happy as hell that you obviously don't want her. But if Rissa sent you a letter, too, I assume that kinda narrows it down—"

"And who's to say you and I were the only chumps to get letters?"

Tony shot to his feet, even though he couldn't punch out the guy's lights through the phone. More's the pity. "And maybe this isn't about us, it's about Josie—"

"You can't force me to get a test, Vaccaro. And since *you* obviously don't want to give her up…" He heard a sigh. "I'm just trying to make this easier for everyone. My wife, my kids…they can't find out about this."

Tony almost laughed. "Yeah, well, maybe you should've thought that through a little harder three years ago. You really are a piece of work, aren'tcha? Although not a very bright one, since you kinda outted yourself when you showed up at my house."

"I panicked, okay? I didn't know what she'd told you, didn't want you coming to *my* house—"

"Yeah, I got that. And the thing is, we *don't* know if she told anybody else." Tony blew out a sharp breath. "Which means there's a real strong possibility this is gonna come back to bite one or both of us in the butt one day. No, I can't force you to take a paternity test. And yeah, in the short term it would definitely be in my best interests if you didn't. But neither do I want this hangin' over my head for the next however many years, wondering if and when you're gonna suddenly have a change of heart—"

"That won't—"

"And if God forbid something happened to Josie and I couldn't donate bone marrow or whatever because I'm not the kid's father, you better believe at that point? I *would* hunt you down and get a piece of your hair or a chunk outta your backside, it wouldn't matter to me, and get that proof. And *then* I'd go in and get whatever it was Josie needed!"

"You're insane."

"Yeah, like that frightens me. So you think about it. In any case, you don't wanna contest the fact that my name's on her birth certificate, then you send me some sort of affidavit to that effect, giving me full and permanent custody."

"Then you have to swear not to tell her about me."

"Ever? You know I can't do that."

"Then no deal," Cole said, and hung up.

As Tony sat there, softly banging the phone against his forehead, he heard the screen door open, saw out of the corner of his eye Rudy come out onto the porch.

"Where're the boys?" Tony asked.

"In their room, playing some video game." He crossed to the railing, leaned against it. "Wanna share?" the big dude asked quietly, folding his arms over a white T-shirt probably a size smaller than it should've been.

Tony's mouth pulled tight. "How much did you hear?"

"Enough to wanna smack you upside the head for not sayin' anything." Those weird blue eyes seared right through him. "Rissa *cheated* on you?"

Leave it to Rudy to not mince words. "Yeah. I didn't find out until a few weeks ago. The day of the party, actually." He filled Rudy in on the few details he had—although he left Cole's name out if it, for the moment—then sagged back in the chair, spent.

Rudy muttered a choice word, then shook his head. "Violet swore something was off, but I figured what does she know, the two of you have only met a cuppla times. Today, though, up at the falls? Hate to tell ya, but you were doing a damn lousy job of hiding your feelings."

"Thanks."

"No problem. But let me guess—nobody else knows, either."

"No. Well, Lili. But that's…" *Another mess entirely.*

"What that is, is something else you suck at hiding your feelings about." When Tony's eyes shifted to his cousin's, the other man smirked. "And yes, it's that obvious."

Tony sighed. "She's…"

"Yeah, can't wait to hear how you're gonna finish that sentence."

"It doesn't matter how I finish that sentence—it's all the rest of it I can't finish!"

The words practically exploded in Tony's brain. Rudy's lips curved.

"Why? Because it's *too soon?* Or were you plannin' on waitin' twelve years like I did?"

"I wasn't *plannin'* on anything. I—" His lips pressed together, Tony leaned forward again. "If being with Rissa taught me anything, it's how much energy relationships take. You lose focus, you're screwed. With everything else goin' on in my life right now? Starting a relationship…not gonna happen. And why're you lookin' at me like that?"

"You honest to God think you're to blame for Rissa's havin' an affair?"

"You sound like Lili."

"Knew I liked that woman."

Tony almost smiled, then sighed again. "These things don't happen in a vacuum, Rudy—"

"And maybe your wife had issues that had nothin' to do with you." Rudy downright glowered at him. "We grew up together, Tone, I know you better than I know at least half my brothers. I watched you with the girls, watched you with Rissa…" Shaking his head, he looked away, his mouth set. "True, nobody knows what goes on inside a marriage except the two people involved. Hell, sometimes even *they* don't. But…" He faced Tony again. "Whatever reasons Marissa had for doing what she did? It wasn't you, Tone. It just wasn't."

Tony got to his feet, walking over to the top of the steps. Dark gray clouds had begun to slide in from the north; a damp breeze whipped through Tony's T-shirt, chilling his skin. "Whatever. It doesn't change anything. That I'm in no position to, to…"

"Get something goin' with Lili?"

"Yeah. Or no, in this case." He frowned at Rudy. "There's the kids, for one thing. And Rissa's parents, for another." Sighed, he looked out over the front yard. "Even if I was ready, they're not."

"Not so sure Daphne'd agree with you there," Rudy said, and Tony smiled.

"Just because she gets along with Lil doesn't mean she's ready to accept her as her mom. Claire wears all her emotions on the outside—I may not totally understand *what* she's feeling, but I always know *that* she's feeling. Daph, though…she's like me. Show must go on and all that crap."

Rudy chuckled. "Kids are bizarre, aren't they?" Then he said, "Okay, I know the timing sucks. But it just seems to me…" He crossed his arms high on his chest. "We both fell hard the first time, when we were too young to know what hit us. Sometimes that works out and sometimes that doesn't. But when things happen that early, that intensely, you don't realize for most people, it doesn't come that easy."

Grunting softly, he rubbed his bristly head. "Until suddenly you're alone again. Only, like you said , there's all this *stuff* in the way there wasn't the first time, most of which is all in here—" he tapped his temple "—all these expectations and anxieties and crap, and suddenly building a nuclear reactor seems easier than finding somebody to share your life with."

"But I'm not—"

"Shut up, I'm not done. Maybe you don't think you want or need somebody right now, or the kids can't deal, whatever. But let me tell you something—one day you're gonna wake up and realize you've done everything for everybody else and haven't done a damn thing for you, and you're gonna be pissed. *Especially* when it hits you what you let slip through your fingers—"

"And maybe you should just butt out, okay? I get what you're saying. I do. But right now, it's *not* about me. And even if…" Tony shoved out a breath. "I'm not sayin' there's not a spark. I'm not even sayin', if things were different, I wouldn't mind acting on that spark. But I gotta think about Lili, too, you know? She's just now getting back on her feet after all that time she spent with her mother, the last thing she needs is to get dragged into this craziness."

At the sound of Violet's minivan crunching down the gravel path, both men turned. A few seconds later, doors popped and slid open and females poured out, laden with bags. Naturally Tony's gaze swept over both his daughters first, but they settled on Lili, laughing about something with Violet as they brought up the rear, and she looked so…honest and real, with her don't-give-a-damn hair and kitty-wampus glasses. Then, still laughing, she looked up and their gazes caught, her smile faltering slightly, like she could read his mind.

Or maybe sort out the mess inside it. Because it was hard to look at her and feel her presence and not think about everything that Rudy'd said, not wonder if maybe she'd bring a little bit of normalcy to the craziness, maybe…

"Maybe," Rudy said quietly beside him, before the rest were close enough to hear, "you should give the woman the chance to make her own decisions." When Troy glared at him, he lifted his hands, smiling. "Just sayin'." Then he grinned for his daughter, stomping up the steps wearing a printed top with the designer name taking up most of the front.

"Huh. That's new."

"See?" she said, turning to Violet. "Told you he'd notice. Like it?" she said, twirling. "It's Tommy Hilfiger."

"I *can* read, Stace," he said, and she stuck her tongue out at him, just as Lili and the girls reached the top of the steps and Tony noticed they were wearing nearly identical, enormous hoodies in different retina-searing colors. With beads. And stuff. Lili in beads? *Claire* in beads? Noticing his gawking, Claire looked down, then back up, blushing.

"Lili bought 'em for us—"

"No, no…it's okay…" Smiling, Tony hugged her to him. "It's just I've never seen you in anything like that before. It looks good on you."

Lili grinned, looked pleased as all hell. "Doesn't it? The color's so pretty with her hair—"

"Mom said we could do cookout tonight," Stacey said to her father.

Rudy squinted up at the nasty sky; a late day storm was quickly bearing down on them. "Not sure about that. But I suppose I could make a fire in the gathering room, we could do hot dogs and roast marshmallows and—" The rest of his sentence was lost in the roar of approval from Daph and the boys. "Then everybody inside," Rudy said, waving them all through the door. He looked back at Tony. "You coming?"

"In a sec," he said, walking back over to the porch steps. A second later he heard rustling bags as Lili settled one hip on the railing.

"Stupid question, I know," she said, "but how are you doing?"

His chest actually ached when he hauled in a lungful of rain-and-pine scented air. "You know, it would help if you weren't so damned nice all the time."

Chuckling, she looked out as the first fat drops began to pounce on the rhododendrons lining the base of the porch. "I could say the same thing," she said quietly. "It would definitely make things easier."

"Dammit, Lil...I didn't expect...I can't..."

"You don't have to explain. In fact, I'd rather you didn't. We both know all the reasons why this can't work. But sometimes, knowing someone cares..." She turned, smiling slightly. "It's lovely, Tony. Truly." She set down the bags to prop her back against a support post, crossing her arms. "But you didn't answer my question."

Tony let his eyes caress hers. "After what you just said? How do you think I'm doing?"

"Sorry. But I wasn't talking about...that. I meant the other."

"Right." Pressing his fingers into the back of his neck, he said. "I called Cole."

Lili's brows shot up. "Already?"

"Yeah. I guess he's been thinking about it and…" He lowered his voice, even though the rain was now pounding the porch roof so hard it was highly unlikely anyone could hear them in the house. "He doesn't want her."

Her head tilted. "Why aren't we sounding happier about that?"

"Because it's not that simple. *Nothing's* that simple," he said on a sigh. "I asked him to put it in writing. He wants me to swear I'll never tell her."

"You can't…" Lili glanced over her shoulder, then whispered, "You can't keep a secret like that forever!"

"Exactly what I said. Bastard hung up on me. So everything's still up in the air." He leaned on his forearms, out far enough to feel a slight spray on his face. "I can just see it now, him showing up out of the blue however many years from now, contrite as all hell and deciding he wants to play dad."

"Surely the law would be on your side, though? If you've been raising her…?"

"You would think. And God knows he'd have a fight on his hands. But that's part of everything I have to sort out." A flash of lightning, then a thunderclap, ripped open the sky. Tony watched the poor rhododendrons cowering in the onslaught, then said, "When are you leaving, exactly?"

He glanced over, saw she wasn't looking at him. "A week from today."

"That soon? Wow."

A smile slid in his direction. "I know, it surprised me, too, when I realized it this morning."

"It'll…be good to get home, right?"

She stretched out one arm, letting the water bounce off her palm. "I suppose," she said, pulling her hand back in and rubbing it on her jeans. "If nothing else, it's time to get serious about sorting out my mother's apartment—" Cutting herself off, she frowned at him. "Do you know I've never lived entirely on my own before?"

"Seriously?"

"Seriously."

"Lookin' forward to that?"

Lili faced front again. "I don't know, to tell you the truth. I always thought I'd like the quiet. The autonomy. Now I'm not so sure. Not that I'm afraid to be by myself, not like my mother was. I just…" Shaking her head, she let the sentence drift off.

Tony cleared his throat. "I—we—should come visit sometime," he said, but she shook her head a second time.

"People always say they'll come visit, but they almost never do." Her eyes swung to his. "I know you're going through hell right now. But you will get through it. You, and the girls. And then you'll go on with your lives and this summer will become another memory." She smiled. "As will I."

His chest seized up. "You sayin' you're never comin' back?"

"Oh, I wouldn't rule it out. But probably not for a long time." She paused. "For obvious reasons."

"I'm sorry, Lil," Tony breathed out.

"For what? For something you can't control? For not being in a position to be what I'd need you to be?"

"Yeah, actually," he said, more pissed about it than he'd expected. "Because you were wrong, the other day, when you said I look at you and just see an older version of the kid I played five million video games with that summer. Believe me, that's not who I'm seeing, Lil. Not who I—"

He jerked away, the rest of the sentence caught in his throat. Thank God she didn't press him to finish it. Instead, she sighed.

"There was a time I used to envy some of my girlfriends, the ones who could fall in love without thinking it to death. It all seemed so easy for them. Until I realized how rarely those relationships stuck." She smiled. "Even a wildflower has to have deep roots to survive. And these gals…so often they looked to the other person to complete them, or they confused love with admiration or infatuation or lust or…" Another sigh. "Or sympathy."

"You feel sorry for me?"

"No," Lili said on a half laugh. "But I am angry for you, which I'm not sure is much better. Angry for the mess you're in, especially angry for what your wife did to you…" She sighed. "I suppose I'm too pragmatic for love to be simple." A pause, then: "And I want to be absolutely sure I'm not confusing it with something else."

"Yeah," Tony said on a breath. "I know what you mean." He rubbed his jaw, then said, "So what now?"

"Now? We go back to Springfield tomorrow and get on with our lives."

"And that's it?"

She smiled at him. "Seems a better alternative to constant frustration, don't you think?"

"Not really, no," he said softly, and she averted her gaze again. "The girls will be with their grandparents again on Saturday, though—"

"And you want me to come clean your bathrooms?"

"Oh, for God's sake, Lili! No, I don't want you to come clean, I want to take you out to dinner! To a real restaurant with tablecloths and candles and everything." Yeah, he had no idea that was coming, either. But as soon as he said it, it made total sense. As much sense as anything made these days, at least. However, judging from her frown, maybe it wasn't making as much sense to her as it did to him.

"W-why?"

"Because I don't want to inflict dry hamburgers on you a second time?"

"No," she said, smiling. "I mean—"

"I know what you mean," Tony said gently, wanting to cup her jaw, to touch that soft skin, to feel her mouth open and warm and giving underneath his again. Still wanting more than he had any right to want. "I just wanna show my appreciation for everything you've done, okay? Just you and me. No kids, no grandparents, no dog. Nobody but us."

Finally, she nodded. "Okay."

"Really?"

"Honestly, Tony…yes. Really."

"You like Italian? Because there's this great little place not far from me, close to the park. We could eat, then go for a walk. Or the other way around, I don't care."

She smiled. "I don't, either. I'll leave it up to you," she said, as a just-awake Josie came barreling outside to graft herself to his legs. Claire stood in the doorway, still in her new hoodie, looking from Tony to Lili, then back.

"You didn't hear her, so I got her up."

"Thanks, honey," he said, flying Josie up into his arms.

"I had a good sleep, Daddy!" the baby said, hugging his neck, and he realized he would kill for her. For all of them. For Lili, too, although he'd keep that to himself.

"Good for you!"

"An' guess what? I went potty, too!"

"No kidding?" he said to Claire.

"No kidding," she said, and they shared a quiet moment of triumph. Every woman in the family had been giving him grief because the kid wasn't potty-trained yet—Susan, especially, had been quite vocal on the subject, insisting she could have Josie out of diapers in a week if Tony would just leave the baby with her—but forcing a kid to use the toilet hadn't been high on Tony's list. He'd figured when she was ready, she'd train. Apparently she was.

Good to know, he thought, looking from Claire to Lili, that somebody was ready for *something*.

* * *

Claire lay awake for a long time, listening to the rain pound the inn's roof and thanking God they were going home tomorrow.

Not that she hated it here or anything—the inn was actually kinda neat and the food was good and it was fun hanging out with Stacey and stuff—but she was *really* tired of feeling like something was going on but nobody would talk about it. Like when they'd been at the falls, and Dad suddenly got that phone call? Don't tell *her* something bad hadn't happened, she could feel it in her bones.

Then there'd been the really strange thing with Lili, after dinner. Since Stacey was, like, texting everybody in the entire universe, Claire'd gotten bored, so she'd gone out onto the porch. The rain had made it darker than usual, except for the light from the gathering room coming through the screen door and windows. So she didn't realize at first Lili was there, too, sitting in the glider at the end of the porch. When the glider squeaked, Claire'd nearly jumped out of her skin.

A second later Claire realized Lili'd been crying, which seemed really weird since she'd been so happy and stuff when they'd gone shopping. Claire hated when grownups cried, because if they weren't in control of things, who was? She meant to go back inside, but instead she heard herself ask Lili if she was okay. Of course Lili said she was fine, trying to make her voice sound normal. But it made Claire uncomfortable and more confused than ever, so she left. Lili came back in a couple minutes after that, but she went up to her room without saying much to anybody—

"Claire? You awake?"

Feeling like she'd gotten an electric shock, Claire rolled over, barely able to see Daphne lying in the other bed, hanging onto the ratty-haired Barbie doll Mom'd given her when she was like two or something. "Yeah, I'm awake."

"C'n I get in bed with you?"

"Sure," Claire said, holding up the covers so Daph could crawl in beside her. The rain had made it so cold, it almost felt like fall. "You have a bad dream or something?"

"Not 'xactly," Daph said, wriggling around until she got comfortable. "I just woke up and felt weird, that's all." Settled, she curled herself around the doll, facing Claire. "And Dad is *seriously* snoring, I can hear him right through the wall."

Claire might've giggled if she hadn't felt so empty inside, sorta like she was hungry except it wasn't food she wanted. She put her arm around her sister and pulled her close, tickly hair and all. "That better?"

"Uh-huh," Daph said with a huge yawn, probably already halfway back to sleep. To tell the truth, having Daph there made Claire feel better, too. She was almost tempted to go get Josie and put her between them, but for one thing the bed wasn't that big, and for another, the rule was once the baby was asleep you did not wake her up unless there was a fire or earthquake or something.

Lightening flashed, followed by a low rumble of thunder. Daph snuggled closer, then whispered, "Today was fun, huh? With Lili?"

"Yeah, I guess," Claire said, although admitting it made her feel bad. Like she was being disloyal to Mom or something. Except Mom wasn't here, for one thing, and the hoodie really was neat—

"Do you think Dad's been acting funny?"

Claire's heart started beating so hard she could hear it in her head. "Don't talk nuts."

"I'm not! Ever since that strange man showed up, it's like he's all the time worried about something."

"You're just imagining stuff." She sneezed, then swiped Daph's hair out of her face. "Go to sleep, everything's fine."

After a few seconds, her sister's breathing slowed down. But Claire's thoughts were running around in her head like that freaked gerbil they had in her second grade classroom that, like, never stopped running on its wheel. Even when it wasn't moving, you'd go to touch it and it would jump and scare you half to death. She felt like that all the time these days, like she never knew when something was gonna jump out at her—

"I think Dad likes Lili," Daphne said, making Claire jump like something *had* popped out at her.

"Jeez, Daph—I thought you were asleep. And of course he *likes* her—"

"I mean *really* like. In fact…" Daph sat up, dragging half the covers with her as she leaned over to looking at the door between Dad's and their room, like she was listening to make sure he was still asleep. Then she snuggled back down and whispered, "I saw Lili and Dad *kissing*."

Now Claire's skin get cold and sticky, like she was about to throw up. "You're lying."

"Nuh-uh, cross my heart! I came up to get something and the door was open and there they were. And it wasn't a little kiss, either, it was like how he used to kiss Mom."

"That's disgusting, Daphne! Take it back!"

"You can't take something back if it's true!" Daph said, bouncing up a second time and messing up the covers all over again. "I only told you because I thought you'd want to know. Now I'm sorry I did."

With that, she stumbled out of the bed and back to her own, where she yanked her own covers over her shoulders, facing away from Claire. Who was totally confused. If that was true, why had Lili been crying? Of course, maybe she was crying because of something else, maybe…

Claire squeezed shut her eyes, wishing the thoughts just *stop*, already. Then she pushed herself up onto her elbow and whispered, "I'm sorry I got mad. You just surprised me, is all."

After a moment, Daphne flopped back around. "What if Dad asks Lili to marry him, an' she ends up being our new mom—"

"Don't be a bonehead, Daph—Dad would never do that."

She could sorta see her sister's frown in the strange gray light coming through the window. "Why not?"

"Jeez, Daph—she *just* died!"

"She didn't *just* die, that was like before Thanksgiving. And it's not like she's ever c-coming back, is it?" Claire saw her wipe her eyes with the edge of the sheet. "Aren't you tired of feeling sad all the time?"

Claire laid her cheek on her hand. Tired of it? Sometimes she felt like it was going to crush her, it was so heavy. "Sure. But I don't know how to stop it."

"Me neither."

"Really? You don't act like you're sad very much."

"I'm just good at keeping it inside me. Because I hate the way Dad looks when I cry and stuff. But wouldn't it would be nice to feel *really* happy, instead of just pretending?"

Yeah, it sure would. "C'mere," Claire said, moving over so Daph could get in bed with her again. Then she stretched out behind her, whispering, "It's gonna be okay, I promise," over and over until she knew Daph was really asleep, this time.

But Claire stayed awake for a long time after that, now thinking mostly about Lili crying, and how wrong that felt, and Dad kissing her—and how *really* wrong *that* felt—but how, just for a little while, when they'd been shopping, Claire had felt almost okay again. Normal. Not exactly happy, but close enough to remember what it felt like.

And she hated feeling so mixed up, one second just wanting Lili to go away, to go back to Hungary, the next minute not wanting her to leave at all. *I don't want to like you!* she thought, brushing away first one tear, then another, running down her cheeks and tickling her nose as she realized how mad she was at Mom, for dying, for leaving her, for making Dad so sad all the time.

Pulling Daph closer, Claire squeezed shut her eyes, holding in the pain, wondering if she'd ever, ever feel like she used to, before Mom got sick.

Before everything had gotten so stupid and messed up and awful.

Chapter Eleven

By the time they got back to Springfield, of course, Lili had gotten over her little pity fest. The funny thing was, she hadn't even known why she was crying when Claire surprised her out on the porch. Not really. Because she *was* practical. She did know—and accept—that she and Tony weren't meant to be, that her feelings for him were, at the very least, muddied with all sorts of emotions that had nothing to do with love.

Not that she didn't love him. That much she'd admitted to herself long before she'd bought those condoms, still buried underneath a half ton of detritus at the bottom of her bag. But life—and love—wasn't like the romantic comedy films her mother had adored, where little kept the couple apart aside from a few misunderstandings. Clear those up and ta-da! Hearts and flowers. In real life, however, issues happened. Sometimes people were simply on different paths, or the timing sucked, or whatever.

Sometimes—

"Tony's here," Uncle Benny yelled up the stairs.

"I'll be right down!"

Sometimes, she thought as she spritzed on the only one of her aunt's perfumes she actually liked, it really was about seizing the day. Or, in this case—she slipped on her ballerina flats, then reached underneath the loose, gauzy top she'd bought in New Hampshire to readjust her first ever truly sexy bra—seizing the moment.

Although honestly—she felt more like a schoolgirl going out on her first date than a nearly thirty-year-old woman hoping to get lucky.

When she reached the bottom of the stairs, Tony turned from talking to their uncle, his eyebrows lifting, only to immediate crash over his nose.

"What's different?"

Me, Lili thought, then smiled. "Highlights," she said, tossing her hair. "Magda dragged me to her hairdresser yesterday. Said I needed a new look to go with my new life. And no, I'm not going to ask if you like it, because *I* like it so what anybody else thinks is immaterial."

The two men exchanged a look, Uncle Benny shrugging and muttering, "Women, whatchagonna do?" before giving Lili a fond grin. "This one's somethin' else, you know that? Gonna miss her like hell when she goes back."

"Aw…I'm going to miss you, too, Uncle Benny," Lili said, giving him a peck on his whiskery cheek, before Tony opened the door and ushered her outside, his hand on the small of her back sending many, many tingles throughout her entire being.

"So," he said, "walk first? Or eat?"

"Walk, I think," she said. "It's such a lovely evening."

"Yeah. Not too hot."

"No. And a good breeze."

"God," Tony said, laughing softly. "We're talkin' about the weather, for cryin' out loud. Is that pathetic or what? Tell you what—" He took her hand. More tingles. "How about we not talk at all?"

"About anything?" Lili asked, hiking her bag up onto her shoulder.

"Nope, nothing. More than that, how about we pretend, just for the next cuppla hours, like there's nothing else except us, bein' together—" he lifted their linked hands, pointing toward a dense thicket of trees a few blocks down "—going for a walk in the park?"

Lili smiled. "Can you really do that?"

"I sure as hell am gonna try."

So, wordlessly, they walked hand in hand until they reached the expansive park, as lush as anything Lili'd seen in Europe. In the viscous light, thick with humidity and small swarms of gnats, they passed the usual contingent of runners, people walking dogs, parents with kids, until their meanderings eventually took them to the edge of a large, glittering lake, teeming with geese and ducks. Within seconds the water rippled like liquid gold as dozens of the creatures glided toward them begging for a handout, honking like Parisian taxis on the Champs Elysees.

Lili laughed and Tony slipped his arm around her waist, and she leaned into him, savoring his scent, the scene, the bittersweet moment. Then his other arm wrapped around her as well, holding her close, and Lili shut her eyes, loving him, and as if he heard her he gently kissed her temple, making tears crowd her eyes. For a long time they simply stood in each other's arms, afraid to move, to breathe, to break the spell, until a sudden, insistent breeze whipped through the trees, snatching at their hair and clothes. Holding her hair, Lili looked around, noticing that all the leaves had flipped over, baring their gray-green undersides.

Tony looked up. "Holy crap—where'd that come from?" he muttered at the huge, menacing black cloud overhead.

"Come on," he said, grabbing her hand, "my house is closer than Magda's. If we haul ass we just might make it before we get dumped on."

Although Lili was wearing flats, her shorter legs were no match for Tony's as, the thunder taunting them, they sprinted out of the park and through the neighborhood, dodging the first big, fat raindrops. A few blocks from Tony's house the sky burst, instantly drenching them. Blinded, soaked, Lili shrieked with laughter when Tony dragged her through the deluge down the alley behind his house, the garden little more than a battered, soggy blur as they ran across.

Once inside, Tony slammed shut his back door, the rain pummeling against it like thwarted demons. Slicking rain from his eyes with both hands, he shook his head and panted out, "Okay…so maybe…that didn't turn out exactly…the way I saw it in my head."

So wet she was unable to move, Lili started laughing all over again when the dog plodded in, took one look at them and quickly backed out of the room.

"I'll get towels," Tony said, his eyes bouncing up from Lili's chest before he ducked out of the room faster than the dog. Frowning, Lili looked down.

Oh, she thought, blushing so hard her roots hurt.

Stripped to the waist, Tony returned a minute later with the towels to find Lili standing at the sink with her back to him, wringing out the front of that flimsy little top, exposing a whole lot of glistening skin in the process. Tony flexed his hands, mesmerized by a single water drop dangling from the end of a delicate rope of hair that'd worked loose from the helter-skelter knot on top of her head. He watched, barely breathing, as the sparkling drop quivered, then jumped, mating with her neck.

And trickled crookedly down.

At his sucked in breath, Lili jerked around, the mangled shirt hem clutched in her hands. The wet fabric clung to her breasts, her dark nipples clearly visible through her wet bra. Flesh-colored lace, from what he could tell. Not what he would have expected.

But then, nothing about this evening so far had gone according to plan, so…

The aching silence pounded inside his head, elsewhere, as they stood barely five feet apart, the rain battering the windows. Lili swallowed, still fisting the top's hem. Then, clumsily, fiercely, she peeled it over her head and let it drop to the tile floor. Her nipples strained against the bra's flimsy lace, rising and falling with her every breath.

"Lil, you don't—"

"I know," she said, smiling slightly, blushing furiously, as she unhooked the front of the bra with shaking fingers and let it drop, too.

Tony let out a long, pained sigh. "Oh, man…" Then he forced his eyes up to hers, wide and determined and bright with nervousness, and let out another, even more pained sigh. "You sure about this?"

Still trembling, Lili fumbled behind her to brace herself against the edge of the counter. "Okay…I got this far but…could you take over now, please?"

"Lil, sweetheart…I don't have—"

"I do," she whispered, flushing even more. "In my bag." She nodded off to the side. "An assortment. Different sizes, different…kinds. I didn't know what…" She cleared her throat, tried to smile. "What you liked."

What he liked was *nothing,* Marissa had always been on the Pill or used a diaphragm. So it looked like this would be a night of firsts for both of them.

"We never got dinner," he said, inanely, and she let out a short laugh.

"Dinner, I can have when I go back home," she said, her eyes locked in his. "You, I can't."

Slowly, so slowly, Tony approached her, until he was close enough to skim an unsteady finger along her jaw, to capture that strand of wet hair, to gently touch his lips to hers, tasting her trembling, her anticipation.

Tasting his own.

Then he gathered her close, the feel of her nipples against his damp, chilled skin like tiny, hot kisses…the feel of her in his arms making his heart pound. He tucked her head underneath his chin, rocking her slightly. "Why?" he whispered into her wet hair.

She lifted her eyes to his. "Does it matter?"

"Yeah. It does."

Several seconds passed before she said, "I've never regretted any of the choices I've made along the way. But I know if I leave here without finding out what…" Lowering her eyes to his chest, she skimmed her hands down his arms before catching his gaze in hers again. "What it would be like to make love with you, I'll regret *that* for the rest of my life."

Tony paused. "You mean, love as in a figure of speech? Or love as in—"

"What I feel now started a long time ago," she said softly. "Even if I'd convinced myself the seed had died before it fully took root…" She shrugged. "Apparently, it hadn't."

Slowly, Tony lifted his hand, the mix of frustration and need and tenderness practically burning him up inside as he trailed one finger down the cool, still damp skin on her neck, barely…touching, barely moving, watching her breath catch as she once more clutched the counter edge behind her. Without her glasses, her gaze was luminous, curious, a mind-blowing blend of innocence and trust and arousal. Gritting his teeth, ignoring the sweet ache in his groin, he let his finger continue its journey, skimming first one shoulder, then the other…then across her collar bone, dipping his knuckle between her breasts…then across the top of one breast…around the outside…and underneath, gently lifting the soft, warm flesh before gently, so gently, grazing her nipple with his thumb. A funny little sound burbling in her throat, Lili caught herself as her knees buckled. Tony smiled.

"Responsive little thing, aren't you?"

"This is not a s-surprise," she said, biting her lower lip when he gently plucked at the nipple.

Lifting his hands to bracket her jaw, Tony skimmed his thumbs across her cheeks. "Thought you were inexperienced," he whispered, brushing his lips over hers.

"Inexperienced," she said into his mouth. "Not clueless. I know what—" her tongue touched his "—everything does. How it w-works." She reached up to yank the clip out of her hair; it fell over his hands, heavy and wet and smelling of something that turned him on so much he saw stars. "I know my own body, even if no one else does."

Tony realized he didn't have a single thought in his head that wasn't gonna sound stupid the instant it came out of his mouth. And this woman didn't deserve stupid. When he stayed quiet, though, Lili dipped her head to look up at him, the honesty in her eyes nearly doing him in. "Are you worried about breaking my heart?"

"Actually…" On a deep breath, he smoothed his hands down her shoulders. "I'm more worried about you breaking mine. Because I know…" He touched his forehead to hers. "You want honesty? It was gonna be hard enough, letting you go. Letting you go after we have sex…that might kill me. There was nobody before Marissa, okay?" he said to her frown. "Obviously there's been nobody after her. You do the math."

At that, Lili tried to back away. Except pinned against the counter there was nowhere she could go. "Then maybe we shouldn't—"

"Yeah, we should," he said, and she met him halfway in a frantic, openmouthed kiss that nearly blew his skull off, more than making up in enthusiasm what she might have lacked in expertise, her earlier nervousness vanishing like snowflakes on a heated sidewalk.

On autopilot now, Tony hauled Lili up onto the counter, pushing himself between her open legs, which she wrapped obligingly around his hips to pull him in tighter, her breasts pressed against his chest for barely a second before she pushed him away, but only far enough to undo his belt, and he thought, *They sure don't make virgins like they used to.* He palmed one breast, soft and heavy and warm, and angels sang as he seized her mouth in another wild and crazy kiss that went on for a nice little while until she shifted, practically shoving her breast into his mouth—like he needed encouragement—clutching his hair as he tongued and swirled and sucked, harder and harder and harder until she groaned, then gasped, then sighed, a small, sweet sound that broke his heart, that she'd waited so long…waited for him…

Don't be stupid, Tony thought, grazing the taut nipple with his teeth, and she yanked up his head and said, "Take me to bed," and he grinned—a little crookedly, probably—and said, "What, you don't want your first time to be in the kitchen?" and she said, "Not especially, no, although we could put it on the list for later," and Tony moaned, lunged for her bag with its cornucopia of condoms, then wrapped her around him and lifted her off the counter to stagger toward the stairs.

Lili laughed, an unexpectedly throaty sound that seriously threatened his control. "If I put your back out, I'd rather it not be before the fun part of things. I can walk, thank you."

"Not sure I can," Tony muttered, even as he grabbed her hand and hustled up the stairs and into his room, not bothering to shut the door before they crashed onto the bed, kissing like a pair of teenagers and ripping off what was left of each other's clothes. However, through the haze and despite an erection that was soon going to need its own zip code, he realized he couldn't just go for it, that you don't send a rookie out into the big game without at least *some* training.

"What's wrong?" Lili asked when he sat back on his knees, streaking one hand through his hair. "And why aren't you wearing a condom yet?"

"Because you're not ready."

She frowned. "And how would you know this? You haven't even touched me, um, down there." When he frowned, she blew out a sigh. "I told you, I do know how everything works. It's not as if I've never done *anything*. Just not…everything."

Tony cleared his throat. He'd always thought he was pretty easy-going, when it came to talking about sex. So much for that. "So you've, um…"

A blush swept over her collarbone and up her neck. "It's called—"

"I *know* what it's called, for God's sake. What I mean is…" He pushed out a breath. Honestly. "Were batteries involved?"

Her brow puckered for a moment until the light dawned. Then she burst out laughing, looking so damned adorable and sexy and trusting with her hair a mess around her head and her skin all pink and her lips swollen— "No."

"Okay, then." Tony stretched out beside her. "Knees up, honey."

"What are you—? Oh," she said when, smiling, he kissed her, then slipped two fingers inside her. And yes, she was *very* ready. A little stroke there, some pressing there, now for a little stretching…

Lili arched, eyes shut, sucking in a breath, letting it out on a soft, beautiful, "Oooohhhh…."

"You good?" Tony asked, which got a tiny, squeaked, "Mmm-hmm."

He smiled, pulling back, dipping deeper, going where no man—or, apparently, anything else—had gone before. "Let go, Lil," he murmured between kisses. "Let it happen."

"But…but….but—" Oh, man, was she close. "But I want—"

"And you'll get," he murmured, speeding up, shifting to flick his tongue over one tight little nipple. "And it'll be so much better with a little warm-up, trust me…" He tugged and teased and tugged some more, listening for his cues, speeding up and slowing down and speeding up again until—

Yeah, like that.

Then he scooped her close, kissing, gentling, until the tremors subsided. After a moment, Lili looped an arm around him.

"Holy mackerel."

"Somebody's definitely been watching too much American TV. From the freaking *'fifties*. Hey—where ya goin'?"

"Nowhere," she said, sitting up cross-legged with her back to him. As Tony trickled his fingers down her spine, she sighed. "It really is different. As a social activity, I mean." Then she twisted to meet his gaze. "And that was just a *warm-up?*"

Tony grinned. "So it was good?"

"Okay, forget I said that," Lili said, laughing, pretending to escape, laughing even harder when Tony yanked her back down on top of him, threading his hands through her hair and kissing her six ways to Sunday. Then she laid her head on his chest, sighing, and the emotions swamping him…oh, man. And it had nothing to do with her being a virgin or any of that crap. It was just…her. Lili. Lili and him together.

Tony sucked in a deep breath, shutting his eyes. What he'd said before? About how hard it was going to be to give her up?

Yeah. In spades.

He shifted her off him, only to gather her close her again. Pushing her hair out of her eyes, she looked around. "Nice room."

"Marissa did it all herself—" On a groan, Tony shoved his face into the pillow, then gave her *sheepish*. "That was really bad form. Sorry."

That got a tiny smile. And a quick kiss. "I know you shared the room with your wife, Tony. She had very nice taste. We can move on now."

Tony nodded, then said, "So…I gotta ask—this dude you were engaged to? You and he never even fooled around?"

Lili shrugged. "A little, of course. But he—we—never let things get out of hand."

One side of Tony's mouth tucked up. Judging from what he'd just witnessed, how the hell she'd been able to rein herself in this long, he had no idea. "And I still say the man was an idiot."

Lili's fist had been knotted on his breastbone; now her fingers unfurled to toy with the thatch of hair there. "No, I think Peter and I simply weren't right for each other, even though it looked good on paper. He married someone else, a few years ago. I ran into them last year." Propping her chin on her hand, she smiled. "She seemed normal enough. And from everything I could tell, they're quite happy."

"But…?"

"No 'buts.' Not about that, anyway. However, seeing them only confirmed what I'd already realized, that what I thought we had wasn't enough. Wouldn't have been enough, in the long run. I want to be with someone who…" Her lips curved. "Who *can't* say no if I'm saying yes. I want someone who *needs* me. Desperately. Madly." Her gaze speared his. "I want something *real*."

Tony stilled. "Is this real?"

"Yes," she said simply. "For this moment, it's very, very

real." She hesitated, then reached for a condom, handing it to him.

"Now?" he whispered, taking it from her.

"Now is all we have," she said, lifting her knees.

In the velvety, early evening light, as the rain thrummed overhead and a warm, honeysuckle-scented breeze swirled around them, Lili felt deliciously bombarded. By her emotions, her senses, more acute than she ever remembered before…by a razor-sharp awareness of every atom of her being as Tony guided himself inside her with excruciating care, until, suddenly, there he was, filling her, loving her, and she sighed, thinking nothing had ever felt this good.

Until, that is, he eased out, then pushed back in, and the sweet joy of it brought tears to her eyes.

"You okay?" he whispered, and she laughed and said, "You have no idea, how okay I am," and he brought her legs up to wrap around him and joined them more tightly, deeply, closely still, and something fierce and hungry rose up inside her, making her feel lightheaded, reckless, apart from herself as she tasted his saltiness, then let her head drop back, sucking in a breath when Tony tongued first one hyper-sensitive nipple, then the other, the ache building and building until she thought she'd burst with it.

Then she did, so hard she half wondered if she might die, not much caring if she did or not…until she heard Tony's breathing quicken, and somehow she both relaxed and tensed at the same time, welcoming, absorbing his release.

Afterward, his smile flashed in the near dark, half cocky, half tender, before he softly kissed her forehead, her cheeks, her mouth. "Don't move," he said, carefully withdrawing, and she murmured, "Not a problem." Seconds later they were again a tangle of combined scents and off-sync heartbeats and warm, damp limbs, wrapped in silence and their own thoughts until Tony whispered, "What's goin' through your head?"

Lili laughed softly, even though reality was beginning to creep back in like the moonlight over the windowsill as the clouds, now spent, dispersed. "About how I just lucked out, I suppose." She snuggled closer, kissed his chest. "We could have been terrible together."

"Somehow, I doubt it."

"Not that your ego's overblown or anything."

He chuckled, the sound all rumbly in her ear, then pressed a kiss into her hair. "Sex is a funny thing," he said over the *plonk, plonk* of water dripping from the eaves. "Despite all that crap you read about in magazines or whatever, technique doesn't have nearly as much to do with whether it's good or not as…the other stuff."

"You mean…feelings?"

"Yeah." He paused. "If it's more about being together, bein' close? Then you can have good sex even if it's lousy, if you know what I mean. But if you're just doin' it to do it, then you can hit all the right buttons and still get that 'Is that it?' feeling when you're done. Of course, in an ideal world you can have both, and then it's freakin' fantastic."

Lili paused, then said, "And…?"

"I think that's called fishing, sweetheart," he said on another soft laugh. "But yeah. That was pretty damned good." Another pause preceded, "I could listen to you cry out like that all night."

Toying with his chest hair, Lili said, "You'll have to feed me first."

Silence. "You sure?"

"That I need to eat—?"

"That you wanna spend the night?"

"I'm sure," she said, even as she shooed away the stinging behind her eyes.

* * *

Tony groaned and swore when an obnoxiously cheerful sunbeam stabbed his eyelids the next morning. Batting at both the light and Ed—who'd apparently been waiting patiently for any sign of life—he sat up, at once realizing two things: A) he was naked, and B) the person he'd been naked with was nowhere to be seen. However, both the muted thumping of the dryer in the mudroom and the blissful scent of brewing coffee gave him reason to believe Lili hadn't gone far. Whether she was still naked or not, however, he had no idea.

She wasn't, as it happened, wearing one of his old shirts at she sat at the kitchen table with her chin in her hand and her glasses perched on her cute little nose, engrossed in the Sunday paper, spread out all over the table. Ed trotted over, tail wagging, to nudge her hand; smiling, she leaned over and messed with his soft, floppy ears, talking nonsense to him. Tony's throat clogged at the sight, at how natural and right it seemed, her sitting there at his table, wearing his shirt, talking stupid to the dog. Just as natural and right as falling asleep with her tucked against his chest after a night of playing catch-up.

"I'm surprised you can move," he said from the doorway, startling her. And that was before she realized he hadn't bothered to put anything on. God, he loved when she blushed.

"I can't, actually," she said when she recovered. Eventually her eyes moved up to his face. "Which is why *you* get to do breakfast."

Smiling, Tony ambled over to give her a kiss. "Not a problem." And another. "So why don't you go take a hot bath while I rustle up some toast or something?"

"Good idea." She braced her hands on the table and pushed herself upright. "I put our wet things in the dryer, by the way, so I'll have something to wear when…um, later."

Their gazes caught. "This is totally up to you," Tony said, "but the kids don't come back until tonight. The rest of the day is ours."

She paused, her eyes twinkling. "You think we should go to church?"

"And get struck by lightning? I think not."

Laughing, she stood on tiptoe to kiss him, then sort of hobbled away.

As Tony poured himself a cup of coffee, he heard the water thunder into the bathtub upstairs. Whining, the dog dropped a disgusting tennis ball at Tony's feet, then backed away, daring him to grab it as the dryer buzzed. "Forget it," he muttered, going to pull out their clothes. Boxers were dry, jeans weren't. Whatever. He put them on, barely getting the jeans zipped when the dog went bonkers out in the entryway.

"Shut up, ya stupid mutt!" Tony yelled, figuring it was somebody walking another dog or kids on bikes or a leaf falling off a tree. But no, he realized as his front door flew open and Daphne barreled into the house, followed by her sisters and grandparents.

What this was, was a catastrophe.

Chapter Twelve

"What are you guys doing home?" Tony asked as his precious time alone with Lili vaporized right in front of his eyes. And thanking *God* the dryer had buzzed when it had, otherwise he'd be flashing his in-laws.

"Claire and the baby both caught colds," Susan said, handing Josie to Tony with a brief frown at his bare chest. Thumb in mouth, the baby curled into him, sniffling. Tony strained to hear upstairs—no water running, no singing, no telltale footsteps. With any luck he could at least get rid of Susan and Lou before Lili was finished with her bath. How he'd explain her to the kids, however…

He looked at Claire, the picture of misery with the splotchy face, puffy eyes, the works, and Daddy mode kicked in.

"You don't feel good, baby?"

"Not really," she said in a scratchy voice as Josie—who'd never let a thing like a runny nose actually stop her—wriggled to get down. "Move, dog!" she said, her voice more gravelly than usual as she shoved the overjoyed mutt out of her path on her way to the kitchen.

"We would've gladly kept 'em," Lou said, hands in pockets, "but Claire said she wanted to come home." He gave Tony a meaningful look. "So we didn't push it."

"Come on, Nana," Daph said, waving her grandmother toward the kitchen. "I'll show you were we keep all the cooking stuff—"

"Cooking stuff?" Tony said, thinking, *Oh, hell no.*

"Yes, I told the girls I'd make pancakes here—"

"*No!* I mean," he said at Susan's frown, "I haven't been to the store yet this week, I don't have any mix or anything—"

"That's perfectly all right, dear," Susan said, gliding past him toward the kitchen, hauling a bulging tote bag. "I brought everything we need. It's just not Sunday without pancakes," she said, nearly tripping over the baby when she suddenly popped back out into the hallway…shuffling merrily along in Lili's shoes.

Okay, no need to panic, Tony thought, panicking, *maybe nobody will notice, maybe I can somehow get Lili's clothes to her and she could just slip away—*

Tony herded everybody toward the kitchen, figuring there'd be so many people nobody would notice if he disappeared for a couple of minutes, only to spot Lili's bag on the counter.

About the same time Claire did.

She turned, accusation sharp behind puffy lids. "Why's Lili's bag here?" she asked, just as Lili herself appeared in the kitchen doorway, hair dripping wet, wrapped in a towel, gingerly dancing only to music she could hear through the tiny plug in her ear from Tony's MP3 player which he'd left on the bathroom sink. All heads turned in her direction the same instant she realized they weren't alone.

"Lili!" Josie squealed, shuffling toward her with her arms outstretched. "I gots your shoes—!"

"Oh, dear God," Lili whispered, blushing furiously. "I'm so sorry, I…" She vanished, as, behind him, Susan muttered a soft, "Oh, Tony," and Claire yelled, "You *said* nothing was going on! Both of you! You *promised*—!"

"*Enough!* All of you!" Tony bellowed, earning him a roomful of shocked expressions. He stormed to the mudroom and snatched Lili's clothes off the top of the dryer, then strode back through the kitchen, pausing only long enough to grab Lili's bag and lift Josie out of her shoes, adding them to the pile.

"I'm sure everybody's got plenty to say," he said, backing out of the room, "but I'm afraid it'll hafta wait for a few minutes. Try not to talk *too* badly about me while I'm gone."

Claire's wails followed him as he took the stairs two at a time to find Lili in his bedroom, sitting on the edge of the bed, clutching the damp towel to her breasts and staring at nothing in particular. As Tony shut the door behind him, she shook her head and whispered, "That was the most mortifying moment of my life. I never meant…"

"I know, I know," Tony said, sitting beside her and swinging an arm around her cool, bare shoulders. It was like hugging a statue. "It'll be okay, honey, I swear—"

"I'm not deaf, Tony. I can hear Claire from here, even through the closed door. From her standpoint, I did exactly what I told myself—what I told *her*—I'd never do. And the look on your mother-in-law's face—"

"We just caught 'em off guard—"

"Then you really don't understand just how deep something like this goes." She grabbed the clothes out of his hand, dumped the towel and unceremoniously stepped into her panties, then clumsily put on her bra. "Last night," she said, jerking up her skirt and fumbling with the back zipper, "was a dream. *This* is reality. Your reality, at least. Claire would never accept me as a replacement for her mother. And your in-laws…" Grabbing her blouse from the bed, she shook her head.

"And none of that matters because you're leaving anyway, right? Because—how did you put that?—what you feel is all mixed up with a bunch of other stuff?"

Lili's eyes darted to Tony's, her trembling hands stilling on the crumbled top's pearl buttons. They watched each other in brittle silence for several seconds before she rammed her feet into her shoes and grabbed her bag from where he'd dumped it on the dresser. When she reached the bedroom door, however, she turned and said quietly, "Face it, Tony...I—*this*—was an interlude. Which we both knew, so no hard feelings. But boy," she said, her eyes watering, "if there was *any* doubt that I don't belong here, in this house...in your life..."

She shook her head, then slipped from the room and ran down the stairs. Moments later the front door slammed. Tony didn't move, Lili's words echoing in his head. Eventually, however, his breathing returned to something resembling normal and he went back downstairs, only to have Lou waylay him in the hallway.

"We need to talk, Tone."

"I should really see to Claire—"

"She can wait," his father-in-law said, taking him by the arm and steering him out front. "Susan's got things under control for the next little while."

Outside, Tony sank onto one of the wicker chairs on the porch, leaning forward with his hands clamped together and staring toward the street. "Obviously Lili and I never meant for anybody to find out," he said. "Or to hurt anybody—"

"You including yourself in that equation?"

He frowned up at the older man as anger bellowed inside him, drowning out the hundred other emotions all screaming for attention. "Twenty-four lousy hours to ourselves," he bit out. "*For* ourselves. Was that so much to ask?"

Finally, Lou sat in the nearby matching loveseat, his fingers laced over his potbelly. "Is it serious?"

Tony snorted. "Would it matter if it was?" He blew out a sharp breath. "When you're eighteen it's all about you. Parents, other people…their opinions mean squat. Then you grow up, have some kids of your own, and it's never just about you anymore. It can't be, if you're a decent parent." When Lou remained silent, Tony's gaze slid back to his. "Why aren't you sayin' anything?"

The other man pushed himself back up, his hands rammed into his chinos' pockets as he crossed to a straggly pot of moss roses that had pretty much been left to their own devices. "Believe it or not, Susan and I really are concerned about you, that this…thing is a whaddyacallit. A rebound. A way to deal with the shock."

"It's been nearly ten months, Lou—"

"I'm not talkin' about Marissa's passing," Lou said quietly, turning, and for the first time Tony saw an anguish of an entirely different kind in his father-in-law's eyes. Tony's stomach plummeted.

"Holy hell…you knew?"

"Yeah."

"When—?"

"Rissa broke down, confessed to her mother not long after she found out she was sick. Susan begged her to tell you the truth then, but she said she couldn't, that she'd take care of it in her own time." He paused. "So about a month ago, we get this note through your guys' lawyer. All it said was, 'By the time you get this, Tony will know.' Susan and me, we kept waitin' for you to say somethin'—"

"Yeah. Like I could've done that." At Lou's slight smile, Tony took a deep breath. "How much did she tell you?"

"That she had an affair, although she didn't mention names." He scratched behind his ear. "That she wasn't sure the baby was yours."

"She's not," Tony said quietly, and Lou swore. Which he

did again after Tony explained everything that had transpired on that front.

"She cheated on you with the Jamison kid?"

"He's not a kid anymore, Lou."

"Whatever. Thought he was a sleazeball then, now I know why. Look, you need any legal help—about keeping the baby, I mean—I know more'n one pitbull lawyer. Don't worry about the money, we'll foot the bill. Anything to make sure you keep Josie." Lou blinked, clearing his throat. "I don't know why the hell Rissa did what she did. I do know she was sorry for it, said it wasn't your fault, that you'd been a good husband. I also know if she said it once, she said it a million times, what a good father you were. Are. If we overstepped— about wantin' to take the girls off your hands, I mean—I apologize. We were just tryin' to help, but…" He shrugged.

Knowing what it took for Lou to say all of that, Tony smiled. "Thanks, I appreciate it. All of it. But God willing we won't have to sic any of your lawyer buddies on the guy…" Tony cupped his mouth, his eyes burning.

"Dammit, Tone—you don't deserve to be goin' through this crap," Lou said gently, then sighed. "And Susan and me, we wanna see you happy. See you married again someday. But now…" He shook his head. "Look, it's not hard to guess what you've been going through the past few weeks. That you're probably not thinking real straight. I mean, gettin' news like that—who would, right?" Lou rubbed his mouth. "Not the best time to start a relationship, that's all I'm saying."

"I know that," Tony said softly. Aching. Once again trying to make sense of something that didn't. "So did Lili. It wasn't… There weren't any expectations on either side, okay? She's leaving in a few days, anyway. So that's…that."

"It's for the best, Tone. Believe me. Because you've got a lot on your plate right now. And you're gonna have even more when you tell Claire and Daphne about…that Josie's only their half sister."

Tony's head jerked up. "The kid's *ten,* Lou. And nowhere near over her mother's death. Why on earth would I dump even more crap on her?"

"I'm not saying you hafta to go into any great detail or anything. But it's gonna come out, probably sooner rather than later. And I'm just guessing here, but if Claire doesn't hear it from you, there's gonna be hell to pay down the road when she does find out."

"No argument there. But she's my kid. And it's up to me to break the news to her. When it feels right."

"Yeah, yeah, of course. Totally your call. But Claire's a sensitive kid, she already knows something's up. She even said as much to her grandmother. So you might wanna think about heading things off at the pass. Just sayin'."

The soft whine of the screen door brought Tony's head around. His mother-in-law, twisting her wedding ring, worry in her eyes. Which Tony saw flick to Lou, silently asking the Big Question, no doubt. About Josie. Saw, too, the older man's slow head shake. He'd witnessed that telepathic communication thing between couples before, although rarely in his own marriage. Lili and he, however—

"Where're the girls?" he asked, turning away from Susan's wretched expression. His own, even more wretched, thoughts.

"Daph and Josie are out back with the dog, Claire's up in her room." She came up to him to wrap one arm around his shoulders, bending over to give him a brief hug. "I'm so sorry, honey. About…about all of it." She paused, then said softly, "Claire's pretty upset—you should probably go talk to her."

Tony stood, looking his mother-in-law in the eye. "Yeah, well, she's not the only one," he said, then banged back the screen door and went inside to go upstairs, desperately wanting to do the right thing by everybody and having no earthly idea how to do that. Hell, at this point he didn't even know what the "right" thing *was* anymore.

Claire was lying on her side on top of her covers, hugging Clifford The Big Red Dog and suddenly looking impossibly small. Tony sat beside her, palming her forehead.

"It's okay," she said, "I don't have a fever. I just feel like crap."

He let it slide. "You eat any breakfast?" She shook her head, not looking at him. No surprise there. On both counts. "Wanna talk?" he asked gently, stroking her hair away from her face. Another head shake.

Seeing her so tiny and vulnerable and tender beside him, he knew no way could she deal with the stuff about her mother and Josie. Not today, at least. Even so, he knew Lou was right, that the longer Tony put this off, the harder it was gonna be. On everybody. God knew acting like nothing was wrong sure hadn't done his marriage any favors, he thought as this brutal sense of loss roared through him—of his wife, in more ways than one; the threat of losing Josie, despite Lou's legal connections; the horrible, gaping hole in his chest when Lili walked out of his room earlier.

That he might somehow lose Claire, too, through his own idiocy—

"C'n I ask you something?" she asked.

"Sure. Anything."

She rolled over, her eyes slightly unfocused without her glasses. "And you *swear* to tell me the truth? Cross your heart?"

"Yeah," Tony said, crossing that heart, banging like hell in his chest. "I swear."

"Why was Lili here?"

Tony took a deep breath. "Because she spent the night."

"Like a sleepover?"

"Sorta."

"Did she sleep in your bed?" When Tony hesitated, Claire let out a sigh of her own. "My friend Jocelyn at school? She told me how her mom sometimes lets her boyfriend sleep over."

"Often?" Tony said, horrified despite himself.

"I don't know, she didn't say. Well?"

"Yeah, baby. She did. But you weren't—"

"Supposed to find out?"

"No, actually." When she made a face, Tony said, "The last thing either of us wanted to do was upset you, baby, I swear—"

"So she's your girlfriend?"

Uh, boy. "Lili's going back to Hungary, cupcake. So it doesn't matter."

Claire sat silently for several seconds, her brow knotted, before she climbed off the bed and went to her dresser to get something out of the top drawer. When she turned, clutching the crumpled piece of paper, Tony felt like he'd been struck by lightning.

"Where…when did you find that?"

"A couple of days ago. Daph'd used up all my pencils, so I went to your office to look for some. I found this in the drawer. I would've put it back, but I was afraid Daph might find it…she p-practically reads better than m-me now…"

"Oh, God, baby…come here." Once he had her safe in his arms, he set Marissa's letter on the bed beside them, then asked, "Why on earth didn't you say something then?"

"It was right before Nana and Gramps c-came to pick us up, there wasn't time." She pulled away, tears crested on her lower lashes. "Is it true?"

After a moment, Tony nodded. "Yeah, honey. It's true."

"Even the part about Josie?"

"That, too."

She threw herself back into Tony's arms, the tears coming

fast and furious now. "Wh-why? Why would Mom d-do that?"

"I guess we'll never know, baby," Tony said, rubbing between her shoulder blades and feeling like he was being ripped apart.

He had no idea how long he held her, letting her cry her eyes out, until she said, in a tiny, shaky voice, "I just wish everything would stop f-feeling like a roller coaster you can't get off of."

In silent agreement, Tony pulled her closer.

"Vat are you doing?" Magda asked from Lili's doorway.

"Packing," she said, shoving a half dozen folded tops into her largest traveling bag, splayed on top of Mia's old bed.

"But your flight isn't for three days yet."

"I'm on standby for an earlier one."

Magda *smack-smack-smacked* across the carpet, clamped her hands on Lili's arms and swung her around. "Vat happened?"

"Nothing," Lili said, on the verge of exploding from trying to hold in her emotions. "I'm just ready to go home, that's all."

"And I don't suppose zis hes anysing to do vis you staying out all night?"

"N-no."

Magda sighed, pushed Lili down onto the pale pink chenille bedspread, ball fringe and all, then sat in the rose-patterned chair across from her, her hands folded on her lap. "I hed hoped you vould hef better sense zen that," she said, not unkindly.

"Yeah, well," Lili said, realizing how much Tony had influenced her speech, "you were the one who said Tony needed me."

"Not exactly vhat I hed in mind," her aunt said, then sighed. "Do you love him?"

Lili nodded.

"So…vas last night worth ze heartache?"

In spite of everything, Lili smiled. "Not that I have a lot to compare it with…but yes. It was."

Eyebrows lifted. "Don't tell me zat vas your first time?"

"Then I won't tell you."

Magda crossed herself, muttering in Hungarian, then squinted at her.

"Yes," Lili said wearily, "we used protection, don't worry." The squint didn't let up. The squint, apparently, was a living thing. "It's not meant to be, okay? There's far too much going on in Tony's life right now…and the girls—well, Claire, anyway—aren't ready…and anyway, I'm supposed to be figuring out what my purpose is in life, and—"

"And zis is all BS and you know it."

"What it is," Lili said softly, getting up to continue her packing, "is a case of the pieces not fitting. I can't wedge myself into his life, Magda," she said when her aunt snorted. "And damned if I'm going to do to Claire what Mama did to me."

Her aunt gave her a look both sympathetic and curious before she sighed again. "I told Sonja she was making a huge mistake—"

"It's okay, we worked through all of that. Eventually. But I refuse to be the bad guy between Tony and *his* daughter."

"And you can spare me ze melodrama, okay?"

"I'm not being melodramatic. I'm being…practical," Lili said, tucking a pair of jeans into the bag.

"Vat you're being," Magda said, slamming her palms against her thighs before she stood, "is a big, fat coward, running avay instead of taking five minutes to see if maybe zere's a solution you heffen't thought of." When Lili frowned at her, she huffed. "You think zere veren't issues ven I fell in love vis Benny? Zat my femily didn't hef a cow ven I said I vas leaving ze circus, leaving behind everyzing I efer knew to marry some stranger? But my heart," she said, pressing her bosom, "told me to take zat risk. Marrying somebody ven your heart is broken, like your mother…" Her lips pressed together, she shook her head. "But if your heart is whole, zat is somesing else entirely."

Lili zipped her bag closed, then hauled it off the bed to set it on the floor. "And what makes you think *Tony's* heart is whole?" she said softly, turning to her aunt.

Who, amazingly, had nothing to say to that.

Chapter Thirteen

Tony nearly jumped out of his skin when he rolled over in bed to find JoJo and Ed staring at him. In rapid succession, Tony glanced at the clock—holy crap, it was nearly nine!—bolted upright, shoved the dog out of his face and pulled Josie onto the bed. She was dressed in shorts and a little top and her hair looked like it'd been combed. Sorta. Ed crawled up, too, to burrow under the sheet, leaving his butt on Tony's pillow. Nice.

"How long've you been up?" he said to Josie.

"Since morning," she said, shrugging. "Claire got me. We had f'osted f'akes." She patted his face, only to jerk her hand back, frowning. "Ick. You gots pokies."

Probably because he hadn't shaved in two days. Might not, either, for the rest of the summer. As rebellions went, it was kinda lame. But a guy can only work with what he's got.

The baby molded herself to his bare chest, well underneath the pokies, as Tony rubbed his gritty eyes. Wasn't until after two before he'd finally talked Claire down off the ledge, five before he finally fell asleep himself. Then it was one rotten dream after another, over and over, a continuous loop of anger and worry and anxiety and regret—

A poor James Brown impersonation came in through the open window. Hauling Josie onto his hip, Tony climbed out of bed and padded over to the window in his boxers to see Hollis and Daphne already out in the garden, doing…stuff.

"Hi, Hollis!" Josie called, which of course brought the kid's grinning face up to look at the window.

"Hey, there, pretty baby." He winced. "And not so pretty daddy. Your five o'clock shadow lose track of time or what?"

"Shut up," Tony grumbled, then looked at Josie, regarding him curiously. "Don't say that. Ever."

"'Kay," she whispered, all that trust in her eyes, and he reminded himself for the thousandth time, that the kids came first. That he had his priorities straight, dammit. That it didn't matter that he already missed Lili with an intensity that went way beyond painful—

"Came over to see how the garden did with the storm, but I see it came through just fine. 'Cept you probably should've brought those tomatoes in."

"Thought about that," Tony said, although of course veggie rescue missions hadn't even been a blip on the old radar that evening, a thought which only made him grouchier than he already was. "Then I decided since I'll be eighty before we use up the tomatoes we already picked, it wasn't worth the bother."

"Good point," Hollis said, adding, "I went ahead and put on coffee," and Tony's mood lifted a little.

A half hour later, beard banished, caffeine mainlined and Josie happily watching Elmo and his little furry friends, Tony and Ed wandered out onto the back porch, Tony toting his second cup of coffee as well as a glass of orange juice for

Hollis, who didn't do "that hard stuff." As the kid righted storm-battered tomato cages, Daphne the Mud Puppy happily yanked weeds on the other side of the garden. Hollis threw him a grin.

"Gardening really ain't your thing, is it, Mr. V.?"

"What was your first clue?"

Straightening, the kid moseyed over to the porch and sank onto the bottom step, taking the glass from Tony. "Daphne said Lili was here yesterday morning." He took a sip of the juice. "Wearin' a towel."

"Brat," Tony muttered, and Hollis chuckled.

"So, you two…?"

"No. I mean…" Tony pushed out a sigh. "She's leaving in a couple of days."

"You don't sound too happy about that."

Tony grunted.

"So you just lettin' her go? Man," he said, wagging his head, "talk about *dumb*."

"Hollis. Stop. It's complicated."

"No, it's not. You love the woman, you do whatchu gotta do to keep her, you hear what I'm sayin'? You been through a whole lotta crap this last little while, Mr. V., doncha think it's time you grab a little happiness for yourself?"

"It doesn't work that way. And who says I love her?"

"That look on your face right now, for one thing. What? You think it's too soon? That people might talk smack about you because you're not honorin' your wife or something?"

"It had occurred to me."

"Hell, Mr. V.—it's not like you cheatin' on the woman. She dead. She not comin' back. And you know how you were always on us to grab opportunities, to not let 'em slip through our fingers? Seems to me maybe you should take your own advice." He got up, handing Tony the empty glass. "I gotta go, signing up today for some classes today at the community college." He extended one hand for Tony to slap and grab, then sauntered off around the side of the house.

While Tony was irritably musing about how straightforward everything seemed when you were eighteen, Claire appeared at the back door. Frowning. Although her cold was better today, her outlook on life was not. Tony couldn't say as he blamed her.

"Mailman says you gotta sign for something."

With a weary sigh, Tony got up, handed her the empty glass and dragged himself through the house to the front door, frowning at the large brown envelope the carrier held hostage until Tony signed the little green card and handed it back. He'd barely shut the front door before he ripped it open, scanning the very legal-looking papers with the notary's seal on the bottom. And the handwritten letter accompanying them.

"Holy crap," he whispered when the important parts sank in, the relief that rushed over him so strong it knocked the wind right out of him. He dropped to the bench to read the affidavit a second time, savoring every word. By the third read-through the words on the page began to dance around the thousands of other words in his head—Lili's and Claire's and Hollis's and Lou's, all those words from all those people who either had a stake in or opinion about what Tony should or shouldn't do with his life…and when he should or shouldn't do it. And through all those thousands of words, he only heard—

"Dad? What is it?"

Not those.

But when he looked up and saw Claire standing in the living room archway, Josie in her arms, and another wave of relief surged through him as he grinned at his baby—*his* baby, who nobody could ever take away from him, not now, not ever—a thought slammed him right between the eyes:

That he could no more let Lili, and what they had together, go without a fight than he could Josie, or Claire, or Daph.

That this wasn't an either/or thing. That—and here was the kicker—this wasn't really only about *his* happiness.

"We have to talk, sweetheart," he said, patting the bench beside him.

"Yeah. I know," she said, startling him, before saying to Josie, "How about you watch one of your movies?" before carting her away, saying to Tony over her shoulder, "I'll be right back."

Wait. What?

Sorry, Mom, I know you hated us watching too much TV, but this is an emergency, Claire thought as she set JoJo in front of the flat screen television with one of her Elmo DVDs. Although between her stuffy nose and all the stuff about Mom—she and Dad had talked for like *hours* last night—she hadn't slept much. But weirdly, when she woke up? Her head felt completely clear. About some things, anyway. Like about how, even though Claire still didn't understand why Mom had done what she had, and it hurt, that couldn't ruin the good memories, or change how Claire felt about her. Not if she didn't let it.

And that—if she was being really, really truthful—the only times she hadn't felt like total crap the past few weeks had been when Lili'd been around.

And she was guessing if you asked Dad? He'd say he felt pretty much the same way.

Claire walked back out to the entryway, her arms crossed over her new hoodie. Dad smiled. "A little warm for that, isn't it?"

"I'm fine," she said, shrugging. "So. What was in the envelope?"

"Excellent news," Dad said, smiling bigger than she'd seen in a long, long time. "We don't have to worry about giving Josie up." He waved the papers. "Ever."

Claire felt her eyes go all buggy. "Really?"

"Really. But…" He leaned forward, looking right into her eyes. "When I realized how good I felt about knowing I was never gonna lose Josie," he said in this real quiet voice, "I realized something else. And I know you might not like it, and God knows your grandparents are gonna have a fit but—"

"But you don't want Lili to leave."

She'd never seen that look on Dad's face before, like he was so shocked he didn't know what to say. Then he held out one arm, waving Claire over to sit on his lap. "It's killin' me, the thought of her leaving," he said, all soft and stuff, then touched his forehead to hers. "Just like it would've killed me to lose Josie. Like it would to lose any of you guys. I love her, baby," he said, giving her a squeeze. "Not more than you or your sisters, not more than Mom, but…just as much."

Okay, just say it— "I don't want Lili to leave, either."

Dad looked at her really hard. "Not exactly the vibes you were giving off yesterday."

"I know, I…" Claire pinched her mouth together, then pushed out, "When I saw Lili standing there in the towel, it really freaked me out…" She looked up at Dad. "I got scared."

Dad hugged her shoulder. "Yeah. I know. But now you've changed your mind?"

Claire frowned so hard it hurt. "It's more…I think I figured out which were the good thoughts and which one's weren't. And I decided to go with the good thoughts."

"Sounds like a plan," Dad said.

After a moment, she said, "Does Lili love you, too?"

"I think so."

"So…if you asked her to marry you and stuff, she'd say yes?"

Dad got a funny look on his face. "That, I don't know."

"What do you mean, you don't know? If you love each other—"

"Loving somebody doesn't mean everything automatically falls neatly into place," Dad said, then let out a big breath. "Or that you can't get hurt down the road."

"You mean…like what happened with Mom?"

He nodded, then said, "But Lili and Mom are very different people, with different ways of looking at things, so…"

When Dad didn't finish his sentence, Claire figured that meant he didn't want to say anything bad about Mom, but she got it, anyway—that he didn't think Lili would ever do what Mom did. Claire didn't know why, but somehow she didn't think she would, either. Because Lili and Dad together felt way different than Mom and Dad had. It wasn't a happy thought, but it was an honest one.

Looking down at her hands on top of Dad's, Claire said, "One day, before Mom got sick, I found her crying. She wouldn't tell me why. But she said…" Claire felt her jaw wobble. "She said not to tell you, it would only make you unhappy." Her eyes burning, she looked at Dad. "Do you think she was crying because of what she did?"

Dad pulled her into his arms and laid his cheek on her head. "Maybe. I think she felt really, really bad about it."

Claire leaned into him, liking how he smelled, like soap and the stuff he used after he shaved. It made her feel safe. Sort of. Because then she sighed and said, "It's so scary, letting yourself love somebody."

She felt Dad's quiet laugh in her hair. "Ain't that the truth?"

Sitting up, she pushed her glasses up on her nose. "If…if Lili…" She frowned, not even sure what she was asking. "This would mean a *lot* of changes, huh?"

"Oh, yeah," Dad said. "Lots." He bent his head slightly to look into her eyes. "Could you deal with that?"

Claire thought for a moment, then shrugged. "It's sure worth a shot."

Dad laughed, then held her tight again for a long time, not saying a word.

Of course, Tony's first impulse—with Daphne's shrieked encouragement—was to go straight over to Lili's and make a complete idiot of himself. But it seemed only right that he make an idiot of himself with Lou and Susan first. So he shooed the girls upstairs, hauled in a breath, and hit number "1" on the old speed dial.

"Tony," Susan said when she answered, "what—"

"Could you put Lou on, too? I got something to tell you. A couple of somethings, actually."

Took a few seconds to get the whole conference call thing worked out, but once everybody was connected Tony told them about Josie, including a lot of stuff he hadn't told Claire—that Cole had apparently come clean to his wife and set up a money market account in Josie's name. That while he'd be willing to get to know her someday, if Josie wished it, he saw no reason to disrupt anyone's lives more than they'd already been. That he left it up to Tony, whenever he felt the time was right to tell Josie the truth.

When the relieved congrats died down, he said, "And now for the hard part."

"What hard part, dear—?"

"Suze, for godssake, let the boy talk. What is it, Tone?"

Deep breath. "You know, we have so little control over what happens in our lives, no idea when somebody's gonna come into it that…" He rubbed a hand over his face. "Okay, cut to the chase—I'm sorry, you guys, but I can't just let Lili walk out of my life. I thought I could, I thought it was the right thing to do, but…it isn't. At all."

Silence. Finally, Lou spoke.

"But…Claire…?"

"Totally on board. They all are." Tony paused. "The girls love Lili. As much as I do. And when I see what she's done for Claire…I know it's…what's that word?"

"Precipitous?" Susan put in.

"Yeah. That. And I don't even know if this is a definite thing, if *she's* ready for this. For us. But I've spent far too much time recently feeling bad about stuff that wasn't my fault. And Lili's the only person with the guts to not let me get away with that crap. How can I walk away from somebody like that? So I gotta find out, if there's a chance. Not just for me, for the girls, too."

"Oh, Tony," Susan started, but Lou said, "Are you even listening to the boy, Susie?"

"But—"

"Here's a news flash, sweetheart," Lou said gently, "this isn't about us. But, Tone—are you absolutely sure?"

God knows Tony couldn't tell them the seed for what he felt now had lain dormant for nearly fifteen years. And if Marissa hadn't died, if they'd been able to fix their marriage, it would have never blossomed. He knew that as well as he knew his own name. But not going after something because of what might have been made no sense whatsoever.

"You know I loved Rissa with everything I had in me," he said quietly. "I feel exactly the same way about Lili. And believe me, I'm thinking straighter than I ever have in my life. This isn't a rebound, Lou, or about me being lonely or whatever. It's…." He heard Lili's voice in his head. "It's real."

He heard muffled conversation for a few minutes before Lou came back on the line. "Then I suppose we got no choice but to trust you're gonna make the right decision."

"Thanks," Tony said, trying not to tear up. "I really do love you guys—"

"Oh, for God's sake—get the hell off the phone and go get the girl!"

Grinning, Tony went back inside. "Anyone up for goin' over to Aunt Magda's?" he called out, and assorted little girls thundered down the stairs.

"*Please* tell me we're not walking," Claire said, shoving Josie's sandals onto her feet.

"Like I'm gonna take twenty minutes to get there instead of a minute and a half? No way."

But when Magda answered her front door shortly afterwards, jumping back in slight alarm when Daph, Claire and Tony all yelled "Is Lili here?" she pressed a hand to her chest and let out a small, distressed cry.

"No, she's not—Benny took her to ze airport an hour ago!"

"What time does her plane leave?" Claire said, worried.

"Magda said two-thirty."

"But it's already—"

"I know what time it is, baby," Tony said, veering around cars on I-91 like he was playing Grand Theft Auto. Keeping one eye on the road with *all those stupid cars in his way, dammit,* he spared her a quick smile. "It's okay, we're gonna make it."

"You swear?"

"On my life," he said through gritted teeth, zooming down the road leading to airport parking. "Okay, here's the plan— we park, I get the baby, Daph takes Claire's hand, Claire takes mine, then nobody lets go of anybody until I say so. Got it?"

"Got it," both girls chimed beside and behind him, Josie echoing her own a soft "Got it," a second later.

Then they were running through the terminal like a possessed, lopsided bug, Daphne and Josie laughing, Claire panting, until Tony came to a screeching halt in front of an Arrival/Departure screen, whipping the other two around him.

"Has her plane left yet?"

"No," Tony said, heart in throat. "But it's boarding. Come *on!*"

And they were off again, only to come to another screeching halt in front of the squat, tough-looking security gal checking boarding passes.

She held out her hand, bored.

"We're not passengers, we're trying to reach someone about to leave on the British Airways flight to Amster—"

"Then you can't go past this point, sorry." Looking around them, she motioned for the next passenger.

"You don't understand, her cell's apparently dead, I don't have any way of getting hold of her and this is important—"

"No, *you* don't understand that I cannot let you through without a ticket or special permission from the airlines." She checked the man's printout and waved him through to screening. "British Airways' counter is right over there. Next! Keep it moving—"

"The plane's freaking boarding, lady! If I don't get to her—"

"And if you don't stop impeding these people with actual tickets trying to make their flights, I'ma hafta take action, mister...*what?*" she said with an irritated huff when Claire tugged on her sleeve.

"I'm sorry my Dad's acting crazy, but see, our mom died last year? And none of us thought we'd ever want somebody else to be our mother? Or in Dad's case, his wife? Only then Lili—she's the lady we're trying to keep from getting on her plane?—came to visit and, well, we all fell in love with her." She shrugged as Tony watched, stunned. "Especially our Dad. And if we don't get to her before she gets on the plane, she'll go back to Hungary and we'll never see her again."

The woman's eyes shot to Tony's. "You put the child up to this?"

"No. Swear to God—"

"Daddy!" Daph shrieked, blasting his eardrums. "Look! Way down there!"

Everybody—and he meant everybody, passengers, security personnel, the works—turned to look where Daphne pointed. And there, trudging up from the gates, dragging a suitcase the size of Rhode Island behind her, her hair a bedraggled mess and her glasses crooked, was Lili.

His Lili.

Okay, he hoped *his* Lili. Nothing in writing yet.

"That her?" the security lady said, and Tony's heart burst in his chest.

"Yeah," he said as the kids started screaming "Lili! Lili!" at the tops of their lungs and Lili's head popped up, her flummoxed expression almost immediately giving way to that huge, sun-coming-out smile he'd grown to love more than life itself, and she startled hustling toward them faster as all the other security peeps started in on old Ironsides, bugging her to let the kids go, at least, for heaven's sake, what did she think *they* were gonna do?

So she did, and Claire and Daph streaked through the arches and down the concourse, flying to a kneeling Lili's arms. She kissed them both, over and over and over, calling them her darlings and her babies, all her in her wonderful, wonderful accent, before her eyes—watery behind her glasses—touched Tony's.

"I suppose you want to go on, too," Ironsides muttered.

"It's okay," Tony said, feeling hugely magnanimous. Grinning so hard his face hurt. "I can wait."

He didn't have to wait long. Because moments later the woman he loved was in his arms, hugging him, hugging Josie, who kept going "Goop hug, goop hug!" and then Lili said, "I was sitting there waiting for the plane to load, and I suddenly thought, Why on earth am I going back to Hungary, there's nothing for me there, I can do my work anywhere and my damn *brothers* can close up my mother's apartment, and if…" Smiling at the girls, she cupped first Claire's, then Daphne's heads. "If you're not ready, I'm perfectly okay with just hanging out together for a while—so we can get to know each other better, yes?—and see where that takes us." She looked at Tony, her eyes soft. "That goes for you, too."

His heart swelled. "You would take that risk?"

"After what I just went through to get my luggage off the plane? I'll probably never be able to fly British Airways again. Of course I haven't exactly thought any of this through, such as how I'm going to stay here without a visa—"

Tony kissed her. And grinned. "You won't be needing any of that."

"Mmm, yes, I will—"

"Not if we're married, you won't."

Her mouth dropped open. "You can't be serious," she said. Eventually.

Tony lowered his gaze to the girls. "Are we serious?"

"Uh-huh," they both said, nodding like a pair of bobble-head dolls. Except then Claire sighed and said, "Da-ad."

Tony frowned at her. By this time, a nice little crowd had gathered. "What?"

"Aren't you forgetting, like, the most important part?"

"Um, I thought askin' her to marry me—"

"Marry *us.*"

"Okay, marry *us*…I thought that *was* the important part."

After a prize-winning eyeroll, his oldest daughter yanked him down and whispered, loud enough to hear in Montpelier, "You forgot the L word, silly."

Tony cleared his throat. "Right here in front of God and everybody?"

"Yep," Claire said with a brisk nod.

"O-kay." Then he met Lili's amused eyes and thought, *Who am I kidding? Give me a bullhorn and I'll tell all of New England.* "Lili Szabo, in the past few weeks—you don't mind if I get all sappy?"

She choked back a little laugh. "Not at all."

"Just checking. Okay—in the past few weeks, you've brought somethin' back into our lives I wasn't sure we'd ever see again. Happiness, sure—who can be around you for more than five seconds and not feel happy?—but more than that, you brought back hope. And hope…that trumps logic every time. What I feel for you is solid, and sure, and…" He chuckled. "Not scary at all, now that you're standin' here." He took her hand, holding it to his chest. "I love you, Lili—"

"Me, too!" Daph yelled, letting out an "Ow!" that echoed through the entire concourse when Claire smacked her shoulder.

"Girls! Jeez!" Tony said, then looked at Lili. "You *sure* you want to sign on for this?"

She laughed, taking the baby from him. "Yes," she said softly, squeezing his hand. "Very, very sure. Can we go home now?"

Tony grinned. "Thought you'd never ask," he said. Then he yanked her close and kissed her, to a great deal of applause and cheering.

Even from Old Ironsides, bless her grumpy soul.

Epilogue

*H*ome.

Lili realized that, before she'd marched up to the British Airways counter two months ago and said she'd changed her mind—and would they mind terribly getting her bag?—that she'd never really sorted out what that word meant to her. Just as she'd never completely clicked into that whole "purpose" thing, either.

Until two *hours* ago when she'd looked into Tony Vaccaro's eyes as they stood in front of the priest and promised to love and cherish each other forever, and he'd smiled down at her, his eyes filled with equal parts gratitude and mischief, and she saw "home" in those eyes…and in his smile and his touch and the simple but profound feeling of *Yes, this is good, this is right,* whenever the girls hugged her.

That was home. And, in her case, home *was* her purpose. Not the cooking and cleaning and daily trivia that kept a household running—although there was something to be said for that sweet sense of closeness that came from sharing the mundane—but whatever she could be for the girls, for her new husband…well. Violet had hit it dead on when she'd said it's the people we're close to who have the biggest influence on our lives, our characters.

That Tony and the girls had entrusted her with their hearts…

What a gift. An incredible, completely unexpected gift.

She heard a giggle behind her. Turning, she smiled for Claire, truly lovely in her jade colored bridesmaid dress and her new rimless glasses. "What's so funny?"

"You look weird standing in the kitchen in your wedding dress."

"Hey. I waited a long time to wear one of these," Lili said, twirling. Magda had been thrilled when Lili asked her to help her shop for the gown, a fairytale confection if ever there'd been one with its off the shoulder, beaded bodice and full tulle skirt. Just as Benny had been touched when she'd asked him to walk her down the aisle. "I'm not taking it off until I absolutely have to."

Still giggling, Claire swished in and sat at the table, staring at the paint splotches, still on the far wall. Although things had eased a great deal between them over the past weeks, Lili knew it would take time for Claire to come to terms with everything that had happened regarding her mother, to fully accept Lili as a stepmother. The wedding dress might feel magic, but the woman inside it was still only human.

"You know," the child now said, chin in palm, "I think we seriously need to paint this kitchen, already."

Tony walked in, loosening his bow tie and winking at Lili. My goodness, the man looked good in a tux. Of course, he looked good out of it, too—

"Yeah?" he said, hugging his daughter from behind and propping his chin on her head. "Which color?"

Claire looked at Lili. "Which one did you say you liked?"

She turned, trying to focus on the swatches through the blur of tears. "That one," she said, pointing to the pale blue green she'd originally liked.

"Yeah," Claire said, nodding. "Me, too—"

"Claire!" their grandmother called. "We're about ready to go…oh, for heaven's sake," she said when Claire left the kitchen, "why aren't you out of your dress yet…?"

Chuckling, Tony came up to Lili to slip his arms around her waist. "I could ask you the same thing," he said in a low voice, nuzzling her neck, and she laughed, thinking, *This isn't a fairy tale, this is real…*

The girls all rushed in to give them goodbye hugs and kisses, then rushed out again. A moment later, the front door shut and the house was theirs. All theirs. Even Ed was gone, spending the next few days with Magda's and Benny's two pups. Sleepover camp, Tony called it.

"Aren't Rudy and Violet expecting us by eight?" Lili asked as—with surprising dexterity—her husband began undoing the many, many buttons on the back of her gown.

"They can wait," he whispered, kissing her. "I can't."

Joy shuddered through Lili as the gown whooshed to the floor and her husband gathered her in his arms. "I love you," he said, and she laughed.

"Me, too," she said, melting into another kiss.

Home.

She was so there.

* * * * *

THE FAMILY HE WANTED

BY
KAREN SANDLER

Karen Sandler first caught the writing bug at age nine when, as a horse-crazy fourth grader, she wrote a poem about a pony named Tony. Many years of hard work later, she sold her first book (and she got that pony – although his name is Ben). She enjoys writing novels, short stories and screenplays and has produced two short films. She and her husband live in Northern California. You can reach Karen at karen@karensandler.net.

To the real "Sam," my dad, a hero beyond compare.
I love you, Dad!

Chapter One

Eyes burning with exhaustion, butt sore from the long drive, Jana McPartland pulled her ramshackle white sedan up to the security gate of Sam Harrison's Sierra Nevada foothills estate. If Sam had changed the gate code since last year, she was sunk. With her cell phone disconnected and not a pay phone in sight, she'd have to sit out here in the gloomy early January drizzle until he next passed through the gate.

She couldn't make out Sam's house—never mind that it was the size of Nebraska. The big, white two-story was around a curve of the asphalt-paved drive, hidden by a row of cypress trees. She'd spent a month there last May, right before she became Tony Herrera's assistant at Estelle's House. Sam had gone off on a book tour for his latest crime thriller and had asked Jana to house-sit. Talk about the lap of luxury.

She rolled down the driver's-side window, her arm tiring

as the hand crank resisted. She had the security code memorized, but still she pulled out the slip of paper Sam had written it on. She liked seeing that almost illegible cursive, the words *Gate Code* reading more like "Goat Cake." He'd laughed when she'd pointed that out to him, had chucked her under the chin like he had when she'd been ten years old.

She knew that touch had meant way more to her than to him. That was why she'd saved the slip of paper, so she could remember that moment.

Tucking the slip of paper back inside her purse, she punched in the five-digit code. A moment of silence, then the gate mechanism clicked and clacked as it rolled aside. She smiled with relief as she continued up the driveway, the gate shutting again behind her.

As she traveled the last curve of the road, her stomach started a two-step, threatening a redo of the nausea that never seemed limited to the morning. She'd eaten lunch at twelve-thirty in Redding, downed a few crackers when she'd stopped for pee breaks in Corning and Sacramento. The only time her stomach cooperated was while she was eating. At three-thirty, with all the crackers gone, it wasn't looking good.

She tucked the sedan alongside the six-car garage, out of the way in case Sam wasn't here and had to pull in. Even on a nasty, rainy Friday afternoon, he could be out running errands. Sam had a thing about keeping his six cars out of the elements, especially the five to-drool-for vintage models in his collection.

Her back aching, she unfolded herself from the sedan, brushing cracker crumbs from her elastic-waist jeans. Snagging her thrift shop jacket from the passenger seat, she shoved her arms into the sleeves. Nothing to keep her head dry, but hopefully she wouldn't be out in the wet for very long.

She'd always loved Sam's house—the wraparound front porch shaded with oak trees, the wide front lawn that sloped gently along the drive. She would have killed for a lawn like that as a kid, a place to run, a million nooks and crannies for hide-and-seek. She'd made do with Estelle Beckenstein's tiny front yard and backyard. She'd sneak over there from the small apartment where she and her mom lived, play rough-and-tumble games with Estelle's foster kids. But Sam's sixty-acre estate was a kid's dream.

Relieved to be under the porch overhang, she tried the doorbell first, pressing her ear to the front door to make sure the three-note gong sounded. Then she knocked, just to be on the safe side. Still no response. Of course, if he was out back somewhere, he wouldn't hear the doorbell or her knock.

Walking along the porch, Jana made her way around the house. She could kill two birds here—one, look for Sam, and two, brave the wet to see if he still left the little bathroom out by the pool unlocked. That would save her the indignity of using the bushes. She'd taken care of business at the service station when she eked out another quarter tank with the last of her cash, but that was a good half hour and a soda ago. Caffeine free, of course.

He hadn't locked the bathroom. That gave her a chance to not only use the toilet but also wash her face and finger-comb her stick-straight chin-length hair. That was a laugh, considering the way the damp strands clung to her face. Hopefully, she wouldn't terrify him when he got home.

Nothing to do but wait. Trotting back to the porch as the rain started in earnest, she retraced her steps to the front. He'd added a porch swing out here, giant-size, big enough for even six-foot-four Sam to stretch out on. A blanket lay folded over the back, and the seat was piled high with pillows. It looked too comfy to pass up.

Shucking her wet jacket, she flopped it over the porch rail then sank onto the soft cushions. The swing swayed as she tugged the blanket over her. Warmth suffused her, the patter of rain a pleasant accompaniment to the motion of the swing.

Since the day the test stick turned blue, stark fear had been her constant companion. Sometimes her terror grew so fierce it all but choked her. But now that she was here, safe at Sam's, she could let it go.

A sudden thought speared her mind, wrenched her from her peace. What if Sam was off on another tour? What if he was a thousand miles away from here and out of reach? No phone, her car nearly on empty—what would she do?

Tears ambushed her. Fighting them back, she turned over, burrowing her forehead into the back of the swing. Squeezing her eyes shut, she tightened her hands into fists and pressed them tightly against her chest. She refused to cry. Refused to be all red-eyed when Sam got home.

And he would come home. He had to. Because she needed him. Because she didn't have anywhere else to go.

Water rolling off his high-tech jacket and rain pants, Sam Harrison hiked up the wooded hill behind his house, satisfied he'd cleared enough brush to keep his creek from overflowing its banks. He'd spent an hour pulling deadfall from the roiling water, hauling soaked branches high enough up the bank to keep them from falling back into the creek. Now when the next storm arrived later tonight, the creek's flow would continue downstream rather than collect at the tight bend behind his house.

Not that the approaching deluge could have dumped

enough water to risk flooding his house. It had been built at the top of the rise, well out of the flood zone. But after a rough, wakeful night, his skin had crawled with the kind of toxic, restless energy that severe sleep deprivation always gave him. He'd had to burn it off with something physical.

He'd been all ready to head into town, his power tools loaded into his pickup, gripping the keys to what he privately referred to as his secret folly. He'd told no one about the little storefront in Camino he'd closed escrow on six weeks ago—not his best friend Tony, not his former foster mom Estelle. He feared they'd laugh at his whimsical idea. Even worse, Estelle would know immediately from what sad, wretched place his harebrained notion to open a Christmas store had come.

It was contemplation of their judgment, as well as the strengthening deluge, that changed his mind. The retrofit of the store could wait for yet another day. He'd be better off with the punishing misery of pulling rain-soaked deadfall out of an icy creek.

Reaching the porch steps, he headed for the back door, then remembered he'd left it locked. He'd have to go around to the front. Which meant he'd have to slip off his muck-covered boots outside the door. He might not give a damn about muddy footprints on the travertine tile entry, but his cleaning lady would have a hissy fit.

About to tug open the screen door, his gaze drifted over to the porch swing, then to the rain pouring buckets beyond it. Then in a double take, he fixed back on the swing. Who the hell was curled up on his cushions, snugged down all comfy and cozy under his blanket?

For a flash of a heartbeat, he wondered if it was Faith, come to beg him to take her back. Except he'd seen the acceptance in her eyes last week when he'd handed over the coup de grâce in the form of a diamond tennis bracelet. Faith had seen it coming. She was good enough friends with one of her predecessors to know how Sam would end it: a pricey gift, a kiss on the cheek, a firm goodbye.

So he wouldn't have the messiness of Faith's return to deal with. He crossed the porch to the swing. It swayed ever so slightly when a gust of wind curled under the overhang and hit it. The woman had her back to him. She'd buried her face into the swing's cushions as if she'd wanted to close out the world.

With the blanket pulled just past her chin and her light brown hair fallen partway onto her cheek, he couldn't see the woman's face. But something familiar about her tickled the back of his mind.

Could she be a foster kid, someone who knew about his history? Maybe she'd heard about Estelle's House, Tony's independent living program for emancipated fosters. Could be she wanted Sam's help getting a spot at the ranch. But how'd she get past the wrought-iron fence and security gate? She looked far too delicate to have jumped the fence.

Lightning sparked in the sky, and it must have been nearby, because the thunder that followed hit like an explosion. With a gasp, the woman's eyes snapped open, and she jolted upright on the swing. Her gaze locked on him, her brown eyes so huge they seemed to fill her face.

"Sam."

Her voice trickled down his spine. His brain finally engaged. "Jana."

She pushed aside the blanket and fussed with her hair. In quick succession, he registered the changes, the differences that had foiled his recognition of her. No more bleached-blond, pink-streaked hair. Her short, spiky cut had grown out long enough to cover the nape of her neck, its natural honey-brown color reminding him of that pugnacious kid he knew from Estelle's. She hadn't been a foster kid like him, but her mother had neglected her enough that Jana spent more time at Estelle's than she did at home.

Not only her hair but also her body had changed from the tomboyish twenty-three-year-old's he'd known last year. Her face was rounder, her hips a little broader and her breasts—

Okay, better not to think about her breasts. Yeah, he'd noticed around the time Jana turned twenty that she wasn't a little girl anymore. She had a lot less meat on her bones than most of the women he dated, but her lean-as-a-racehorse body nevertheless intrigued him. But she was a friend and he'd known her since she was a child. Breasts shouldn't even be in his lexicon with Jana, even though the ratty blue V-neck sweater she wore shaped them so nicely.

He dragged his gaze back up to her face. "You came back." Nothing like stating the obvious.

His staring must have made her jittery, because she jumped to her feet. She went green the moment her sneakers hit the deck, clutching the chain suspending the porch swing and swaying with its motion. He grabbed her, hooking her arm around his waist and supporting her across her shoulders.

"Let's get inside," he said as he walked her to the door. She leaned against him, damp but warm, softer in places he remembered being bonier.

As they crossed the entryway—so much for keeping his cleaning lady happy—Jana tried to wriggle away from him. "I'm fine. Let me go."

"You looked ready to pass out a minute ago."

"Just let me sit." She glanced down at his feet. "Mrs.

Prentiss will go ballistic if you walk on her carpet with those muddy boots."

"It's my carpet. I can walk on it any way I want."

Jana lifted one brow. "She scares you spitless. You lock yourself up in your office when she comes to clean."

"I'm just trying to stay out of her way."

Jana smirked and he knew he'd lost the argument. It was only a few steps from the entry to the recliner anyway. She made the short trip without incident and eased herself into the chair.

Hooking his jacket on the coatrack, he bent to unlace the offending boots. "Can I get you something?"

The leather upholstery creaked as she reclined. "Some saltines. I'll get them myself. After the month I spent house-sitting, I probably know better than you where to find them."

He was contemplating the fact that she probably was right when a game show ding-ding-ding went off in his head. Despite his chosen career as a novelist, he'd always had a fair mind for math. He could generally add two and two and come up with the correct answer.

He listed the clues mentally. The soft rounding of Jana's body. Her obvious nausea when she stood too fast. The request for saltines.

He skimmed off his rain pants and tucked his long-sleeved henley more securely into his jeans. "You stay put. I'll get them." He marched off to the kitchen, catching himself worrying whether his damp socks would leave prints on the carpet.

Stepping inside the walk-in pantry, he started scanning the groaning shelves arranged in a U around the narrow space. When Jana spoke behind him, he nearly jumped out of his socks.

"I've seen mini-marts with less merchandise."

He turned and found her inches away, leaning to one side to see past him. "Don't you ever listen to what you're told?"

"Where's the fun in that?" She edged around him toward the bottom of the U, smelling of rain-dampened flowers. "Does Mrs. Prentiss still alphabetize everything?"

"She doesn't alphabetize." Trying to shake her scent loose, he backed away and came up hard against a shelf full of pasta. "She just organizes it to make it easier for me to make a meal."

"Like boxed mac and cheese or canned chili? There they are."

She went up on tiptoe to snag the saltines from the top shelf. But the shelf heights accommodated his six-foot-four frame, not Jana's five-six height. Wannabe five-footer Mrs. Prentiss used a stepladder to off-load groceries onto the highest shelves.

All Jana managed to accomplish was another apparent bout of dizziness that tipped her toward him. Her hands slapped against his chest for balance as he gripped her shoulders. He had a three-second grace period to enjoy the feel of her hands clutching his henley before he got a good look at her face. This time she was even greener about the gills.

As she sagged against him, he lifted her carefully into his arms. She whacked him on the chest and said feebly, "Put me down."

He kept walking out to the living room. "I'd just as soon you not upchuck on my floor."

Her throat worked as she swallowed. "I might do the honors on your shirt."

He put her on the sofa, then emptied the small plastic wastebasket Mrs. Prentiss kept tucked under an end table. He thrust the wastebasket into Jana's hands. "Be right back with the crackers."

His stocking feet nearly went out from under him when he hit the kitchen, the slippery tile color-coordinated to the travertine entryway. Snatching up the saltines, he retraced his steps, then stopped short in the doorway as the sound of Jana being sick reached his ears.

If he knew Jana, the last thing she'd want would be a witness to her indignity. Cracker box tucked under his arm, he went back into the kitchen, tore a couple paper towels off the roll and wet them at the sink. Then he brought the towels and saltines out to Jana.

Lolling against the sofa back with her eyes shut, she had the wastebasket propped on her knees. He took it without comment, handing her the paper towels and dropping the crackers on the coffee table, then took the mess to the guest bathroom for cleanup. When he returned, she was swiping her face with the towel.

"You want to rinse your mouth?" She nodded in response to his query. "Can you make it to the bathroom?" Another nod.

He helped her to her feet; then when she shook off his hand, he let her go on her own speed to the bathroom. She walked the short distance carefully, as if she expected the floor to tilt at any moment.

If not for the math he'd done earlier, Jana's illness would have worried him. Not that he wasn't wrestling with some class-A anxiety, considering the likely reality of her situation, but he'd had a little prep on just this kind of female condition. Tony had just regaled him about how his wife,

Rebecca, had had her first bout of morning sickness just last weekend. Sam would have begged off on hearing all the gory details, but he knew how excited the couple were about the baby.

When Jana emerged from the bathroom, she didn't look much more cheerful, but her color was a little better. The problem was, instead of letting her flop onto the sofa, he wanted to pull her back into his arms, cradle her on his lap. Maybe even press a kiss against her forehead.

What the hell was wrong with him? Faith's departure, never mind that he instigated it, must have impacted him worse than he'd thought. Otherwise he wouldn't be entertaining such crazy ideas about Jana.

He waited until she'd seated herself cross-legged on the sofa, then took the recliner for himself. She scooped the box of crackers from the table and took her time tearing open the end flap. She took the same deliberate care in ripping open the packet of saltines.

A cracker in her hand, she eyed him warily. "I'm pregnant."

"So I gathered." He helped himself to a cracker. Just to be sociable, not because he could brush her fingers in the process. "So where's Ian? I presume he's the proud papa."

"Not so proud." She finished her cracker and plucked out another. "When he got the news, he left skid marks in the carpet while running out the door." Her laugh was hollow. "Believe it or not, neither one of us had ever been with anyone else. I guess he couldn't handle hitting the jackpot with his first relationship."

A compulsion filled Sam to pound the feckless boy into the ground. He tended to limit homicide to the pages of his books, but he could make an exception for Ian.

With an effort, he kept his tone light. "So you got tired of Portland, Oregon, and came home."

"It was either that or live in my car." She smiled, but he didn't miss the desperation in her brown eyes. "The pub I was working at closed. Couldn't afford the apartment without Ian. Not that he was helping a whole heck of a lot."

Sam's murderous impulse transformed into an icy rage. He remembered Ian as a bit of a slacker, mid-twenties with no discernible goals in sight. Maybe not one hundred percent dependable, but to cut and run, leaving Jana holding the bag, was despicable.

"Any idea where he is now?" Sam asked, teeth clenched, jaw aching.

"Not a clue. Midwest somewhere? Maybe back with his family in Indiana." Second cracker finished, she set aside the packet and fixed her gaze on him. "I'm dead broke, Sam, and in big trouble. A buck-fifty in my pocket, two months pregnant and sick as a dog."

His heart squeezed tightly in his chest. Over the fourteen-plus years he'd known her, she had asked him for almost nothing. Even now, she was hanging tough, doing her best to hide the panic that seeped around the edges. But she was all but on her knees here. And she'd come to him. Not Tony, not Estelle or Rebecca. Him.

It took almost more willpower than he possessed to resist throwing his arms around her. That kind of sappy comforting would only acknowledge that he saw her weakness. So he stayed in his chair, linking his hands in his lap to keep from reaching for her.

"What is it you need?" he asked.

She hunched in on herself a little bit. "After the way I walked out on Tony, left him in the lurch…" The first threads of tears stitched her words. "I just can't face him on my own. I thought if you went with me, talked to Tony, he'd give me my job back. Give me a place to stay."

"With the Estelle's House program." A stone settled in the pit of his stomach. "At the ranch."

Hope lit her face. "I'll bunk with one of the students if I have to. Take a cut in pay. Anything."

"Jana." He did take her hand then. "There have been some changes since you left. The work you were doing… the kids do that now. Rebecca's taking care of fund-raising. Estelle fills in as needed. Your job is gone."

"But I could stay at the ranch… Maybe find a job in town…"

"Every bed is filled, and then some. Estelle's sharing with Ruby in the main house. There'd be no place to put you."

Her eyes welled; her hand trembled. "Sam, I've got nowhere else to go." Tears spilled down her cheeks.

Shaking her head in denial, she yanked her hand free and jumped to her feet. Swiping the wetness from her eyes, she took off across the foyer, fumbling for her purse, groping for the door. He caught her before she could turn the knob.

At first she resisted, slapping his chest to get free of him. Then she tumbled into his arms and sobbed her heart out.

God, he wanted to bottle her pain and throw it far out into the ocean. Where he'd felt maybe an ounce of sympathy for Faith when she'd opened that jewelry box, he staggered under the weight of Jana's sorrow. Where he wouldn't in a million years want Faith back, he overflowed with gratitude that this quirky, wise-mouthed friend had returned home.

"We'll work it out, kid," he murmured. "We'll find a way to make it right."

Chapter Two

Jana didn't know why she'd expected anything different, considering the hell-in-a-handbasket mode her life had been in the past couple months. Really, it had been all downhill since she'd walked out on Tony and the Estelle's House program last Labor Day weekend to run off with Ian. Of the four months since then, she'd had maybe one good week before her rat boyfriend showed his true, lazy colors.

This was no way to start her homecoming, no matter how good it felt to have Sam's arms around her. She had to claim some space, get her head clear so she could figure out what the heck she'd do next. She'd never manage it with Sam thinking he had to save her just like his Trent Garner character would save the world in one of his thriller novels.

Palms pressed against Sam's chest, she pushed away from him, closing her mind to the feel of hard muscle under soft knit. He'd hugged her plenty of times, when she was a skinny ten-year-old brat, when she was a hormone-crazed teen, and more recently during those far-and-few-between visits he made to the ranch. She'd felt nothing but kindness in the gesture all these years, never mind how she'd fantasized about something more when she was a starry-eyed sixteen-year-old and he was twenty-seven. She'd given up that adolescent dream years ago. She reminded herself that now, just as he had then, he just wanted to comfort her.

Feeling as wrung out as a tatty old rag, she returned to the sofa and collapsed into its deep cushions. Her mind was numb with exhaustion. She had to figure out what to do next, but she didn't have the energy to put two brain cells together.

She scrubbed at her face. "If you could just give me a few minutes, I'll get out of your way."

He switched on a table lamp, illuminating the storm-darkened living room. God, he looked good, even in holey jeans and a plain knit shirt, his overlong hair in need of a good cut.

Sitting in the recliner, he leaned toward her, elbows on his knees, large hands linked. "It's pouring rain. Not exactly traveling weather."

"I'll figure out something." She wanted so much to take his hand, hold tight against the torrent inside her.

"When are you due?" he asked quietly.

"End of July." Seven long months filled with a thousand unknowns waiting to trip her up.

"And then?" he asked.

This was the place she didn't like going to. Because it stole her breath, stabbed her heart with hot regret. Unplanned or not, fathered by a jerk or not, this was beyond unbearable.

She tried to say it as if it were a matter of little concern, except it tore her voice into shreds. "Then I give the baby up for adoption."

She waited for him to argue with her. Tell her she was a terrible person to give her baby away. She glanced over at him sidelong when he didn't speak. "I have to. I'm twenty-four years old. No job, no money, no education. I can't support a child."

He continued to stare at her for long silent moments. Outside, the wind picked up, howling through the trees. A dark, lonely sound.

Finally, he spoke. "If you think it's best, for you and the baby, that's what you should do."

His acceptance of her decision only made her feel worse. The thought of pushing to her feet, walking out the door and to her car utterly overwhelmed her. She'd left her jacket on the porch rail. It would be soaked by now. No protection against the deluge.

Nevertheless, she reached down deep for the strength to get up. Might have made it if not for one large hand closing around hers, keeping her on the sofa.

"You're not going out in that," he told her. When she would have protested, he put a finger to her mouth. "You're staying here, in the downstairs bedroom. Tomorrow morning, we'll figure out what happens next."

She tried not to focus on where he was touching her. The warm contact took her mind on a one-way trip to crazy. "It's my mess, Sam. I have to be the one to take care of it."

"I'm just giving you a place to sleep tonight, not a

solution to your problems. You're welcome to work that out on your own."

Except even as Sam said it, Jana could just about see the wheels turning in his head. He was a rescuer, had been since he was a boy, according to Estelle. He'd bring home stray dogs, lost kittens. As an adult, he gave buckets of money to Tony's independent living program, helping Tony rescue aged-out foster kids instead of cuddly kittens.

She was pretty sure that somewhere in that awesome brain, he was ticking away, coming up with a way to save her from herself. It was tempting to let him—she knew she was just as much a first-class screwup as her mom. But her mother, who had flitted from one crisis to the next, waiting for some man to fall at her feet and fix everything, had been beautiful and a born charmer. Jana had no illusions she had the womanly wiles to lure any man.

Jana pulled free, unfolding herself from the sofa. Immediately light-headed, she teetered, falling against the rock that was Sam. He actually picked her up in his arms again, just like in his book *Crash* when Trent Garner swept the heroine off her feet to save her from the bad guys. Except the heroine wasn't mortified the way Jana was. Probably didn't feel like upchucking either.

He carried her to the downstairs bedroom and laid her on the bed. Level and motionless, she managed to ward off the nausea. Last thing she wanted was a repeat of her earlier indignity.

He pulled off her still-damp sneakers, then covered her with the comforter folded at the foot of the bed. "Take a nap. We'll talk about this when you wake up."

She wanted to argue the point, would have if she could have kept her stomach under control. Not to mention that when she started feeling cozy under the thick comforter, her eyes got so heavy she didn't have a prayer of keeping them open. She'd have to let him win this one. She could leave later, when she was rested. Walk out to the car and say her goodbyes. Later…

Sam waited until her breathing grew even and deep and her body relaxed. Then he left her, reckoning the more distance he put between them the better. She'd felt too damn good cradled in his arms when he'd carried her, her hair sweetly scented by the rain, her body warm against his. When he started contemplating pulling off her jeans—because they were damp and mud-splattered—he knew he had no business staying in that room.

He had to keep her here, at least for the night. She wasn't an idiot and would probably see the logic of putting off her next steps until the weather cleared. If she gave him guff, he'd call Estelle and let her talk some sense into Jana.

Maybe if he brought her things into the house, that would be an extra inducement to stay. She'd want to change out of her damp, muddy clothes anyway. With any luck, she'd left her little Honda Civic unlocked so he could carry in her suitcase and whatever.

Of course, it could be she had her keys stuffed in the pocket of her jeans and he might be able to fish them out without waking her. His mind fixated on that possibility, displaying a full-color video of him reaching under those warm covers, fingering his way inside her pocket.

He clamped a lid on those images, marching himself over to the entryway for his boots and rain gear. Outside, he circled around to the far side of the garage and stared in confusion at the battered white sedan there. What happened to the late model red Civic she'd left here in last September? He'd cosigned the loan to help her buy it, and she'd been damn proud of the car.

Had she wrecked it? His stomach clenched at the thought of her being in an accident, especially in her current condition.

At least the beater was unlocked. During a quick look through the passenger cabin, he didn't find much. A sweater and a pair of sandals were tossed on the backseat alongside a half-dozen scattered paperbacks—all of them his books. All of them dog-eared, likely from multiple readings.

A plastic market bag under the driver's seat gave him a place to stash the books, sweater and shoes. He popped the trunk and found a small duffel bag, an even-smaller cosmetic bag and a box filled with books. A DVD with a cracked case was wedged in the box—an adaptation of his first novel and his favorite of the six that had made it into film.

The day he'd received his prerelease copy of the movie from his agent, he'd taken it to Estelle's. A rainy Saturday afternoon in February. Jana was there, helping Estelle ride herd on three new foster girls as they cleaned house.

Jana, fourteen and skinny as a rail, had wisecracked that the lead actor wore a toupee and she hoped he didn't lose it in the action scenes. But when they'd all sat down to watch it, she'd been enthralled, grabbing his hand during the high climax, holding on so tightly he'd thought his fingers would pop off.

When the movie had officially came out on DVD, he'd given her a copy, had autographed the cover. She'd made a smart remark about how much she might be able to get for it at a flea market, but she'd hung on to it these past ten years. That it meant so much to her, that maybe she even treasured it, set off an ache, an emotion inside him he didn't even want to name.

With market bag and duffel hooked on his fingers, cosmetic bag on top of the box of books, he elbowed the trunk shut and hurried toward the house. If not for the books, she could have fit everything in a paper shopping bag, the luggage of choice for a foster kid. She hadn't experienced that transient, unpredictable life as he had. She'd had a mother, no matter how undependable. But he'd ended up living on a sixty-acre estate, while it seemed Jana still hadn't found her way.

She wasn't his responsibility. She was a close friend, and he did everything he could for good friends. But that didn't mean he should step into her business and try to make everything better.

Back in the house, he set aside the small pile of Jana's worldly goods and stripped off his now-soaked boots, jacket and rain pants. The quiet told him Jana was likely still sleeping, but he nevertheless checked on her. She'd rolled on her side, her silky hair just long enough to spill across her eyes. He itched to smooth it back, but besides the fact that it would tick her off if he touched her while she slept, he couldn't risk waking her when she so obviously needed her rest.

Backing from the bedroom, he climbed the stairs to the second floor. His office overlooked the slope leading down to the creek; with the windows open, he could hear the rush of water below. Oaks, pines and cedars crowded the banks on either side, red-barked manzanita filling the spaces in between. Sometimes, when he drew a blank on what dark hellhole to next send Trent Garner into, he'd gaze out the windows, watch hawks circle in the sky or deer leap through the trees.

Sitting at his desk, he punched in Tony's number. Rebecca answered, laughter in her voice. "Estelle's House."

"It's Sam."

She giggled, then whispered, "Tony, stop it," before returning to the phone. "Sorry, Sam. Tony's not behaving. I'm guessing it's him you want to talk to."

As she handed over the phone, he heard more laughter, then more scolding before Tony came on the line. "How's it going?" Tony asked, his happiness evident in his voice. Tony's life had been one hard-luck story after another, but since his and Rebecca's remarriage and her pregnancy, he was a changed man.

Sam had no right feeling any kind of envy for his friend. Sam had a hundred times more than many people had—a burning hot career as a thriller novelist, a gorgeous home, a garage full of high-ticket automobiles. His pick of women. But sometimes Sam felt he'd give anything for Tony's riches—his wife, Rebecca; his five-year-old daughter, Lea; and their baby-to-be.

"Sam?" Tony prodded.

Sam returned his attention to the phone. "A little something has come up. Jana's back."

A few moments of silence ticked away. "How is she?"

"Pregnant." He told Tony the rest of it, how she'd turned up on his doorstep with barely more than a junker car and the clothes on her back.

"Where's Ian?" Tony asked.

"The father of the year is AWOL. She was hoping I

could intervene to get her position back at the ranch." Before Tony could state the obvious, Sam added, "I told her how things have changed."

"You know I'd help her if I could," Tony said. "But once they all arrive, we'll have double the participants we had the first session. There'll be students stuffed away in every nook and cranny on the ranch."

"We could build another modular." They'd added two to the property when they ran out of space in the existing structures.

"To be honest, I don't think the teens in the program can stand the disruption. They've been arriving since the day after Christmas, a tough time of the year for any foster."

Sam had lived that heartbreak, had the scars to prove it. Before he could stop himself, his mind drifted to his secret folly, the Christmas shop. In his imagination, it was filled to the rafters with glittering ornaments and decorated trees. A tree for every year after his mother left.

Sam shut the door on the past as Tony snagged his focus again. "Not to mention Becca's pregnancy just about has her whipped."

"No worries. Jana's safe here for the moment."

He said his goodbyes, then listened again for any sign that Jana was stirring. All quiet below. At loose ends, he went through his e-mail, replied to a query from his agent about a radio interview, skimmed several dozen notes from fans. Three were from aspiring writers he'd met at conferences or signings, and he felt a twinge of guilt that he hadn't yet replied.

His agent had suggested he hire an assistant, but that was another to-do he'd yet to cross off his list. He didn't like the thought of letting someone into as intimate a part of himself as his writing life. How could he trust handling his fans to a total stranger?

The idea that blindsided him was so brilliant he felt like a doofus for not thinking of it sooner. Who could he better trust than Jana? She already knew the stories of some of the budding writers he was mentoring—the twenty-two-year-old kid whose raw talent had knocked Sam's socks off, the seventysomething grandma who'd written a devious and hilarious cozy mystery.

Could he persuade her to take the job? It wasn't really full-time work, and even a fair wage wouldn't be enough to live on. Maybe if he padded her salary…

Outside, the drenched day had darkened to black. He wandered back downstairs to see what he could scare up for dinner. The doorway to the room where Jana slept might as well have been a magnet, pulling him off his intended path. He only lingered there a few moments, watching her chest rise and fall, thanking God she was here and safe.

His quick scan of the refrigerator told him what it usually did—that he didn't know a damn thing about cooking. Rebecca, Tony's wife and the head cooking instructor at Estelle's House, could throw together a feast using air and fairy dust. His lone specialty was scrambled eggs and toast. Maybe if he added sliced oranges like they did at restaurants, he could call it a complete meal.

He laid out the eggs, bread and fruit on the granite-topped island, then checked the clock. Five-thirty. Should he wake Jana? Let her sleep herself out?

On his way back to the living room, the phone ringing made the decision for him. He dove for the handset on the coffee table, but there was little chance the bedroom extension hadn't rung in Jana's ear. Then it turned out to be a wrong number.

As he set down the phone, Jana emerged, sleepy-eyed, from the bedroom. Her pale blue sweater was rucked up on one side, revealing nothing more than the elastic waist of her jeans. He imagined sliding the hem up that one more inch necessary to bare her smooth skin.

Then she tugged the sweater down, and he gave himself a mental slap. "Are you hungry?"

"Sick as a dog," she said. "Which means I better eat. That's the only time I feel human."

Her attention strayed to the pile of belongings he'd arranged beside the entryway. Color rose in her cheeks, anger and shame warring in her face. "What are you doing bringing my things in here?"

"I wasn't sure what you'd need, so I just brought it all."

"I never said I was staying." She strode across the living room to the entryway. "Did you go through it all?"

He could feel heat rise in his face even though he hadn't touched a thing. "I just carried it from the car. What happened to the Honda?"

She zipped open her duffel, pushed aside the clothes piled on top. "I let Ian talk me into selling it for some extra cash."

He caught a glimpse of a stack of papers held together with a rubber band in the duffel. Then she dropped a pair of skimpy red panties onto the tiled entryway, short-circuiting his brain. The image of Jana in those panties played out in Technicolor in his mind.

Faith had only been gone a week. Between his travel, her travel and the writing on the wall, it had been at least a month since they'd slept together. Was he that sex-deprived to be lusting after Jana? When she'd been nothing but a buddy to him before now?

With barely a glance at them, Jana stuffed the panties back in the duffel and thankfully out of sight. Taking her time, she got to her feet, duffel hooked over her shoulder. She snagged the cosmetics bag with her other hand. She looked ready to walk out the door.

He stepped into her path. "Don't be stupid, just because I pissed you off."

For a moment she looked as if she wanted to blast him. But then she took a breath, her chin tipping up in defiance. "I'll stay. But just for tonight." Shoulders flung back, cosmetic bag and duffel clutched to her chest, she snatched the packet of crackers from the coffee table and retreated into the bedroom.

Once she'd shut the door behind her, Jana tossed the duffel onto the bed and grabbed a handful of crackers. Stuffing a saltine into her mouth, she ferried the cosmetic bag to the adjacent bathroom. She was pretty desperate for food, but a hot shower sounded too good to pass up, especially since Sam had brought in a change of clothes for her. The crackers would tide her over.

Thank God he hadn't seen the letters. She'd managed to hold on to them for ten-plus years, had kept them safe from Ian's prying eyes for four months. Not an easy task when her donkey butt boyfriend wasn't the least ashamed of opening her mail or digging through her dresser drawer in search of a check or some ready cash.

The duffel had a reinforced bottom that lifted out; she slipped the letters underneath for more security. Good thing she hadn't left them under the seat or Sam might have found them when he did his Trent Garner-style search of her car. Bad enough he saw she'd saved the movie and every autographed book he'd ever given her.

Despite the beginnings of queasiness, the hot shower felt amazing. She scrubbed herself twice, squeezing out every last drop of shampoo to make sure her hair was squeaky clean. Ian always had dibs on the shower before her, and by the time she had gotten in, there was never anything left but lukewarm water.

Wrapping herself in a thick bath sheet with another towel around her head, she knelt to search the cabinet for the hair dryer. There had been one in here when she'd house-sat last May, although as short as her hair was then, she'd never used it. Sam must have moved it.

Padding barefoot through the bedroom, she cracked open the door and called out, "Sam."

Music blasted from the kitchen, the Eagles rocking out a song about heartache. Wasn't that the story of her life.

Sam must not have heard her over Glen Frey. She edged out the door, gripping the bath sheet more tightly. The towel on her head slipped, falling to her shoulders, then to the floor.

She stopped about halfway to the kitchen and shouted over the din of the music. "Sam!" When there was still no response, she filled her lungs with air for another try.

She screamed his name just as he switched off the music. An instant later, Sam came flying out of the kitchen. Closing the space between them, he threw his arms around her and pulled her off her feet.

Flinging her hands out for balance, she lost her grip on the bath sheet. Now the only thing holding it up was the pressure of his body against hers.

Chapter Three

Well, wasn't this an adolescent boy's fantasy. Except he was twenty years past that overheated time of life and the fragrant, delectable female in his arms was Jana. Pregnant, good-buddy-and-not-his-girlfriend Jana.

He started to release her, but she tightened her hold on him. "Wait," she gasped. "The towel."

A downward glance revealed the source of her distress. The bath sheet had loosened, and now hung precariously just above her breasts. Or rather, just above that part of her breasts that had likely hooked it and slowed its descent.

Damn it, don't think about her nipples. Except that was all he could think about now.

"I'll close my eyes," he told her, "and you can fix it."

He not only closed them, he covered them with his hands. He waited as he heard her shift, then walk away from him, presumably in the direction of the bedroom.

"Okay," she said, sounding breathless. She stood in the bedroom doorway, half-hidden by the door.

"When you yelled like that, I thought something bad had happened."

Her cheeks, already red, flamed even brighter. "I just needed the hair dryer. You used to keep it under the sink."

"Faith took it when we split."

"Faith?" she asked. "What happened to Shawna?"

"She left," he said cautiously.

Jana's gaze narrowed on him. "You mean you showed her the door. Like Cyndy. And Patricia. What'd you give Shawna? The emerald choker? Or the tennis bracelet?"

His cheeks burned. "There's another hair dryer in my room. I'll get it for you."

He took the stairs two at a time, feeling as if he was outrunning every one of Jana's unspoken accusations. He didn't know why it was any of her damn business how many girlfriends he'd sent packing. As long as it wasn't her he was kicking to the curb.

He stumbled in his bedroom doorway, knees weak at the thought of sending Jana away. She was the only one in his life, Tony and Estelle included, that he felt he could tell just about anything to. Which was why she had an inventory of every girlfriend to whom he'd bid au revoir.

He stared at himself in the bathroom mirror, wincing against the glare of the track lighting. He just wasn't ready to settle down. Yeah, he was thirty-five, past the age that many men married. But with Shawna, Patricia, Cyndy and Faith, with all their predecessors, he'd start sensing their first steps over that invisible line. The one between fun and games and commitment. And inside him a door would slam shut. Then it was time to call his jeweler.

Digging out the hair dryer from the back of one of the bathroom cabinets, he carried it downstairs. Jana was still waiting by the door, shivering a little.

She snatched the hair dryer from him and shut the door with a muffled "Thanks."

Sam returned to the kitchen. He switched on the Eagles again but toned down the volume. The eggs were cracked in a bowl and ready to scramble, the oranges sliced and ready to put on the plates. Digging around in the freezer, he'd unearthed the chocolate cake he'd tried to forget was there. No reason he and Jana couldn't enjoy it tonight, he'd thought as he'd set it out on the counter to defrost.

Jana's fragrance seemed to drift in before she did. In her stocking feet, she wore another pair of jeans and a pink sweatshirt with a surly looking pig on the front. The slogan across the shirt read Give Me the Latte and Nobody Gets Hurt.

She caught him reading it. "Thrift store. I gave up caffeine when the stick turned blue."

"Have a seat. I'll scramble the eggs."

She tore a slice of bread in two and inhaled half of it. Mouth full, she held up a finger to stop him, then went to the refrigerator. She collected a block of cheese, some tomatoes and an onion. In a quick circuit of the kitchen, she pulled a grater from the cupboard, unhooked a frying pan from its wrought-iron hanger and set the pan on the stove. With a flick of her wrist, she splashed olive oil into the pan and twisted on the gas.

She slapped the cheddar and the grater into his hands. "Shred it, Dano."

Before he could figure out which end of the grater to use, she was chopping the onion and dicing the tomato. The onion fell into the pan with a sharp sizzle, filling the kitchen with an incredible aroma.

Sam juggled the grater and block of cheddar with much less grace. "Looks like you picked up a few tricks from Rebecca." Tony's wife taught kitchen skills as part of the independent living program.

"A few." Jana glanced at him over her shoulder as she flipped the browning onions in the pan. "But I cooked for my mother more often than she cooked for me. It was a matter of survival."

A respectable pile of golden shreds had accumulated on the cutting board and he'd only nicked himself twice. "This enough?" he asked.

She set the frying pan on the granite countertop. "Looks good. Grab me one of those small cereal bowls."

He turned to the cupboard, staring in indecision. "Which ones are cereal bowls?" Behind him, Jana laughed, her amusement putting a smile on his own face even though the joke was at his expense.

"You don't ever use your own kitchen, do you?"

"I nuke stuff in the microwave sometimes. I know where the forks are." He opened a cupboard at random and found neat rows of water glasses. Next door were platters the size of Alaska and bowls big enough to bathe in.

"To your left. No, farther left."

He finally put his hand on the requested item and set it on the counter. She scraped the cooked onions into it, then returned the pan to the stove.

As the oil heated up again, she nibbled on the rest of the slice of bread. "You can start the toast."

"Finally, something I'm competent at."

She laughed again, and the light in her eyes stole the

breath from his lungs. Something burned in his chest; he couldn't tell if it was pain or joy. Either way, he knew it was trouble. Thank God this was just Jana and not a member of his girlfriend parade.

As she poured the scrambled eggs into the hot oil, he kept his attention on the four-slice toaster, lowering the bread, fidgeting with the doneness knob. Anything to stuff down those baffling feelings toward Jana that kept wanting to bubble up.

As he buttered the first of the four slices, Jana tossed cheese, onions and tomatoes into the pan. "Plates in the same cupboard as the bowls."

"I knew that." He set two out onto the counter for her. Using the spatula, she cut the perfect golden omelet in two and served up half on each plate. Sam added the toast and orange circles.

They took their plates to the breakfast nook, a half-octagonal room walled with windows. It was dead-black night out now, nothing visible beyond the white rail of the wraparound porch.

Jana settled in her chair with a sigh, grabbing a slice of toast even as she scooted toward the table. "I forgot milk. I'm supposed to have at least one glass a day."

"I'll get it." Two months pregnant and she'd made dinner for him. The least he could do was bring her something to drink.

He set two glasses of milk on the table, then took his first bite of omelet. "I think I've died and gone to heaven."

"Just eggs and cheese, Sam." But she seemed pleased by the compliment, which set off that glow inside him again.

He directed his thoughts back to the brilliant idea that had visited him earlier. "I think I have the answer to both our problems."

She swallowed a mouthful of omelet. "You have a problem?"

Certainly not one he'd given much thought to until this evening. "You could work as my assistant. Respond to e-mail, get me organized. Make my travel plans, my appointments."

"I thought you already hired an assistant."

"I never got around to it." He scraped his fingers through his hair, the overgrown length of it irritating him. "I get a million e-mail messages every day that need dealing with, a big stack of letters every week."

She gave him an assessing look. "You desperately need a haircut."

"See what I mean? I never remember to call the stylist. You could go through my e-mail, sort it all out for me. Tell me what I should deal with personally, handle the stuff I don't need to. It's plenty of work. You'd earn your salary."

Her gaze narrowed. "How much?"

Feeling like a deer in the headlights, he blurted out a figure. Her jaw dropped; then anger flashed in her eyes. "That's too much."

"It isn't the only work I want you to do for me." The words spilled out in a rush.

There was no missing the suspicion in Jana's face. "You're making this up as you go along, aren't you?"

Heat rose in his cheeks. "Not all of it."

"My life isn't one of your books, Sam. You can't just write me into your stories."

Damn straight. The characters in his stories were much better behaved than Jana.

So what else could he have her do? What would keep

her busy enough to satisfy her pride, so she'd be willing to let him pay her what he wanted to pay her?

The notion that coalesced in his mind didn't seem nearly as brilliant. Because it pried open a door he still wasn't ready to crack, even for Jana.

But as he rolled it around, he had to admit it was probably an ideal solution. Flicking a glance at Jana, he took the leap. "There's a project I've been working on."

Her plate clean, she leaned back in her chair, nibbling the last triangle of toast. "A writing project?"

He shook his head. "I bought a storefront in Camino. A gift shop, pretty successful until the owner got sick. It's a wreck now, needs a ton of work before it can open again."

"You're going to run a gift shop?" She swiped her mouth with a paper napkin, missing a crumb of toast. His mind temporarily jumped the tracks as he contemplated brushing that crumb from her bottom lip.

He shifted his brain back into gear. "I thought that eventually the Estelle's House kids can run it. For now, you could help me get it ready. Supervise the foster teens when they come into the picture."

She nodded. "Sounds good. Gives them experience in a different kind of business than food service."

Her approval warmed him, but now came the dicey part. In all the heart-to-hearts he'd had with Jana, he'd managed to omit any details of his time before he arrived at Estelle's. No one but Estelle knew about how his world had ended that December night.

He looked at Jana sidelong, not wanting to face her. Just in case she laughed. "I was thinking of turning it into a Christmas store. You know, Christmas decorations available year-round."

Her brow furrowed. "Just Christmas stuff?"

Defensiveness put an edge on his tone. "I like Christmas. Lots of people like Christmas."

"Sure they do. Me, too. Still…"

Was she going to press him? Ask him to explain? Well, he wasn't going there, not even with Jana.

She gazed at him thoughtfully, then set her crumpled napkin on the plate. "Even if I worked for you, I can't stay here."

He let out a breath he hadn't even realized he was holding. "You wouldn't have to. There's a small apartment above the shop. Needs work, too, so you would have to bunk here for a few days until we could get it livable. But it's got a small kitchen, a bathroom, sleeping area."

She nodded. "That could work."

Relief and anxiety warred within him. As glad as he was that she was considering staying in the area and working for him, he was already regretting the impulse to include her in the plans for the shop. Until now, he could have backed out on the idea any time. Now he felt committed.

He shoved back his chair, grabbed their plates and empty glasses. He slotted the plates and glasses into the dishwasher. "You could stay there rent-free, plus I'd pay you."

Leaning against the dishwasher, hands gripping the cold edge of the granite countertop, he watched her. In that moment, he wasn't even sure if he wanted her to say yes or no. After all, they could find her an apartment in Sacramento, and he could help her with the rent. His friend Darius, a private investigator, could maybe come up with some busy work for her in his Sacramento office. Darius ran a small operation, with only one investigator besides himself, but Sam could pay Jana's salary under the table.

Except, besides the dishonesty of it, he didn't want her fifty miles away in Sacramento. He wanted her close by, under his nose so he could make sure she was taking care of herself. If she was down in Sac, he'd be worrying about her every day. He had to balance that with the risk of her discovering more about him, and his motive for buying the shop, than he wanted her to learn.

Wariness still tightened her mouth with tension. "Why would you do this, Sam?"

He groped for a response. "You're a friend, Jana. Shouldn't I take care of my friends?"

She laid her hand against her still-flat belly. "I don't have a whole lot of choices. I can't live on the street until July."

"I would never let you do that."

For an instant, he thought he saw the glimmer of tears. Then she glanced out the window, face hidden as she stared into the darkness.

"Fine. I'll take the job." She pushed to her feet. "Jobs. Both of them."

Another knife of anxiety speared through him. "Great."

"Until the baby's born and maybe a little after, if that's okay. In the fall I'll want to start classes at the junior college down in Folsom. I'll probably need to get a job down there."

That she'd be here only until September set off a twang inside him. "You can stay as long as you want."

"Then I'll start cleaning up the apartment tomorrow."

"We can do it together."

Frying pan in one hand and spatula in the other, she elbowed past him on the way to the sink. "Don't you have a deadline or something?"

"I have a month off before I start my next book." When

she gave him a fishy look, he raised his hands, palms out. "Gospel truth. You can call my agent and ask him."

Jana shrugged, then started swishing some soapy water in the frying pan. "We'll go over together, then. Get the work done quicker." She tossed him a look over her shoulder. "So I can get out of your way faster."

She rinsed the pan and spatula and set them in the drainer. The bowls they'd used for dinner prep she loaded into the dishwasher. He would have stepped in to do it himself if he wasn't sure she'd bite his head off at the shoulders.

Finished with washing up, she dried her hands on a kitchen towel. "What's with the cake?"

"Birthday cake from last October. Faith made it for me."

"Oh."

"It's been in the freezer ever since. We kept meaning to pull it out and share the rest of it."

"But she got the Rolex and the kiss-off instead."

He squirmed at Jana's near nose-on assessment. "It was a tennis bracelet."

She grinned and tossed the kitchen towel aside. Then her grin faded as worry put shadows under her eyes. "It's the right thing to do, isn't it? Having the baby, giving it up for adoption."

A dozen bromides flitted through his brain. If Jana were a character in one of his stories, he'd have any number of comforting lines to feed her.

But this was real life. He couldn't lie. "I don't know, Jana."

Tears glimmered in her eyes. Without thinking, he pressed his hand against her face. A teardrop escaped, trailing down her cheek as she stared up at him.

That was as far as he should have taken it. Except she took that last step and wrapped her arms around his waist. All the times he'd hugged her, held her, it had felt like friendship. But today, right now, she was a woman in his arms.

That didn't mean he had to let his mind wander along any of those crazy paths temptation suggested. She only needed his comfort, just as she had dozens of times over the years.

But then she looked up at him, eyes wide, lips parting, breath hitching in her throat. A devil perched on his shoulder, calling out instructions, goading him into doing something he damn well shouldn't do. Not when it was Jana in his arms, hurting and confused.

Then her eyes drifted shut. The sight of those delicate lids, the way she'd tipped her face up to his, blew all his good intentions out of the water. All he could think about were her lips and lowering his mouth to hers.

Chapter Four

Holy crap, what was she doing?

Getting all wussy and teary and all but falling into Sam's arms. Yeah, her heart just about felt split in two every time she thought about handing over her baby to someone else, but that didn't give her the right to hang all over Sam, expect him to fix everything for her. She was acting just like her mother used to.

And tipping her head back, closing her eyes—she wasn't asking him to plant a big wet one on her, was she? Even though the world would have tipped end over end on its axis before it crossed Sam's mind to lip-lock with her. Even though getting him to kiss her was exactly what her mother would do. Step one, get a man to make your problems go away. Step two…

Open your eyes, Jana ordered herself. Except now she was terrified to look, afraid of the expression she'd see on

Sam's face. Complete bewilderment, most likely. Or even worse, embarrassment.

She pulled out of his arms, escaping the warm circle of his embrace with her eyes still shut. She opened them as she turned on her heel, the move upsetting her fragile equilibrium. Dizziness washed over her, goading her to reach for Sam. No chance she'd tiptoe into that sand trap again. She grabbed for the island instead, gripping cool granite as she slid a sidelong glance toward him.

He was rubbing the side of his face, maybe trying to figure out what the heck had just happened. Worry creased his brow. Her sissy tears had probably put those lines there. With confusion spinning a hamster wheel in her stomach, inexplicable tears still clawing the back of her throat, she stretched her mouth into a smile.

"I'm dead on my feet." She sidled along the island, keeping it between them. "You mind if I give Faith's wonder cake a pass?"

His X-ray stare bored through her. "Are you okay?"

"Great. Just tired." With a sketchy wave, she scooted from the kitchen. He called her name, but she wasn't about to turn around again.

She heard his footsteps behind her but had the door to the guest room shut before he caught up. Nausea, regret and grief braided themselves into an intricate knot inside her as she pushed herself toward the bed. She shucked her jeans and climbed under the covers, reaching up to shut off the bedside lamp before curling into a ball.

She still had to brush her teeth and pee. After her nap, she wasn't really all that sleepy anyway. But she felt torn apart in a million directions, even though she had no right to feel that way. She had a job and a place to stay. The huge weight that had ridden piggyback all the way here from Portland had taken a hike. But there was still all this emotional junk floating around inside of her that made no sense.

It all revolved around Sam and the moment she thought she wanted him to kiss her. It made her cringe inside, not just because he'd think she was still that fourteen-year-old kid with a crush on him, but also because of her mother.

She never wanted to be like her mother, always finagling the men in her life to solve her problems. Then came the payoff—a few days or weeks or sometimes months of mattress wrestling before she sent her savior on his way.

Yuck. Jana had sworn she would never live her life that way. She might be the world's worst screwup—she had to admit she'd inherited that crappy set of genes from her mother—but she wasn't bartering her way out of anything with sex.

Now, scrunched up in bed, she replayed that impulse to kiss Sam. Did she have more in common with her mother than she wanted to admit? Sam gives her what she needs— boom, give the boy a smooch. She could even see the same pattern with Ian. She'd been longing for someone to see her as special, to care about her and only her. Ian put on his show of love, and within days she was tumbling into his bed.

Her skin crawled at the thought, her nausea deepening. She gritted her teeth, bound and determined not to lose the meal she'd just shared with Sam. Gulping in a breath, she managed to get her stomach to settle somewhat.

She didn't care how strong a grip her mother's genetics had on her DNA. No way, no how was Jana going to mess things up with Sam. He was her all-time best friend in the world. She would die if she stepped over the line, made some stupid pass at him and destroyed their friendship.

KAREN SANDLER   47

Pushing back the covers, she padded into the bathroom to take care of business. She still didn't feel very sleepy, so she dug through the box of books Sam had brought in. She'd read them all more than once, but she could always find something new each time through.

She found the one he'd given her for her twelfth birthday. Angling the book up to the bedside lamp, she turned to the title page. Above his signature he'd inscribed, "Jana, try to stay out of trouble." Advice well worth following.

Settling back against the pillows, she turned to the book's prologue and immediately immersed herself in the story. Just past midnight, when even the riveting story couldn't keep her eyes from drifting shut, she dropped the paperback on the bed and switched off the light. Her dreams were full of Sam—as Trent Garner. It was just like a movie, Sam chasing down bad guys. Except instead of fighting with a gun like Trent would, Sam threw pieces of chocolate cake.

She woke at seven, tired and cranky and more than a little bit sick to her stomach contemplating that chocolate cake. And the French toast she made for her and Sam's breakfast proved to be a bad choice. All that butter and sugary maple syrup didn't sit right. Not to mention Sam barely said a word the whole time they ate.

He continued the silent treatment as they drove into town in his 1946 Hudson pickup, with Jana gulping to keep that breakfast down. It wasn't that he seemed angry or anything. More likely she'd screwed everything up last night with that moment of weakness, and now Sam was probably too embarrassed to talk to her.

Then as he reached the last stop sign before pulling onto

Carson Road, he reached across the bench seat, took her hand and squeezed it, his quiet voice matching the stillness of the poststorm mist. "It's all going to work out, Jana."

That just made her want to cry like she had last night, which she was absolutely not going to do. She pressed her lips tightly together, gave him a squeeze back, then tugged free to drop her hand in her lap.

Sam took a side road, pulling in behind the row of businesses that lined the south side of Carson Road. He parked the Hudson behind the third building down, carefully nosing the moss-green classic truck beside a Dumpster.

"Wait," he told her as he opened the door.

He was going to help her out of the cab as if she were some kind of invalid. She felt a smidgen of pleasure at the gesture but mostly irritated that he felt the need. Squelching pleasure, she pushed open her door and jumped out before he got halfway around the back of the truck. She caught his scowl as her feet hit the asphalt pavement.

Shouldering past him to the bed of the truck, she grabbed the caddy of cleaning supplies and tucked a roll of paper towels under her arm. "Can you get the tools? Or do you need a hand?"

She saw the objections dancing in his eyes. He didn't even want her to carry the lightweight caddy, with its couple of bottles of Windex and 409. He wasn't about to let her lift a finger to tote a power tool inside.

"I've got it," he muttered, reaching in the bed for a gigantic toolbox. The way he narrowed his gaze on her, she wondered if he was assessing whether he could tuck her under his arm and carry her in as well, like a roll of paper towels.

She sidled off toward the back door. A set of stairs angled above the door, leading to a second story.

Sam headed for the stairs. "We'll want to start up here."

She followed, waiting a step or two down from the postage stamp–size landing as he opened the door. Behind her, beyond the screen of ponderosa pines, she could hear traffic whipping by on Highway 50 a quarter mile away.

"Like I told you, it's a mess," he said as he set his toolbox inside. He opened the door wider to let her in.

He wasn't kidding. The place looked more like a storage room than living quarters, with boxes piled waist-high along the walls. More boxes and trash littered the kitchen area at one end. The threadbare carpet that led down the hall was a dust bunny habitat.

But with its living room-kitchen combo maybe ten by fifteen feet in dimension, this part of the apartment wasn't a whole lot smaller than what she'd shared with Ian in Portland. And when she headed down the hall, frightening the dust bunnies into the corners, she saw that the bedroom might even be a little bit bigger.

She checked across the hall and wrinkled her nose. "The bathroom is disgusting."

Sam edged in beside her. "I'll have it gutted. Down to the studs. Replace everything with new."

She squinted up at him. "It just needs a good cleaning." With trepidation she lifted the toilet lid. "Okay, new toilet. But the rest is okay."

Sam got a mulish expression on his face. "I don't want you living in a rattrap."

"And I don't want you spending buckets of money on me." She backed out of the bathroom, again herding dust bunnies down the hallway. "It's bad enough you're giving me this place, this job. I can't let you turn it into a Jana McPartland charity case."

Towering over her in the living room, he shoved his hands into the pockets of his jeans. But as he spoke, he wouldn't quite look at her. "I would have had to fix this place up anyway."

He sounded as if he was trying to convince himself as well as her. As if he wasn't even sure himself why he'd bought this white elephant.

"A complete remodeling would take too much time," she pointed out. "I don't want to have to hang out at your place that long."

He scowled. "This bathroom looks like a toxic waste dump."

"Let me see what I can do with some cleanup. If it's still gross, you can bring in the sledgehammer."

Except she would work her fingers to the bone excavating those layers of dirt before she'd let him empty his bank account on her behalf. Okay, he'd have to plate everything in gold to put a dent in his fortune, but still.

Sam shrugged. "I'll start moving those boxes downstairs. Give us some room. We can go through them later."

He retreated down the hall, shoulders still hunched over. Jana stared after him, wondering what was bugging him. Was he having second thoughts about making the job offer now that he saw what a disaster this place was? Was he considering how to let her down easy, tell her this wasn't going to work after all?

Panic stabbed her, competing with her nausea. She refused to let herself give in to it. She'd just work her buns off here, get the bathroom in tip-top shape so Sam could see it wasn't so bad after all. That she could be trusted to do her part. She couldn't give him a reason to change his mind.

Grabbing the scrub brush and cleanser, she folded her-

self over the edge of the tub. Wetting the brush and sprin-
kling it liberally with cleanser, she attacked the worst of
the stains.

Sam stacked the last two boxes from the living room on
top of one another and elbowed open the door. It had started
to drizzle when he had returned from carrying the previous
load down. As he carefully made his way downstairs, the
raindrops beaded on his face and eyelashes, making it hard
to see. Slipping inside the shop's back door, he hoped that
whatever was in the top box could stand a little moisture.

He supposed it wouldn't matter if anything was ruined,
since he'd be buying new supplies and merchandise anyway. Except he hadn't the first clue what exactly he wanted
to fill this boondoggle of a shop with. Christmas stuff.
Decorations. Lights. Ornaments. Where he'd find them,
how he'd choose them, he had no idea.

That Jana was here to help him through the minefield
of his cockeyed notion filled him with both relief and
dismay. Relief because he could trust her not to belittle his
idea and because given her crazy imagination, she'd get
this shop together in no time. Dismay because of the armpit
of an apartment he was saddling her with.

He'd done only the most cursory walk-through when
he'd closed on this place. Stupid, yes. He'd been scrupu-
lous about every detail when he'd bought his estate. But
the dream of what the shop could be had lodged itself
inside him, locking rose-colored glasses over his eyes. He
hadn't been back since he'd signed the paperwork, had forgotten how nasty the bathroom was.

With the last set of boxes dumped in the middle of the
cluttered shop, Sam locked up and returned upstairs. He

should have just insisted on bringing in a crew to rehab that entire bathroom. He didn't like the thought of pregnant Jana living in squalor.

But when he poked his head inside the bathroom, he was surprised to see that the tub just about sparkled it was so clean. Looking up at him over her shoulder, Jana smiled, the pride in her work shining in her face. His heart kicked in his chest, and he was swamped by the urge to sit beside her and gather her in his arms.

Pushing on the edge of the tub, she folded her feet under her to rise. He reached for her arm and helped her up. But he let her go right away, not liking the ache in his chest.

She gestured at the tub. "Told you it would come clean. The toilet's a loss and the floor is curling up in the corners, so those definitely need replacing. But I think I can get the stains out of the sink and a little paint should fix up the vanity."

"Let me take a look at that floor." They danced in the small space, him edging in toward the far wall, her taking his place in the doorway. He pressed with his toe where the old linoleum curled up. "Dry rot." He showed her how it gave under his foot. "I'll have to call someone to fix it."

"You told me you worked construction all through college. Why can't you do it yourself?"

Out of long-forgotten habit, his mind went through the steps needed to repair dry rot. He shook his head. "Why should I when I can pay someone?"

She made a face at him. "You've gotten so used to throwing money at a problem. Are you afraid of a little hard work?"

"Of course not." He remembered dragging deadfall from the creek yesterday morning, how good the physical labor had felt. "You said yourself you wanted this place finished as quickly as possible."

"I do." With a sigh, she leaned against the doorjamb. "But I don't want you spending tons of money. Plus, this is your shop—don't you want to be the one who fixes it up?"

Did he? He hadn't really thought that far ahead. He'd gone completely on impulse when he'd bought the shop, with a fuzzy, distant dream of Christmas leading him by the nose. Now that he was here, with Jana's arrival and her and her baby's needs factoring into the picture, he was going to have to start fleshing out his amorphous fantasies, pronto.

"It makes sense I should do some of it," he agreed. The feeling of gratification that welled inside surprised him. It wasn't as if he avoided hard work—constructing a thriller novel took a hell of a lot of brain power. But he felt a sense of renewal throwing himself into this project.

"I'll still have to hire out some of the work," he told her. He wasn't going to touch the electrical work and he hated plumbing.

"Give me another half hour or so to finish the sink. Then we'll go through and get all the tasks organized and prioritized."

"Watch the floor in that corner," he warned her. He put his full weight on it. Soft, but it wouldn't give way. He felt a chill at the thought of her falling through.

She sidled back into the bathroom, carrying her cleanser and scrub brush to the sink. "I'm glad we're doing it ourselves. It'll seem more like a home then."

He looked around at the ratty bathroom, then down at the shredded carpet that lined the hall. His chest tightened a third time, and he started wondering about heart problems.

It amazed him that this meant so much to her, that she seemed so happy in this ragged-around-the-edges studio when she could have been living in his much nicer guest room.

He knew Jana had grown up with as little as he had. But where he'd enjoyed increasing wealth over the past decade, she'd struggled from the moment she'd turned eighteen when her mother tossed her out. To appreciate so little, to see this apartment's potential as a home, just emphasized the difficult place she'd found herself in when Ian walked out on her.

Stepping across the hall to the bedroom, Sam left her to her work. There were more boxes stored in here, several more loads to transfer downstairs. As he lifted the first two and started down the hall, he heard Jana belting out "The Star-Spangled Banner," flat and off-key. She never could sing a note, but, damn, did she sound happy.

Chapter Five

By the end of the day, the sink and tub were clean, the vanity sanded and ready for paint, the dry rot in the floor repaired and the toilet removed. They'd taken stock of the kitchen—cart away the refrigerator, oven okay, but the dishwasher smelled like a petri dish culture. Sam had an extra microwave at the house that Jana could take—he would have bought her a new one, but she talked him down from that position. There wasn't a stick of furniture in the entire place, so that required a shopping spree.

With a trip agreed to for the next day while the contractors were in working on carpet and such, Jana made her way, zombielike, through take-out pizza back at Sam's, then all but fell into bed in exhaustion. She seemed to spend the night in constant motion in her dreams, waking in the morning feeling more sapped of energy than when she'd gone to bed.

When she stumbled into the kitchen and discovered Sam at the stove flipping pancakes, a pile of misshapen flapjacks behind him on the island, she nearly burst into tears. She had to turn away before he saw her, step back into the great room so she could pull herself together. She couldn't quite reason why she wanted to sob, but it had something to do with being pregnant, wiped out and completely overwhelmed by Sam making pancakes for her for breakfast.

She hated pancakes. A fact she'd never had the opportunity to mention to Sam. Unlike French toast, pancakes got all soggy and gummy when you poured syrup on them. Her stomach was already doing its usual gymnastic floor routine of backflips and somersaults. Now she'd have to drop pancakes into the mix. Because no way, no how could she refuse what Sam had made for her.

Swallowing back tears and nausea, Jana reentered the kitchen. This time, Sam grinned at her over his shoulder. She felt so darn lucky to have a buddy as great as Sam and couldn't help but smile in return. Then as their gazes locked and Sam's smile reshaped into something softer, sexier, her heart thumped heavily in her chest. Suddenly, it was a little hard to breathe.

She tore her gaze away, shifting it to the sagging stack of pancakes, grateful when the nausea returned. She had no intention of going down that same path she'd tripped down the night before last. She couldn't risk the friendship she so desperately wanted to keep intact.

Grabbing an overripe banana from the bowl on the island, she stripped off the peel and chomped a bite of the fruit. "So, you can make pancakes at least," she said over a mouthful of banana.

"From a mix." He gestured at the box lying on its side next to the cooktop.

Jana picked up the box. "You used it all?" she asked, feeling its featherweight.

"A lot of trial and error my first time out." He pressed a toe on the pedal for the trash can, showed her the burnt pancakes lining the bottom. "Mostly error."

She got out the syrup and the eggs, figuring the more she filled her stomach with other stuff, the fewer pancakes she'd have to eat. By the time they sat down in the break-fast nook, she'd already wolfed down two scrambled eggs straight from the skillet. The two pancakes she ate didn't seem to settle as badly on a mostly full stomach, especially since she dipped each bite in the puddle of syrup on her plate rather than pouring the stuff on top.

Sam inhaled the last of his stack of six, then leaned back in his chair, fingers locked on his belly. "I was thinking…"

Her radar shot up. "What?"

She saw the wary look in his eyes. "While we're out, I wanted to pick you up a few things."

She pushed her plate aside, not liking the direction he was going. "Such as?"

"Stuff for the apartment, of course. Linens, towels, shower curtain, miniblinds."

"We already talked about all that last night." She could accept those purchases because she'd be leaving them all behind after the baby was born and she moved out.

"I also thought you'd need some other odds and ends." Now his gaze drifted out the window where the sun fought for supremacy with scattered clouds. "Clothes. Shoes."

She squashed her irritation. "Why do you keep wanting to buy me stuff?"

"You need clothes, Jana. I didn't have to go through that duffel to know you don't have more than a couple of changes. And you're going to need more than T-shirts once you get…" He flapped his hands out in front of himself.

He was right, she didn't have nearly enough to get her through her pregnancy. Two pair of maternity jeans and a few large T-shirts. "Take me to the thrift store, then. I can find some stuff there."

He shook his head. "I want to buy you new."

"Why spend all that money when hand-me-downs work just as well?"

"Because it's all I know how to do!" He shoved back his chair, jumping to his feet. "It's the only way I know how to help you. I can't cook worth a damn. I can't transform Ian into the world's best father. I can't answer even one of the questions I know you've got racing around in your head."

He picked up his plate and all but tossed it on the counter beside the sink. "But I have money, and spending it is something I know how to do. Just let me spread a little of that wealth on you."

She carefully considered her response, not wanting to offend him. "I appreciate it, Sam. Really I do. I just don't know why you'd want to."

"We're friends."

"I'm glad you think so." Even more than she was willing to admit to him. "But I feel a little like…" She considered how to say what had been eating at her. Then just blurted it out. "I can't give back to you the way you're giving to me. And don't you say a word about how I'm working for you. You know everything you're offering me is way above and beyond."

He leaned against the center island, arms crossed. "You

don't have to give me anything in return. All these years I've known you, since you were a kid… You have to know you're like a sister to me. Family."

That took the wind out of her sails. It sure made it crystal clear that she didn't have to worry about the sex thing with him, even if she'd wanted to follow in her mother's foot-steps. She ought to be relieved. She was, really. It was per-fect, wasn't it, for him to think of her as a sister?

For Sam to consider her family…a cartoon heart took off from her chest. She'd never known her father, had been an afterthought to her mother. The only family she'd had all those years growing up was what she'd found at Estelle's. She'd always hoped she meant more to Sam that just some twerpy kid always clinging to his coattails.

"Okay, big brother." She got to her feet and walked over to him. "If blowing a few bucks on your little sister makes you happy, go for it. As long as you don't go overboard."

He smiled again, that same drop-dead gorgeous grin that probably sold more books than the actual stories he wrote. No wonder they plastered his face on the back dust jacket.

He threw his arms around her and tugged her close. She reluctantly wrapped her own arms around his waist in turn. Just because it felt so good rubbing her palms against the back of his thick wool sweater didn't mean there was anything to their hug other than brotherly-sisterly affection.

Except that her imagination was marching out sugges-tions that didn't feel the least bit sisterly. She swatted them aside, resisted the urge to snuggle even closer to Sam, to press her mouth against his chest and kiss him.

She might never have had a brother, but she was darn sure that wasn't something she might have done with one. She took a big step back. "You made breakfast. I'll clean up." Her hands, looking for an excuse to touch him again, got busy filling the sink with hot soapy water.

She could feel him behind her, still rooted to the same spot. When she sneaked a peek, he was staring at her.

A tremor shivered up her spine. "What?"

He seemed to shake himself, then took the long way around the island. "I'll get the car."

"I'll meet you outside in just a sec," she called out. "Okay?"

No answer from Sam. He just skittered out of the kitchen and toward the garage.

Had she done it again? Somehow let slip her thoughts through her actions? Was he able to decipher her fantasies from the way she'd rubbed his back?

She squeezed her eyes shut, trying to remember just how she'd touched him. It had seemed innocent, but who knows how Sam might have interpreted it?

She'd have to stop touching him altogether. She couldn't trust herself not to do it wrong. If she screwed things up with Sam like she'd messed up so much else in her life, it would break her heart.

So from now on, it was hands off. No excuses.

Sam backed his 1960 Edsel Villager Wagon from its slot in the garage, taking care not to nick the car's finish on the side of the garage door. Considering where his mind was— certainly not on the pristine turquoise-and-white paint job of his cherished nine-passenger Edsel—he wasn't sure he should be behind the wheel at all.

It had been an innocent gesture, taking Jana in his arms for a hug. What he'd said about thinking of her as family, as a sister, had been gospel truth. He'd never fully articulated that to himself before that moment, but as soon as he spoke it out loud, realization had shot up like a flame.

Then he drew her in his arms and felt her softness pressed against his chest. And started going way off course. Contemplating kisses along her brow. Exploring that shadow behind her ear. The tenderness of her slender throat.

Sam slammed on the brakes, a bare inch from ramming the back of the Villager into a cypress tree. He pounded the heel of his hand into his forehead a few times, wishing he could reset his brain the same way he did with his computer's power button. But he'd let those thoughts in, and now he'd have to deal with them. Box them in a corner, throw a heavy blanket over the box and a boulder on top of the blanket. Maybe the Empire State Building atop the boulder.

As he pulled up in front of the house to wait for Jana, another worry squirmed inside his stomach. Just because he considered her family, that didn't give him any guarantees. She could still walk out the door like his mother had, disappear from his life as his sister, Madelena, had. Betray him the way Aunt Barbara had when she'd drop-kicked him into foster care.

Except Jana wouldn't…would she? Leave him, disappear, betray him. Of course not. She was different than that. He could count on her.

Yeah, she'd experienced that momentary insanity and gone off with Ian. But she'd realized her mistake, had come to her senses. And it was him she'd come to when she knew she needed help. Not Tony or Rebecca. Not even Estelle. She came to him. That meant something.

He'd be okay as long as he kept his head on straight. As long as he didn't start thinking about her like he had about

Faith. Or Shawna or Cyndy or Patricia. Or any of the other women who had drifted in, then out of his life.

The front door opened and Jana stepped out, locking up with his house key. This was far too much heavy thought for so early in the morning. He was making this thing way more complicated than he needed to. Too used to dreaming up complex plotlines for his thrillers, he sometimes let that tendency creep into the real world. He'd overthink things.

He and Jana were friends. Close as family. Nothing more to it.

Then she climbed into the car, her smile so radiant he felt its effects clear to his toes. Without a word, she sent him into another maelstrom of confusion.

Before Jana could again throw out the suggestion that they make their purchases at the local thrift store, Sam made a big deal out of insisting they buy furniture at a high-end designer home store in Sacramento. As predicted, Jana went ballistic and demanded he take her to the local big-box discount place instead. Satisfied that he'd gotten her off the thrift store bandwagon, he crossed his fingers that she wouldn't figure out she'd been snookered until the Villager was safely parked.

They pushed separate carts, which also got an argument out of Jana. Even after Sam patiently explained that the stuff they were picking up was bulky and would require two carts—for example, for the bedding and window coverings—she still kept up the scowl. That sunny smile she'd greeted him with when she'd first climbed into the wagon had vanished.

Her mood darkened as they proceeded through the store, as he made arrangements to have the futon sofa and easy chair delivered tomorrow, as he pulled out his credit cart to check out. She turned so pale when she saw the total that he would have taken her arm to support her if she hadn't already had such a death grip on the counter.

When they finally pushed the towering pile of purchases out to the parking lot, Sam waited until they'd unloaded and Jana had a chance to climb in the car and get her seat belt on. Then he turned toward her, cocking one leg up on the bench seat.

"You want to explain the Dr. Jekyll and Ms. Hyde bit this morning?"

To her credit, she gave him a straight answer. "You're doing too much for me. You even got me a cell phone, for heaven's sake."

"It's just a few extra bucks on my current cell plan. Besides, I thought we agreed on this." He gestured at the packed rear seats.

"We did. But the reality of it…" She locked her fingers together. "Up until now, the only things you've given me were copies of your books."

"I took you out to McDonald's a few times."

"When I was eleven." She huffed an impatient breath. "Don't minimize this, Sam. You just dropped a lot of bucks on me and plan to spend more. Stuff for the apartment, maternity clothes. And so far I haven't done a darn thing to earn any of it."

"Why do you feel you have to earn it? Why can't I just give it to you?"

"Because…" She opened her mouth as she seemed to grope for an explanation. Then her gaze skittered away from him, out the Villager's broad windshield. When she looked at him, a beguiling wash of pink colored her cheeks.

Jana's lips were still parted, moist from where her tongue had wet them. The chilly interior of the wagon spiked with heat, as if their bodies were warming it. Her soft brown eyes widened as she stared up at him. Sam's good intentions threatened to take a powder, and he was nine-tenths of a second from reaching for her.

At the last instant, he wrapped his fingers around the steering wheel, focusing out the windshield instead of on her. "I never gave you stuff before because you didn't need it. You need it now. You've got to have sheets to sleep on and a blanket to keep you warm. You'll need to wear something for the next seven months."

She sighed. "When it's over, I can just leave the stuff with you, okay? Maybe donate the clothes to the thrift store?"

"Sure. That makes sense." She wasn't likely to need those voluminous shirts and stretchy jeans again any time soon. But a part of him wanted her to keep what he'd given her. Even that silly little Eeyore bedside lamp they'd found in the children's section.

Which confused the hell out of him. He couldn't care less if Faith had thrown that outrageously expensive tennis bracelet into the Sacramento River after she'd left his house. But he wished Jana would want to keep a cheapo Eeyore lamp.

Well, he'd known Jana longer. She meant more to him. As a friend, of course. As a close-as-family, almost-like-a-sister friend.

Tucking away his confusion, Sam headed back out to Highway 50. Last night on the Internet, he'd scoped out the best price for a dishwasher and fridge and found a place in Folsom, twenty miles west. The appliances he chose wouldn't be the cheapest, which he refused to buy no matter how much Jana squawked, nor the most expensive, which should keep her complaints to a minimum.

Once they got to the store, she ended up wandering off to the music aisle, leaving him to deal with the oversolicitous salesman. Jana met up with him again just as they finished writing up the sale, two CDs in her hand.

"I want to pay for these," she told him, "so take them out of my first check."

The twentysomething salesclerk, tall and skinny with a smudge of hair on his chin, gave Jana the once-over with a grin. "So you two are together?"

Jana didn't show even an iota of interest in the eager young man, but annoyance boiled up inside Sam nevertheless. He wanted to hustle Jana out of there, away from the salesclerk's avid gaze. A guy didn't want another guy looking at his sister like that, right?

Before he could tug Jana toward the exit, remind her they had one more stop to make for a bed, a woman's voice called out to him. "Sam?"

He turned to see Faith at the other end of the aisle of dishwashers. Behind her, a short, stocky man with thinning hair was studying a microwave.

She murmured to her companion, then approached Sam with a tentative smile. The man followed. Jana had shaken off the salesclerk and eyed Faith with curiosity.

"This is Ed," Faith said.

A light of recognition flickered on. "From your law office," Sam said, shaking the man's hand.

"On the real estate side," Ed said with a proprietary touch to Faith's shoulder.

Not just coworkers, then. Barely more than a week since he'd ended things with Faith and here she was with Ed.

Now the resignation in her face that day made more sense. He supposed he couldn't blame her, considering his benign neglect at the end of their relationship.

Except he ought to feel something more than indifference, shouldn't he? He nudged Jana forward. "You remember me mentioning Jana McPartland."

Smiles and handshakes all around, then Faith gave Ed's arm a squeeze. "Excuse me a minute, sweetheart. Can I talk to you, Sam?"

Jana's gaze narrowed on his ex-girlfriend as Faith walked with him out of earshot. He wouldn't put it past Jana to put on some kind of superradar so she could follow the conversation.

With a side-by-side refrigerator obstructing their view of the others, Faith took her stand. "I want you to know Ed was a perfect gentleman those last few months before you kissed me off. He let me cry on his shoulder, never made one wrong move."

"It's okay. I understand."

Her face hardened. "Don't think it didn't hurt, even knowing what I was getting into with you."

Well-placed sucker punch, he thought. But who could blame her? "I'm sorry, Faith. I never meant to—"

"I gave that damn bracelet away. Donated it to Goodwill."

He almost laughed but kept the impulse down with an effort. He couldn't wait to share the joke with Jana. Leaning back to get a clear line of sight between refrigerators, he managed to make eye contact with her. She looked about ready to die from the tediousness of making conversation with Ed.

Despite his inattention, Faith kept talking. "At least now you've got what you always wanted."

His head whipped back around to her. "What?"

"Jana. As much as you waxed euphoric over her while we were dating, Jana this and Jana that, I'm glad the two of you are finally together."

"We're not together." Anxiety at the thought marched through his stomach. "She's an old friend. And just a kid."

Faith gave him a long considering look. "Okay."

He felt the need to clarify. "She showed up a couple days ago. I'm just helping her out."

Another long look, then she patted his arm. "I have to get back. Ed and I are on lunch hour."

They all parted company, then Sam paid for Jana's bargain bin CDs—a loan, she insisted again—and they returned to the car. He told her how Faith had donated the tennis bracelet to Goodwill, expecting her to laugh at his expense. But Jana was quiet as they continued west on Highway 50 toward the mattress store, her expression thoughtful.

They'd just pulled into the parking lot when she delivered a finish to the one-two punch Faith had started. "You buy women things because it's safer."

"I don't know what you mean," he said, although he suspected that was a lie.

She turned to him as he nosed the car into a slot. "It's safer than giving them more of yourself."

"Maybe buying them things is my way of giving myself."

She stared at him, and he could see her working out that possibility in her mind. Then she shook her head. "I don't think so."

He wanted to tell her she was wrong, that she didn't know a damn thing about him. Except wouldn't that prove her point, that even after all these years she didn't really know him, because he gave her so little of himself?

Better to just ignore what she'd said, pretend it didn't apply to him. So he held his tongue as he and Jana climbed out of the car, headed for the store. As he prepared himself to buy his way out of an honest look at himself once again.

Chapter Six

Jana felt a little better figuring out what she had about Sam. She was still worried about all that money she had no way of repaying. But in a strange way, she guessed he was getting something out of his generosity. Protection against anyone—in this case, Jana—digging any deeper.

She would have preferred it if he'd trusted her enough not to need that kind of distraction. But in a way it provided her protection, too. Because he was buying her stuff to make him feel better and certainly not—insert laugh track here—because he was hot for her bod.

In any case, she let him choose the double bed, didn't even look at the price. She tried it out because he insisted, although that was pretty awkward, lying on the bare mattress with Sam and the saleswoman standing over her. The chic-to-the-max saleswoman recognized Sam and was gushing all over him, telling him she'd read everything he'd written. Sam seemed to forget Jana was there as he scrawled his autograph on a piece of printer paper and turned on that million-watt smile for the woman.

Not that Jana was jealous, any more than she'd been when she'd seen the gorgeous Faith in the appliance store. She knew what kind of women Sam went for, and they weren't tomboyish and boobless with mousy brown hair. Like her.

Of course, Sam talked the saleswoman into arranging delivery for tomorrow, just as he had all the other stuff. Paid extra for it, too. Which was great—all the sooner for her to get out of Sam's place and into the apartment.

Sam had cheered up by the time they got back into the car. He was smiling as he carefully pulled the Villager out of its space.

"Did you ask her out?" Jana asked, even though she really didn't want to know.

"Who?" He had his eyes on the road as he merged the vehicle onto the freeway.

"The saleswoman. Ms. I'm-your-biggest-fan."

Now he glanced over at her. "Why would I do that?"

"Did you?"

He actually blushed. "She gave me her number."

Jana laughed even though she felt hollow inside. "Of course she did."

He scowled. "I didn't ask for it."

She forced herself to laugh again. "You know, as your assistant, I could buy the parting gifts early. That way when you're ready to call it quits, you're all prepared."

She knew the instant the words were out of her mouth that they would hurt him. It was like something her teenage self would have said, the unthinking screwup she'd always been. Apparently still was.

She saw how tightly his hands gripped the steering wheel, the way his jaw worked with tension. "I'm sorry. That was stupid. It's hormones or tiredness or just that I'm a complete idiot."

He was quiet as they passed Folsom, then continued past the foothill towns west of Placerville. "You have a point," he said finally. "My track record sucks."

She let out a long breath of air, grateful he wasn't totally mad at her, that he wasn't about to pull over and boot her out of the wagon. She cautiously suggested, "Maybe you should give the whole girl thing a rest for a while."

He pulled off the freeway at the Golden Arches, glanced over at her at the red light and stared at her for a long time, until the guy behind him honked at the green. "Maybe so," he said quietly as he pulled through.

There was a message in those blue, blue eyes, one she couldn't decipher. But it sent a finger of sensation up her spine and started her imagination all over again thinking of possibilities.

After lunch, Sam could see Jana was beat. He drove her straight up to the house rather than stopping at the apartment as he'd originally intended. They could always drop off their purchases tomorrow. The contractors finishing off carpet and vinyl installation in the apartment were probably still working anyway. He and Jana would just get in their way.

While Jana napped, Sam holed up in his office. The wind had picked up, gusts sending puffy white clouds scudding across the deep blue sky. The oaks and pines visible through his office window moved in a free-form dance as the breeze punched through them.

What Jana had told him earlier about how he bought women stuff to keep them from getting close was still sifting through his mind. It wasn't anything he hadn't realized himself, deep down. He just had never chosen to acknowledge it.

Why shouldn't he keep some of the crap inside to himself? He'd gone through some pretty heavy-duty mojo during his childhood. Did he have to be all touchy-feely and lay that mess on everyone he met? Jana ought to be grateful he hadn't burdened her with his personal nightmare. She knew his mom had walked out on his sister and him—did she have to hear the gory details of the whole terrifying experience?

So it made him feel good to buy stuff for people, to spend his hard-earned money on them. That didn't mean he was substituting money for truth. He didn't owe the truth to everyone in the world. Considering how things had ended up with Faith, it was just as well he'd kept some things to himself.

What about Jana?

Over the years, she'd laid out a lot about her own life, how her mom was such a flake. How her mom was always getting herself into fixes that other people would have to pull her out of. And how her mom had been leaving her alone all hours of the day and night since Jana was eight. Sam hadn't needed that confidence from Jana to know she was a lost soul and a lot like him.

So why not confess some of his old garbage to Jana? She wouldn't go blabbing it to, say, Tony and Rebecca. He could trust her to keep his secrets just as he had his foster mom, Estelle, although even she didn't know every last detail.

But why tell anyone? That was ancient history. It wasn't as if it had anything to do with who he was today.

Turning back to his computer, he opened up a document filled with notes for his next book. He hadn't planned to start working in earnest until March, but when ideas popped up, he felt compelled to type them in so he wouldn't forget. These past couple days spent with Jana had sparked an inspiration, and he wanted to see where it would take him.

Trent Garner had been a lone wolf for eight years and ten books, loving 'em and leaving 'em by the end of each action-packed story. For the most part, women had always been window dressing in the complex plots. There was a female police chief in the jurisdiction where the fictional P.I. lived, as well as a female judge who drifted in and out of the novels, but they were both older women and more sounding boards than actual intimates.

But a new character was trying to insinuate herself into his consciousness. A smart-mouthed female journalist, sharp as a tack, always trying to weasel her way into Trent's business. She wasn't drop-dead gorgeous like the arm candy Trent liked to keep company with. But she was cute and appealing, a fresh-faced twenty-five-year-old to act as a foil to Trent's world-weary midthirties.

By the time he came up for air, it was nearly four o'clock and he could hear Jana moving around in the kitchen. Saving the file and exiting his word processor, he padded downstairs and across the living room. He stopped just out of sight of Jana in the kitchen. She'd changed into the red-and-purple-striped sweater he'd bought her today and had tied one of Mrs. Prentiss's aprons around her waist.

As she chopped onions at the island, she did a clumsy two-step, her voice a dissonant accompaniment to Don Henley's on Sam's vintage Eagles CD. She never could sing worth a damn. He made a mental note to add that trait to the character description of his new Trent Garner sidekick.

He waited until she'd pressed the hold button on her off-key singing and dropped the onions into the sizzling frying pan. Then he strode into the kitchen. "Hey, what's cooking?"

Tossing the last few diced onions into the pan, she gave him a wary look. "Chili. I found some ground beef in the freezer and thought I'd make some."

"I love chili." Which she knew. That much he'd told her.

She gave the onions a stir, then glanced at him sidelong. "Are we okay?"

"Sure. We're fine." He fussed over the selections in the fruit bowl, finally settling on a golden delicious apple. He wasn't hungry, didn't want it, but had to do something with his hands.

"I'm sorry about the bad joke. That was mean of me."

"Hey, it was funny. Right on the mark." Except it had cut deep. He took a savage bite of the apple. "Anything I can do to help?" he asked around a mouthful.

"Open those cans," she said, pointing with the wooden spoon at a lineup on the center island of chili beans, tomatoes and tomato sauce.

Setting aside the apple, he dutifully carried the cans over to the opener, near the sink. Over the whine of the motor, he brought up the touchy subject that had crossed his mind while he was working upstairs.

"You know you're going to have to contact Ian sooner or later. Get his permission for the adoption."

With her back to him, he couldn't see her face, but her shoulders stiffened. "I know."

He tiptoed a little closer to the minefield. "I could call Darius, my private investigator friend. Tracking missing persons is one of his specialties."

"Not yet."

"Jana—"

"Not yet, please." She faced him. "I know it's something I have to take care of. I'm just not ready."

He got it, then. Contacting Ian, having him sign off on parental rights, would take her one step closer to finalizing her decision to put her baby up for adoption.

Another thought dropped an anchor in his stomach. "Are you hoping he'll come back?" he asked. "That the two of you will get back together?"

Her lip curled in disgust. "Yuck. Absolutely not. I might have been stupid to have hooked up with that loser in the first place, but I'm not completely brainless." She snatched up the cans he'd opened and dumped the contents into a massive pot.

Relief eased the knot in his belly. He'd hated it when she'd disappeared with Ian last year. Not knowing where she was, if she was okay. That sister-brother thing again. It was the same way he used to worry about his sister, Madelena, when she was living with Aunt Barbara and he was in foster care.

Second time in one day he'd thought of Maddie. It had been, what? A decade at least since that phone call from her, one night while Aunt Barbara was out of town. And that had been brief. She'd been a giggly seventeen-year-old, giddy over the fact she'd tracked down the phone number for her forbidden elder brother.

Then five or six years ago, she'd tried again, this time through his agent, since his number was unlisted by then. But he'd been an arrogant horse's ass, recently stung by a girlfriend only interested in his money and a piece of his fame. He'd sent a message back through his agent, refusing Maddie's overture.

Nothing since then. Which probably meant she'd given up on him. She was an adult now, no longer under Aunt Barbara's thumb. She could track him down by e-mail through his Web site, but she hadn't bothered. Or maybe she figured the ball was in his court.

So why hadn't he contacted her? He'd like to think it was because his life was too busy and he just hadn't gotten around to it. But in his heart of hearts, he knew the truth—that he still harbored that stone of resentment inside that he went to foster care but Maddie didn't.

Jana was waving a chili-coated spoon in his face. "Earth to Sam."

He shook off thoughts of his sister. "How long before the chili's ready?"

She eyed him speculatively. "Couple hours at least. I want to make cornbread, too."

"Enough time to play some cards, then."

She set aside the spoon, apparently willing to go along with his change of subject. "Cribbage? Russian rummy?"

"Cribbage first. We'll see where we go from there."

As she untied the apron, slipped it from her body, his mind took off in an entirely unexpected direction. Before he could stop himself, he was picturing Jana taking off her clothes, piece by piece, as they played strip poker.

Lagging behind her so she couldn't see, he slapped himself in the head a couple times to knock some sense in. He'd been doing well the whole day, keeping his distance, avoiding touching her even in the close confines of the car. He'd even kept a strict muzzle on his imagination while she was trying out beds at the mattress store, focusing instead on the endless nattering of the salesclerk so he wouldn't get dragged along by his adolescent libido.

Cribbage. We're playing cribbage, he reminded himself as he tracked down the board and a deck of cards from the sideboard in the living room. But when she settled opposite him on the sofa, feet curled up under her, the sleeves of her sweater pushed up to her elbows, all he could think about was how it would feel to run his finger slowly from the inside of her wrist to the crook of her arm.

Sam didn't have a prayer of winning. Not with his mind handicapped by misplaced lust and Jana playing her usual cutthroat game. It didn't take her long to peg to a win, double-skunking him as winter darkness settled outside and the delectable aroma of chili filled the house.

When they checked out the apartment the next morning, Jana could see the contractors had made a ton of progress. They hadn't finished repairing the kitchen cabinets, and a couple of light fixtures were down to correct code violations, but the new carpet and the flooring in the kitchen and bathroom looked great. It was actually starting to look like a home.

Jana had wanted to repaint the bathroom vanity herself, but Sam nixed that idea. He had a point, though—breathing in paint fumes in that small space wouldn't be good for the baby. So, while Sam gave the contractors a hand in finishing up the final repairs, Jana went downstairs to inventory what was in the boxes.

Before she even started with that chore, she gave the shop a thorough going-over, a pad and pen handy to make notes. The main space, about twenty by twenty, looked as if the previous owner had packed away the merchandise but left everything else right where it stood. The empty shelves were thick with dust, the walls full of holes, big and small, with outlines visible where pictures had hung. The wood floor was stained and in need of refinishing. One of the front windows was cracked and would have to be replaced. Two of the fluorescents in the fixtures above were out.

Listing all the needed repairs on her pad, she moved on to the restroom and office/storeroom situated on either side of the back door. The bathroom was in good shape, but there were a dozen more boxes tucked away in the storeroom that she'd have to go through. The cardboard in the corner of one had been chewed through. She shivered. Rats. The actual, literal kind. She made a note, then returned to the store to start opening boxes.

The slam of the back door at lunchtime announced Sam's arrival. "How's it going?"

"Great. Just finishing the last box."

She turned to smile at him and felt as if the breath had been knocked out of her. Good grief, the man looked good in jeans and a T-shirt—even with his hair a little sweaty from hard work, flecks of white paint dotting his arms and face.

A couple small specks of paint had landed on his forehead. Before she could think better of it, she reached up to rub them away, fingers itching as they drew closer. "You've got some paint—"

He grabbed her wrist, stopping her cold. "I've got it. Thanks." He slipped into the bathroom.

She wanted to kick herself and would have if she didn't have the baby to consider. She'd done great all of yesterday, keeping her hands off him even when she'd won her third game of cribbage and longed to give him a celebratory hug. She couldn't mess that up now.

He returned, face a little damp from washing. "Did you figure out what's what?"

She turned her focus on her morning's work. "I've got everything sorted out into five categories." She pointed as she ticked off what she'd found. "Supplies, like TP for the restroom, register tape, pens, pencils, that sort of thing. Generic merchandise we might be able to use in the store—scented candles, potpourri, silk flowers. Over there's stuff we don't need but is worth selling on the Internet for a few bucks."

"We can give the proceeds to Tony's program."

"Sure. I'll need a computer to set up an account at one of the auction sites and a digital camera."

"I've got an older laptop and camera I don't use anymore. What else?" he asked.

"In those boxes—" she pointed "—are a fair number of smaller odds and ends that might not be worth selling but are still good enough to donate to the thrift store. Those boxes over there are Dumpster fodder."

"You're amazing. Great work."

His words set off a glow inside her. That urge to give him a thank-you hug for the compliment bubbled up inside, but she ignored it.

Instead, she showed him her pad. "You might want to go through and double-check this. I may have missed something."

He scanned the list, then glanced up at her. "You think I'm crazy buying this run-down store? My wacky idea about turning it into a Christmas shop?"

She sensed he was asking more than the surface question and didn't want to say the wrong thing. "I never knew Christmas was such a big deal for you."

He looked away, out the front window at the traffic passing by on Carson Road. "Why wouldn't it be?"

"You never came to the Christmas parties Estelle gave

for the kids. I mean, you'd send all kinds of presents, but you'd never be there."

The pad of paper bent under his tight grip. "You know I'm busy."

She should leave it alone. Sam had drawn a line in the sand enough times for her to know that she'd get nowhere trying to cross it. But if this shop was so important to him, shouldn't she know why? Wouldn't that make it easier for her to help him make it a success?

She gulped in a breath. "Except Estelle told me that even when you were a kid living with her, you never liked Christmas. All the other kids would exchange presents, and you'd be sitting in your room, alone."

He whipped around on his heel so fast that Jana took an involuntary step back. "That's none of your business."

His anger tore into her. He'd been irritated with her enough times, impatient, but never enraged like this. He was shaking he was so mad.

Jana hugged herself. "I'm sorry."

Just like that his anger washed away. "Oh, God, I'm sorry, Jana." He crossed the room and wrapped his arms around her. "That was inexcusable."

It took about three seconds for Sam to soothe her; every moment after that was pure elation. Not good if she was going to keep her head on straight. She pulled back, giving his arm a pat before she stepped clear.

"You're totally forgiven if you'll feed me. I forgot my crackers and my stomach's a little dicey."

"One of the guys went for sandwiches." Unease still cut a line in his brow. "Are you sure you're okay?"

More than okay with him so close, staring down at her. "I'm fine. Except for the ready-to-upchuck part."

He scrubbed a hand through his already messed-up hair. "The whole Christmas thing is kind of complicated for me."

She thought he might tell her more, but then the younger of the two contractors knocked at the back door and stepped inside. He held a bag out to Sam. "There's a couple of sodas on the bottom." He headed back out again.

Sam arranged a couple of boxes sturdy enough to sit on beside a third they could use as a table. Jana wolfed down half her turkey and provolone sub with barely a pause, then took a break to make sure everything settled okay.

"I had a thought last night while I was falling asleep," she said as she sipped her orange soda. "Kind of a variation on your idea for the store."

He split open a bag of chips and laid it out for them to share. "Tell me."

"I do think a Christmas store is cool. But to give it a better chance, what if we made the shop more of an all-around holiday place?"

He munched a potato chip, then took a swallow of cola. "How so?"

"There are always holidays to celebrate. Valentine's Day, Easter, Independence Day. We could stock decorations and other merchandise for holidays year-round. And besides the biggies like Thanksgiving and Christmas, there are all these wacko days like Hug Your Cat Day and Rocky Road Day."

He laughed. "You're making this up."

"Looked it up on the Internet this morning, on your office computer. Before you were up. I hope that was okay."

"Sure. No problem." He looked distracted, as if he was considering her suggestion.

She crossed her fingers. She wasn't exactly known for coming up with fabulous ideas. Sam was too nice to tell her it was stupid, but he might not be able to hide that look in his eyes if the thought crossed his mind.

But his grin told her his opinion even before he spoke. "You are brilliant."

She just about swooned at the second compliment from Sam in less than an hour. Not that he was stingy with them; in fact, he'd always been her biggest booster. But after so many recent stumbles in her life, hearing Sam's praise was overwhelming.

"So we'd rotate the stock depending on the season?" he asked. "We'd have to get creative to come up with the right merchandise for some of your wacky days—"

"Like stuffed cats and bags of chocolate, marshmallows and nuts."

"Excellent. The Valentine's and Easter products would be a piece of cake to come by."

"We could do an e-mail newsletter to keep people up-to-date on what holiday is coming up and some of the stuff we'll have in the store."

"I like it. A lot." He took a last bite of his roast beef sandwich, his expression thoughtful. "What if we sold some of the Estelle's House baked goods here?"

The students in Tony's independent living program ran a bakeshop in Apple Hill, creating all kinds of yummy treats under Rebecca's direction. "Simple stuff like coffee cake and turnovers."

"And I still want to get some of the kids over here once the shop is open, expose them to another type of retail business."

They spent the rest of the lunch hour tossing ideas back and forth, feeding on each other's enthusiasm. Some of Jana's suggestions were goofy and outrageous, but Sam never made fun of them. He said they were brainstorming, just like he did with his books. He told her that anything goes when you're brainstorming, that there's no such thing as a stupid idea. That took some getting used to—that she could say anything she wanted and Sam wouldn't think she was a screwup.

After they'd cleaned up from lunch and Sam returned upstairs, Jana still felt that glow inside from his compliments. With paper towels and a bottle of spray cleaner, she tidied up the shop, bathroom and office as best she could, cutting through a few layers of dust. She knew she was overdoing it, working past her desperate need for an afternoon nap. But she wanted to please Sam, maybe get another one of those kudos from him.

When she finished around five, grubby and exhausted, she wanted nothing more than a shower and a good night's sleep. But when Sam showed up with yet another grin on his face and tugged at her arm to urge her upstairs, she did her best to put aside her cranky bad temper. As she climbed the stairs to the apartment, she saw that the contractors' truck was gone, leaving only the Villager behind the store.

When she first stepped inside the living room, she almost thought she was in the wrong place. The furniture had all been delivered. The living-room walls and kitchen cabinets all had a fresh coat of paint. The blinds were hung, with frilly little curtains across the top that were pulled back on either side.

"Come look in here," Sam said, the excitement clear in his voice.

He towed her along to the bathroom, showing her he'd hung the shower curtain they'd picked out, with its giant sunflowers on a sky-blue background. There was a brand-new toilet, and the spanking-new paint on the vanity matched the shower curtain's pale blue. Then in the bed-room, he'd made up the bed with the bedspread and com-forter they'd bought the day before. The Eeyore lamp shone bravely on the nightstand beside the bed.

It was the silly lamp that did it for her. Eeyore, with his hangdog expression holding up the lightbulb, the lavender lampshade glowing with warmth.

"It's all so beautiful," she said. Then she collapsed on the foot of the bed and burst into tears.

She shouldn't have let him sit next to her. She should have jumped to her feet and run from the room instead of allowing him to put his arms around her. And she abso-lutely, positively never should have buried her face in his neck and bawled her eyes out.

He rubbed her back. "This whole crying thing is getting to be a real habit."

"When i-is it gonna s-stop?" she sobbed, embarrassed to the max and wanting to crawl under the bed.

"Maybe when your hormones settle down."

Except with his chin resting on top of her head, with his hands stroking her from shoulder to waist in slow arcs, she didn't think her hormones would ever mellow out. In fact, she thought maybe he was riling them up even worse.

He shifted—thank God he was pulling away—and she readied herself to stand up the moment he let go. But he didn't release her, just kept up that oh-so-pleasant pressure of his arms, his breathing long and deep against her ear.

Then he buried his mouth in her hair, the soft heat against her scalp sending her heart into a two-step. She couldn't see, could only feel— Good God, was he kissing her? His mouth moved along her hairline, down her brow, his lips settling at the sensitive place between her eyes. Her heart screamed in her chest, a hot, flaming phoenix.

Her hands clutched his sides so hard she was probably hurting him. She wanted his mouth on hers so badly she could hardly bear its absence.

Somehow, his T-shirt had scooted free of his jeans—had she done that?—and she could feel bare skin against her fingertips. She couldn't help herself—she stretched her fingers longer, drew them across that warm, taut smoothness.

He grew still, his mouth still on her, his breathing ragged. Then he just about pole-vaulted out of her arms. Stood over her, staring down, shock clearly on his face. She dropped her own gaze, mortified, again wishing she could creep under the bed out of sight. She thought of apologizing, then realized if she did, she'd have to admit she'd been groping him.

Before she could even draw a breath, he'd left the room. She heard him talking and realized he was on the phone ordering Chinese. Then she heard the front door open and close, and she figured he'd left.

But as she returned to the living room, he came back inside. Didn't quite look straight at her. "With the new stuff we brought over, you have a change of clothes for tomorrow, right?"

"Yeah." She'd seen it all hanging in her bedroom closet.

"Would you be okay sleeping here, then?"

"I'd like to sleep in my own place." She'd also like to do a total rewind on the past ten minutes.

"Good." He tucked his hands under his armpits, still not looking at her. "Dinner should be here in about thirty minutes. I gave the guy my credit card, so it's all paid for."

"Aren't you going to eat with me?"

"Not tonight. I have to…" He scanned the apartment, as if for an excuse. "Have to do stuff."

Then he grabbed up his sweater from the futon and walked to the door. For half a second, she thought he might give her a goodbye hug. But he must have been afraid she'd put the squeeze on him again if he did.

So he walked out, leaving her to mentally kick herself around the room like a soccer ball.

Chapter Seven

He'd been ready to kiss her, to touch her everywhere, to strip off her clothes and pull her down onto that bed. The sudden hurricane-force temptation had shocked him, the lightning-fast switch from comforting yet another Jana meltdown to raging lust. When he'd felt her inadvertent brush against his bare skin, it had both sent sensation jolting through him and knocked some sense into him. He'd skedaddled out of there as quickly as humanly possible.

And as luck would have it, the next morning fate stepped in to save him from himself. His agent's call woke him at 10:00 a.m.—long after he usually woke, but he'd been staring at the ceiling most of the night—and offered him a sanity-saving lifesaver. A writers' organization in Phoenix had lost its conference keynote speaker at the last minute to a nasty case of flu. Could he step in to give the opening speech tomorrow, Wednesday, and appear on a few discussion panels?

He gave a tentative yes, then called Tony and Rebecca to arrange for a few of the teens in their program to give Jana a hand in the shop while he was gone. Last thing he wanted was pregnant Jana schlepping around heavy boxes. Next, he called his accountant and insurance agent and set Jana up as an official employee with medical benefits. He arranged for the insurance agent to send the paperwork directly to Jana.

Reassured that Jana would have backup, he gave the conference organizers a thumbs-up and made his airline reservations. Then he dug the laptop computer and camera he'd promised Jana from his office closet. He'd wait until the afternoon to drop it off. By then Tony would have sent one of the boys over to help with the heavy lifting.

Sure enough, when Sam arrived at the shop at three-thirty, a familiar navy-blue sedan was parked out back. Tony had purchased the small, used four-door for the kids in the program to use. Two of them had turned up, a boy and a girl, and Jana had them opening boxes and itemizing the contents on a list.

When Jana first saw him, her expression was wary, but then she saw the laptop tucked under his arm. "Tell me that's for me. If I have to write one more thing by hand, my fingers will fall off."

"Set it up in the office or out here?" Sam asked.

"I think the Internet cable in the office is long enough to reach out here. Ray?" she called to the wiry, dark-haired boy digging through a cardboard box.

"I'm on it." He trotted off to the office, returning with a coil of blue cable.

Jana set up the computer beside the cash register on the

front counter. Ray plugged in the cable. "I can get you set up," the boy told her.

"Thanks, Ray."

Stepping aside to let Ray work, she asked Sam, "Here to help?"

Guilt twinged inside him, but sexual attraction danced right next to guilt like a naughty younger brother. "Something came up." He told Jana about the writers' conference. "My agent piggybacked a Sunday-morning signing at a local bookstore, so I won't be back until that afternoon."

Was that relief he saw in her eyes? He felt even worse seeing it. That meant she'd figured out where his dirty little mind had been straying last night. Trying to be casual about it, he stepped back to give her some more breathing room.

"Can you check on the house while I'm gone?" He dug in his pocket for the extra set of keys he'd brought. "Bring in the mail, look through it. Open whatever you think needs attention."

"Sure." The keys might as well have been a snake, considering how gingerly she took them.

He gave her another foot of clearance. "I'd appreciate a call once a day. I can let you know what time works once I've seen the conference schedule."

"Call once a day. Check."

"And I set up medical insurance for you." He slipped a folded piece of printer paper from his back pocket. "This is a temporary card off their Web site."

"Thanks." She took the paper.

"Did you see an OB doctor in Portland?"

"At the free clinic." He saw a flicker of challenge in her eyes.

"Rebecca can probably recommend hers. I want you to make an appointment, ASAP."

She just nodded, not even arguing the point, which worried him even more. It was as if they were dancing around the room, keeping an invisible buffer between them. All because he'd stepped over the line last night and no doubt made her feel vulnerable.

He looked around him at the mismatched clutter arrayed across the shop floor. "You think you'll be able to sell some of this stuff the Internet?"

She reached into the nearest box and pulled out a stuffed toy, a fluffy, big-eyed kitten. "Should be able to. Ian and I used to hit the garage sales on Saturdays. Then we'd sell the stuff online. My boss at the pub would let us use his computer to upload the pictures and set up the ads."

She clutched the kitten close, like a barrier. He wanted to tear his own head off as punishment for being responsible for that uneasiness in her. He glanced over at Ray, working at the computer, and the blond girl categorizing a box full of figurines. No way they could discuss this with the two teens there. It would just have to wait until he returned.

"When are you leaving?" she asked.

"Early tomorrow. I've got plenty to do to get ready, so I won't see you again until I get back."

He held his breath, trying to parse what he saw in her expressive face. Except she was holding her cards close to the vest now. If she was relieved or disappointed that he'd be away five days, he couldn't tell.

"The contractor should be done refinishing the floor in here by the time you get back." She stroked the silky fur of the stuffed kitten. Damned if he didn't wish he was the one being stroked. "One small problem, though. My car is still at your place."

Sam didn't feel comfortable with leaving the kids here while Jana went with him to pick up her car. Not to mention the peril in being alone with her at his house, considering his current frame of mind.

"Ray, you have a license?"

The boy looked up from the computer. "Yeah."

"Ever ridden in a DeLorean?"

Now his eyes got as big as saucers. He just about fell over when Sam took him out back and he saw the stainless steel gull-wing. Ray lifted the door reverently and slid into the low-slung car, looking as if he'd died and gone to heaven.

A grin splitting his face, Ray sat in stunned silence as Sam took the curves back to his estate. When Sam was Ray's age, he would have given ten years of his life to ride in a car like the DeLorean. He felt a spark of joy giving a fellow foster kid that experience.

After Ray left in Jana's car, Sam packed, then checked his e-mail for updates from Melanie, the conference organizer. Based on Melanie's information, he wouldn't have to do much prep. He had a stock speech he gave at conferences, and he'd never given it in Phoenix. He'd print it out and give it a quick once-over on the plane. The panel discussions would require only a short bio. The rest of the five days he'd be schmoozing or maybe seeing a little of the Phoenix area.

Melanie had made it clear she'd be glad to show him around. Had made a point of mentioning she was single. Had even directed him to the photo on her Web site. The woman was a knockout, just his type.

But as he imagined shopping in Scottsdale or hiking

Dreamy Draw, his mental movie starred Jana, not Melanie. It was he and Jana who would share the stark desert beauty. He'd show her the towering saguaro cactus, and she'd make jokes about their many-armed freakishness. It would be her hand he'd reach for to help her up the craggy boulders as they climbed to Piestewa Peak. Then once they'd reached the top, they'd stand together and admire the spill of scarlet in the sky as the sun set.

He had his hand on the phone, ready to call her, before he realized he couldn't invite Jana to Phoenix. Not until he got his head on straight with her. Bad enough he'd let his physical attraction to her get so out of control just because they'd spent a few days in close quarters. Who knew what would happen if he took her with him to a conference? Even if he booked her in her own room, she'd be only steps away.

He let go of the phone and slumped in his chair, then thought about how his libido was mucking up this great friendship with Jana. He spent a few minutes feeling like a complete rat for even considering taking advantage of a mixed-up young woman who was pregnant and in need of his compassion, not a come-on.

He couldn't have Jana tonight, but he could have her alter ego. He opened up his notes document on his computer and spent the next couple of hours fleshing out his new character—he'd named her Lacey—and laying some meat on the bones of his new plot.

Lacey was still with him when he went to bed—early in deference to his 3:30 a.m. wake-up time—weaving herself into his dreams. In one fragment of sleeping fantasy, he made love to her, and in the midst of climax her face transformed from the one he'd imagined for his fictional character to Jana's.

* * *

The days Sam was gone moved so slowly for Jana that they just about went in reverse. It was as if he fed her a continuous electrical charge when he was around, an energy main line she couldn't live without. His absence meant she fell back into herself, sinking into her self-doubt, reliving the mistakes and screwups that riddled her life. She pictured him surrounded by adoring fans, the beneficiaries of his charisma.

Despite her doldrums, she made great progress at the shop. She and Ray and Frances were able to group the stuff for sale so they could be sold in bunches rather than one item at a time, which would make the whole thing easier and quicker. The contractors worked on the floor Wednesday through Friday, sanding, staining and varnishing the beautiful old oak boards. She'd filled a legal pad with merchandise ideas for six months of holidays starting with their mid-April opening date. One full page listed name possibilities for the shop to replace the choice Sam currently had registered with the court—The Christmas Store.

Like any of that would really distract her from her "Sam obsession." Here she was at Sam's house, Saturday afternoon, staring at the digital clock above his desk, watching it tick off the minutes until four o'clock—five o'clock Phoenix time. That was the slice of time between when his conference day ended and he was dragged out to dinner with those gaga fans he kept complaining about.

When the clock display read four, she forced herself to wait another few minutes before calling by playing another game of solitaire on Sam's computer, hand on the mouse instead of the phone. When it rang at five after four, she threw the mouse as she lunged to answer.

"Hey," she said, out of breath. "Thought I was doing the calling."

"I didn't want to take the chance I'd miss you. They're transporting a bunch of us up to Sedona for dinner. The bus leaves in a couple minutes."

"I've always wanted to see Sedona." She said it lightly so he wouldn't think it meant a lot to her.

"I wish you were the one coming with me."

There was nothing light in the way he said it. The simple statement seemed heavy with meaning. *I miss you,* her mind cried out. There was a time she could have said that out loud—such as when she was twelve and he'd gone off to Utah for a summer—but now those words seemed to mean so much more.

So instead she talked about trivialities. "I bought the printer today. Put it on the Amex card." He'd given her the card during their shopping spree, having told her it was for business expenses.

"Anything interesting in the mail?"

She flipped through the stack, although she'd already looked it over. "A couple fan letters forwarded from your publisher. A royalty check from your agent. Did you check your voice mail? He called yesterday evening while I was here, and I heard part of the message."

"He had the details of that new movie option."

"Congratulations." As if she needed another reminder of how out of her league Sam was. Last week while they'd been so buddy-buddy, she'd forgotten the circles Sam usually traveled in. His latest film deal brought home the fact that, little sister or not, she was such a minor player in his life.

She heard a woman in the background call his name. "In a minute," he responded, his voice muffled.

Was that exasperation in his tone? Or just eagerness to be finished with Jana so he could join the woman and the others? Or maybe it would just be this woman and him in a private car while everyone else rode in the bus.

She would make herself crazy thinking that way. "I'd better let you go." Her thumb hovered over the disconnect button.

"One more thing," he said, stopping her from hanging up. "I'd planned to land around three tomorrow afternoon. But Melanie's putting together a dinner for some of the local authors."

"Melanie?" Jealousy stabbed her, sharp as glass.

"The conference organizer. Should I stay another night? Or come home?"

Come home! Her heart all but yelled it. "Whatever you want."

"But do you—" He hesitated. "Is there anything I'm needed for at home?"

Was he asking if *she* needed him? She did, desperately. But she wasn't about to beg him. She had some pride. Plus she knew how important it was for him to keep promoting himself, even though he was Mr. Blockbuster Bestseller. Certainly more important than her wanting him home.

"Nothing going on I can't handle." The literal, if not emotional, truth.

She heard the woman again; then Sam made his apologies and signed off. As she stared at the phone, loneliness sat on her shoulder, crooning a sad little song in her ear.

Back at the apartment, she had little appetite for dinner, but she knew she had to eat. So she sautéed slices of chicken breast and tossed them with rigatoni, olive oil and Asiago cheese, then threw together a green salad to go with it. She ate as much as she could manage, remembering there were other needs besides hers at stake. Except that she didn't want to think about the baby and the inevitable loss she'd face when the adoption was final.

Sunday morning she woke to a brilliant blue sky and the glitter of frost kissing the pine trees outside. Bundling up in layers from the wardrobe Sam had bought her, she headed down the hill to Old Sacramento, a touristy section between the capitol and the Sacramento River.

She didn't like the sounds her engine was making as she drove down Highway 50 and considered turning back. But there were a half-dozen shops in Old Sac she wanted to check out. She'd arranged to speak with some of the owners about where they bought their merchandise, which companies were reliable sources and which weren't. In the back of her mind, she read Ian the riot act for talking her into selling her beautiful red Civic and buying this junker. He'd pocketed most of the profits in the transaction.

But the car got her safely to Old Sac, and she had a great time wandering around. Of course, it would have been way, way better exploring with Sam, asking his opinion about whether they should stock T-shirts and sweatshirts with seasonal slogans and sharing a chocolate-covered caramel apple from the candy place. But she took tons of notes and got plenty of good info. All the shopkeepers loved the idea of a holiday shop and thought the location up in El Dorado County's Apple Hill was a great one. She had such a good time that she didn't get back to the car until nearly three.

The noise started up again just as she hit the interchange between Interstate 5 and Highway 50. She did okay for another ten miles or so; then the engine started bucking and surging. With a death grip on the wheel, she pressed on, hoping and praying that the evil spell her life seemed to be under might not hold for just this once.

Sam was jammed in the jet aisleway between a stout woman and a couple of squirmy kids when his phone rang. He had to wriggle past his carry-on to free the cell from his back pocket, where he'd shoved it after turning it back on. When he saw the caller ID, his heart shifted into overdrive.

"Jana? Are you okay?"

"No." Her voice shook and terror ratcheted up another notch. "I'm stuck." He heard the roar of what sounded like a semi. "On the freeway."

"How— Never mind. Where are you?" As she described which exits on the freeway she was stuck between, dread oozed up inside him. The flight attendants still hadn't opened the damn door.

"Stay in the car, Jana. Call 911. I'll get a tow truck." The door finally open, Sam inched forward along the aisle. "I should be there in thirty minutes. Don't you move from that car." He refused to let himself imagine Jana walking along the freeway, exposed to the fast-moving traffic.

Once he was in the Jetway, he punched a preset on his phone for his auto club. More juggling of his carry-on to retrieve his wallet, but he got a tow truck ordered. He grabbed his checked bag the moment it popped out onto the conveyer belt, then took off like a tight end through the crowd.

He topped the speed limit by only ten miles per hour, whipping in and out of the light Sunday-afternoon traffic. By the time he pulled his Prius onto the shoulder behind Jana's junker, the tow driver was there and she was standing safely beside the freeway embankment.

He threw his arms around her, holding her close, feeling her heart thunder against his. "You're not driving that car anymore."

She tipped her head back, a faint wash of color flagging her pale cheeks. "I suppose you're going to let me use the DeLorean."

He couldn't help his grin. "In your dreams. You can borrow the Prius."

She buried her face in his chest. "Thank you for being here when I needed you."

He thought his heart would leap from his chest. "I'm just so glad you're safe. That the baby's safe."

Seeing the tow driver getting ready to roll the old junker up onto the bed of his wrecker, Sam let go of Jana. They got the rest of her belongings transferred to his Prius.

As they merged back onto Highway 50, Sam could see she was still shaken by the breakdown. Her throat worked as she seemed to struggle against tears. "I thought you weren't coming home until tomorrow."

So did he, until he found himself packing like an automaton this morning, loading up the rental car so he could head for Sky Harbor Airport the moment his bookstore appearance ended. All the while he spoke to the crowd of readers, he could think of nothing but seeing Jana again. Thank God he'd listened to his instincts.

His gaze linked with hers, just for an instant before he returned his attention to the road. But with just that brief visual contact, realization hit him with the force of a skip-load of bricks.

What he was feeling for Jana—it was the same single-minded obsession he'd felt for Faith when he'd first met her. And for Shawna before Faith and Cyndy before Shawna. He was laying his usual modus operandi on Jana, as if she was just one in a long line of women he professed to love and then later left.

Panic filled him. Was that what all this sexual attraction was about? Him taking himself down that same ambush-riddled path to disaster? Was there some twisted part of himself that wanted to turn his relationship with Jana into something physical so he could travel that same rutted road before discarding her?

No way. He wasn't going there. Because Jana was better than that. She was his friend, his sister. If he let himself follow his usual habitual pattern with Jana, she could be lost to him forever. His gut burned at the thought.

Jana pulled him from his dark musing. "You want to stop in at the shop? See what we got done while you were gone?"

Of course he did. Because now that he was back home, with Jana again, he wanted nothing more than to be with her.

He had to take a step back. Get some space, clear his head.

He leapt to the first excuse that popped into his mind. "Actually, during the flight I got some ideas on the new book. I want to get them down before I lose them."

"How about dinner, then?"

A fist of longing settled in his chest. Spending an hour sharing a meal with Jana would be a little piece of paradise. "Too much to do. Unpacking and laundry and…stuff. In fact, I've been thinking…if the kids have been working out at the shop—"

"They've been great. They hardly let me lift a finger."

"I want to get started on this book early. While every-thing's fresh in my mind. Which means you might not be seeing much of me for a while."

A few beats of silence settled in the car before she spoke again. "Okay. No problem."

She said the words so casually, as if it didn't matter to her at all that he was retreating back into his shell. As if she could take or leave his company.

He pressed on past the ache inside him. "You can access my e-mail from the shop. Follow up on fan mail, let my agent know about any speaking requests."

"Sure."

"And, you know, I'll pop in sometimes. It's not like you won't see me at all."

"Whatever, Sam. We'll be fine." She sounded as if she meant it.

He drove straight to his place, then after he'd retrieved his luggage from the trunk, watched her drive away. He stood on his front porch a long time, imagining her wending her way back to the security gate, then passing through. Wishing he could call her back.

Then he walked inside his lonely house and faced an endless time without Jana.

Chapter Eight

If Jana thought those five days Sam was in Phoenix had slogged by, that was nothing compared to the rest of January and all of February. It didn't help that it poured like Noah's flood twenty-six out of the forty-odd days during his absence. At the tail end of February, a cold front from Canada dropped in on Apple Hill with subfreezing temperatures and six inches of snow.

She kept herself busy with the shop, handling Sam's snail- and e-mail, forwarding on whatever she thought needed his attention. By previous agreement, she'd pick up the mail that arrived at the post-office box he kept for fans, leaving the correspondence that arrived at the house for him to deal with. He'd also provided her with a stack of autographed books, author copies for donating to worthy fund-raising causes.

So, while they talked during those long weeks, by phone

and e-mail, occasionally face-to-face at the shop, the conversations were short and sweet, leaving her aching for more. It was like when she was a kid and Sam's visits to Estelle's were few and far between. Sam was the only bright spot in her life.

She distracted herself with Frances's and Ray's antics, with visits to the Estelle's House ranch. At first she thought Tony would never forgive her for deserting him to take off with Ian. But after a couple of deluge-soaked weekends helping Rebecca and her students clean the bakeshop kitchen and dining room, he started to come around.

The last Sunday in February, while Ray, Frances and the other teens whiled away the rainy afternoon working on pie dough in the bakeshop's big commercial kitchen, Rebecca and Jana put their feet up in the dining room. With the bakeshop on hiatus until April, only a couple of the eight-foot folding tables were set up in the dining room, each one ringed with chairs. The rest of the tables and chairs were neatly stacked to one side.

"I like the pictures," Jana said, admiring the photos that filled one wall. The portraits featured the ten participants in the Estelle's House program's first session.

"Tony thought it would be a nice tradition to put the students' pictures up once they graduate." Rebecca turned from the photo gallery to eye Jana's still mostly flat belly. "I'm only a month further along than you. How come I already look like I'm carrying a watermelon and you're still svelte as ever?"

"How come you have actual boobs and mine look more like apricots?" Jana stared down at her chest. "If I can't get a good bust out of this, what good is pregnancy anyway?"

Rebecca smiled, but Jana saw a tinge of something

sadder in her friend's eyes. "How are you and Sam getting along?" she asked.

"Great. I never see him." She'd meant to say it as a joke, as if she preferred their separation. But her throat tightened up at the end.

Of course, Rebecca heard that little catch. "What's going on with you two?"

"Nothing. He's busy with his book. I'm busy with the shop. I work for him, Rebecca. There's nothing else between us than that." She did better that time, keeping the words matter-of-fact. "I mean, yeah, we're friends, but that's all."

"He seemed thrilled that you'd come back."

Jana laughed. "You don't have to exaggerate to make me feel better."

Rebecca fixed her steady gaze on Jana. "He's coming this evening. That's why the kids are working so hard on making the perfect apple pie."

"He never mentioned it."

Jana could see the uneasiness in Rebecca's face. "He's been having dinner over here most Sundays."

That knocked the air clean out of Jana's lungs. Because she was here so late some weekends, she'd shared Saturday-night dinner with the Estelle's House crowd and the occasional Friday night as well. But she'd always headed home by four or so on Sunday.

A sharp pain curled up in her stomach. "He's been waiting for me to leave?"

"No," Rebecca said. "At least not the way you think."

"What other way is there to think about it? He stays away when he knows I'm here, then shows up when I'm gone."

"Jana." Rebecca took Jana's hand, held it against her round belly. "I think Sam's pretty confused."

"And I'm not?" She patted her stomach. "Kinda got a few things on my mind myself."

"He's just always found it easier to keep people at arm's length."

"Tell me something I don't know." She flung her hands out in frustration. "I wish I'd never asked him for help. I wish I'd just gone some place in Portland, found a doctor who would—"

A hand might as well have closed around her throat. She couldn't say the words, couldn't even allow herself to think them. She stroked her belly in apology.

"Maybe I should have tried harder with Ian to get him to step up to the plate. Then I never would have had to dump my problems in Sam's lap."

Rebecca put an arm around her shoulders. "Sam's glad you came to him. Glad you're nearby. He might not want to let people get too close, but he likes to know that those he cares about are okay."

Jana knew Rebecca was right, but the fact that Sam seemed to be actively avoiding her still stung. She started to get up. "I guess I should get going. Before he gets here."

Rebecca's hand on her shoulder kept Jana in her chair. "Stay for dinner." When Jana tried again to rise, Rebecca didn't let up the pressure of her hand. "You might have Tony convinced to let bygones be bygones, but I think I still have some payback coming from you for deserting me last September. This is the first meal the kids are preparing for Sam entirely on their own. I need you here to soothe nerves."

Almost as if Rebecca had planned it that way, one of the girls—Frances maybe—shrieked in dismay from the kitchen. With a grin, Rebecca pushed to her feet and gave

Jana a hand up. Arms linked, they walked into the kitchen to see what culinary creation needed saving from the jaws of catastrophe.

Sam's first heads-up that Jana might still be at the ranch came when he detoured into town to see if the Prius was parked behind the shop. She could have been out running errands somewhere—wondering about where she might be and who she might be with gave him heartburn—but he figured it was most likely she was still hanging out with Rebecca. So when his candy apple–red 1968 Mustang slogged through the puddles in the ranch's gravel parking lot and his headlights picked out the Prius alongside Tony's pickup, he knew there'd be a moment of reckoning served up with his dinner tonight.

Parking his car with plenty of clearance on either side, he trotted across the wet, muddy gravel toward the warm glow of the bakeshop. The kitchen door was closest, so he entered that way, then wished he hadn't when he saw the mass hysteria playing out. Two of the teens were screaming at each other at the stove, two others with a glaze of panic in their eyes were garnishing plates on the center island and Ray was up to his elbows in dirty pots.

Rebecca spared Sam one quick glance, then called to Jana, "Get him out of here."

Jana grabbed his arm and towed him away, slipping through the madly moving bodies. After so many weeks of self-imposed exile from her, having Jana's hands on him was just about sending his circuits into overload.

"Sorry. Freak-out time. It was all going well until Liz put orange juice instead of lemon in the chicken piccata."

He unzipped his rain jacket. Before he could stop her,

Jana was behind him, helping him off with it, her fingers brushing the nape of his neck, then the length of his arms. He shuddered, hoping she'd assume it was a chill from the icy deluge outside.

She nabbed his hat, as well, then pushed a lock of hair back from his eyes. Still recovering from the contact on the back of his neck, the near-instantaneous graze across his forehead poleaxed him. He stood frozen as she crossed the room, hooking his hat and jacket on a coatrack with several others.

Even the warning that she was here hadn't been enough to build any defense against her. Not when he'd spent the past six weeks alternating thoughts of his new book with fantasies of her. Write a paragraph, think of Jana, write a sentence, imagine Jana, type a word…

It was a testament to his professionalism that he'd gotten as many pages written as he had. But that was likely because his fictional journalist, Lacey Willits, might as well have been Jana. Every moment he wrote about Lacey, he felt as if he were spending time with Jana.

"Anything I can do?" he asked.

Busywork might keep his mind off how incredible Jana looked in jeans and that thick wool sweater, as vivid red as the Mustang outside. She'd never been much for makeup, but she and Rebecca must have spent some girlie-girl time together, because she wore lip gloss just a shade lighter than the sweater.

And damn his overactive imagination, he wanted to kiss the lipstick off. See what it tasted like, how her mouth tasted. Feel the changing curves of her body under that sweater.

"Just sit," she said, pointing to the head of the tables set end-to-end. "Tonight you're not a helper bee—you're a customer. It's our job to please you."

Then she returned to the kitchen, leaving him gasping for air. He sat himself down, taking a slice of French bread from the basket in front of him and slathering it with butter just to give his hands something to do.

Within a few minutes, the teens started ferrying out the main dish—chicken à l'orange instead of chicken piccata. They served him first, then quickly set plates around the table. In far less time than he thought possible, considering the insanity of a few minutes ago, everyone was seated—eight teens, Rebecca, Tony, Estelle and Jana.

Jana sat to his right, her knees bumping against his. She wasn't nudging him on purpose, nor was she trying to avoid touching him. She kept smiling, laughing, joking with him and with the others around the table, her expression never changing whether her knees were in contact with his or not. He, on the other hand, could barely focus on his meal, waiting for her to touch him again, holding his breath until she moved away.

He praised the meal and ate every bite, although considering his distraction, he could have been eating pabulum. He didn't want the kids thinking he didn't appreciate their efforts. It was not their fault that Jana had stayed for dinner and he just couldn't handle being near her.

At seven-thirty, after they'd all finished their apple pie à la mode and the kids had started the cleanup, Sam pushed back from the table, ready to make his escape. Jana was in the kitchen with Rebecca and the others. He could give them a quick wave through the pass-through and leave by way of the dining-room door.

But he'd barely raised his hand to give his goodbyes when Jana called out, "Sam, I need to talk to you."

She wove through the busy students toward him, snagging his arm and all but perp-walking him outside to the front of the bakeshop. The rain had let up, the clouds gusting away to reveal a sliver of moon overhead. Neither the moon nor the lights inside provided much illumination, leaving him and Jana in the mysterious dark.

Whatever imperative had driven her to bring him out here seemed to have stalled. She kept glancing over at him, whether to gather courage or to abort her mission, he wasn't sure. He didn't exactly want to give her encouragement, but if she had something to say, he felt he owed it to her to give her the time to speak her piece.

There was a wood and wrought-iron park bench set outside, tucked under the overhanging eave. Sam tested the seat with his palm and found it was dry to the touch. "Sit?"

She settled on one end, hands tucked between her thighs, no doubt for warmth. He was sure he could do a better job of warming her hands; in fact, he could slip his hands around hers between her legs and—

He sliced off that notion with a mental machete. Sitting beside Jana, he shoved his own hands under his armpits to keep them out of mischief. "Well?"

She took a good, long breath. "Here's the thing. I am grateful to the max for everything you've done for me. The way you've taken me in, given me a job and place to stay."

Something about the tone of her voice thrust a sudden crazy idea into his mind. This was the big farewell. With all the work Jana had been doing here at the ranch, Tony had realized what a find she was and had eked out a job and living quarters for her. Or even worse—Sam's heart just about stopped beating in his chest—Ian had been in touch with her again. He'd had an epiphany about what an ass he'd been and now was ready to be a father.

His panic went up another notch as she continued. "That gratitude is what kept me from saying anything before now. But it just isn't right to keep going the way we have been."

He would start hyperventilating any minute now. He could cope with her returning here to the ranch—he'd still see her often enough. But if she went back to Ian, moved off to the Midwest or God knew where…

He wanted to grab her, to keep her here, but he just kept his hands where they were. Still, the frantic energy inside had him bouncing his legs, shaking the bench and Jana as well, no doubt. But he couldn't sit still.

"You have to do what you think is right," he told her, his voice sounding rough to his ears.

"Exactly." She turned toward him. Her face was more shadow than light, her expression impossible to decipher. "So here's the deal."

He gulped in a breath. Dug his fingernails into his sides.

Then she turned him upside down again. "It's time to cut the crap."

"What crap?"

She waved a finger at him. "Stop hiding from me, avoiding me, turning yourself into a hermit because you've got some brainless idea it's best for me. We are friends." She poked him in the arm with each word. "We do best when we spend at least a little time together, talking, arguing, sharing good Mexican and bad Chinese. If you've gotta work, you know I understand. Because I've got plenty of my own work to do. But during the in-between times, we can both squeeze in a little time for each other."

His legs stopped bouncing as he struggled to take in what she'd just said. "You want to spend more time with me."

She gave him a sharp nod. "Because I need your input on

the shop. Because I'm not sure I know how to answer every fan letter you get. Because I just plain enjoy your company. And I'm tired of sitting around at home alone because you have some goofy idea you need to set me free to spread my wings on my own." She flapped her hands in parody.

That she wasn't leaving was good. That she hadn't figured out why he'd been staying away—that his physical attraction for her threatened to mess up everything good about their relationship—was stellar. He'd missed her so desperately these past several weeks. He was such a self-centered SOB that it hadn't even crossed his mind that she might miss him, too.

"Come here," he said, reaching across the bench for her. He wrapped her in his arms, tucking her head under his chin. He felt the flare of attraction, but he blanked it as best he could and just let himself enjoy her nearness.

God, he cared so much for her. She was his best pal, the one he could tell anything to. Someone he could trust with his secrets, if he ever felt ready to share them. The whole sexual thing was an aberration, the side effect of a couple of months without a significant other. It was probably time to start scouting for a new girlfriend so he could stop those inappropriate thoughts.

Her breath on his throat grew warmer, her mouth moist against his skin. He wove his fingers into her hair, enjoying the length of the silky strands, the way they tickled his palms. He brought his other hand up to cradle her jaw, tipped her head back so he could see her face and trailed his thumb along her lips to see if he could make her smile.

Her dark eyes seemed enormous, rich with enigma and riddle. He brought his mouth gently down on the lids of her eyes as they fluttered closed, wishing he could solve the puzzle of Jana with that slight touch. She sighed and he spread his hands wider, feeling her heat soak into him. Then his lips drifted lower, along her high cheekbone, across her cheek, zigzagging back toward her mouth.

He only wanted to know her better. To understand what lay in his friend's heart. Tease out what she kept hidden inside. It wasn't a kiss. It was an exploration, a discovery.

He heard, he felt her sigh the moment his mouth covered hers. Felt her lips soften, felt them part. Tasted the first damp moisture within with the tip of his tongue. Dipped inside ever so slightly with a quick sweep.

He thought he'd come apart right there, just from a kiss. But, no, it wasn't a kiss. Just a touch, just an exploration.

A blast of wind spattered them both with the runoff dripping from the roof. He let Jana go and rose clumsily, tangling his feet on the leg of the bench. Groping for balance, he slapped his hand on one of the broad windows that fronted the bakeshop. Inside, Rebecca was just turning off the dining-room light switch, plunging him and Jana into a deeper darkness.

He could see the faintest glint in Jana's eyes. "I didn't mean to… I wasn't trying to…" He tried to order his thoughts. "Hell, I don't know what I was doing."

Silence swirled around them with the breeze. "What I said about more time together—"

"I know. That wasn't what you meant." He put his hand out for her. "Ready to go?"

"Let me grab my purse. I'll get your jacket and hat."

When she came back, she kept a buffer zone between them. She kept her goodbye hug brief, tentative, and he could feel her holding her breath. He wanted to try again to explain what he'd done on that bench, but he wasn't exactly clear on the concept himself. Yeah, his libido had been wagging its naughty little tail, whispering suggestions. But there had been something more, something deeper in those charged moments.

It wasn't as if she was a lover. But it was a hell of a lot more than friendship. And how that interlude would fit into the world he and Jana shared he had no damn idea.

Chapter Nine

The first few weeks of March, Jana saw so much of Sam that she would have thought they'd get tired of each other or start to bicker about stupid things. But those twenty-something days were like some kind of magical interlude. The last of her morning sickness had vanished. She'd never smiled so often, never laughed as much, never told so many really awful jokes in her life. All that time, she kept looking over her shoulder for her old companion, disaster, but so far he was a no-show.

Sam would work on his book for several hours starting early in the morning, while Jana and one or two of the teens would set up the display shelves or unpack merchandise that was arriving daily. Then he'd join her, helping the teens with the heavy work that he absolutely refused to let her do.

They'd all have lunch; then she and Sam would often spend the afternoon brainstorming ideas for the shop or plot complications for his book. Or they'd head down the hill to run errands, sometimes stopping for dinner and a movie before returning home. If she made him dinner at the apartment, they'd play cards afterward or watch some television.

With all the conversation that flew fast and furious between them, there was one topic of discussion they wouldn't touch with a fifty-foot pole. That night at the ranch. Her in his arms. His kiss.

A part of her wondered if she'd imagined the whole thing. Another part, that wishful-thinking part, wondered what it had meant. Because although she'd burned from head to toe with the feel of his mouth on hers, there was something about his touch that had seemed…well, not chaste exactly. But not really sexual. There had been something more to it. Something deeper, more complex. Something she most definitely didn't understand.

But he hadn't shown even a smidgen of interest in a repeat performance. She told herself that was good, that the last thing she wanted was to follow in her mother's footsteps. But some nights, as she lay in bed alone, the longing for Sam just about killed her.

Now, sitting at the apartment's kitchen table, her feet up on the second vinyl dinette chair, Jana stared into her peppermint tea, replaying for the millionth time every moment of Sam's kiss. She was alone this morning, the teens all too busy preparing for the big Easter carnival and egg hunt at the ranch. The fund-raiser was scheduled for Saturday, the 27th of March, and only two days away. The kids had been going crazy baking, building game booths and decorating. Jana and Sam had been able to get them a good deal on the decorations and game prizes, but Rebecca was insisting the teens do everything else themselves. Which left Jana out of the loop.

There were a few things she could have done downstairs this morning, but it just wasn't the same without Sam. He usually showed up by noon; it was a quarter after.

She moved to the living-room window to watch for him to pull up out back. Holding the mug of tea, her gaze out at the pine trees shielding Highway 50 from her sight, she almost missed it. She wouldn't have even known what she was feeling, if Rebecca, a month ahead of her, hadn't described it a few weeks ago.

"Oh," she whispered, setting the mug of tea down on the windowsill. She stared down at her belly, at five months now pooching out far enough that no one could miss the fact that she was pregnant. She held her breath, afraid breathing would keep her from feeling it again.

Then she felt it, clear as day. Like a bubble inside her, kind of a swish. Too subtle to feel or see from the outside yet. Not like it would be later, according to what Rebecca had told her.

She plastered herself against the window, willing Sam to come. When he finally arrived five minutes later, she flung open the door and hurried out to the landing.

"Sam!" she all but screamed down at him as he climbed from the Mustang.

He slammed the car door and raced up the steps. "What's the matter? Are you okay?"

She smiled so he wouldn't worry, so full of joy she could have floated off the landing. "I felt the baby move."

A mix of expressions danced across his face, so quickly she couldn't figure them all out. But happiness settled last, and he threw his arms around her. "That's great, fantastic."

As they walked inside, a dose of reality slapped Jana upside the head. Her joy faded even as the little minibun tumbled again inside her.

She sat on the sofa as Sam shut the door. "It's probably not such a great idea getting so excited about the baby moving."

He settled on the armchair beneath the window. "Maybe not."

She curved her fingers around her belly. "It's just hard sometimes to think about it. Watching the baby grow all these months. Then saying goodbye."

He leaned forward, elbows on his knees. "You don't have to, Jana."

"Nothing's changed. I still don't have a dime to my name except what you give me."

"You work for that money."

"I do." As hard as she could. And she'd saved every penny she could, a part of her still wishing she could build enough of a nest egg to keep her baby.

But not even those tight-fisted savings would last beyond a few months. She'd still be scraping by for food and diapers for the baby. She couldn't begin to afford day care, which would allow her to work. Wouldn't it be selfish to raise her child in poverty just because she wasn't strong enough to give it up?

The baby moved yet again, as if to express an opinion. But darned if Jana could figure out what that was. She only knew she didn't want to think about it right now.

"Did you want to go through the Christmas catalog again, finalize our order?"

The holiday season might be more than eight months away, but it would be a big one for the store. She wanted all the details nailed down way in advance. Especially since she probably wouldn't be here past September.

It was as if the last of the air seeped out of her little balloon of happiness. September was a mere five months away. By then the baby would be born. And gone, living with another family. The balloon went flat.

Sam had been looking off into the middle distance, his thoughts impenetrable. When he zeroed in on her again and said, "Why not?" it took her a few seconds to remember the question he was answering.

They went downstairs, the brisk early spring breeze stealing under Jana's roomy long-sleeved T-shirt. She wrapped her arms around her middle, wanting to keep her belly warm.

Melancholy descended again as she waited for Sam to unlock the back door. Would she have a chance to hold her baby? Should she? Maybe it would be best if she never saw it.

"I like the sign," Sam said as they walked inside.

The lighted window sign, spelling out Celebration Station in colorful neon, had been delivered and installed yesterday. A couple weeks ago, when Sam was still digging in his heels about changing the shop's name, she wasn't sure if they'd get the sign finished before their April 10 opening. But then one night, he'd abruptly changed his mind, and Jana was able to get the wheels turning with the neon artist.

They sat together in the office, flipping through the catalog. Sam nodded in all the right places, even threw in a comment or two, but Jana could see his mind was somewhere else. The feel of the baby's movements still so fresh, her heart still tender and grieving, she wanted all of Sam here with her. She thought of grabbing him and shaking him, demanding he pay attention to her, now. Then she gave herself a mental kick in the butt and told herself to buck up.

They were almost finished anyway; then they could go get some lunch. She reached into the filing cabinet and pulled out a file folder. She'd been clipping photos of decorated rooms from old magazines for the past several weeks.

She spread the pictures across the desk. "I was thinking we'd set the store up kind of like a living room. One big Christmas tree in the corner with presents piled underneath. Garland and ribbons everywhere, small tables set up with seasonal tablecloths, Christmassy shades on the lamps, standup Santas and snowmen. Of course, everything on display would be available for sale."

It was as if she'd lassoed him and brought him back from outer space. He riveted his gaze on those happy, gorgeous photos, the rooms perfectly decorated for Christmas. She'd clipped each page for only one or two ideas. They were mostly way too busy for her taste. But she might as well have waved a magic wand over Sam's head. She could see that from his soft smile, the light in his eyes, he loved every overdone bit of glitter in the pictures.

He picked them up, one by one, taking his time, his gaze moving from one feature on the page to the next. Once he'd examined them all way more closely than Jana had ever expected, he went back to the second one in the array.

"This is what I want," he said, setting the magazine page in Jana's hands.

It was the most garish of the bunch, a riot of vivid color. Most of the others were themed—all silver, all gold, variations on bells, Santas, snowmen. But that particular room had been decorated with just about every Christmas symbol on the planet, many of them animated. Reds and greens and blues and purples screamed from the page. It was like a child's fantasy of Christmas.

"A little over the top, don't you think?" Not to mention a headache to set up in the shop the size of Celebration Station. She got vertigo just thinking about all those animated pieces moving at once.

"It's perfect," Sam said, a familiar stubborn set to his jaw. "This is how I want to decorate the store."

"Okay," Jana agreed, drawing out the syllables. What did it matter, anyway? She wouldn't be here for the final setup. "Ready for lunch?"

Now guilt flickered across his face. "I have plans."

A boulder of disappointment dropped in her stomach. "An appointment with your accountant?" With the April 15 tax deadline approaching, maybe there were some details they had to iron out.

"Not my accountant. Someone else." He wouldn't look at her. That set off alarm bells she tried to ignore.

She ordered herself to breathe. "No biggie. I can throw together something here. Or maybe go up to Mae's Diner."

He checked his watch, pushed to his feet. "How about dinner instead?"

How about you tell me who you're seeing? "I've been craving spaghetti and meatballs."

"Great." He gave her a kiss on the forehead absent-mindedly, like he used to when she'd been a twerp and he a grown man. Then he was out the door without so much as a look back.

She stacked up the magazine pages and stuffed them back into the folder, with Sam's choice on top. Without him for company, she didn't have much of an appetite. But she heated a can of tomato soup and made a peanut butter and jelly sandwich and finished both as if they were medicine she had to take.

A quick survey of her fridge told her she'd need to go to the market for some ground beef for the meatballs. If she went down to Placerville, she could spend a little time browsing the shops. It'd be kind of lonely without Sam, but she ought to get used to doing stuff without him. Friend or not, they weren't exactly attached at the hip.

Deciding to save her marketing for later so the meat wouldn't spoil, she drove into Placerville, parked the Prius and headed up the north side of Main Street. The late-March sunshine spilled down yellow as butter, warming the breeze, cheering Jana despite her longing for Sam. Maybe she'd get herself some gelato from the little place she and Sam often stopped in for lunch.

She'd just reached the café, had been about to turn for the entrance when a familiar silhouette caught her eye. Sitting by the window, his back to her, was Sam. She recognized the forest-green T-shirt he'd been wearing, of course, but even if he'd changed clothes, she had those broad shoulders memorized.

And opposite him, her pretty face animated as she spoke, was a woman.

It was as if someone had poured hot oil over her, inside and out. Sam had made plans for lunch with someone else, hadn't wanted to tell her with whom. He had every right to date someone new, but why wouldn't he just tell her? She might not have wanted to know, but better fair warning than this surprise.

Calm down, idiot. This could be anyone—a fellow author, a friend, his accountant's married daughter. There didn't have to be anything special between them.

But then Sam reached across the table and took the woman's hand. Held it in both of his. Cradled it as if it was precious, the most wonderful gift. Jana could imagine the way Sam was looking at the woman. It was the way she wanted Sam to look at her.

Jana tried to drag her gaze away, but it was as if her eyes were stuck on the image, like a movie on pause. She studied the woman's face, her dark wavy hair, the blue eyes. The black Irish look of her, the familiarity of her smile.

It hit her with the force of a wrecking ball. This wasn't Sam's new love. And no distant cousin either. She looked so much like Sam that Jana would bet a million dollars this was his sister.

His real sister. Not a fake, you're-just-like-a-sister figure like Jana. The woman in the restaurant was Sam's blood relation, a real link to his past. Someone that would mean about a hundred times more to Sam than Jana did.

Jana racked her brains—what had Sam said her name was? Maddie? He'd only mentioned her the one time, when he'd come over to Estelle's after yet another breakup. Jana was seventeen at the time, during her madly-in-love-with-Sam phase. Sam had been a little drunk, and he'd let slip that he had a sister named Maddie whom he hadn't seen in years.

And here he was meeting her again in the flesh, but he didn't say one word about it to Jana. Why was that? Why not share that good news? Maybe because now that he had the real McCoy, he didn't need a pale imitation. Probably this afternoon, when he'd been so distracted, was just a taste of how he would start withdrawing from Jana's life.

No wonder Sam was in another world. He was planning

to meet his sister. That had to be big for him, huge. Way more significant than spending yet another lunch with Jana Not-Really-His-Sister McPartland.

Jana ordered her feet to move, backing away from the café. She'd lost her taste for gelato. Had no heart for window-shopping. She'd just go to the market, then head home again.

Pulling into the supermarket parking lot, she tried to push down the pain inside her. But it stayed lodged in her chest all the time she shopped, all during the drive home, the entire afternoon while she made dinner for Sam. A dinner he would probably wish he was sharing with Maddie instead of Jana.

Sam stared across the table at his sister, no doubt a goofy grin on his face, and wished to hell he'd brought Jana along. But he hadn't known how it would go today, if it would work out or be awkward and uncomfortable, so he'd thought it would be better to fly this one solo.

Still he'd hated to leave her behind. The past few weeks had been great, better than great. His book was just about writing itself, the time he spent with Jana energizing his creativity. And although that zing that shimmered between him and her never went away, he'd managed to box away that night at the ranch, the kiss outside the dining room, and not obsess about it. Not too much anyway.

"God, I'm glad I e-mailed you," Sam said to his sister for about the hundredth time.

And for about the hundredth time, she smiled at him across the table. "Me, too."

Other than when they were eating lunch, they'd barely

let go of each other's hands. He hung on, a little afraid she'd disappear, that the past hour and a half had been a dream.

"I wish things had been different, Sam. That Aunt Barbara hadn't kept us apart the way she did."

"I wish I hadn't been such a jerk when you contacted me five years ago." He was still kicking himself over that, regretting the time lost in getting to know his sister.

He couldn't wait to introduce Maddie to Jana. He was sure Maddie would love Jana. That they'd instantly click the way he and Jana had all those years ago.

That pleasant prospect was sidetracked by the question that had been lurking in the back of Sam's mind. The one he didn't know if he'd ever get a chance to ask. The one he wasn't even sure he wanted answered.

He took a breath. "When Mom left, those days we were alone…"

He saw the sympathy in Maddie's eyes. "That was a long time ago, Sam."

"I just need to know," he went on before he could chicken out. "How much do you remember?"

"I was two years old," she reminded him.

"So you don't remember anything?"

"No, except…" Her brow furrowed. "The bathwater running."

Sam's stomach clenched as the memories flooded him. Maddie's fever spiking, the cool bath the only thing he could think of to bring it down. He'd left her for only a minute, less than a minute.

Maddie must have seen something of his inner torment, because she gave his hand a squeeze. "We both came out okay, Sam. What does it matter what happened twenty-five years ago?"

The server returning with his credit card saved him from having to answer. As he signed the slip, Maddie asked a question of her own. "Have you ever looked for her?"

He didn't have to ask who she meant. "No."

"But haven't you ever wondered—"

"No, I haven't." A big fat lie. Few days went by that his mother didn't at least drift into the periphery of his mind.

"It would be nice to know," Maddie said quietly.

Darius could find her, probably in a heartbeat. But that was yet another question he'd just as soon leave unanswered.

They walked along Main Street. "That woman you're helping. Jana."

"What about her?"

"To take her in like that, to help her get through her pregnancy… I kind of wondered if there was more between you."

"More?" They stopped at the crosswalk, waiting for traffic to clear. "More like what?"

"The way your face lights up when you talk about her, it reminds me of Matthew. He looks at me that way sometimes."

"Matthew, your fiancé?" He put a hand on her arm as they stepped into the street. "As in, the guy who's madly in love with you?"

When they reached the other side where their cars were parked, she stopped him, looked up at him. "Are you in love with her?"

He went hot, then cold, then hot again. "No! Yes, I think the world of her. Like I do Estelle, and my friend Tony. But, no, I'm not in love with her."

Of course he wasn't. Because if he fell in love with Jana, it wouldn't be long before he fell out again. Then he wouldn't want her in his life anymore and would send her away. He couldn't bear the thought of seeing Jana leave.

The contradicting thoughts collided with each other, leaving him even more confused. He tried to figure out how to explain things to Maddie as they stopped beside his Mustang. "When I first met Jana fourteen years ago, my life was pretty upside down. I'd been on my own for three years, was still scared to death I'd end up on the street. School was way harder than I thought it would be."

Maddie leaned against the car beside him. "I wish I could've been there for you."

"Aunt Barbara never would have let you."

"Still…" Her arms wrapped around her, Maddie stared down at the sidewalk. "I don't remember much about when Aunt Barbara sent you away. I wondered what happened to my brother. But I was so young, I kind of forgot you for a while."

"She didn't talk about me at all?" It shouldn't matter after all this time. But it cut so deep that he'd been discarded that way, even though he'd been such a juvenile delinquent.

"Just that you'd gone to live somewhere else." Distress lined her face as she seemed to grasp for the old memories. But then she smiled, looking up at him again. "So you met Jana at Estelle's?"

"Yeah." He told Maddie about the first time he saw Jana's pugnacious young face. "She had a way of taking my mind off everything that was eating me up inside. She'd tell some ridiculous joke that should only have been funny to a ten-year-old girl, but somehow I'd be laughing with her."

He let the storyteller in him take over, describing the trips to the river to collect tadpoles, the snowball fights up at Lake Tahoe. It occurred to him that during those years, Jana had given him the childhood he'd never had.

Then there was that day when everything changed. When he showed up at Estelle's and Jana, now a willowy twenty, was there showing off the dress she'd borrowed for a date with her latest boyfriend. Seeing her in that electric-blue, strapless cocktail dress had sucked the air right out of his lungs. Yeah, she was still just a friend, but she was a woman, not a little girl anymore. And to be honest, that was the first time he'd wondered about kissing her.

Maddie was studying his face, and damned if she wasn't poking into his mind again. "Just friends, huh?" He saw the laughter in her blue eyes, so close a match to his they were like his own reflection in a mirror.

"I think you're so in love with Matthew you want to see that same passion in everyone else."

She shrugged. "What do you think of her giving up her baby?"

That was another path he didn't really want to walk down. He hated the idea but knew he couldn't ever breathe a word to Jana about how he felt. Taking a page out of his sister's book, he shrugged. "Her decision."

"True. But has it crossed your mind…" Maddie turned toward him, fixing him with that familiar blue gaze. "Have you thought about having kids?"

Her whiplash-inducing question left him stuttering. "I…ah…yeah, as a matter of fact. I want kids." Not the usual male thing to do, but having kids, a family, had been a distant dream for a long time. But problematic, the way he couldn't keep a woman in his life.

One corner of Maddie's mouth dipped down, and he had a sudden flash of déjà vu, of two-year-old Maddie frowning that way. "You'd have to think long and hard about it. It's not something you'd ever take on lightly. But if she's determined to give up her baby…"

As Maddie verbally danced, prescience prickled up his spine. "What the hell are you talking about?"

"About Jana's baby." Maddie laid her hand on his arm, the seriousness of her expression sending another wave of foreboding through him. "Why not adopt the baby yourself?"

Chapter Ten

Maddie's bombshell suggestion pretty much knocked the stuffing out of Sam. He, in turn, felt both stupid for not thinking of it himself and completely terrified at the thought. Mixed in that stew of emotions was an unexpected joy that he could have a child of his own. Even better, a child that came from Jana, the one person he cared about most in the world.

Sure, he had no clue about how to be a father—he certainly couldn't emulate his own absent dad, who spent far more time with his job as a long-haul trucker than with his family. And he wasn't certain he could pull off the mothering side of the equation either—except to do it differently than the confused and messed-up mother who deserted him and Maddie.

Amidst all that heavy thought, he completely forgot about his promise to have dinner with Jana that night. It wasn't until two-thirty in the morning, as he stood at his bedroom window, staring out at the darkness, that he recalled his broken commitment.

By then it was too damn late to call and apologize. He wondered why Jana hadn't called him to remind him, then got riled up worried about her, that something had happened to prevent her from reaching the phone. When he still couldn't get that thought out of his mind an hour later, he dressed and drove down to the apartment, parking on the Carson Road side, where her bedroom window faced. He drifted off a couple of times in the cramped driver's seat, but finally at five-thirty or so, her light came on. He took that as a sign that she was okay and went back home to scrape together a few hours of sleep.

The moment his eyes opened at just past eleven, he called her. When her cell went to voice mail, his sleep-deprived brain crafted a barely coherent message; then he stumbled to the shower.

Now fully awake, he dithered with the phone in his hand. Should he mention Maddie's suggestion? No, bad idea. He hadn't come close to making up his mind. Whether his adoption of Jana's baby would thrill her or chill her, he shouldn't be giving her grief until he was sure. So he'd keep it to himself for now.

He pressed her speed dial key again. This time, she answered.

He didn't even bother with hello. "I'm sorry. I'm a jackass."

Her response was polite and prim and entirely un-Jana-like. "I'm sure you have plenty on your mind."

Good God, did she know? Had Maddie somehow tracked down Jana's cell number and called her, laid out her outrageous suggestion? He shook off the crazy, impossible notion. Jana was probably just ticked off that he'd forgotten dinner.

"Let me make it up to you," he told her. "Come over here for dinner tonight."

"You're going to cook?" Now she sounded like the old Jana.

"A caterer friend owes me one. I'll have her send over dinner."

"Is she one of your kiss-offs?" Now she sounded nasty, even more out of character for Jana than the politeness.

What alien has stolen my good buddy? "I met the caterer and her husband at a chamber of commerce event. Seven o'clock sound okay?"

"I guess. What about lunch? I seem to have an excess of spaghetti and meatballs in my fridge."

"Yeah, I can— No, wait." He checked the calendar on his phone. "Damn. I've got this thing at noon with my agent. I can come over after, maybe around two."

"I have a doctor's appointment. Then I'm meeting with a lady. At that agency." The last three words came out raw, as if dragged from her throat.

About to ask what agency she meant, it hit him like a semi. *The adoption agency.* "You finally made the appointment."

"I thought I better."

Should he tell her now? But he still wasn't sure. What if he got cold feet? If he couldn't commit to a woman, for God's sake, how could he commit to a ten-times-more-needy baby?

The best he could come up with was an offer. "You want me to go with you?"

Silence for five long seconds. "I'd rather do this alone."

Now he felt like a real heel for keeping quiet. But although he could impulsively offer her money, could change his life on a dime to help fix up the apartment for her and give her the job preparing the shop for opening, blurting out, "Hey, why don't *I* just adopt your baby," would be beyond wrong.

"Then I'll see you at seven," he said.

"Okay."

He hung up, wishing he could have reached through the phone and given her a hug. He went into his office and sat at his desk in preparation for the conference call with his agent. God only knew how he'd focus on the negotiations for film rights on his next book. He would have rescheduled if his agent hadn't gone through so much trouble setting this up with the Hollywood producers involved.

So when the phone rang, he did his best to shift gears, to take his mind off Jana. But she was always there in his mind's eye, the image crystal clear—her looking up at him, her expression serious as she placed her baby in his arms.

Jana's was the last appointment of the day at the adoption agency. It was a Friday on top of that, and the lady Jana talked to must have planned a big weekend, because she seemed in an awfully big rush to get through the preliminary interview. But despite her speediness, the woman managed to work in the same question about a dozen times in as many versions.

Are you sure you want to give your child up for adoption?

Jana nodded yes every time, saying it out loud for extra emphasis. It didn't change the screaming no inside her, but she'd stopped listening to that voice when it couldn't come up with a solution for how she'd manage to raise a baby while working and going to school. When she would barely be able to support herself, let alone pay for a sitter.

After the emotional roller coaster of the adoption agency visit, she would have just as soon stayed home. Eaten a third meal of spaghetti and meatballs. But she had a feeling that if she called and canceled, Sam would be on her doorstep about ten minutes later.

The way he'd insisted on her coming over for dinner had made her kind of suspicious. Maybe he wanted to tell Jana that since he'd gotten in touch with his sister again, he wouldn't be able to spend as much time with her. He'd rather use the time he'd been spending with her to see his sister instead. This could be a kiss-off, sort of like the ones he did with his girlfriends, except without the expensive jewelry.

That lit a campfire in her stomach, a burning pain worse than anything the month of morning sickness had thrown at her. Still, she pulled on jeans and what she thought was her cutest maternity top, a short-sleeve, rose-patterned scoop neck, and headed over to Sam's. She knocked to give him warning, then let herself in when she discovered the door was unlocked.

He was halfway down the stairs as she stepped inside. He wore a black dress shirt, the sleeves rolled up, and black slacks that looked custom-made. Despite the sense of impending doom hanging over her, or maybe because of it, all the longing, wanting, hot desire she'd refused to acknowledge these past few months surged in a sudden ambush. So vulnerable after her visit to the adoption agency, laid low by her fear that Sam was about to show her the door, she had nothing in reserve to contain her reaction.

His hurrying steps slowed as he crossed the room toward her. "How'd it go?" Something flashed in his eyes behind the question, but she couldn't figure it out. Hopefully not pity. She'd be pissed if that was all he had left for her.

"It went," she said, fighting to keep the mess inside her out of her voice. "I've got another appointment in a couple weeks."

She followed him into the dining room, then had the breath knocked out of her when she saw what he'd done. Tall white candles in crystal holders, what had to be his best china and actual silver silverware, a gorgeous arrangement of spring flowers and a white tablecloth, for heaven's sake. She stared at the flickering flames, the coral glads with their fuzzy red centers, and just wanted to start bawling. Because this might not be a diamond tennis bracelet, but it was close.

And competing with the tears, a rush of desire washed over her again, completely turning her brain inside out. It made no sense that in the same moment she wanted to break down and cry, she also wanted to beg him to carry her off to his bedroom and make love to her.

Was it because she was more like her mother than she wanted to think? With good old Mom, every road from gratitude would lead to sex, because she didn't know any other way to say thank-you.

Except in that moment, with Sam looking back at her, that expression on his face asking if it was okay what he'd done, if she liked it, Jana didn't care if she'd turned into a clone of her mother. Because Jana wanted him so desperately, to ease the pain inside her, to express how much she appreciated all he'd done for her. She wanted him because he was Sam, because she loved him so damn much and had forever.

He served the meal, kept warm in the oven. Shrimp scampi and pasta, a Caesar salad and crunchy French bread. Tiramisu for dessert, coffee for him and herbal tea for her. They talked about the shop, the latest merchandise that had arrived that day, the big Easter extravaganza at the ranch tomorrow, the progress on his book. She thought he might ask again about her appointment, but although he asked how it went at the doctor, he avoided the other topic.

They moved to the living-room sofa, Jana stretched out at one end, Sam at the other with his feet on the coffee table. Outside, a spring storm rattled the windows.

Should she ask him about his lunch? Introduce the subject so she could be put out of her misery sooner rather than later? He'd been dancing around something all evening. She'd just as soon get it out into the open.

Then he took a big breath and saved her from asking. "I saw my sister today."

Jana's stomach lurched. "Maddie?"

"Madelena. I'm surprised you remember the name. I know I never talked much about her."

The disaster monkey perched on her shoulder, Jana focused on making polite conversation. "How long since you saw her last?"

"Twenty-three years ago, when she was four. We spoke over the phone about ten years ago, but nothing since then."

"I guess you'll be off with her a bunch," Jana said, trying to be casual. "No biggie. I'm fine on my own."

He stared at her as if she'd grown antlers. "She only flew in for the day. She's already back in San Diego."

The rolling turmoil inside Jana came to a screeching halt. "What? Why?"

He shrugged. "Neither one of us was sure how the reunion would go. So she figured she'd just do a day trip this first time. I didn't tell you before now for the same reason. But when she's able to get away again, she's looking forward to meeting you."

He told her more about Maddie, about how she'd attended University of California at San Diego for her nursing degree and now worked at a research hospital. Her fiancé, a marine, would be permanently deployed in San Diego after this last tour of duty.

"Maddie suggested I bring you to her wedding."

Still reeling from the revelation that Maddie hadn't replaced her in Sam's affections, Jana stuttered out, "When is it?"

"First weekend in December."

She felt like one of those guys in the old Western movies, tied to four horses to be torn apart. There was the horse that wanted to meet Maddie and the one that feared tying herself even more tightly to Sam. The one who would love to go to Maddie's wedding and the one who thought she'd be better off walking away after the baby's birth. At least until she was on her own two feet, to show Sam she could take care of herself.

"We'll see," she said finally.

A powerful gust of wind slammed rain against the back windows. The trees beyond the pool whipped their branches in a crazy dance.

Sam glanced at his watch. "It's nearly ten."

"I should get going." But she didn't move, exhausted by the emotional ruckus of the past few hours.

"Maybe you should stay over. In the guest room."

Why not? She'd slept there any number of times, back when she house-sat for Sam and more recently, when she'd returned from Oregon. But somehow the decision to stay tonight seemed weightier. More dangerous.

Another bucket of water gushed against the window. She thought about slogging out to the Prius, driving back to town, with the wind shaking the small car on the winding roads, getting even wetter racing up the stairs to her apartment.

"I could stay."

"Good."

The decision made, they lapsed into silence. Sam turned, straightening his legs alongside hers. At one time, that would have been the most innocent of gestures. They would have rubbed each other's feet and cracked jokes over whose socks were the smelliest.

But tonight, there was no grade-school humor. The tension between them was too taut, too loaded. Jana's skin felt hot, too tight. It was hard to breathe.

Sam's gaze fixed on her, the blue of his darkening nearly to black in the dim room. His hand fell on her leg, his fingers dipping under the hem of her jeans, stroking from the top of her ankle sock to her calf. Fire followed in the wake of his touch.

As if she were his mirror image, helpless to resist imitating him, she trailed her fingers under the cuff of his slacks. Her heart hammered in her ears as she touched skin, halfway up his calf, felt the coils of hair against her palm. He shifted his leg so she could push the slacks up, allowing her access to the crease of his knee, the beginning of his muscular thigh.

Her snugger jeans restricted how far he could touch her, leaving her aching, wanting his hands to move higher, along her thigh, to the juncture of her legs. With the loose elastic around the waist, it would be easy enough to slip the jeans from her hips, give him better access. Her head swam with confusion, with flame, as she imagined herself undressing for him.

A tiny piece of common sense floated to the surface, but her throat felt so dry she could barely speak. "What are we doing?" she whispered.

"I don't know. Honestly. I don't have a damn idea."

"We're friends." She swallowed, trying to work a little moisture in her mouth. "Do friends do stuff like this?"

She hadn't even felt this way with Ian, and he'd supposedly been her lover, her boyfriend. But things had never been this way between her and Sam. Not until the past few months, since she came back from Portland.

And yet she didn't stop touching him, leaning forward slightly to graze the crease behind his knee. His breath caught; she could hear it. He shifted again, and she could see his erection pushing against the fly of his slacks. A movie reel of images spilled from her mind—her unhooking his slacks, slowly lowering the zipper, pushing down slacks and shorts. He wore boxers; she'd seen a pair left on the floor outside his bedroom once.

She could so clearly see how he'd look with his clothes pushed out of the way, the way he'd react if she kissed along that hard length. She'd never liked doing that with Ian, had gone along with it because she thought she should. But she was dying to taste Sam that way.

"Damn it to hell," Sam muttered, shoving off the sofa and striding across the living room. He practically pulled the hair off his head as he paced back and forth across the carpet. Jana couldn't drag her eyes away from him, still fixed on that enticing bulge at his fly.

He caught her looking. Turned his back on her. Managed to make it to the stairs without ever revealing the front of him. Of course that gave her his butt to fantasize about.

He wouldn't have known because he didn't look her

way again. "I'm… I've got… Don't think I'll be down again tonight. You know where everything is."

She watched until he disappeared at the top of the stairs. She sat for several more minutes, trying to gather herself. She might as well have been a feather out in that storm, tossed every which way until she didn't know which end was up.

Finally, she levered herself up from the sofa and padded off to the guest room. She thought she'd never fall asleep, but her body took charge and tipped her off into dreamland the moment her head hit the pillow.

Not that he'd really expected to fall asleep when he went upstairs at ten, but he didn't think he'd still be a jittery mess of nerves at two in the morning. The two-hour session at his computer from ten to midnight had only wired him more than Jana's touch had, although he did have a damn good love scene written between Trent and Lacey. Too accurate a description of all the things he'd like to do with Jana, the seven pages would never see the light of day.

When he finally shut down his computer, when he should have had better sense, he'd crept downstairs and to the guest room. When he couldn't hear a sound from within, he'd made another boneheaded move and nudged the slightly ajar door open and cautiously stepped inside. Jana was so dead asleep that she didn't so much as stir as he tiptoed across the floor to stand over her bed.

It reminded him of the story of Cupid and Psyche, except with the gender roles reversed. He was the awe-struck mortal, gazing down at the heart-stoppingly beautiful goddess sleeping in his house.

That whimsy had been enough to kick his butt back upstairs. He went through the motions of his nighttime ritual, sliding between the sheets alone when he wanted to be anything but. Then he proceeded to tangle up the bedclothes with tossing and turning when he'd much rather rumple the covers with the sleeping goddess downstairs.

As the digital clock ticked over to two-eleven, he dropped his feet to the floor and pushed out of bed. Maybe a belt of scotch would relax him enough to go to sleep. In his bedroom doorway, he dithered over whether to pull pajama bottoms on over his boxers. But why bother digging them out of his dresser drawer? When he'd checked on her, Jana had looked so lost to the world a herd of Disney hippos in tutus wouldn't have wakened her.

He took the carpeted stairs as quietly as he could, with only the sixth step from the bottom squeaking under his weight, as usual. Certainly not loud enough to reach as far as the guest room.

He was halfway across the living room before the pale glow of a kitchen light registered. Not as bright as the overhead fluorescents—maybe the downspot over the sink. Maybe Jana had left it on before she went to bed. He hadn't noticed it when he'd come down earlier. In fact, he'd bumped a toe on one of the side tables because it had been so dark.

So, if he accepted the concepts of gravity, the sun rising in the east, the Sacramento River Cats being the best Triple-A ball club on the face of the planet, he should acknowledge that the light in the kitchen was on only because Jana was in there and not asleep in the guest room. And he most definitely shouldn't go in there to check, just to be sure.

And yet his feet started moving toward the kitchen, irresistibly drawn to the compulsion that was Jana. All too aware of the cool air on his body, the vast areas of skin the boxers didn't cover. How it might look to go popping into the kitchen nearly naked.

But then he stepped inside and saw her, and he didn't give a damn. She was leaning against the counter by the kitchen sink, a glass of milk cradled in her hands. She wore a worn-out T-shirt, one of his, if he wasn't mistaken. And although the kitchen island blocked his view of her below the waist, he suspected that other than maybe panties, she wasn't wearing anything but the shirt, not if those two little points pressing against the soft knit were any indication.

His erection came on hard and fast, threatening to push itself out of the open fly on the boxers. He stepped up to the island to shield himself, which had the side benefit of giving him a great view of her bare legs from hip to knee.

"What are you doing up?" She gazed at him warily, clutching her glass to her chest, her bent arms framing her breasts.

Stay put! Don't you dare go over there. As extra enforcement, he gripped the smooth granite of the island. "Couldn't sleep. Thought you were down for the count, though."

That was a mistake; he could see it in the narrowing of her eyes. "How do you know whether or not I was asleep?"

"You seemed tired. Like you'd fall asleep pretty quick." He forked his fingers through his hair, wishing he could reach in and pluck out the randy thoughts dancing through his mind.

"I did. But I heard this big bang. It woke me up. I couldn't fall asleep again, so I thought I'd go for the warm milk."

She took another sip, her eyes drifting shut. His eyes drifted, too, down her body to her breasts, to those faint bumps in the T-shirt that told him where her nipples were. Somehow, he'd moved around the island, closer to her.

Anchoring his ankles in imaginary shackles, he gave himself a mental slap. "Where'd you find the shirt?"

She opened her eyes again. "From that giveaway bag you keep in the coat closet. I figured you wouldn't mind."

"Sure. No problem." Damn, he'd moved closer again. Now he stood two feet from her, could scan her delicious body from head to toe. Her slightly swollen belly only added to her allure, tempting him to run his hand over it, imagine the baby within.

A baby that could be his. That idea went through him like a bolt of lightning. Should have derailed him from the sex track but somehow instead added coal to the roaring engine.

Her gaze locked with his, she set the glass on the counter, nearly upsetting it. He grabbed for it to set it into place, in the process gathering up her hand, drawing it to his mouth. He pressed a kiss to the back of her fingers, then traced his tongue along the middle one to its tip.

Her soft sigh galvanized him, tugging his attention to her mouth. After that brief kiss at the ranch nearly a month ago, he'd relived it a thousand times, embellished it, extrapolated it. He could follow through on all those fantasies right here, right now.

His lips brushed hers softly at first, just in case she wanted to object. When she leaned in closer, her mouth opening to his, he knew he was going to have to take his own sweet time exploring, tasting. He dipped his tongue inside, groaning at the honeyed warmth, feeling her hum of responding pleasure vibrating against his lips.

As he wrapped his arm around her, her free hand settled on his chest. A part of him, the part that still clung to a microgram of sanity, hoped she'd push him away. But instead, she trailed her fingers through the curls of hair, her nails scudding against his heated flesh. His erection throbbed so powerfully he wondered if he'd lose control right there in his kitchen, shame himself in a way he hadn't since he was eighteen, making out with Melinda Barker in the backseat of her dad's Chrysler.

Damn, her hand was moving lower. Down the center of his torso, to his navel, pausing there to send a shiver through him as she stroked inside. Then he felt her fingertips at the elastic of his shorts. She didn't slide her hand beneath, and regret and relief duked it out inside him. But then she drifted lower, to the gap where the fly opened. In the next explosive instant, she'd worked her fingers inside and wrapped them around him.

He gripped her even harder, turning to lean against the counter to keep his knees from buckling. He reached for her shoulders, tried to push her away, to give his lungs a chance to drag in a little air. But then she was gone as she bent, going to her knees, and took him into her mouth.

He couldn't, he wouldn't let her—he couldn't stop her. Had no strength to pull away from her and the explosion building in his body, the brilliant light and heat and sensation. That this was Jana pleasuring him, the one person he'd felt more connection to than any other, tipped mind-blowing into miraculous.

Just when he thought he might step away, her hand gently cupped him, stroking as her soft mouth blasted him to infinity. His body arched as the climax hit like a semi from heaven, Jana moaning as if she came, too, just from the contact high. Her tongue licked one last time along his length, imploding his lungs; then she sat back on her heels.

Straightening his boxers, too shell-shocked to put two thoughts together, he stared down at her. Since he blocked the downspot, her face was mostly in shadow and he couldn't quite read what might be going on inside her. But damned if he wasn't ready for round two, except this time turnabout was fair play.

He helped her up, felt her tremble. Didn't like the troubled look on her face. The way she avoided meeting his gaze.

"I…" she glanced at him sidelong, then away "…shouldn't have—"

"Stop." He tried to cupped her chin, make her look at him, but she wriggled away.

"I have to go to bed."

He could hear tears in her voice as she hurried from the kitchen, and he felt like the lowest form of animal. Even lower, like a worm. What the hell was he thinking, traipsing into the kitchen the way he did, knowing she was here? After what had happened on the sofa earlier?

Because this is exactly what you wanted, he told himself and felt even worse. A worm wouldn't even want to keep company with him.

He rushed after her, at a loss as to how to fix what he'd broken. But by the time he'd reached the guest room, she'd already locked herself inside. She wouldn't answer his knock.

After ten minutes of trying, he dragged himself off to bed, skin crawling with remorse. Wishing he could somehow replay the past half hour. And hoping against hope that he hadn't ruined everything with her.

She curled herself up tightly into a ball—at least as tight as she could, considering the cantaloupe-size lump in her belly. She spread her hands over her eyes in a vain effort to block out the memories. The luscious feel of Sam against her mouth, the exhilaration of feeling his climax against her lips.

Her body tightened at just the memory. She'd nearly gone over the edge herself. Just from holding him, touching him.

But how could she? This wasn't the relationship she and Sam had. They were friends, not…what? Lovers? Pleasure pals?

She could only hope, pray that her actions hadn't totally messed up everything with Sam. She didn't even know how she'd face him in the morning. Or tomorrow at the Easter egg hunt. Or ever for the rest of her life.

Stop thinking about how good it felt. She shouldn't have done it. It was a completely brainless move. And she absolutely, positively should not be thinking about how much she wanted to do it again.

Chapter Eleven

Jana crossed the front lawn of the Estelle's House ranch, her sandals squishing a little in the rain-soaked grass, dodging kids from toddler size to middle-graders as they zipped around searching for eggs. Good thing the storm had quit dumping the wet stuff by six, when Jana had crept out of Sam's house. And since the hunt had been scheduled at one, there had been time for the lawn to dry out a bit.

They couldn't have asked for a more gorgeous day. If Jana wasn't so turned inside out and upside down, that bright blue sky and sweet light breeze that fluttered the full skirt of her maternity dress might have lifted her spirits. But the sky reminded her of Sam's eyes, the puffs of wind of his touch. In fact, everything she'd seen and smelled and tasted today, from the apple fritters the Estelle's House teens had made for breakfast to the dark hot decaf she'd warmed her hands with, reminded her of the explosive fire of last night.

It had been like watching one of the Trent Garner action movies or reading one of Sam's books. Everything happening at once, boom, boom, boom. Never a chance to catch your breath. Never a chance to think and consider just how stupid your actions might be.

Jana paused as Tony and Rebecca's daughter, Lea, and another five-year-old girl dashed madly across Jana's path. They were both screaming with laughter, the eggs in their baskets threatening to bounce right out. What a difference from the sad-eyed Lea that Jana had babysat only last year.

With the coast finally clear, Jana reached the booth for the beanbag toss game and stepped inside. She and Frances would be manning the booth when it opened after the kids finished the egg hunt.

A small commotion caught Jana's eye, and a moment later she heard a kid wailing. A little boy, maybe three, had slipped on the wet grass and dropped his basket of eggs. Sam was right there, asking the kids around him to gather up the little guy's eggs, sending one of the teens for a towel to wipe some of the mud off his bottom. In nothing flat, the three-year-old was giggling up at Sam, his basket a few eggs heavier because the older kids had added one or two of their own.

No doubt because of Sam. She could see even from across the lawn how the kids adored him. The littlest ones stared up at him in awe, heads cranked way back to see the top of six-foot-four Sam. The middle-graders flocked around him as if he were Harry Potter, Spider-Man and Luke Skywalker all rolled into one. The teen girls were madly in love with him, and the boys all wanted to be like him.

He crouched to give the muddy little guy a hug, his long arms just about able to wrap around the kid twice with some to spare. She couldn't quite make out Sam's face, but the way he held the kid in his embrace, the way he patted his back before letting him loose to run like a maniac across the lawn again, tugged at Jana's insides. She'd never thought about it much, but she realized he'd always been good with kids, had always liked them. Lucky for her or he might have never noticed her at Estelle's all those years ago.

He straightened, his jeans wet from kneeling beside the toddler. Her heart flip-flopped seeing that. He didn't care about messing himself up if it meant comforting a child.

Then he turned to scan the crowd. A prickle danced up and down Jana's spine as she realized he was looking for her. She was half-tempted to dive behind the booth's counter. She could tell Frances she was going through the prizes so she could sort them by color or something equally ridiculous.

But she didn't. She let him find her, felt the prickle turn into a torrent of heat as his gaze locked with hers. She struggled to breathe as he strode purposefully in her direction.

She wasn't ready to talk to him yet. She'd avoided him this morning when she had skipped out early, had conveniently ignored his calls on her cell phone and had arrived here at the last minute when the place was totally cuckoo with the impending egg hunt. Unless Frances turned up quickly or she had a sudden influx of customers at the beanbag toss, it was time to face the music.

He leaned toward her across the counter. "We should talk."

She fidgeted with the skirt of her dress. "Could we just forget it ever happened?"

His gaze grew so hot she thought he might laser-zap her to a crisp. "Not something I'm ever likely to forget. But I don't want you thinking… You damn well shouldn't be blaming yourself for anything." He reached into the booth, took her hand. "Are you?"

"I don't know why I did it, Sam. I mean I do know, except…"

"Except neither of us wants to go there. Right?" His warm hand enfolded hers, his thumb stroking the back of it. For someone who didn't want to go someplace, he was sure laying out the map and drawing the route.

She forced herself to blank her mind to his touch, although her body wasn't going along with it. Sensation rippled up her arm.

She had to work hard to keep the trembling from her voice when she spoke. "Just tell me we're still friends."

"The best of friends." He took a breath, as if about to add something else. But Frances arrived just then, ducking behind the booth with a wide grin, her lip ring bobbing. Sam let go of Jana's hand, then walked off with a wave.

Jana still felt funny inside about what had happened last night. Partly because she didn't yet know how it was all going to shake out with her and Sam's friendship, partly because her mind kept replaying every sensual moment. To be gospel-truth honest, she wanted to do it again. That and more.

But as the kids started lining up and she put beanbags into small hands, she knew a repeat performance was never going to happen. Never should happen. Because it was pretty obvious that was a direction Sam just didn't want to go. She had to return to her original plan—stay with Sam for the time being, have her baby, move on with her life. Maybe move away from the area again to make a clean break.

It didn't matter that the thought pretty much destroyed her heart. She'd find a way to survive the pain.

* * *

He could barely take his eyes off her the whole day. Whether she was lifting up a four-year-old to help her get her beanbags into the frog's mouth or spinning cotton candy at one of the snack stands, his fascination with Jana filled every ounce of his awareness. He'd managed to do a passable job at the goldfish game, sneaking a Ping-Pong ball into a water-filled bowl if it didn't bounce in on its own, keeping the relish and chopped onions filled by the hot dog stand. But more than once, one of Tony's teens had to yell at him to get his attention when he was preoccupied with gawking at Jana.

She was so damn good with the kids. It broke his heart that she was having to give up the baby. She really ought to be raising it herself.

It was seven by the time the last cranky kid had been bundled into his parents' car and the teens started the cleanup operation. When Rebecca wouldn't let Sam lift a finger to help, he scoped out the grounds to see where Jana had gone. When he didn't see her immediately, his gaze jumped to the parking lot. The Prius was gone.

Rebecca nudged him aside so she could pick up some trash under his foot. "She was beat. She went home."

He considered playing it cool and asking who she meant. But Rebecca wasn't stupid. She'd never go for it. Instead, he asked, "Where's Estelle?"

"In the house. Where I'll be in about five minutes. Ruby's got these kids well in hand."

Ruby had been a student in the first session of the Estelle's House program and was now employed as house-mother. "See you in a few, then," Sam said as he walked toward the house.

Tony must have seen him approach through the window because he had the door open before Sam hit the porch. "Come on in. Can I get you a beer?"

"No, thanks." He didn't dare drive the Mustang down the curving foothill roads with a beer in his system. "Estelle in her room?" Estelle shared the downstairs bedroom with Ruby.

"Yeah. Pretty tired, though. I don't think she's up to a long visit."

Anxiety for his former foster mom bubbled in his stomach. "Seems like she's always tired."

Tony made a face. "Whatever her doctor's been telling her, she's not sharing it with me or Rebecca. Just keep it short with her."

Sam nodded in agreement, then headed for the bedroom. He knocked and called out, "It's Sam," then slipped inside when she invited him in.

One look at Estelle, and his concern for her rose another notch. Propped up in the bed with a book in her lap, she had dark circles under her eyes and her hands and ankles were swollen. She looked years older than the last time he saw her, only a month ago.

He hovered by the door. "I hate to bother you. If you're too tired—"

"Oh, come in, for goodness' sake. That Tony wants to mother me to death."

A chill traveled up his neck at her use of the word, but he moved to sit at the foot of the bed. "I need some advice."

She set aside her book with a smile. "I haven't had the chance to butt into your life in a long time."

With her smile, she looked younger again, the way he remembered her. The knot in his stomach eased. "I've been in contact with my sister, Maddie."

Now she beamed. "That's great."

"It's fantastic. We had a long lunch the other day. I told her about my career, about the ranch program." He took in a long breath. "And about Jana and the baby."

"And?" Estelle prodded.

"Maddie had kind of a crazy idea. Except I haven't been able to think about anything else." Sam met his former foster mother's gaze, so he could be sure to see her reaction. "Maddie thinks maybe I should adopt Jana's baby."

Estelle folded her hands in her lap. "To be honest, Sam, I'd considered the same thing. You certainly have the wherewithal to bring up a child. You're a good man and you'll make a good father."

"But?" She hadn't said it, but he could hear it in her tone.

"But…" She sighed, her gaze falling to her linked, swollen hands a moment before she looked up at him again. "You grew up without a mother." She held up her hand against his protest. "I did my best with you, but I was not your mother. I gave you all the love I could, but we both know how many others there were in the house."

He moved beside her on the bed, took her hand. "I never felt cheated or shorted. None of us did."

"In any case, do you want your own child growing up without a mother? When you have a choice and could choose otherwise?"

He struggled to parse out what she was trying to say to him. "You mean don't adopt the baby? Let someone else, a married couple, take the baby?"

She shook her head. "No, I think you should. But you need to come up with the rest on your own," she finished cryptically. She leaned back in the bed. "Now I do need to rest."

He gave her a gentle hug, then left the room. Too full of

his own thoughts, he passed on Rebecca's offer of dinner and headed out. But instead of turning toward home, he pulled onto the freeway and started up the hill toward Lake Tahoe.

He got as far as Desolation Wilderness, pulling the Mustang into the turnout and climbing from the car. The moonless sky had faded to nearly black, with only the occasional passing headlight providing illumination. The air was chill this high up and dirty snow still lined the sides of Highway 50.

He wanted Jana with him here. Wanted to gaze up at the mountainside with her, listen together to the roar of Horsetail Falls in the distance. To soak up the cool night air, talk about how in the summer, after the baby was born, they'd hike to the top together.

He tried to imagine what it would be like to have Jana hand her baby over to a pair of strangers. It just about killed him. The child was part of Jana and, in a way, a part of him, even though he'd had nothing to do with the creation of it. How could he let the baby pass out of his life?

He couldn't. Even if he would be raising the baby alone, without a mother. Even if—especially if—Jana left again afterward. He'd need the baby then, a reminder of her.

He got behind the wheel again, turning the car around and heading back down the hill. It was past eight—too late to go to Jana's as tired as she'd been? He'd have to play it by ear, check to see if her lights were still on.

He felt ready to burst with anticipation by the time he pulled off the freeway in Camino. He drove down Carson Road, saw her street-facing bedroom light glowing. Parking behind the store, he climbed the steps two at a time, rapped on the door.

He had it all detailed in his mind, how he'd present the

adoption idea to her, the arguments she might make against it and how he'd counter them. He rehearsed his opening as he listened for her footsteps, editing it as he would a paragraph in one of his books.

Then the dead bolt clattered and the door swung open. Her fragrance hit him first, the faintest dream of honeysuckle. Then his eyes filled up with pink—her ruffly pink babydolls, the flush on her throat where her pulse beat. And his mind wiped clean, as empty as the day he was born.

He couldn't breathe. Heat exploded in his body from the center out.

"Sam." She whispered his name so softly it was a caress against his skin. An invitation she seconded with her eyes, with her hand reaching across the space between them.

In one motion, he stepped inside, kicking the door shut behind him as he gathered her in his arms. She spread her hands across his chest, sliding them up to lock her fingers behind his neck. The swell of her belly between them filled him with an irrational pride. This would be his child, his baby. He knew it with a dead certainty.

But her mouth eagerly accepting his, her fingers threading through his hair pushed aside that needed conversation. As he kissed her, his hands stroking her through the thin fabric of her babydoll shirt, he backed her down the hall toward the bedroom. She stayed with him each step, her touch as urgent, her mouth as hot as his.

Impatient, mindless, he tugged off her top, tossing it aside. Drinking in the sight of her breasts, still small but rounded with her pregnancy, he bent his head, taking one nipple into his mouth as he stroked the other with his fingers. She gasped, throwing her head back. He felt her knees give way.

He caught her, easing her back onto the bed. Standing over her, he splayed his hand over her belly. "So damn sexy."

She started to shake her head, then he let his fingers drift lower to the elastic waist of her shorts. He watched her eyes widen as he pushed inside, cupping the soft curls at the vee of her legs.

"Incredibly sexy," he murmured as he lowered to kiss her.

While he brushed her lips with his, he explored her folds, the silkiness, the moistness between them. She moaned into his mouth and he drank in the sound.

He stroked her, rubbed her, dipping a finger inside her to feel her slick, wet heat. Reveled in every purr of pleasure, the way her breathing grew rough with passion. As mind-blowing as last night had been, touching her this way, feeling her rise up against his hand, her fingernails digging into his shoulder, was an even greater paradise.

Then she came, her body clenching around his finger, her legs squeezing around his arm so tightly he half wondered if he'd ever pull it free. Then she fell back against the bed, as if every muscle in her body had turned to jelly.

Her eyes drifted open, and he worried that she might be as ashamed of what he'd done as she'd been last night. But then she whispered, "Take off your clothes."

He hoped he wouldn't need his heart, because it had just slammed out of his chest. He stripped off his polo, his jeans and boxers, threw them every which way. Tugged off her dainty pink shorts.

Then he stalled. Kneeling between her legs, still touching her because she felt so damn good, he hesitated.

"What?" she asked, worry beginning to creep into her face.

"I've always used a condom."

Her mouth curved in a beguiling smile. "I think that ship has sailed."

He stroked her belly. "Not the only reason."

"He was my first, Sam. I was his. He was a jerk but not a sleep-around jerk." Her eyes half closed as he found a particularly sensitive spot on her body. "So, if you've been careful…"

He had. Had been tested, declared A-OK. And he could only be so noble as she reached for him, her hands on his hips urging him toward her, into the cradle of her thighs.

With his first stroke inside her, his eyes just about rolled back inside his head. He had to stop, gasp for breath, find a way to balance himself on his elbows to keep from collapsing on her and the baby. Thought he might die in that instant from the pleasure of it.

Then she shifted, pulling him even deeper, her fingers digging into his hips. Her legs wrapped around him, ankles locking at the small of his back. The moan low in her throat, her musky smell, the feel of her breath on his cheek scraped every nerve raw.

Then he started to move, pulling out, then thrusting in, forcing a slow rhythm, battling for control. Even as she squirmed against him, reaching for her own climax, he fought to hold off, wanting every exquisite moment to last, not ready to give in to his body's imperative.

Then she came, jolting, hips thrust up against him, her body vibrating with pleasure. His own body took over, shoving him abruptly into his climax, tossing him into a formless space filled with sensation. Jana was his only anchor, his path back to earth. He clung to her as bit by bit he returned to himself. As bit by bit, the reality of what they'd just done crashed in on him.

He kept his face buried in her throat, inhaling honey-suckle, terrified to look at her, see her expression. Where had he just taken their friendship? Had he blasted it to hell with his compulsion to have her? Could they crawl back up this cliff, get back on solid ground again?

He eased back from her, just enough to shift to the mattress and release her from his weight. Kept his eyes shut as he steeled himself for whatever might have changed. This was different from last night because he'd started it, he'd been running things from beginning to end. They could have considered last night an aberration, but not after tonight.

He'd dived too deep. He'd plunged so far inside her—not physically, but emotionally—that their relationship was beginning to feel different. More like what he'd felt with Faith, with Shawna and Cyndy.

Except so far beyond what he'd experienced with them, it might as well be in a different dimension, a different universe. And that shot hot lead through him, a familiar irrational fear he could no more hold back than he could have held back his climax moments ago.

"Sam?"

He hated the anxiety he heard in her voice, hated himself even more for putting it there. He damn well better be man enough to face her and see if there was a hope of backing away from this brink.

He lifted his gaze to her face. And with a shock, realized things were even worse than he'd thought. It was written, clear as day, in her eyes.

But maybe he was mistaken. Maybe that glow, that smile, didn't mean what he thought it did.

Then she took a breath and foreboding crept up his

spine. He would have covered her mouth if he could to keep her from saying the words.

She propped herself up with her elbow, tipped her chin up, defiant. And said it, even plainer and stronger than Faith or Shawna ever had.

"I love you, Sam." And just in case it wasn't clear enough, she added, "As more than a friend. As a lover. As a partner. I love you."

Just like that, the bottom dropped out of his world.

Chapter Twelve

To his credit, he didn't jump up and run out the door like she expected. He just lay there, staring at her, that snakebit look on his face. His hand still lightly stroking her belly, making her ache for another taste of his lovemaking.

She'd known it was a calculated risk coming clean that way. She hadn't even realized she was going to do it until those moments after she'd climaxed the second time. It had been too gigantic to hold inside her, too perfectly beautiful to keep to herself. Even though she might lose everything with those three simple words.

Her heart thundering in her ears, she waited for disaster to catch up with her. Called up every bit of strength in her body to keep her eyes on him, kind of daring him to deny what she'd said. But still he didn't speak. He just had that someone-ran-over-my-dog look in his eyes, so much pain she wondered how he could bear it.

Then he half sat up and she thought, *This is it: he's going.* But he only reached across her for the light, switching it off, plunging them into darkness. No moon outside, the streetlights blocked by her blinds—now they couldn't see each other at all as he settled back beside her.

Then she figured it out. That was exactly why he turned off the lights. So he wouldn't have to look at her. See whatever was in her face that she just couldn't hide anymore.

But he stayed. Gathered her up in his arms, pulled the covers up over them. Spread his hand across her belly as if to lay claim to what was inside. She puzzled over that. Not for long because even though it was barely ten, the long day overcame her. With Sam so close, she could inhale his scent with each breath. His warm body a comfort, she fell asleep.

He stayed all night. When she got up at midnight to pee, she could see the glitter of his open eyes in the faintest bit of light seeping in from outside. And when she woke closer to morning, she could still feel him beside her, although he wasn't holding her anymore.

When she jolted awake at six-thirty, he was gone. Fumbling as she put on her babydolls, she raced out to the living room, catching her toe on a side table when her belly made her clumsy. She said a few words her baby shouldn't hear, then pushed aside the front curtains to look.

His Mustang was still there. It didn't look as if he was behind the wheel. Was he downstairs? She couldn't let him leave, not without talking to him, figuring out what was happening next.

She dressed in about nine seconds, throwing a T-shirt and jeans over her babydolls. Her feet stuffed into fluffy yellow-duck slippers, a silly thrift store purchase she'd made right after Ian had left, she raced down the stairs. The shop door was unlocked, so he had to be here. She took a breath, pulled the door open and stepped inside.

Sam was over by the summer display she'd set up in the window. She'd filled the shelves with colorful teddy bears in sunglasses and whimsical resin animal figures reclining on tiny chaise longues. To one side were outdoor flags with smiling suns, gorgeous flowers and sailboats on the water, their wooden poles poked in a sand-filled lime-green bucket. A Day-Glo pink bucket on the other side held garden art— butterflies, frogs and dragonflies on metal rods.

He turned as she walked quietly toward him. "You've done a great job here."

"The kids have helped."

He scanned the rest of the shop, much of it still in disarray. She'd focused on the front window so people would get a hint of what the shop was about. "Will it be ready to open in two weeks?" he asked.

"No worries. All the stock is here. Just a couple more shelves to assemble."

Now he faced her, hands shoved into his pockets. "What happened last night… That wasn't my intent."

"It's okay."

He shook his head slowly. "I think we've been letting our relationship go in directions that we…that we probably shouldn't."

A fist squeezed her heart. "Okay." She kept using that word, even though things were a million miles from being okay.

His face got so serious she thought, *This is it. He's gone from me forever now.* Then he reached for her hand.

"I've got something important to say to you. I want you

to think about it, give it some real consideration before you make a decision. It's what I'd planned to talk to you about before we…"

She had no idea where he was going, but she had a feeling she wasn't going to like it. She just nodded, her free arm around her middle, wishing she had some real armor to wrap herself with.

It wouldn't have helped. Because what he said next hit her like a sucker punch from left field.

"I want to adopt your baby."

She hitched in a breath. "Where did that come from?"

"My sister first." Jana pushed down the pain she felt at the mention of his sister, the reminder that he had someone new in his life who probably meant way more to him than she did. "Then Estelle," Sam continued. "When I asked her for advice yesterday. She'd considered suggesting it herself."

It was wrong to feel betrayed by Estelle, the woman who was more mother to her than her own mom. She didn't even understand why the thought of Sam taking her baby hurt so much.

Because he wants your baby but not you. She couldn't forget his rejection last night of her declaration of love.

"But, Jana, this was building up in my subconscious even before Maddie said anything. Every time I'd think about your baby, about seeing him sent off to strangers, of never seeing him again—"

"It might be a *her,* damn it!" The defense, made ragged by tears, made no sense. But she was grasping for one thing she could control, even if her baby's gender wasn't even it.

He kept going. "Or her. Either way, my heart would break thinking about it. Not only that I would never see the baby, but that you wouldn't either. Because you could be in his…her life. Visit whenever you wanted."

Talk about half a loaf. Maybe it was just the moldy, weevily heel. Because there would be this baby she adored, this man who she loved with every fragment of her being, and she was just a visitor.

But it was far more than she would have otherwise. The woman at the adoption agency was talking about a couple in Boise, another one in Arizona. There was no telling if either one would be willing to have an open adoption.

He took a step toward her. She retreated. "Don't. Please. I can't think if you're too close."

"You don't have to decide now. You've got four more months."

Except how could she possibly turn him down? When she knew he'd give her baby a fabulous life, would be a wonderful father?

She breathed against the rock weighting her chest, fixed him with her gaze. Before she could decide about the baby, they had another little matter to clear up. "What about last night?"

She'd never before seen a man turn beet-red like that. "It was…"

"Incredible." She narrowed her gaze, daring him to contradict her.

"Yeah. Beyond that." He swiped his hands over his face. "You know about me and women, Jana, when they get too close. I care about you so much. I don't want you ending up like them."

"Then just don't. Why does my loving you have to mean you're gonna throw me away?"

Outrage lit his face. "I wouldn't do that! Send you away.

But you have to know… I can't love you that way. And the fact that you think you do—"

"Know, not think."

Now he stared her down. "It means I want to run about a hundred miles in the other direction. That I want to give you a wad of cash and set you up down in Sacramento to get some distance. And I don't want to lose you that way."

She shook her head, struggling to understand. "This makes no sense, Sam."

He paced off toward the cashier's counter and settled on the stool behind it. "It doesn't. I know. It's completely irrational. But if you felt what's going on inside me…it's stark terror, Jana. Complete panic. I'm holding it in. Not letting you see the worst of it. But it's taking everything in me not to jump in my car and take off for Texas."

Now she saw it, the tension around his mouth, how stiffly he sat on the stool. All the times she'd poked fun at him about his love-'em-and-leave-'em ways, she'd never known that the whole commitment thing was such a freaking big deal for him.

And she'd pushed his panic button.

Barely able to hold her own self together, she walked slowly toward him. "I need some time to think about this. About your offer to adopt."

He gave her a brusque nod. "Of course."

She moved to the other side of the register from him, putting the waist-high counter between them. "I've been going one way in my mind about the baby. I've gotta readjust."

Another nod. He looked miserable, as if a fire was burning him from the inside out.

"Sam," she said quietly. "I wonder…maybe if you told me about what happened when you were a kid—"

"No."

"I know your mom left you. Your dad died. Your sister got adopted, but you ended up in foster care—"

"Not open to discussion," he snapped.

"But you gotta know it's all connected," she persisted. "Whatever happened—"

"Damn it, Jana, drop it!"

Now he shoved back from the stool so hard it fell backward. He dragged his fingers through his hair as he paced.

"Rehashing old history won't make a damn bit of difference. It's not like it'll pass a magic wand over me and suddenly I'll love you!"

Jana gasped in pain, all the air leaving her lungs. Shaking all over, she backed away from him and turned toward the back door. He shouted her name, grabbed her arm when he caught up. "I'm sorry. I'm the world's biggest jerk."

She let her tears fall. "You can't stop me from loving you, Sam Harrison. So you'll just have to deal with it."

She tore away from him, running up the stairs. She got to the top well before him. If he came after her, she wasn't about to let him in.

But as she leaned against the locked door, his footsteps stopped halfway up. There was a long pause; then she heard him descend again. Moments later, the back door to the shop slammed shut; sometime after that, the Mustang's engine roared to life.

Feeling desolate, she wandered into her bedroom and tugged open the top drawer of the little dresser Sam had bought her. She'd hidden Sam's letters under the underwear when she'd first moved in and hadn't looked at them since.

She pulled them out now, slipping each one from its envelope, reading them all, from the short, one-paragraph notes to the two- and three-pagers.

Her love for him spilled out as she read each precious word. And she realized there was no better person to raise her child than the one she loved so dearly.

The following Sunday, on Easter, after she'd spent an exhausting, draining week getting the shop ready for opening, she called him. She didn't bother with hello.

"You can adopt my baby, Sam. Just tell me what I need to do."

She hung up after about thirty seconds of awkward conversation, went into her bedroom and sobbed into her pillow for the next hour.

By opening day the following Saturday, Sam had Darius tracking down Ian Wilson. His attorney was drawing up the adoption papers and he'd figured out about a hundred million ways to call himself a coldhearted jackass. On the plus side, his book was going great, his female foil, Lacey, giving Trent hell, a literary expiation of Sam's personal sins.

Because Celebration Station's profits would be benefiting the Estelle's House independent living program, Sam's publisher had donated fifty hardback copies of his most recent book to be used as giveaways. Sam's publicist had sent press releases to the *Mountain Democrat* in Placerville and the *Sacramento Bee* stating that the first fifty customers would receive a free autographed book. Sam wasn't sure if they'd reach fifty customers for the entire weekend but figured it was worth a try.

The books were gone in the first two hours on Saturday. True, some of the happy fans made a beeline to Sam's table, tucked in a back corner, and left just as quickly with only the book in hand. But at least half of the fifty lingered in the store to browse the flamboyant spring whirligigs, the gorgeous silk flowers for Mother's Day and the patriotic Memorial Day banners. Several of the shoppers had walked out with their arms full of the clever and sometimes wacky seasonal decorations Jana had filled Celebration Station with.

Since Sam was done signing at noon, he offered to pitch in. Jana sent him out for lunch, then tasked him to handle the press when they arrived. Two of the local network affiliates actually sent news vans to cover the opening. Not only were both the local newspapers eager for interviews, but the *San Francisco Chronicle* had tapped a stringer to drive up to the foothills. Sam spent the entire afternoon yakking with them, doing stand-up interviews with the TV people, grinning like an idiot in front of the store while the photographers filled their digital camera memory sticks.

Every time he tried to bring Jana into the conversation—damn it all, she was the one who'd done ninety percent of the work—she waved him off. Too busy, too tired, too preoccupied. Too pissed at him was more like it. And too hurt, too terribly wounded by what he'd said.

Finally, when the newspeople had scampered off to file their stories, when Ray and Frances had ushered the last customer out the door and then left themselves, Sam thought he might finally have a chance to talk with Jana. Except that when he crossed the store to where she was ringing out the register, she looked tempted to bolt.

But she stood her ground. "We're completely out of the

garden art. There's one dragonfly left, but one of its wings is broken. I just about had to put a lady into a half nelson to keep her from buying it. Had to promise I'd save her one from the next shipment."

She took a breath, as if to launch into another recitation. He put up a hand to stop her. "Can we get another shipment by tomorrow?"

"We'd have to pay extra to bring them in from a warehouse in Reno."

"Go ahead and call. Use the AmEx card. Anything else we'll be short on tomorrow?"

She pushed a sheet of paper over. "Same warehouse has most of these."

"Get what you can. The rest will just have to be on order." He glanced out the front window as a logging truck moved slowly down Carson. "How long before you're done?"

"Another ten minutes. Ray and Frances will be here early to help with setup."

The two teens had arranged with Tony to use work in the shop as their training, rather than the kitchen work that Rebecca taught. They were both taking online business classes with the nearby junior college. Celebration Station fit better with their future plans.

"I'm taking you out to dinner." He put enough emphasis in the words to make sure she understood he wasn't taking any arguments. "I'm going to run home to change, then be back in thirty to pick you up."

She shrugged, then nodded. He headed out, half tempted to demand the car keys to the Prius so she couldn't escape. But she'd agreed. He'd have to trust her. Which, of course, was not one of his strong suits.

But she was there when he climbed the stairs to her

apartment a half hour later. When she opened the door, wearing the same flowing flowered dress she'd worn at the Easter egg hunt, honeysuckle teasing his nose, he was a heartbeat away from backing her into the apartment as he'd done two weeks before. Maybe she saw it in his face, because she quickly stepped past him onto the landing, then down the stairs.

Damn, he had to get a grip. It didn't help that her scent drifted across the small space of the DeLorean. Or that he could see the shadow of her cleavage down the front of her scoop-neck bodice. He stole a quick glance before he put the blinkers on and just drove, but it was enough to start the inner X-rated newsreel.

He turned the car over to an ecstatic attendant at the Sequoia in Placerville, then, with his hand on the small of Jana's back, he escorted her into the upscale restaurant. The maître d' seated him and Jana at a table so secluded he'd need a trail of bread crumbs to find his way back to the front door. As packed as the popular restaurant was, their back table could have been in a private room. But that was exactly what he'd asked for when he'd made his reservation.

He ordered a beer; she asked for cranberry juice. They left their menus closed on the table.

Once the drinks arrived, he figured his moment of truth had, too. "Whatever you want to know about me, I'll tell you."

Sipping her juice, she lifted her gaze to his. He saw the wary surprise give way to determination.

"Tell me about your mother."

He should have expected Jana wouldn't pull any punches. But he might as well get the worst of it out of the way first.

He took a swallow of beer. "She had problems. She didn't like that Dad was a long-haul trucker. He wasn't when they married. He just sprang it on her one day a couple months after I was born."

"So he was away a lot."

He could almost hear tucked away in the back of Jana's mind, *At least you had a father.* Her dad had walked out before Jana was born, kind of like Ian had skipped on her.

"Gone a couple weeks, back a few days, then gone again. Part of the reason it took so long for my sister to come along. Dad just wasn't around to make another baby."

He'd never understood that about his father. He was pretty closemouthed when he was home, as if he just didn't know what to say to his pretty young wife. He was fifteen years older than her, thirty-six to his wife's twenty-one when they'd married.

Almost like him and Jana. That was a kick in the teeth.

"I think there was more to it than Mom just missing Dad. Knowing what I know now, I'm guessing she was depressed. She tried self-medicating with alcohol at first. Moved on to weed, coke. After a while she was buying any kind of crap she could get off the street."

His stomach roiled at the memories. His mother coming home high on God knew what. Needle marks on her arms, which she'd cover with long sleeves even in the summer.

"I think she'd worked her way up to heroin. Don't really know."

"Your father had to have known something was wrong."

"Sometimes they would argue in their bedroom. She'd be in tears, promising things would be different." He shook his head. "Then Dad would head out on another long haul, and it was as if the promise had never been made."

Jana reached across the table and took his hand. "What happened when she left?"

This was where it got ugly. The rest of the story, so to speak, that he'd told no one. Only Aunt Barbara knew the truth, and she'd cut him out of her life long ago.

Still, he'd promised Jana he'd tell her anything. He at least kept his commitments. "It was four days before Christmas. I was ten, Maddie two. Mom hadn't bothered with a tree or decorations. Too caught up in her own private escape."

He saw the flicker of understanding in Jana's eyes. His obsession with Christmas probably made sense to her now.

"She went out that night like she did plenty of times. Except this time, she wasn't back by morning. When she wasn't back by nightfall, I was scared spitless."

Maddie kept crying for her mommy, growing fussier by the hour. By the middle of the second day, she wouldn't eat, and that really scared Sam.

"Wasn't there anyone you could call?" Jana asked.

"My dad's sister. Aunt Barbara. The one who—"

"Adopted Maddie." He'd told her that much of the story. "So did you call her?"

"Couldn't get hold of her at first. Then I left a message with my thirteen-year-old cousin. Not the most reliable kid."

She folded his large hand in both of hers. "I've never understood—why did she adopt Maddie, but not you?"

Here was the worst of the story. The part Maddie didn't remember.

His jaw cramped with tension as he pushed the words out. "Because I nearly killed my sister."

Chapter Thirteen

Sam could see Jana try to wrap her mind around his bald statement. Maybe she was thinking he was exaggerating. But even if he could hide the bone-deep guilt in his eyes, he wasn't about to. She wanted to know; he was telling her.

He'd already passed judgment on himself twenty-five years ago. Surely Jana's condemnation couldn't be any worse.

But this was Jana, the most fair-minded person he knew. Not Aunt Barbara, who'd thought the worst of him from the get-go.

Jana's tone was neutral, gentle, as she asked, "What happened?"

He let the silence stretch a few more moments as he took another pull of his beer. Then he continued. "By Christmas Eve morning, I figured out why my sister was so cranky and wouldn't eat. She was burning up with fever. She started getting kind of glassy-eyed and after a while she wasn't even crying anymore."

It was like a knife in his chest remembering that listless little girl. She'd always been so cheerful, such a happy baby. Seeing her like that had been painful beyond bearing.

"I knew enough not to give her the grown-up medicine, but I couldn't find the baby aspirin. She kept getting sicker. I called Aunt Barbara again, but she must have gone out to dinner for Christmas Eve. I should have called 911, should have gone to a neighbor, but I just wasn't thinking clearly."

The waiter hovered nearby; Jana waved him off with a dark look. Sam shut his eyes, just letting the memories resurrect themselves, his voice foreign to his own ears.

"I'd seen my mother put Maddie in a cool bath once when she had a fever. So I ran a little water in the tub. Just a couple of inches. Not too much because Maddie was so small."

Now it felt as if he was talking about something that had happened to someone else, a movie or a scene in one of his books. How Maddie had cried as he swished the water on her, how her temperature seemed to spike even higher. How he'd left her sitting up in the tub while he raced to his parents' bedroom, thinking maybe the aspirin was in there.

"I was about to go back to the bathroom when someone knocked. I heard Aunt Barbara yelling through the door and ran to answer it. I guess my cousin finally remembered to give her the message."

He sucked in air. "She asked where Maddie was. When I told her, she pushed past me. Yelled at me for leaving her alone. By the time we got back to the bathroom—"

The rest of it spilled out. Maddie had tried to climb out of the tub, had slipped and hit her head. She'd landed facedown in the water.

Jana's warm hand on his brought him back to the busy restaurant. "How long was she under?"

"I don't know. Aunt Barbara got her out, squeezed the water from her lungs. Maddie started coughing. Aunt Barbara screamed at me. *'You could have killed your sister! You stupid boy!'*"

"But she was okay."

"But she could have died." He pulled his hand free, scrubbed at his face. Wished he could wipe away the images, still sharp after two and a half decades. "If Aunt Barbara had been a few minutes later, Maddie might have been dead."

Jana stared at Sam, wondering how she could pull him out of his self-imposed hell. "You were ten years old."

"I should have known better."

Jana resisted the urge to reach across the table and shake him. "How could you have?"

He sighed, sliding his beer bottle back and forth across the table. "All those years I avoided contacting my sister, I told myself it was pride—if she and Aunt Barbara didn't want me, I didn't want them either. But to be honest, I was terrified that when I talked to Maddie, when I saw her again, I'd see some lasting effect. Brain damage or something."

"But you didn't."

He smiled. "She's smart and funny and kind. I never should have wasted all those years."

The waiter looked their way again. Sam picked up his menu and Jana followed suit. She picked the least expensive item. Sam zeroed in on something as quickly as she did, and the waiter hurried over to take their order.

Jana got back to business as soon as the waiter left. "That can't be why your aunt Barbara sent you away."

He shook his head. "The first two years after my mom left, Dad left us with Aunt Barbara when he was on a haul. I was incorrigible. Lying, stealing from her. Flunking out at school. Then Dad had his wreck. With my dad dead, my behavior got even worse."

"Geez, Sam, you were hurting. I think your aunt could have cut you some slack. Got you some counseling."

"She tried. I wouldn't talk to the counselor. After a while I think she was afraid of me. Afraid of my influence on her own son. Afraid of leaving me alone with Maddie." Jana could hear the shame in his voice. "I think she started wondering if what happened in the bathtub really was an accident."

That ticked Jana off so much she would have clocked his aunt if the woman had been there. The Sam she knew—a little cocky, way brilliant—was a good man, just about the best person on the planet. How could his aunt have suspected him of trying to hurt his sister?

She reached for his hand again. "So your mom left. Your dad died. Aunt Barbara threw you into foster care and wouldn't let you see your sister. I'm guessing you went through a few foster homes before you found Estelle." He nodded in acknowledgment. "And you were hell on wheels with Estelle at first. She told me that much."

"I did my best to get her to throw me out, too."

"Trying for some control in your life, I guess. Which is what you do every time you buy one of those parting gifts."

"It isn't conscious, Jana. What I feel inside. I don't do it on purpose." She could hear the desperation in his voice. "I've got demons inside me. Pulling me two ways. I'm terrified of losing you. But I'm even more afraid of letting you in."

"But why?"

"Because you won't stay. Either you'll walk away—"

"Not gonna happen."

"—or I will." The lines of his face grew even more tense. "I don't trust myself to not walk out on you. Just like my mother did."

She felt as if she were on a merry-go-round, with Sam as the brass ring. But he kept backing away every time she tried to reach for him.

The waiter brought their salads, a pretty mix of greens and tomatoes that Jana was sure she wouldn't be able to eat. Still, she picked up her fork and poked around among the arugula. "So what now?" she asked.

He pulled a slice of bread from the basket. "We can't sleep with each other anymore."

Of course they couldn't. That would only finish the job of destroying her heart. Then a sudden thought filled her with panic. "What about the baby?"

His gaze swung up to meet hers. "I still want to adopt."

"But will you love the baby? Are you going to let the baby love you?"

She could see from the look on his face that she'd caught him off guard. That he hadn't thought it through. He turned away from her, staring out at the busy restaurant, and she had to fight to keep the tumult inside her at bay.

Then he turned back toward her. "Lots of fathers wonder if they'll love their baby. And they know going in that someday their kid will leave them. Your baby will never, ever feel unloved. Unwanted. Not one day, not one minute. I promise you that."

There was more steel in his voice than a New York City high-rise. Her doubt and fear faded.

They focused on their food then, making their way through the salads and bread, then the entrée when it arrived. Her body had its own idea about whether she should eat, commandeering her through the plate of pasta primavera. Just to give herself some stalling time, she asked for the dessert menu even though she knew she couldn't manage it. Because she knew she wouldn't have a receptive audience for what she was going to suggest.

She gave the menu a cursory look, dreaming briefly of chocolate lava cake, then set it aside. And crossed her fingers. "I think you should talk to your aunt Barbara. And maybe find out what happened to your mother."

He puffed up like a grizzly bear, looking ready to growl. She didn't back down. "You don't have to become her new best friend, eat dinner with her every Sunday night. But for your sake, isn't it time you cleared the air?"

"Maddie made the same suggestion. About finding our mother." He shrugged. "She had a pretty common name. Makes someone much harder to locate, according to Darius. Maybe I'll ask him when we hear back about Ian."

Jana understood enough about Sam to know that much of a concession was huge. Even so, she prodded him. "What about Aunt Barbara? Is she still in the area?"

"According to Maddie. It was Aunt Barbara's car Maddie borrowed to drive up to Placerville for lunch that day." When Jana kept staring at him, he threw up his hands. "Fine. I'll think about calling her. Satisfied?"

Not until you love me, she thought. But it looked as if that was a complete lost cause.

April wore on into May, Sam plunging deep into writing his book to keep the craziness inside him tamped down.

Although it should have been a healing process to reveal all to Jana—at least that's what a shrink would have told him—it seemed as if it had stirred up more than it settled. Nightmares he hadn't had in twenty years returned, him running through his old house, searching for Maddie, finally finding her blue-faced dead. Aunt Barbara screeching at him; the guilt and remorse crushing him.

He couldn't stay away from Jana entirely; it just wasn't in him. He'd share lunch with her and the kids, and they'd go over to the ranch for dinner two or three nights a week. After dinner he'd walk her up to her apartment, give her a chaste hug, then drive home with fantasies running through his head he knew he could never act on.

The third week of May, Sam got the word from Darius that he'd tracked down Ian. The feckless kid had jumped at the chance to sign the termination of parental rights papers. When Sam told Jana, she got quiet, and he wondered if she'd had second thoughts about Ian. Then he realized it was just that it meant the adoption was moving another step forward.

The next week, right before Memorial Day, Maddie got a few days free between shifts and Sam flew her up to Sacramento. The first two nights she stayed with him. He and Maddie and Jana did the touristy thing, heading up to Tahoe one day, the next doing a wine-tasting circuit in Fairplay, with Jana as designated driver.

Maddie and Jana clicked immediately, the way women so often seemed to, joking and teasing, usually at Sam's expense. Maddie tiptoed around the sensitive topic of Jana's baby, asking general questions, readily accepting Jana's offer to feel the baby kick.

That was the only time he let himself touch Jana for

more than a few seconds, resting his hand on her belly, waiting for the nudge and bump of that tiny being that would soon be his son or daughter. That first strong kick shot through him like an emotional rocket, leaving him shaken and awed.

Maddie's last night in Northern California she'd promised to spend with Aunt Barbara. And Sam had told his sister he'd give her a lift to her adoptive mom's Roseville home. If he thought he'd have a chance to simply leave Maddie off at the curb, Jana disabused him of that notion pretty quickly. She'd come with him for moral support, but by God he was going to see his aunt Barbara.

He did his best to delay the inevitable. He suggested they stop at a coffee shop in Placerville for waffles and pancakes, then paid the price when the heavy meal sat like a stone in his stomach. After breakfast he took his time putting the top down on the Mustang so they could enjoy the warm late-spring sunshine. He took the back roads down the hill to Roseville, telling the two women there'd be too much wind at freeway speeds.

When they pulled up to the house, Sam felt as if the skin had been stripped from his body. He was that twelve-year-old boy again, defiant and needy, a heartbroken juvenile delinquent. She'd sent him out with two suitcases filled with his stuff; within a year those possessions had been winnowed down to what he could fit in two paper market bags.

Jana smiled at him across the car. Her hair was a riotous mess from riding in the convertible, and he wanted to smooth it back into place. He'd want to kiss her after that, despite his sister in the backseat and Aunt Barbara watching from the front window—he'd seen the curtain twitch aside. He'd keep his hands off Jana's hair, but in his imagination, there was a golden link between them that would feed him strength during the upcoming confrontation.

Sam climbed out and retrieved Maddie's suitcase from the trunk. With the two women leading, he carried Maddie's baggage—and a fair load of his own—up the walk. Aunt Barbara had the door open before they got to the stoop.

Damn, she was old. Yeah, it had been more than twenty years and she was close to sixty. But he'd had that midthirties face locked in his mind, that last scowl of disapproval she'd directed his way when she'd delivered him to Child Protective Services.

Her hair might be salt-and-pepper and her face creased with wrinkles, but the scowl was still there. It dropped for a few moments while Maddie introduced Jana as Sam's friend; then it fell back into place. After Maddie and Jana were inside, Aunt Barbara stared at him as if he were the same young miscreant she'd banished from her home twenty-three years ago.

It damn well shouldn't hurt. What did he care what this woman thought of him after all these years? He was a grown man, a big success. Control of his life wasn't in this old woman's hands anymore.

"I'd like to put this down," he said, indicating the suitcase.

She finally stepped aside. He entered, took in the changes of two decades. Updated carpet, furniture. A bookcase full of books he'd bet every penny of his fortune didn't include even one Sam Harrison thriller.

Suitcase set down, an array of family photos caught his attention. He crossed the living room to view them—the school pictures featuring Maddie and his cousin Jason, several with Aunt Barbara, all smiles, with her husband and the two kids. There was one photo of his dad holding baby

Maddie, just home from the hospital. Sam remembered that picture used to hang in his parents' bedroom, except he'd been in the photo, too, at his father's side.

No room for Sam Harrison on the bookshelf, no space for him on the wall. Obliterated from Aunt Barbara's life.

She crossed her arms around her stout body. "You've done well for yourself." She said it as if there was something disreputable about his success.

"I've been fortunate."

Jana stepped up beside him. "He's got copies of his latest release in the car." She tugged at his arm, bobbing her head between him and Aunt Barbara.

"I'm glad to give you one." He almost choked on the offer.

Interest flickered in her eyes, just a moment before it was extinguished. "I don't read those kind of books."

He felt Jana stiffen beside him, saw his sister's sympathetic expression. He didn't care what Aunt Barbara might think—he put his arm around Jana. He needed her to hold on to.

Aunt Barbara's gaze slid to Jana's seven-months-pregnant belly. Sam set a proprietary hand there. "Jana is carrying my baby."

He heard Jana's hissing intake of breath. She shot him a glance that he ignored. He directed all his attention toward Aunt Barbara.

"I apologize for being a jackass when I lived here. I was a messed-up kid, and I took it out on you. But everything I am, everything I have, is in spite of what you did to me. And I'm damn well not going to hate you anymore. You're not worth the space in my heart."

He let go of Jana to give his sister a hug. "Let me know when you can come up again." Then he took Jana's hand and started toward the door.

"You look like her," Aunt Barbara called out. "Like your mother."

A rush of cold, then heat, filled Sam. He turned back to his aunt.

"It wasn't because of your behavior," she said, the lines in her face sharpening. "You were a rotten kid sometimes, but I mostly had you under control."

"Then why?"

Although she did her damnedest, she couldn't quite hide her shame. "Because I saw your mother's face in yours every day. I despised her."

"I've done my share of hating her myself," Sam said.

Her gaze narrowed as her face turned meaner. "She told me you were his. And she refused to get rid of it."

Sam swayed a little as he tried to grasp what his aunt was telling him. "She was pregnant with me when they married?"

"My brother said he believed her, but she didn't fool me. I knew she slept around."

Rage bubbled up inside him. "What are you saying?"

"You know what I'm talking about." She flicked a dismissive glance at Jana. "You'd better do a paternity test with this one. She looks like the type that would lie to suit herself."

Sam heard a roaring in his ears. He was only dimly aware of Jana clinging to his arm, Maddie moving in to stand between him and Aunt Barbara. It had never in his life even once crossed his mind to strike a woman, but every atom in his body was goading him to break that sacrosanct rule.

But with Jana's fingers digging into his arm, her full weight anchoring him to the floor, he came to his senses. He let Jana drag him out the door and down the walk.

At the sidewalk he shook her off. "I'm okay." Pressing

both hands on the hood of the car, he dragged in breath after breath, willing away the nastiness of the scene they'd just left. Jana's gentle hand on his back soothed him, brought him round again.

He took her in his arms, and he could feel her vibrating with indignation. "What a horrible, despicable, low-life—"

"Do you think it's true?"

She pressed her palm against his face. "Does it matter?"

"Yes. No." He tried to reach inside himself for an answer. "I don't know."

She gazed up at him, her expression earnest. "Does it change the way you feel about your father?"

Now he could hear the real reason for her question. Would he feel differently about the child Jana carried, knowing he or she wasn't biologically his?

"My father was distant. Not cold, but—always awkward with me. But to tell you the truth, he seemed that way with Maddie, too." He allowed himself to kiss Jana's forehead. "Still, I loved him. And in his way, I think he loved me, too. He tried his best."

He opened the car door for Jana and helped her swing down into the low-slung Mustang. About to round the front of the convertible, he heard Maddie calling him from the house.

She came down the walk, carrying a battered cardboard box. "I'm sorry, Sam. I had no idea."

"No worries, little sis."

She thrust the box into his hands. "Last time I was up here, I found this in the closet of the guest room. I just gave it a quick look then. It's mostly Dad's stuff, but there might be a few things of Mom's in here, too."

"Does she know you're giving this to me?"

"No. Right now I'm so angry with her I don't really care."

Handing the box to Jana, he gave Maddie another hug. After putting the top up on the vehicle, he climbed into the driver's seat.

As he pulled out, Jana's fingers twitched on the box. "What do they say about curiosity and the cat?"

"We'll be home in less than an hour. You can wait that long." And he'd have that much more time to prepare for what new revelations might be inside.

Chapter Fourteen

Sam drove to his house, leery of the cozy intimacy of Jana's apartment. His stomach was still in knots, but he made them sandwiches anyway, mindful of Jana's need to eat for the baby's sake. They sat on the sofa, plates on their laps. He didn't touch his food, and she only nibbled at hers, both of them with one eye on the box they'd left on the coffee table.

"Go ahead," Sam said. "You might as well open it."

She set her plate aside. The tape across the top of the box was yellowed and loose, no doubt from Maddie's cursory inspection. Jana unfolded the flaps. The top of the box was high enough that she couldn't quite see inside, so she set it on the floor between them.

She looked up at him. "Do you want to—"

"You do it."

Jana started digging through, identifying each of her

finds as she withdrew it. "A penknife. A sergeant's patch. Some army medals." She arrayed them on the coffee table.

"I didn't even know Dad was in the military."

"It would be cool to frame these. To show them to…" her hand dropped to her belly "…when he's old enough."

"Or she."

She gave him a sad, wistful smile, then reached into the box again. "What's this?"

She unearthed a painted wooden car from under a manila envelope. The garishly decorated seven-inch-long car tugged an old, old memory.

"My Pinewood Derby entry. From Cub Scouts." He took the lightweight pine car from her. "I was eight. It was my only year in Scouts."

During a rare, weeklong layover, his dad had helped him with the car, showing him how to sand it, helping him choose the paint. He'd brought home decals one day that Sam had plastered on the car from front to back.

"I can't believe he saved it." Sam had figured it was lost, like so much else from his early life.

Jana fished a business-size white envelope from the box. After she asked permission with a glance at him, she removed the contents.

On top was his dad's driver's license, its Commercial Class A rating allowing him to drive the big rigs. Taking it from Jana, he studied his father's photo, searching for some resemblance to his own face.

Jana brushed his arm. "Not everyone looks like both their parents."

He set the license on the table. "What else is in there?"

As she unfolded the two eight-and-a-half by eleven sheets in her hand, a square of cardboard fluttered to the floor. She picked it up absentmindedly, focused on the papers. "Your sister's birth certificate."

"The other one must be mine." His stomach did a dance as he considered whose name might be written under *father*.

Jana handed it over. His gaze scanned rapidly over the information. "His name is here. My dad's."

"Of course it is." She looked down at the card she'd dropped. "It's your mother's Social Security card."

He took it from her, reading his mother's married name, Linda Harrison, typed on the front. He had given Darius the name last week, but his friend had reminded him that someone with such a common name would be difficult to find.

But with his mother's Social Security number, Darius could probably track her down in a heartbeat. He placed the card carefully on the table.

Jana pulled a manila envelope from the box. Flipping the flap open, she slid out a photo. She turned it over, read the inscription. "Their wedding picture." She showed him the date. Four months before his birthday.

Okay, Aunt Barbara was right about that much. His mother was already in a family way on their wedding day.

The portrait of his parents, both of them smiling, happy for once, took his breath away. Again, he studied every feature of his father's face, searching for something familiar.

Jana looked over at him. "You are a dead ringer for her."

"I am," he agreed quietly. He supposed that ought to upset him. But he felt an odd sense of pride that he carried his mother's legacy in his face.

"But then, so is Maddie. Your sister has your dad's mouth, but the rest is pure Mom."

Jana's defense warmed him. She shook the remaining

contents of the envelope out between them on the sofa. A half-dozen smaller envelopes fell to the cushions.

"I think they're letters," Jana said. "From your mother to your father, from your father to your mother." She stacked them neatly in date order. "The first one is from your mother. A month before the wedding date."

A sense of foreboding rolled over him as Jana placed the letter in his nerveless hands. He rose abruptly, knocking a couple of the other envelopes to the floor. "Be right back," he told her as he headed for the stairs.

In his room he lowered himself to the edge of the bed. The letter might be completely innocuous. A love letter. A pouring out of youthful angst. A simple confirmation of the pregnancy and of their plans to marry.

He separated the torn edges of the envelope and extracted the sheet of pale pink paper. Cautiously opened it flat. And read.

Tom,
  You will always have my thanks for getting me out of this fix I got myself into. I promise I will be the best wife I can be if you will only treat this baby as your own....

There was more, something about borrowing a friend's car and a trip to Reno. He barely took it in before dropping the letter to the floor. His vision narrowed to that pale pink sheet of paper between his feet as he hunched on the bed.

He didn't even hear Jana come in. Barely registered her picking up the letter and scanning it before laying it on the nightstand. It was only when she sat beside him and put her arm around him that whatever had frozen inside him started to thaw.

He was blind to everything but her—her warmth, the faint scent of honeysuckle, the silky feel of her hair when he brushed his mouth against it. At first he was only looking for comfort, but as he kissed her brow, then her cheek, her lips, a fire exploded inside him. All the sensual need he'd held at bay for the past several weeks burst through the barriers he'd used to confine it. He was helpless to deny it.

They fell to the bed, pushing clothes aside, unbuttoning and unzipping. When they were skin-to-skin, the swell of her pregnancy enthralled him, and he kissed and caressed every inch. He brought her to climax with his mouth and hands, then stood between her legs as she lay at the edge of the bed. With his arms propped on either side of her, he thrust inside her, feeling her belly against his, locking his gaze with hers. Reveled in the knowledge that this was *his* son or daughter inside her.

Afterward, they lay in bed together, her spooned up against him, his hand on that firm, rounded curve where the baby dreamed. His gaze fell on the letter on the nightstand. And with sudden insight, he knew what he had to do.

"Jana," he murmured before the fear could catch up with him. "I want to get married."

There wasn't an argument she could use to dissuade him. From that stubborn set to his face, Jana could see that Sam had his mind made up. He was ready to dig in his heels and wait for her to come around.

With the afterglow pretty much jolted out of her by Sam's pronouncement, she'd gotten up from the bed, tossed his clothes at him and pulled on her own. She marched from the bedroom and downstairs where her stale sandwich waited to satisfy her now-ravenous appetite. She was wolfing it down when he flopped next to her on the sofa, a just-try-me look on his face.

She sorted through all the reasons that marrying him would be a crazy idea, then settled on the one most important to her. "Why would I marry a man who doesn't love me? A man who doesn't even want me to love him. Unless that's changed?"

Even though he avoided a direct answer, she got the message anyway. "I'll be a good husband, a good father for our baby—"

"And what about that whole terrified-of-commitment story you told me last month? That's suddenly gone, poof?"

"Not exactly."

She saw it now, the same rigid control she'd seen in the shop the day she'd confessed her love to him. Fingers laced together in his lap, the tendons popping in his arms, the backs of his hands. The stiff set of his shoulders.

She set aside her empty plate and scooted herself away from him to rest against the arm of the sofa. It was all she could do to keep the tears from crawling up her throat. "Let me get this straight, then. You want to marry me, even though you don't love me, even though it scares the holy crap out of you, even though you don't have to, to make this child yours."

"My father did the right thing. I can, too."

Pain and anger and desolation built up inside her. She tried to grasp the emotions smashing around, to understand one clear thing. Then realization popped to the surface.

"I want you to love me, Sam. I want that to tie you to me, not obligation. Not 'the right thing.'"

"Marry me anyway," he said, his voice rough.

No was in her mind, on her lips even. But her throat wouldn't cooperate. It just wouldn't let enough air pass to speak the word. Not when he was sitting there, so close, his face so well loved, his scent, the memory of his touch still on her skin.

"Give me time to think about it," she said finally.

"Not too long."

Pulling her gaze from his, she bent awkwardly to find the shoes she'd slipped off earlier. He found them for her under the table and held her feet as he put them on for her.

"Could you take me home, please?" she asked.

"Tony and Rebecca are expecting us for dinner tonight."

"Tell them I can't make it."

They drove to the apartment in silence, Jana not taking an easy breath until Sam was gone. Maybe because she was so edgy, the baby was wide-awake, bouncing around like an Olympic gymnast.

Her brain was mush. There was no way she could think this through clearly on her own. Frances was right downstairs, helping Ray run the shop, but no doubt the eighteen-year-old really wasn't up to having Jana dump her big-girl problems on her. No way could she talk to Tony, and Rebecca was probably way too busy in the ranch's bake-shop. Which left Estelle.

A quick call to the ranch told Jana that the former foster mother was up for a visit. Gathering up her car keys, she headed out, waving to Ray as he came out to dump some cardboard in the recycle bin. She made it to the ranch in record time and found Estelle out in the backyard of the main house, sitting in the pergola under the flowering wisteria.

In the cave of thickly blossoming wisteria, Estelle

folded Jana into a big hug, then patted the seat of the bench. "It seems like months since we've talked."

Despite her smile, Estelle looked tired, her hands more puffy and swollen than Jana's own from her pregnancy. She felt a twinge of guilt for bringing her problems to Estelle when the older woman obviously wasn't feeling well.

"I know, I look like death warmed over," Estelle told her. "I'm fine. I just get a little tired when the weather warms up. Tell me what's going on."

Jana had intended to work her way into it, but instead she blurted out, "Sam wants to marry me."

Estelle beamed. "That's wonderful!"

"But he doesn't love me."

She thought maybe Estelle would argue the point, tell her, but of course he does. Except she didn't. She just said, "Sam has a tough time understanding what he feels."

"I do love him, Estelle. And he wants to be the father of my baby. I'd live sort of happily ever after." It was definitely one up on her mother, who never seemed to be able to get the men in her life to tie the knot. "But he made it pretty clear he'd only be marrying me out of obligation."

"He said that?"

It wasn't her place to reveal what Sam had just learned about his parents. "Let's just say he sees it as the right thing to do."

"So the question is, how can you be happy with that?"

"How can he?" Jana asked. "There'd be no more Shawnas or Cindys or Patricias. He'd be stuck with me."

"He's very fond of you." Estelle fixed her probing gaze on Jana. "But you don't think that's enough."

"I keep wondering, what happens in a few years? When I get some college under my belt and I don't have to depend on Sam for everything. When I can fend for myself, when he's not obligated anymore, what then? If he truly loved me, if he wasn't just *fond* of me, that'd be one thing. But if obligation is the only glue between us and then that's gone…"

Estelle didn't have an answer for that. So they sat there in the quiet of the backyard, concealed from the rest of the world by the wisteria, Jana's emotions as twisted as the vines overhead.

Then Estelle took her hand. "I think the real question, Jana, the one that really matters, is do you want to be a mother to this baby? Because marrying Sam is the only way to be sure of that."

Of course. Leave it to Estelle to lay it out so clearly. It spoke of her turmoil that Jana hadn't asked herself that very question before now.

"That is a no-brainer," Jana said. "Because all this time, when I've thought about giving her up, it's just about killed me. I love her already, more than I can even say. Despite the way she came about, despite her stinker of a father."

"Not anymore," Estelle reminded her. "Because from this point forward, that father is Sam. Maybe he didn't put the baby there physically, but from the moment he took you under his protection, that baby was meant to be his."

As she spoke her piece, Estelle looked even more exhausted than she had when Jana had arrived. Jana helped the older woman to her feet and walked with her to the main house.

On the way to Sam's, she wrestled with second thoughts, third thoughts, an infinity of qualms and uncertainties. But the baby trumped every scrap of doubt, circling her back around to the same decision.

As she pulled up to his gate, it occurred to her that

maybe she should have called him. For all she knew, he could be out. But as she pulled up to the house, she spotted him on the front porch, just coming around from the back.

He waited for her at the top of the steps, hands gripped at his sides. She climbed up, tipping her head back to look up at him, the expression on his face telling her he was filled with just as much misgiving as she was.

She said all she had to say. "Yes, I'll marry you."

He took her into his arms and held her for a long, long time.

Chapter Fifteen

With a waterfall of wisteria blooms as a backdrop, the mid-June Sunday sky so blue it made her heart ache, Jana whispered a shaky "I do" to Sam Harrison. He at least said his out loud, clear enough for the teens sitting in the last row to hear. His brief kiss barely qualified as one, his body so rigid she wondered if his tuxedo was stitched with two-by-fours. But they made it through with a passable imitation of a happy-to-be-wed couple.

Their quickie wedding had turned into a borderline monstrous affair with forty guests—twenty from the ranch alone, plus Sam's agent and publicist; his sister, of course; and even his housekeeper, Mrs. Prentiss. Because Sam wanted both Tony and Darius as best men, Jana had to have two bridesmaids also, so she asked Ruby and the ginor-mously pregnant Rebecca. Jana doubted anyone was looking at her. They were too busy wondering if Rebecca would pop before the ceremony was over.

Besides the expansion in the guest list, Rebecca's offer to have the kids prepare a light buffet brunch morphed into a catered sit-down that probably cost Sam some serious cash. The photographer Sam hired had just shot exclusive photos of some big celebrity wedding. Jana didn't want to see that bill.

By the time the paparazzo finished and the last of the receiving line tromped past, Jana's feet were killing her and her back screamed with pain. Not to mention the wedding dress that chafed around her middle because of her ballooning out the past few days since the fitting. Sam was beside her, his hand gripping hers a little too tightly, his forehead glistening with sweat in the hot sun.

When they finally relocated to the air-conditioned bakeshop dining room, Jana made a beeline for the head table and collapsed in a chair. Almost immediately Sam's publicist—a woman with a figure like a twig—hurried over.

The publicist waved her digital camera. "Could I just get one more shot of the two of you outside?"

"Later, Bridget. My wife needs a break." He all but shooed her away, throwing off his jacket and dropped into the seat beside Jana.

His hand cupped her cheek, turning her to face him. "It'll work out, Jana."

One way or another, she supposed. But would things "work out" to keep them together? Without love as a tie? No point in asking those questions again. She'd made her bed.

He took her hand, running his thumb over the simple golden band he'd placed there such a short time ago. "I wish you'd let me get you a diamond."

"I don't like your history with fancy jewelry." Her joke came out harder edged than she'd intended. "I'm sorry. I'm tired, my feet hurt and my hands are swollen worse than Estelle's."

"The ring seemed like a tighter fit than I'd expected."

She wrinkled her nose at him. "Thanks for confirmation that I'm getting fat."

"It's not that. Your face seems…rounder. Swollen like your hands."

She wasn't about to mention the headaches. Sam would probably freak out, when it was just the stress of the wedding.

She made it through the rest of the reception by staying off her feet as much as she could. She and Sam kept their one dance brief; then she offered herself up to Tony and Darius. Sam waltzed gingerly with Rebecca, then Ruby, finishing with his sister, Maddie. Although Jana felt bad that Maddie had had to attend without her fiancé, she was grateful to have avoided an additional dance with Matthew.

Despite her best efforts to avoid it, Frances caught the bouquet and Ray the garter. The girl wouldn't even look at Ray after that, refusing his offer for a last dance.

When it was finally time to go, Jana changed into maternity slacks and blouse and carefully laid her wedding dress across the backseat of the Mustang. She wouldn't have even gone back inside except that she realized she'd forgotten her purse in the main house.

When she saw Tony, Rebecca, Darius and Sam clustered around Estelle on the sofa, her heart just about stopped. Estelle had had a bad episode last year, shortly after Jana had left the ranch. That she hadn't been here to help was one more tick in the guilt column.

"Is she okay?" Jana asked. "What's going on?"

Estelle was sitting up, but she looked horrible—puffy and swollen, her breathing coming in short gasps as if she couldn't get enough air. She glanced over at Jana. "I'm so sorry to spoil your wedding day."

"Never mind that." Sam gave his former foster mother's hand a squeeze. "Darius and Tony are going to take you to the emergency room."

Estelle didn't argue, which was pretty scary in itself. Jana knew the older woman hated hospitals.

Darius and Tony made a chair with their arms and carried Estelle out to Tony's truck. The two men climbed in with her and drove off, spitting gravel.

No one had the heart to toss rice at Jana and Sam as they made their way to the car. Already on an emotional razor's edge, Jana kept having to blink away tears as worry for Estelle tied her stomach up in knots.

Out of habit, she thought Sam would drop her off at the apartment. When he made the turn onto the road to his house, the realization that they were truly married dropped like a load of bricks. She wasn't going to be able to go back to her tiny apartment and crawl into her bed alone. To try to come to terms with whether she'd just made the biggest mistake of her life.

She didn't bother trying to fight the tears that spilled down her cheeks. Sam would assume she was crying for Estelle. And she was, but there was far more ripping her up inside. She'd had this crazy hope that once they spoke their vows, all her doubts would vanish. That she would be happy enough with the limits Sam had placed on their marriage. At least that it wouldn't hurt.

She kept her gaze out the window as they stopped at the

gate to Sam's property. She was afraid to look at him, feared the rush of love that hurt so much inside. What should have been a day for tears of happiness just filled her with grief. Feeling sick to boot, her stomach aching a little from the rich food, just made her more miserable.

At least they wouldn't be doing that whole honeymoon thing, not yet anyway. Not with her pregnant as a hippo. They'd agreed to wait until the baby was born and old enough to leave with a sitter. The way she felt today, she wondered if she and Sam would last that long.

As he parked in the garage, in the fourth slot over, Jana turned to him finally. "Would you mind if I went in and took a nap? I'm beat."

He reached across to smooth a lock of hair behind her ear. "Not the wedding day you imagined, I'm guessing."

In a way it was, if you counted those days when she was twelve and thirteen, still dreaming that someday Sam Harrison would marry her. "It was beautiful. Thank you for everything."

He turned away, and she sensed all was not well in Sam Land either. Unable to bear one more scrap of anxiety, she climbed from the car and threaded her way through the garage to the house. After passing through the kitchen, she automatically turned right toward the guest room.

Sam's voice stopped her. "You're sleeping in my room now."

He didn't sound too sure of that himself. She glanced his way, taking in his troubled expression, and tried to smile, but her face felt too stiff. "I forgot."

As she walked past him toward the stairs, he followed just behind her. She wanted him with her, wanted him to go away and leave her alone. She wanted to feel normal again. That wasn't likely to happen for a while, certainly not before the baby was born.

While she pushed off her shoes and slacks, wriggled out of her short-sleeved blouse, Sam pulled back the covers for her. She crawled gratefully into the bed, rolling on her side with her back to him. Her arm curved around her bare belly, she felt the bump and grind of her little passenger who was really wearing out the welcome these days.

She'd started to drift off when she remembered Estelle. She raised her head from the pillow. "You'll wake me if you hear anything?"

"I will," Sam said, his voice sounding far away.

As she settled her head back down, she thought she heard the sound of a chair being pulled from the corner toward the bed. Then sleep had its way with her, dragging her into dreams.

Sam settled in the chair, nudging off his loafers and lifting his feet to the edge of the bed. He placed them carefully so as not to disturb Jana. She'd fallen asleep pretty quickly, not surprising considering the demands of the day, and the last thing he wanted was to wake her.

Hopefully she'd feel better by dinner. Mrs. Prentiss had insisted on making a light wedding supper as a gift for them. It was all packaged up in the fridge for later, salad ready to be tossed and main dish ready to be popped in the oven.

He didn't have an appetite, even though he'd been too keyed up to eat much from the wedding buffet. Considering his stomach still felt as if he'd eaten ground glass, he wasn't enthusiastic about whatever grudging labor of love the dour Mrs. Prentiss had prepared. Still, he'd eat it all with gusto if it put a smile on Jana's face.

He let his gaze trail down the lines of her body, the lightweight covers following its swells and curves. He doubted it was an accident that she'd turned her back to him. She'd been ready to go hole up in the guest room, likely would have if he hadn't said anything. Maybe he just should have let her.

He scrubbed at his face with his hands, trying to make sense of the stew of emotions inside him. He'd thought their marriage would throw a magic switch. That his fears would vanish, replaced finally with a sense of security. He would know that Jana was here to stay, that she and her child—their child—would forever be in his life.

But it hadn't worked out that way. Their I-do's raised more what-ifs than they'd answered. What if she stopped loving him? What if her heart couldn't bear his miserly, limited affection for her? What if she left him, just as his mother had? Except Jana wouldn't leave the baby behind. To have them both leave…

Despair battering him, he dropped his hands, drank her in, calming himself with the sight of her in his bed. But there was something even darker chewing at him, an insight into himself he didn't want to acknowledge. It wasn't Jana's leaving him he had most to fear. It was his leaving her.

The way his dad had left his mom again and again. Because even though he'd made the right choice, done the right thing, he found it impossible to live with it. So he picked a job that kept him far away from home, gave himself a legitimate way to escape the ramifications of the decision to marry Sam's mother.

Sam could do the same. He always got far more requests for television interviews and conference appearances than he accepted. He could start saying yes more often, bring a laptop with him to allow him to work on the road. Jana wouldn't say a word, would accept him putting his career first.

But when he thought of upping his travel, spending lonely nights in hotel rooms in Denver or Oklahoma City, the pain in his gut just increased. Maybe his father had felt the same way. Except in his dad's case, the scale tipped more toward escape.

God, he needed to touch her. Even though she'd shown her desire to keep her distance by turning her back to him. He slid his feet from the bed and walked quietly around it. He considered climbing under the covers but didn't want to risk rousing Jana. So he lay on top, on his side so he could face her.

Her hand was balled up at her face, her knees bent up toward her belly. With slow movements he shifted his leg to rest against hers, then laid his fingers lightly against her hand.

If this was all he had to do for the rest of his life—lying beside Jana, watching her sleep—maybe he could manage it. Except it was all so much more complicated. And he knew that if he didn't find a way to solve this riddle between his heart and hers, he would risk losing everything.

Two days after the wedding, Tony called with the latest news about Estelle. Jana recognized the caller ID as being from the ranch, but Sam got to the phone first. After a quick greeting, he said to Tony, "Hang on. Jana's with me. I want to put the call on speaker."

Then Sam reached for her, leading her to sit with him on the sofa. She held on to his hand so tight, she was probably making bruises.

"Estelle's got something called polycystic kidney disease," Tony said grimly. "She may have had it for quite some time."

"Polycyst—what does that mean?" Jana asked.

Tony's answer drifted from the handset. "Cysts have been growing in her kidneys, probably for years, replacing the good tissue. Her kidneys aren't functioning at all."

She glanced over at Sam and saw he looked just as scared as she felt. "So what are they going to do to fix her?" Jana asked. "They can make her better, right?"

"She'll have to have a kidney transplant," Tony said. "Which means we'll have to find a matching donor. Meanwhile, she's got to undergo dialysis several times a week."

"I want to get tested," Jana said. "To see if I'm a match."

"We all will," Tony said. "Darius is already contacting as many of Estelle's former fosters as he can."

After Sam hung up the phone, they sat on the sofa in each other's arms. Estelle's crisis should have brought them closer together—wasn't that part of being husband and wife? Except that even though Sam did all the right things—hold her, rub her back, murmur that everything would be all right—it almost could have been a scene he'd written in one of his books. He was still a million miles away from her, protecting his heart from the pain that losing Estelle would bring.

Jana sleepwalked through the next few weeks. She seemed to grow bigger on a daily basis, her feet swelling along with her belly and her hands, headaches keeping her awake at night. The doctor didn't like the way her blood pressure had crept up and pretty much restricted her to bed rest. The confinement made her feel only more crazed.

The news about Estelle was good and bad—good because she was responding well to the dialysis but bad because they hadn't yet found a match. It turned out that the rare set of antigens in Estelle's blood would make finding a compatible donor difficult.

Whether it was the problems with Estelle or Sam's buyer's remorse about marrying Jana, Sam kept to himself an awful lot. He'd hole up in his room, working until one and two in the morning. Jana saw him less than she had before they were married.

When he finally joined her in bed, she'd pretend to be asleep. That way, he would take her into his arms, snuggle up against her back. If he knew she was still awake, he would make sure not to touch her.

During those long hours alone, waiting for him to come to bed, hamster-wheel thoughts rolled around in her head. One minute she wanted to yell at him, shake him out from behind his iron bars. The next she wondered if she should just admit to him that their marriage was a big mistake. That they should part company now before the baby was born.

Then Sam would creep into the room, slip into bed beside her. Gather her up in his arms so tenderly that her heart would break into a zillion pieces. And she knew she couldn't leave even as she knew staying would tear her apart.

July arrived with a vengeance, slapping them with triple-digit heat on the first day. With nearly a month still to go before her due date, Jana woke on the third day of the heat wave feeling worse than ever. Her head pounded, her hands looked like the Pillsbury Doughboy's and she was crankier than a cartoon-deprived toddler. To top it off, Sam was as usual hiding in his office, working, even though it was a Saturday.

Restless and achy after breakfast, she stretched out on the living-room sofa, directly under the ceiling fan. Darius usually called on Saturday with an update on his search for Estelle's former fosters, so she had the phone at hand as she flipped through a baby magazine.

When it rang, she grabbed the portable, its caller ID confirming it was Darius. "Hey, how's it going?" she asked.

"Is Sam there?" Darius asked.

Jana's anxiety bumped up a notch. "If it's about Estelle—"

"Estelle's fine. Nothing new to report. I'm calling about Sam's mother."

Prickliness danced across her skin. Sam had mentioned he'd finally given Darius his mom's Social Security number a couple days ago. Sam had told Darius to take his time, that the search for Estelle's fosters had top priority.

"Did you find her?" Jana asked.

"Let me talk to Sam," Darius said.

Sam must have sensed something, because he appeared at the top of the stairs. Jana waved him down, then handed him the phone when he came up behind the sofa.

"Yeah?" he said to Darius. He listened a while; then his face bleached of color. "Okay. Thanks."

Looking dazed and lost, he swayed, dropping the phone as he gripped the sofa back. Like a blind man feeling his way, he moved around the sofa, reaching out for Jana as he all but fell beside her. He pulled her into his lap, burying her head in his neck.

He shuddered, his mouth close to her ear. "She's gone, Jana. My mother is dead."

It shouldn't matter. It shouldn't mean a damn thing to him. His mother might as well have been dead the moment she walked out of their house twenty-five years ago. And yet it felt as if someone had run him through with a sword. Because somewhere deep inside, there was a little boy thinking he might see his mother again someday.

He started to shake, and before he knew it would happen, before he could stop it, he started to sob. It was coarse and ugly and had to be terrifying for Jana. He knew that deep inside. But he couldn't let go of her, because she was the only thing that mattered in his life, the only light that shone for him at the other end of this black tunnel he'd burrowed into. He just might die himself if he didn't keep his grip on her.

And she held on just as tightly, her fingers digging into the back of his neck, into his ribs. She murmured soothing sounds, comforting him just with her voice. That she loved him, that she would be with him always, that she would never leave him.

When he finally quieted, Jana's hair wet with his tears, his hold on her loosened, her hands relaxed against him. Yet she snuggled even closer, as much a part of him as his own self. And in that moment insight hit him with freight-train force.

He could never let her go. He would never walk away. She would be in his life for as long as he lived. Because he could trust her love, could count on it. Could rely on its constancy.

Whatever drove his mother to abandon him, that was about as foreign to Jana as antlers on a tiger. And his father's wanderlust had never rubbed off on him—he liked home base, liked the anchor and foundation of it. If he went anywhere, it would be with Jana and their child at his side. He didn't have to drag the shackle of his childhood anymore.

He would tell her. That the walls he kept between them had crumbled, that his heart burned now with a new passion. That from now on, their lives would be different.

"Jana," he whispered, his throat raw.

She leaned back from him, and for the first time he saw she didn't look right. "I don't feel good."

In the next moment she slumped in his arms, deadweight.

The next hour passed in a blur of panic. Calling 911, the excruciating wait for the Advanced Life Support team—only ten minutes until arrival they'd told him, but it seemed forever. Then the controlled chaos as they worked over Jana—checking her blood pressure, starting an IV line, administering medication to bring down her high blood pressure, all the while in contact with the doctor at the hospital.

Jana had come to right after he'd hung up the phone, so he had that small comfort. But it broke his heart seeing her on the gurney as they rolled her from the house, IV line feeding into her arm and oxygen mask on her face.

He rode up front with the paramedic, lights and sirens clearing the way for the ambulance. Another agonizing wait, time crawling as they raced toward the hospital in Placerville. Everything seemed to move in slow-motion when they arrived, Jana pulled from the back, rushed inside and down the hall to Obstetrics.

Sam didn't like the look on the doctor's face when he checked Jana's blood pressure on the monitor. The man looked even more grim when he saw the baby's heart rate on the fetal monitor.

"The medication is not bringing your wife's blood pressure down, and your baby's in distress," the OB told him. "We have to do an emergency C-section."

Sam had no chance to react to the twin blows. They took Jana to the operating room while a nurse took Sam to change into scrubs. Panic surged again inside Sam—what if Jana died, like his father had, like his mother? What if he never had a chance to tell her he loved her?

He sat huddled in the OB waiting room, praying for Jana. He made deal after deal with God, if only He would let Jana and the baby be okay. He offered his own life if God wanted it, in exchange for Jana and the child she bore.

When the nurse appeared in the doorway, he jumped to his feet, taking in the woman's smile. "Are they okay?"

Her smile broadened. "Your daughter is in the Neonatal Intensive Care Unit, but she and your wife will both be fine. Would you like to see your daughter?"

Not even bothering to answer the no-brainer question, he followed the nurse to the NICU, then stared through the glass at the tiny bundle the woman pointed out. He could see only the scrunched-up face and a wisp of blond hair that poked out from the pink cap, but love poured out of him in a flood.

He didn't even realize his face was wet with tears until the nurse offered him a tissue. He hadn't cried in probably twenty years, and yet here he'd blubbered twice in one day.

"When can I see Jana?" he asked the nurse.

"Another half hour or so. I can come get you in the waiting room—"

"I'll wait here," he said, staring through the glass, beyond smitten.

Only the prospect of seeing Jana could have torn him away. As he stepped into the recovery room and saw her there, still connected to tubes but turning to him and smiling, his heart leapt into the stratosphere. Damn, he was crying a third time.

"I'm turning into a complete wuss, you know," he told her, swiping away the wetness. "All your fault. Yours and that little gem of perfection in there."

Jana's face glowed as if lit from within. "Isn't she gorgeous? I love her so much already."

"Me, too." He moved a plastic chair over to the bed and took her hand gently. "And I love you, sweetheart. In every way possible. As my wife, as my lover, as my friend. You've healed me, Jana. I want to spend the rest of my life repaying you for that gift. With my love."

Now tears shone in her eyes. He rose to kiss her cheek, to whisper every endearment he could think of into her ear.

The past faded, vanished, burned away by love and joy.

Epilogue

"**W**hy a blindfold?" Sam asked, with daughter Sophie tucked on his hip, her brown eyes fixed adoringly on him.

"Because it's a surprise," Jana said, giving Sophie a noisy raspberry on her soft baby cheek. The five-month-old giggled, then returned her attention to the one who mattered most in her world—Daddy.

Jana wasn't the least bit offended that sweet Sophie was a Daddy's girl. Truth be told, the kid had both of them wrapped around her pudgy fingers. If Sophie could snap her fingers, she would, to order up whatever her heart desired in the moment—a piggyback ride on Daddy's shoulders, a snuggle with Grandma Estelle, or the quick appearance of the part of Mommy that Sophie loved best, Jana's breast.

Not that Jana would offer that up right now in the chill late-November air behind Celebration Station. She might have resigned herself to feeling like the family dairy, but even she had her limits.

"Stand still," Jana scolded as she reached up to tie the blindfold over Sam's eyes.

"Is this like the surprise you gave me at home while Sophie was napping?"

"In your dreams," Jana said. She pried her daughter from Daddy's arms—if the big lug tripped, she didn't want to risk Sophie's safety—and guided him through the shop's back door.

She held her breath as she and Sam moved slowly along the short hallway into the shop proper. This was what she'd spent much of Thanksgiving week doing, in between writing essays and reports for the two college classes she'd signed up for this semester. Frances and Ray had dropped in yesterday to help add the finishing touches, and with the shop closed today for Thanksgiving, she could finally show Sam.

They had to make their stop brief, with Tony, Rebecca, Estelle and the others expecting them for dinner at the ranch. The get-together would include not only all the students who had been through three sessions of Tony's independent living program but also Sam's sister and soon-to-be brother-in-law, Matthew, finally home from the Middle East.

They had a lot to be thankful for this year—their marriage, Sophie's birth, Matthew's safe return and the success of Celebration Station. Although the doctors still hadn't found a compatible donor for Estelle, she was doing well enough with her dialysis treatment.

"Can I take it off now?" Sam asked.

"Hang on. Give me a sec." She raced around the room, flipping switches, pressing buttons. As the shop filled with light, little Sophie's mouth dropped open in awe.

Jana shifted her daughter to her other hip, mentally crossing her fingers. "Go ahead," she told Sam.

He shoved the blindfold off. Stared at what she'd done. His jaw dropped in such a perfect imitation of Sophie's expression that Jana started to rethink the whole nature-versus-nurture argument. Then he grinned at her and burst into laughter.

The shop was a riot of vivid color, a faithful copy of the magazine picture that had so enchanted him. Jana had decorated it with the wackiest and most outlandish Christmas symbols. A bunch of them were animated, and right now Santas and snowmen and penguins were ringing and dinging and singing with holiday cheer. Just like in the magazine, it was a child's fantasy of Christmas.

Sophie's head had swung around at the sound of Sam's laughter, and now the girl squirmed in her mother's arms, reaching for Daddy. Crossing the room, he lifted his baby girl up and held her against his chest.

He curved his warm hand against Jana's cheek. "Thank you for loving me. And thank you for giving me my family."

Looking up at him, Jana saw the devotion in Sam's eyes shining more brilliantly than any light in the room. She stepped into his arms, into the circle of his love.

* * * * *

Turn the page for a sneak peek at this fantastic new story from Janice Carter, available next month from Mills & Boon® Special Moments™

Samantha Sorrenti is in the business of finding things. But this is the first time anyone's hired her to find someone. And, at twelve years old, Danny is her youngest client ever. With the help of her twin sister, she tracks down Chase Sullivan and complicates his already-complicated life with the news he has a son. A son who needs him desperately.

Don't forget you can still find all your favourite Superromance and Special Edition stories every month in Special Moments™!

A Father for Danny
by
Janice Carter

"I FIND THINGS, NOT people," Samantha Sorrenti repeated. "Things like rare books or antique coins. Art objects. Once I even had to search for an original Winnie the Pooh Teddy Bear." She grinned, hoping to lighten the mood. His brown eyes didn't flicker. Sam sighed. "What you want is a private investigator. Did you check the Yellow Pages?"

"Your Web site says you find anything."

"Any*thing*. Not any*one*."

"It didn't say you just look for stuff like old books."

"I'm sorry, but I really can't help you. My advice is to check out an agency."

He stared at her for a long, painful moment. Then he pushed his chair back and got to his feet so abruptly that it toppled over. The clatter echoed in the small room. When he reached the doorway, he turned around.

"I can't afford a private detective. Your ad says you don't charge anything unless you find it."

It! she felt like shouting. "Why the urgency? I mean, you could probably find him through the Internet yourself."

His face darkened. "I don't have time for that."

"But it might take only a few weeks and it's free. How can you lose?"

He took a step toward the desk. "How could I *lose?*" His voice cracked.

He was going to cry!

"You just don't get it. I need to find him because… because my mother is going to be dead in six weeks. Maybe less." He wheeled around.

Sam swallowed. "Wait," she said.

He stopped, turning slowly back to her. His eyes and nose were red.

"Maybe I can do something," she murmured.

He stared as if he hadn't heard right.

Sam pointed to the toppled-over chair. "Sit," she said quietly, trying not to sound as exasperated as she felt. After all, he was only twelve years old.

He didn't rush back to the chair, but shuffled instead, in that awkward walk of boys wearing ridiculously baggy pants. He slowly righted the chair and sat on it, slouching.

Sam knew this nonchalance was an attempt at face-saving, but it still rankled. He could at least *pretend* to be appreciative. "Look, I'm expecting an important call, so I can't be long, but…uh…I know someone who may be able to help." Sam stopped. Did she really want to take that step? She looked at the light in his eyes and her heart sank. She had to take it now. "Someone in the FBI."

"The FBI?" It came out as a croak.

"Do you have a problem with that?"

"No, but this is going to be just between us, right?"

"Are you talking about confidentiality?"

"Yeah. That's what I mean."

"I think you've got me confused with a lawyer. As I said, I'm not even a private investigator. I look for—"

"Yeah, you told me. Things. Not people."

Sam felt her blood pressure rise. "Do you want me to get you some help or not?"

She saw him flinch, but didn't regret her harsh tone. He might be only twelve, but he'd managed to barge into her office all on his own.

"Yes, I do. It's just that you mentioning the FBI...it sounds serious."

More serious than you can imagine. "Okay," she said, reaching for her notepad. "Why don't you tell me your story and I'll make some notes? Then I'll get back to you."

"When?"

"I don't know. As soon as I can."

He chewed on his lower lip for a few seconds, then began. When he finished, less than ten minutes later, Sam didn't trust herself to look his way. She stared at her notes, the words blurred by tears. She sniffed, blinked twice and finally raised her head.

His eyes met hers, and Sam thought she caught a glimmer of satisfaction in them. *He knows I'm hooked.*

She cleared her throat. "Okay, so let me review this. Your mother has had no contact with your father since you were born."

"Since *before* I was born. She says he never knew about me."

"But she never tried to contact him, to tell him about you?"

He shrugged. "I dunno. She always told me he never knew. I think he moved to another city, anyway."

"Maybe your mother can fill in some of these gaps."

"Why do you have to see my mother? Can't this be just between us?"

"Does your mother know you came to see me?"

He looked away.

"She doesn't, does she?"

"She has enough problems."

Sam had no reply to that. He was right of course. "The thing is, you're a minor. I can't legally help you without your mother's consent."

His eyes flicked coolly back to hers. "But you're not a real private detective, anyway."

And you're no typical twelve-year-old. "I can't do anything for you without your mother's knowledge. Anyway, you told me she was the one who suggested finding your father."

"Kinda."

"What do you mean, *kinda?*" Sam's voice rose.

His gaze dropped to his hands, interlocked in his lap. "When she first found out about the cancer, she said it was too bad my father didn't know me."

Sam felt as if she'd just plunged her other foot into quicksand. "Well, I'd have to talk to her if you want me to help," she eventually said.

"Okay, okay." His eyes met hers again. "But don't upset her. Please? She already feels bad because she knows I'll have to go into foster care after…well, after."

He didn't need to clarify. "I won't upset her, Danny, I promise. But she needs to know. Can you tell me anything at all about your father?"

"His name is Danny, too. I think my mom forgot his last name."

Or never knew it. Sam was beginning to wonder if Danny was the product of a one-night stand. Which meant the task she'd taken on would be impossible. "Anything else?"

His face brightened. "He liked motorcycles. My mom said he had a real cool tattoo on his right arm and long hair, like a rock star."

"Oh," was all Sam could think to say. The picture forming in her mind wasn't exactly a poster for fatherhood. "So Benson is your mother's name?"

"Yeah. Emily Benson." He craned his neck, looking at something behind her.

The clock, Sam realized. "You have to go soon?"

"Yeah. I told Minnie I'd be back about five and I gotta take a couple of buses."

"Who's Minnie?"

"Our next-door neighbor. I've been staying with her for the last two weeks."

"Your mother—"

"She's in the hospital."

"Oh. Is she having surgery or something?"

He shook his head. "Nope. All that's finished. Now she's just waiting. In… I can't remember the name for it. A special room in the hospital."

"Palliative care?"

"Yeah. That's it. Mom calls it the Waiting Room. She jokes about it. You know, how hospitals are always making you wait for something. She says she even has to wait to die." His voice cracked again and he turned his head toward the bookshelves at his right.

Silence shrink-wrapped the room. Sam badly wanted a glass of water. No. Make that a double of any alcoholic drink available. Unfortunately none was.

Finally he said, "Minnie says I can stay with her for now but…well, she's old, you know." He looked back at Sam. His eyes were red-rimmed. "She's living on a small pension and can't take care of me for too long."

Sam cleared her throat. "I'll need her telephone number."

Danny complied, then said, "She's in the apartment across the hall from ours, so I can go back and forth, take care of Mom's plants and stuff." He got to his feet. "So…uh, when should I call you?"

Sam knew she was sinking fast and there was no way out. Maybe a couple of phone calls would convince him she couldn't do much more. "Like I said, I have to, uh, talk to someone who may be able to help and then I'll get back to you."

"Will that take long?"

She felt her face heat. He was persistent. Not one to be put off by lame excuses. "I'll do my best, Danny."

His eyes held hers for a long moment, then he turned abruptly and walked out the door. Sam dropped her forehead into her hands. *What have you done now, Sorrenti?*

© Janice Hess 2008

⊚ SPECIAL MOMENTS™ 2-in-1

Coming next month

DADDY ON DEMAND by Helen R Myers

Left to raise twin nieces by himself, millionaire Collin Masters turned to Sabrina. She accepted his job offer and found herself falling for the reluctant father!

DÉJÀ YOU by Lynda Sandoval

When a blaze sparked memories of a life-changing accident, firefighter Erin DeLuca ran to the arms of a mystery man. But that one night had far-reaching consequences!

A FATHER FOR DANNY by Janice Carter

Samantha finds things for a living and she's been hired to find a missing person! Someone has to tell Chase Sullivan that he has a son – who needs him desperately.

BABY BE MINE by Eve Gaddy

Tucker wants his best friend Maggie to be happy, even if that means a fake union so she can foster a baby girl. Until he discovers he wants this marriage to be real.

THE MUMMY MAKEOVER by Kristi Gold

When Kieran offers to help Erica get her life back on track, he finds himself willing to break the first rule of personal training – no fraternising with the clients…

MUMMY FOR HIRE by Cathy Gillen Thacker

Grady McCabe isn't looking for love – just for a mother for his little girl. But when matchmaking Alexis tries to change his mind, he starts to relent…and fall for *her*!

On sale 16ᵗʰ July 2010

SPECIAL MOMENTS™

Single titles coming next month

THE PREGNANT BRIDE WORE WHITE
by Susan Crosby

When Jake McCoy came home to Chance City, he found a whole new family waiting for him. Was the adventurer ready to become an honest husband?

SOPHIE'S SECRET
by Tara Taylor Quinn

For years it's suited Duane and Sophie to keep their relationship a secret. Then Sophie becomes pregnant – and Duane proposes. Are they ready to make their private affair public news?

HER SO-CALLED FIANCÉ
by Abby Gaines

What possesses Sabrina to tell everyone she's going to marry Jake Warrington? She's sure her ex hates her! Sabrina needs Jake's help – and he might give it. But it comes with some conditions attached...

DIAGNOSIS: DADDY
by Gina Wilkins

Connor Hayes had just started to pursue his dream of being a doctor when he found out he was a father. Mia wanted to help, but was she up to multitasking as best friend... nanny...and love of Connor's life?

On sale 16th July 2010